Edward L. Youmans

The Correlation and Conservation of Force

SALZWASSER
VERLAG

Edward L. Youmans

The Correlation and Conservation of Force

Reprint of the original, first published in 1865.

1st Edition 2022 | ISBN: 978-3-75259-003-6

Verlag (Publisher): Salzwasser Verlag GmbH, Zeilweg 44, 60439 Frankfurt, Deutschland
Vertretungsberechtigt (Authorized to represent): E. Roepke, Zeilweg 44, 60439 Frankfurt, Deutschland
Druck (Print): Books on Demand GmbH, In de Tarpen 42, 22848 Norderstedt, Deutschland

THE

CORRELATION AND CONSERVATION

OF

FORCES:

A Series of Expositions,

BY

PROF. GROVE, PROF. HELMHOLTZ, DR. MAYER,
DR. FARADAY, PROF. LIEBIG AND
DR. CARPENTER.

WITH AN

INTRODUCTION AND BRIEF BIOGRAPHICAL NOTICES OF THE CHIEF PROMOTERS OF THE NEW VIEWS.

BY

EDWARD L. YOUMANS, M. D.

NEW YORK

1865.

TO

JOHN WILLIAM DRAPER, M.D., LL.D.

PROFESSOR OF CHEMISTRY AND PHYSIOLOGY IN THE UNIVERSITY OF NEW YORK.

DEAR SIR:—

IT seems peculiarly appropriate that this volume should be dedicated to you. Knowing the eminent esteem in which you are held in the circles of European science, I cannot doubt that the distinguished authors of the following essays would cordially approve this connection of your name with their introduction to the American public.

There is, besides, a further reason for this in that large coincidence of purpose which is manifest in their labors and your own. For while the pervading design of the present collection is to widen the range of thought by unfolding a broader philosophy of the energies of nature, your own comprehensive course of research—beginning with an extended series of experimental investigations in chemical physics and physiology, and rising to the consideration of that splendid problem, the bearing of science upon the History of the Intellectual Development of Europe—has powerfully contributed to the same noble end; that of elevating the aim and enlarging the scope of scientific inquiry.

I gladly avail myself of this occasion to say how greatly I am indebted to your writings, in which accurate and profound instruction is so often and happily blended with the charms of poetic eloquence. That you may live long to enjoy your well-won honors, and to contribute still further to the triumphant advance of scientific truth, is the heartfelt wish of

Yours truly,

E. L. Y.

PREFACE.

In his address before the British Association for the Advancement of Science last year, the President remarked that the new views of the Correlation and Conservation of Forces constitute the most important discovery of the present century. The remark is probably just, prolific as has been this period in grand scientific results. No one can glance through the current scientific publications without perceiving that these views are attracting the profound attention of the most thoughtful minds. The lively controversy that has been carried on for the last two or three years respecting the share that different men of different countries have had in their establishment, still further attests the estimate placed upon them in the scientific world.

But little, however, has been published in this country upon the subject; no complete work, I believe, except the admirable volume of Prof. Tyndall on "Heat as a Mode of Motion," in which the new philosophy is adopted, and applied to the explanation of thermal phenomena in a very clear and forcible manner. I have, therefore, thought it would be a useful service to the public to reissue some of the ablest presentations of these views which have appeared in Europe, in a compact and convenient form. The selection of these discussions has been determined by a desire to combine clearness of exposition with authority of statement. In the first of these respects the essays will speak for themselves; in regard to the last I may remark that all the authors quoted stand high as founders of the new theory of forces. Although I am not aware that Prof. Liebig has made any claims in this direction, yet it can scarcely be doubted that his original researches in Animal Chemistry tended strongly toward the promotion of the science of vital dynamics.

The work of Professor Grove, which is here reprinted in full, has a high European reputation, having passed to the fourth edition in England, and been translated into several continental languages. It is hardly to the credit of science in our country, that this is the first American edition. The eloquent and interesting paper of Helmholtz, though delivered as a popular lecture, was translated for the Philosophical Magazine, and has been very highly appreciated in scientific circles. The three articles of Mayer, which were also translated for the Philosophical Magazine, will have interest not only because of the great ability with which the subjects are treated, but as emanating from a man who stands perhaps preëminent among the explorers in this new tract of inquiry. The researches of Faraday in this field have been conspicuous and important, and his argument is marked by the depth and clearness which characterize, in an eminent degree, the writings of this extraordinary man. The essay of Liebig forms a chapter in the last edition of his invaluable 'Familiar Letters on Chemistry,' which has not been republished here; and, as it touches the relation of the subject to organic processes, it forms a fit introduction to the final article of the series by Dr. Carpenter, on the "Correlation of the Physical and Vital Forces." The eminent English physiologist has worked out this branch of the subject independently, and the paper quoted gives evidence of being prepared with his usual care and ability. A certain amount of repetition is of course unavoidable in such a collection, yet the reader will find much less of this than he might be inclined to look for, as each writer, in elaborating the subject, has stamped it with his own originality.

In the introduction I have attempted to bring forward certain facts in the history of these discoveries, in which we as Americans have a special interest, and also to indicate several applications of the new principles which are not treated in the volume. It seemed best to confine the general discussion to those aspects of the subject upon which most thought had been expended, and which may be regarded as settled among advanced scientific men. But there are other applications of the doctrine, of the highest interest, which though incomplete are yet certain, and these will be found briefly noticed in the introductory observations—too briefly, I fear, to be satisfactory. Those, however, who desire to pursue still further this branch of the inquiry—the correlation of the vital, mental, and social forces—are referred to the last edition of Carpenter's "Principles of Human Physiology;" Morell's "Outlines of Mental Philosophy;" Laycock's "Correlations of Consciousness and Organization;" Sir J. K. Shuttleworth's address before the Social Science Congress of 1860, on the "Correlation of the Moral and Physical Forces;" Hinton's "Life in Nature," and "First Principles" of Herbert Spencer's new system of Philosophy. The first and last of these works are the only ones, it is believed, that have appeared in an American form, and the last is much the ablest of all; I was chiefly indebted to it in preparing the latter part of the introduction. The biographical notices, brief and imperfect as they are, it is hoped may enhance the reader's interest in the volume.

I have been specially incited to procure the publication of a work of this kind, by the same motive that has impelled me to write upon the subject elsewhere; a conviction of our educational needs in this direction. The treatment of a vast subject like this in ordinary school text-books, is at best quite too limited for the requirements of the active-minded teacher; to such, a volume like the present may prove invaluable.

But a more serious difficulty is that, until compelled by the demands of intelligent teachers, the compilers of school-books will pass new views entirely by, or give them a mere hasty and careless notice, while continuing to inculcate the old erroneous doctrines. And thus it is that from inveterate habit, or intellectual sluggishness, or a shrewd calculation of the indifference of teachers, outworn and effete ideas continue to drag through school-books for half a century after they have been exploded in the world of living science. He who continues to teach the hypothesis of *caloric*, falsifies the present truth of science as absolutely as he would do in teaching the hypothesis of *phlogiston;* in fact, the reasons offered for persisting in the erroneous notions of the materiality of heat—convenience of teaching, unsettledness of the new vocabulary, &c., are precisely those that were offered for clinging to phlogiston, and rejecting the Lavoiserian chemistry of combustion. Both conceptions have no doubt been of service, but both were transitional, and having done their work they become hindrances instead of helps. We can now see that when the true chemistry of combustion was once reached, the notion of phlogiston was of no further use, and if retained could only produce confusion and prevent the reception of correct ideas. So with caloric, and those false conceptions of the materiality of forces, which it implies: not only are they errors, but the ideas they involve are radically incompatible with the higher truths to which science has advanced; so that while the errors are retained the truths cannot be received.

Nor will it answer merely to mention the new views while adopting the old, on the plea that the facts are the same in both cases. The facts are very far from being the same in both cases. It is precisely because the old ideas are out of harmony with the facts, and can no longer correctly explain and express them, that new ideas are sought. Was not phlogiston abandoned because it no longer agreed with the facts? So with the conception of the materiality of the forces; it contradicts the facts, and therefore, for scientific purposes, can no longer represent them. In the workshop it may perhaps be very well to magnify facts, and depreciate their theoretical explanations, but not in the school-room; the business is here not working, but thinking. It is the aim of art to *use* facts, but of science to *understand* them. And it is simply because science goes beyond the fact to its explanation, and is ever striving after the highest truth, that it is fitted to discipline the thinking and reasoning faculties, and therefore has imperative educational claims.

In therefore bringing forward these able and authoritative expositions in a form readily accessible to teachers, I trust I am not only doing them a helpful service, but that they will be led to require of the preparers of school-books a more conscientious performance of their tasks, and that the interests of sound education will be thereby promoted.

New York, *Oct.* 1, 1864.

CONTENTS.

INTRODUCTION.

There are many who deplore what they regard as the materializing tendencies of modern science. They maintain that this profound and increasing engrossment of the mind with material objects is fatal to all refining and spiritualizing influence. The correctness of this conclusion is open to serious question: indeed, the history of scientific thought not only fails to justify it, but proves the reverse to be true. It shows that the tendency of this kind of inquiry is ever *from* the material, *toward* the abstract, the ideal, the spiritual.

We may appeal to the oldest and most developed of the sciences for confirmation of this statement. The earliest explanations of the celestial movements were thoroughly and grossly material, and all astronomic progress has been toward more refined and ideal views. The heavenly bodies were at first thought to be supported and carried round in their courses by solid revolving crystalline spheres to which they were attached. This notion was afterward replaced by the more complex and mobile mechanism of epicycles. To this succeeded the hypothesis of Des Cartes', who rejected the clumsy mechanical explanation of revolving wheelwork, and proposed the more subtile conception of ethereal currents, which constantly whirled around in vortices, and bore along the heavenly bodies. At length the labors of astronomers, terminating with

Newton, struck away these crude devices, and substituted the action of a universal immaterial force. The course of astronomic science has thus been on a vast scale to withdraw attention from the material and sensible, and to fix it upon the invisible and supersensuous. It has shown that a pure principle forms the immaterial foundation of the universe. From the baldest materiality we rise at last to a truth of the spiritual world, of so exalted an order that it has been said 'to connect the mind of man with the Spirit of God.'

The tendency thus illustrated by astronomy is characteristic in a marked degree of all modern science. Scientific inquiries are becoming less and less questions of matter, and more and more questions of force; material ideas are giving place to dynamical ideas. While the great agencies of change with which it is the business of science to deal—heat, light, electricity, magnetism, and affinity, have been formerly regarded as kinds of matter 'imponderable elements,' in distinction from other material elements, these notions must now be regarded as outgrown and abandoned, and in their place we have an order of purely immaterial forces.

Toward the close of the last century the human mind reached the great principle of the indestructiblity of matter. What the intellectual activity of ages had failed to establish by all the resources of reasoning and philosophy, was accomplished by the invention of a mechanical implement, the balance of Lavoisier. When nature was tested in the chemist's scale-pan, it was first found that never an atom is created or destroyed; that though matter changes form with protean facility, traversing a thousand cycles of change, vanishing and reappearing incessantly, yet it never wears out or lapses into nothing.

The present age will be memorable in the history of science for having demonstrated that the same great principle applies also to forces, and for the establishment of a new philosophy concerning their nature and relations. Heat, light, electricity, and magnetism are now no longer regarded as substantive and independent existences—subtile fluids with peculiar properties, but simply as modes of motion in ordinary matter; forms of energy which are capable of mutual conversion. Heat is a mode of energy manifested by certain effects. It may be transformed into electricity, which is another form of force producing different effects. Or the process may be reversed; the electricity disappearing and the heat reappearing. Again, mechanical motion, which is a motion of masses, may be transformed into heat or electricity, which is held to be a motion of the atoms of matter, while, by a reverse process, the motion of atoms, that is, heat or electricity, may be turned back again into mechanical motion. Thus a portion of the heat generated in a locomotive is converted into the motion of the train, while by the application of the brakes the motion of the train is changed back again into the heat of friction.

These mutations are rigidly subject to the laws of quantity. A given amount of one force produces a definite quantity of another; so that power or energy, like matter, can neither be created nor destroyed: though ever changing form, its total quantity in the universe remains constant and unalterable. Every manifestation of force must have come from a preëxisting equivalent force, and must give rise to a subsequent and equal amount of some other force. When, therefore, a force or effect appears, we are not at liberty to assume that it was self-originated, or came from nothing; when it disappears we are forbidden to conclude that it is annihilated: we must search and find whence it came and whither it has gone; that is, what produced it and what effect it has itself produced. These relations among the modes of energy are currently known by the phrases *Correlation* and *Conservation* of Force.

The present condition of the philosophy of forces is perfectly paralleled by that of the philosophy of matter toward the close of the last century. So long as it was admitted that matter in its various changes may be created or destroyed, chemical progress was impossible. If, in his processes, a portion of the material disappeared, the chemist had a ready explanation—the matter was *destroyed;* his analysis was therefore worthless. But when he started with the axiom that matter is indestructible, all disappearance of material during his operations was chargeable to their imperfection. He was therefore compelled to improve them—to account in his result for every thousandth of a grain with which he commenced; and as a consequence of this inexorable condition, analytical chemistry advanced to a high perfection, and its consequences to the world are incalculable. Precisely so with the analysis of forces. So long as they are considered capable of being created and destroyed, the quest for them will be careless and the results valueless. But the moment they are determined to be indestructible, the investigator becomes bound to account for them; all problems of power are at once affected, and the science of dynamics enters upon a new era.

The views here briefly stated will be found fully and variously elucidated in the essays of the present volume; in these introductory remarks I propose to offer some observations on their history and the extended scope of their application.

I have spoken of the principles of Correlation and Conservation of Forces as established; it may be well to state the sense in which this is to be taken. They have been accepted by the leading scientific minds of all nations with remarkable unanimity; their discussion forms a leading element in scientific literature, while they occupy the thoughts and guide the investigations of the most philosophical inquirers. But while science holds securely her new possession as a fundamental principle, its various phases are by no means completely worked out. Not only has there been too little time for this, even if the views were far less important, but the questions started lie at the foundation of all branches of science, and can only be fully elucidated as these advance in their development. The new doctrine of forces is now in much the same condition as was the new astronomy of Copernicus. It is not without its difficulties, which time alone must be trusted to remove; but it simplifies so many problems, clears up so many obscurities, opens so extended a range of new investigations, and contrasts so strongly with the complexities and incongruities of the older doctrines, as to leave little liberty of choice between the opposing theories. Not only does the reception of these views mark a signal epoch in the progress of science, but from their comprehensive bearings and the luminous glimpses which they open into the most elevated regions of speculative inquiry, they have a profound interest for many thinkers who give little attention to the specialties of exact science.

In the history of human affairs there is a growing conception of the action of general causes in the production of events, and a corresponding conviction that the part played by individuals has been much exaggerated, and is far less controlling and permanent than has been hitherto supposed. So also in the history of science it is now acknowledged that the progress of discovery is much more independent of the labors of particular persons than has been formerly admitted. Great discoveries belong not so much to individuals as to humanity; they are less inspirations of genius than births of eras. As there has been a definite intellectual progress, thought has necessarily been limited to the subjects successively reached. Many minds have been thus occupied at the same time with similar ideas, and hence the simultaneous discoveries of independent inquirers, of which the history of science is so full. Thus at the close of the sixteenth century, philosophers had entered upon the investigation of the laws of motion, and accordingly we find Galileo, Benediti, and Piccolomini proving independently that all bodies fall to the earth with equal velocity, whatever their size or weight. A century after, when science had advanced to the systematic application of the higher mathematics to general physics, Newton and Leibnitz discovered independently the differential calculus. A hundred years later questions of molecular physics and chemistry were reached, and oxygen was discovered simultaneously by Priestley and Scheele, and the composition of water by Cavendish and Watt. These discoveries were made because the periods were ripe for them, and we cannot doubt that if those who made them had never lived, the labors of others would have speedily attained the same results. The discoverer is, therefore, in a great degree, but the mouthpiece of his time. Some discern clearly what is dimly shadowed forth to many; some work out the results more completely than others, and some seize the coming thought so long before it is developed in the general consciousness, that their announcements are unappreciated and unheeded. This view by no means robs the discoverer of his honors, but it enables us to place upon them a juster estimate, and to pass a more enlightened judgment upon the rival claims which are constantly arising in the history of science.

Probably the most important event in the general progress of science was the transition from the speculative to the experimental period. The ancients were prevented from creating science by a false intellectual procedure. They believed they could solve all the problems of the universe by thought alone. The moderns have found that for this purpose meditation is futile unless accompanied by observation and experiment. Modern science, therefore, took its rise in a change of method, and the adoption of the principle that the discovery of physical truth consists not in its mere logical but in its experimental establishment. It is now an axiom that not he who *guesses*, though he guess aright, is to be adjudged the true discoverer, but he who *demonstrates* the new truth, and thus compels its acceptance into the body of valid knowledge.

Now the later doctrines of the constancy and relations of forces, and that heat is a kind of motion among the minuter parts of matter, have had their twofold phases of history, corresponding to the two methods of inquiry. They had an early and vague recognition among many philosophers, and may be traced in the writings of Galileo, Bacon, Newton, Locke, Leibnitz, Des Cartes, Bernoulli, Laplace, and others; but they were held by these thinkers as unverified and fruitless speculations, and the subject awaited the genius that could deal with it according to the more effective methods of modern science.

It was this country, widely reproached for being over-practical, which produced just that kind of working ability that was suited to translate this profound question from the barren to the fruitful field of inquiry. It is a matter of just national pride that the two men who first demonstrated the capital propositions of pure science, that lightning is but a case of common electricity, and that heat is but a mode of motion—who first converted these propositions from conjectures of fancy to facts of science, were not only Americans by birth and education, but men eminently representative of the peculiarities of American character—Benjamin Franklin and Benjamin Thompson, afterwards known as Count Rumford. The latter philosopher is less known than the former, though his services to science and society were probably quite as great. The prominence which his name now occupies in connection with the new views of heat, and the relations of forces, make it desirable to glance briefly at his career.

Benjamin Thompson was born at Woburn, Mass., in 1753. He received the rudiments of a common school education; became a merchant's apprentice at twelve, and subsequently taught school. Having a strong taste for mechanical and chemical studies, he cultivated them assiduously during his leisure time. At seventeen he took charge of an academy in the village of Rumford (now Concord), N. H., and in 1772 married a wealthy widow, by whom he had one daughter. At the outbreak of revolutionary hostilities he applied for a commission in the American service, was charged with toryism, left the country in disgust, and went to England. His talents were there appreciated, and he took a responsible position under the government, which he held for some years.

After receiving the honor of knighthood he left England and entered the service of the elector of Bavaria. He settled in Munich in 1784, and was appointed aide-de-camp and chamberlain to the Prince. The labors which he now undertook were of the most extensive and laborious character, and could never have been accomplished but for the rigorous habits of order which he carried into all his pursuits. He reorganized the entire military establishment of Bavaria, introduced not only a simpler code of tactics, and a new system of order, discipline, and economy among the troops and industrial schools for the soldiers' children, but greatly improved the construction and modes of manufacture of arms and ordnance. He suppressed the system of beggary which had grown into a recognized profession in Bavaria, and become an enormous public evil—one of the most remarkable social reforms on record. He also devoted himself to various ameliorations, such as improving the construction and arrangement of the dwellings of the working classes, providing for them a better education, organizing houses of industry, introducing superior breeds of horses and cattle, and promoting landscape-gardening, which he did by converting an old abandoned hunting-ground near Munich into a park, where, after his departure, the inhabitants erected a monument to his honor. For these services Sir Benjamin Thompson received many distinctions, and among others was made Count of the holy Roman Empire. On receiving this dignity he chose a title in remembrance of the country of his nativity, and was thenceforth known as Count of Rumford.

His health failing from excessive labor and what he considered the unfavorable climate, he came back to England in 1798, and had serious thoughts of returning to the United States. Having received from the American government the compliment of a formal invitation to revisit his native land, he wrote to an old friend requesting him to look out for a "little quiet retreat" for himself and daughter in the vicinity of Boston. This intention, however, failed, as he shortly after became involved in the enterprise of founding the Royal Institution of England.

There was in Rumford's character a happy combination of philanthropic impulses, executive power in carrying out great projects, and versatility of talent in physical research. His scientific investigations were largely guided and determined by his philanthropic plans and public duties. His interest in the more needy classes led him to the assiduous study of the physical wants of mankind, and the best methods of relieving them; the laws and domestic management of heat accordingly engaged a large share of his attention. He determined the amount of heat arising from the combustion of different kinds of fuel, by means of a calorimeter of his own invention. He reconstructed the fireplace, and so improved the methods of heating apartments and cooking food as to produce a saving in the precious element, varying from one-half to seven-eighths of the fuel previously consumed. He improved the construction of stoves, cooking ranges, coal grates, and chimneys; showed that the non-conducting power of cloth is due to the air enclosed among its fibres, and first pointed out that mode of action of heat called *convection;* indeed he was the first clearly to discriminate between the three modes of propagation of heat—radiation, conduction, and convection. He determined the almost perfect non-conducting properties of liquids, investigated the production of light, and invented a mode of measuring it. He was the first to apply steam generally to the warming of fluids and the culinary art; he experimented upon the use of gunpowder, the strength of materials, and the maximum density of water, and made many valuable and original observations upon an extensive range of subjects.

Prof. James D. Forbes, in his able Dissertation on the recent Progress of the Mathematical and Physical Sciences, in the last edition of the Encyclopedia Britannica, gives a full account of Rumford's contributions to science, and remarks:

"All Rumford's experiments were made with admirable precision, and recorded with elaborate fidelity, and in the plainest language. Every thing with him was reduced to weight and measure, and no pains were spared to attain the best results.

"Rumford's name will be ever connected with the progress of science in England by two circumstances: first, by the foundation of a perpetual medal and prize in the gift of the council of the

Royal Society of London, for the reward of discoveries connected with heat and light; and secondly, by the establishment in 1800 of the Royal Institution in London, destined, primarily, for the promotion of original discovery, and, secondarily, for the diffusion of a taste for science among the educated classes. The plan was conceived with the sagacity which characterized Rumford, and its success has been greater than could have been anticipated. Davy was there brought into notice by Rumford himself, and furnished with the means of prosecuting his admirable experiments. He and Mr. Faraday have given to that institution its just celebrity with little intermission for half a century."

Leaving England, Rumford took up his residence in France, and the estimation in which he was held may be judged of by the fact that he was elected one of the eight foreign associates of the Academy of Sciences.

Count Rumford bequeathed to Harvard University the funds for endowing its professorship of the Application of Science to the Art of Living, and instituted a prize to be awarded by the American Academy of Sciences, for the most important discoveries and improvements relating to heat and light. In 1804 he married the widow of the celebrated chemist Lavoisier, and with her retired to the villa of Auteuil, the residence of her former husband, where he died in 1814.

Having thus glanced briefly at his career, I now pass to the discovery upon which Count Rumford's fame in the future will chiefly rest. It is described in a paper published in the transactions of the Royal Society for 1798.

He was led to it while superintending the operations of the Munich arsenal, by observing the large amount of heat generated in boring brass cannon. Reflecting upon this, he proposed to himself the following questions: "Whence comes the heat produced in the mechanical operations above mentioned?" "Is it furnished by the metallic chips which are separated from the metal?"

The common hypothesis affirmed that the heat produced had been latent in the metal, and had been forced out by *condensation* of the chips. But if this were the case the capacity for heat of the parts of metal so reduced to chips ought not only to be changed, but the change undergone by them should be sufficiently great to account for *all* the heat produced. With a fine saw Rumford then cut away slices of the unheated metal, and found that they had *exactly the same capacity for heat as the metallic chips.* No change in this respect had occurred, and it was thus conclusively proved that the heat generated could not have been held latent in the chips. Having settled this preliminary point, Rumford proceeds to his principal experiments.

With the intuition of the true investigator, he remarks that "very interesting philosophical experiments may often be made, almost without trouble or expense, by means of machinery contrived for mere mechanical purposes of the arts and manufactures." Accordingly, he mounted a metallic cylinder weighing 113.13 pounds avoirdupois, in a horizontal position. At one end there was a cavity three and a half inches in diameter, and into this was introduced a borer, a flat piece of hardened steel, four inches long, 0.63 inches thick, and nearly as wide as the cavity, the area of contact of the borer with the cylinder being two and a half inches. To measure the heat developed, a small round hole was bored in the cylinder near the bottom of the cavity, for the insertion of a small mercurial thermometer. The borer was pressed against the base of the cavity with a force of 10,000 pounds, and the cylinder made to revolve by horse-power at the rate of thirty-two times per minute. At the beginning of the experiment the temperature of the air in the shade and also in the cylinder was 60°F. at the end of thirty minutes, and after the cylinder had made 960 revolutions the temperature was found to be 130°F.

Having taken away the borer, he found that 839 grains of metallic dust had been cut away. "Is it possible," he exclaims, "that the very considerable quantity of heat produced in this experiment

—a quantity which actually raised the temperature of upward of 113 pounds of gun metal at least 70°, could have been furnished by so inconsiderable a quantity of metallic dust, and this merely in consequence of a change in the capacity for heat?"

To measure more precisely the heat produced, he next surrounded his cylinder by an oblong wooden box in such a manner that it could turn water-tight in the centre of the box, while the borer was pressed against the bottom. The box was filled with water until the entire cylinder was covered, and the apparatus was set in action. The temperature of the water on commencing was 60°. He remarks, "The result of this beautiful experiment was very striking, and the pleasure it afforded amply repaid me for all the trouble I had taken in contriving and arranging the complicated machinery used in making it. The cylinder had been in motion but a short time when I perceived, by putting my hand into the water and touching the outside of the cylinder, that heat was generated."

As the work continued the temperature gradually rose; at two hours and twenty minutes from the beginning of the operation, the water was at 200°, and in ten minutes more it actually boiled! Upon this result Rumford observes, "It would be difficult to describe the surprise and astonishment expressed in the countenances of the bystanders, on seeing so large a quantity of water heated and actually made to boil without any fire. Though there was nothing that could be considered very surprising in this matter, yet I acknowledge fairly that it afforded me a degree of childish pleasure which, were I ambitious of the reputation of a grave philosopher, I ought most certainly rather to hide than to discover."

Rumford estimated the total heat generated as sufficient to raise 26.58 pounds of ice-cold water 180°, or to its boiling point; and he adds, "from the results of these computations, it appears that the quantity of heat produced equally or in a continuous stream, if I may use the expression, by the friction of the blunt steel borer against the bottom of the hollow metallic cylinder, was *greater* than that produced in the combustion of nine wax candles, each three-quarters of an inch in diameter, all burning together with clear bright flames."

"One horse would have been equal to the work performed, though two were actually employed. Heat may thus be produced merely by the strength of a horse, and in a case of necessity this might be used in cooking victuals. But no circumstances could be imagined in which this method of producing heat could be advantageous, for more heat might be obtained by using the fodder necessary for the support of the horse, as fuel.

"By meditating on the results of all these experiments, we are naturally brought to that great question which has so often been the subject of speculation among philosophers, namely, What is heat? Is there such a thing as an igneous fluid? Is there any thing that with propriety can be called caloric?

"We have seen that a very considerable quantity of heat may be excited by the friction of two metallic surfaces, and given off in a constant stream or flux *in all directions*, without interruption or intermission, and without any signs of *diminution* or *exhaustion*. In reasoning on this subject we must not forget *that most remarkable circumstance*, that the source of the heat generated by friction in these experiments appeared evidently to be *inexhaustible*. (The italics are Rumford's.) It is hardly necessary to add, that any thing which any *insulated* body or system of bodies can continue to furnish *without limitation*, cannot possibly be a *material substance;* and it appears to me to be extremely difficult, if not quite impossible, to form any distinct idea of any thing capable of being excited and communicated in those experiments, except it be MOTION."

No one can read the remarkably able and lucid paper from which these extracts are taken, without being struck with the perfect distinctness with which the problem to be solved was presented, and the systematic and conclusive method of its treatment. Rumford kept strictly within the limits of legitimate inquiry, which no man can define better than he did. "I am very far from pretending to know how, or by what means or mechanical contrivances, that particular kind of motion in bodies, which has been supposed to constitute heat, is exerted, continued, and propagated, and I shall not presume to trouble the Society with new conjectures. But although the mechanism of heat should in part be one one of those mysteries of nature, which are beyond the reach of human intelligence, this ought by no means to discourage us, or even lessen our ardor in our attempts to investigate the laws of its operations. How far can we advance in any of the paths which science has opened to us, before we find ourselves enveloped in those thick mists, which on every side bound the horizon of the human intellect."

Rumford's experiments completely annihilated the material hypothesis of heat, while the modern doctrine was stated in explicit terms. He moreover advanced the question to its quantitative and highest stage, proposing to find the numerical relation between mechanical power and heat, and obtained a result remarkably near to that finally established. The English unit of force is the foot-pound, that is, one pound falling through one foot of space; the unit of heat is one pound of water heated 1° F. Just fifty years subsequently to the experiment of Rumford, Dr. J. P. Joule,* of Manchester, England, after a most delicate and elaborate series of experiments, determined that 772 units of force produce one unit of heat; that is, 772 pounds falling through one foot produces sufficient heat to raise one pound of water 1° F. This law is known as the mechanical equivalent of heat. Now, when we throw Rumford's results into these terms, we find that about 940 units of force produced a unit of heat, and that, therefore, on a large scale, and at the very first trial, he came within twenty per cent. of the true

* JAMES PRESCOTT JOULE, born December 24th, 1818, at Salford, near Manchester, England, where he pursued the occupation of a brewer. Long and deeply devoted to scientific investigation, he became a member of the Manchester Philosophical Society in 1842, and of the Royal Society of London in 1850.

statement. No account was taken of the heat lost by radiation, which, considering the high temperature produced, and the duration of the experiment, must have been considerable; so that as Rumford himself noticed, this value must be too high. The earliest numerical results in science are rarely more than rough approximations, yet they may guide to the establishment of great principles. Certainly no one could question Dalton's claim to the discovery of the law of definite proportions, because of the inaccuracy of the numbers upon which he first rested it.

We are called further to note that Rumford's ideas upon the general subject of forces were far in advance of his age. He saw the relation of all friction to heat, and suggested that of fluids, by churning processes, as a means of producing it—precisely the method finally employed by Joule in establishing the mechanical equivalent of heat. He furthermore regarded animals *dynamically*, considering their force as the derivative of their food, and therefore as not created. That Rumford held these views in the comprehensive and matured sense in which they are now entertained is, of course, not asserted. The advance from his day to ours has been prodigious. Whole sciences have been created, which afford the most beautiful exemplifications of the new doctrines. Those doctrines have received their subsequent development in various directions by many minds, but we may be allowed to question if the contributions of any of their promoters will surpass, if indeed they will equal, the value and importance which we must assign to the first great experimental step in the new direction.

The claims of Rumford may be summarized as follows:

I. He was the man who first took the question of the nature of heat out of the domain of metaphysics, where it had been speculated upon since the time of Aristotle, and placed it upon the true basis of physical experiment.

II. He first proved the insufficiency of the current explanations of the sources of heat, and demonstrated the falsity of the prevailing view of its materiality.

III. He first estimated the quantitative relation between the heat produced by friction and that by combustion.

IV. He first showed the quantity of heat produced by a definite amount of mechanical work, and arrived at a result remarkably near the finally established law.

V. He pointed out other methods to be employed in determining the amount of heat produced by the expenditure of mechanical power, instancing particularly the agitation of water, or other liquids, as in churning.

VI. He regarded the power of animals as due to their food, therefore as having a definite source and not created, and thus applied his views of force to the organic world.

VII. Rumford was the first to demonstrate the quantitative convertibility of force in an important case, and the first to reach, experimentally, the fundamental conclusion that heat is but a mode of motion.

In his late work upon heat, Prof. Tyndall, after quoting copiously from Rumford's paper, remarks: "When the history of the dynamical theory of heat is written, the man who in opposition to the scientific belief of his time could experiment, and reason upon experiment, as did Rumford in the investigation here referred to, cannot be lightly passed over." Had other English writers been equally just, there would have been less necessity for the foregoing exposition of Rumford's labors and claims; but there has been a manifest disposition in various quarters to obscure and depreciate them. Dr. Whewell, in his history of the Inductive Sciences, treats the subject of thermotics without mentioning him. An eminent Edinburgh professor, writing recently in the Philosophical Magazine, under the confessed influence of 'patriotism,' undertakes to make the dynamical theory of heat an English monopoly, due to Sir Isaac Newton, Sir Humphry Davy, and Dr. J. P Joule; while an able writer in a late number of the North British Review, in sketching the historic progress of the new views, puts Davy forward as their founder, and assigns to Rumford a minor and subsequent place.

Sir Humphry Davy, it is well known, early rejected the caloric hypothesis. In 1799, at the age of twenty-one, he published a tract at Bristol, describing some ingenious experiments upon the subject. It was the publication of this pamphlet which brought him to Rumford's notice, and resulted in his subsequent connection with the Royal Institution. But Davy's ideas upon the question were far from clear, and will bear no comparison with those of Rumford, published the year before. Indeed his eulogist remarks: "It is certain that even Davy himself was led astray in his argument by using the hypothesis of change of capacity as the basis of his reasoning, and that he might have been met successfully by any able calorist, who, though maintaining the materiality of heat, might have been willing to throw overboard one or two of the less essential tenets of his school of philosophy." It was not till 1812 that Davy wrote in his Chemical Philosophy, "The immediate cause of the phenomena of heat then is motion, and the laws of its communication are precisely the same as those of the communication of motion." When, therefore, we remember that Davy's first publication was subsequent to that of Rumford's, that he confined himself to the narrowest point of the subject, the simple question of the existence of caloric; and that he nowhere gives evidence of having the slightest notion of the quantitative relation between mechanical force and heat, the futility of the claim which would make him the experimental founder of the dynamical theory, is abundantly apparent.

The inquiries opened by Rumford and Davy were not formally pursued by the succeeding generation. Even the powerful adhesion of Dr. Thomas Young—perhaps the greatest mind in science since Newton—failed to give currency to the new views. But the salient and impregnable demonstration of Rumford, and the ingenious experiments of Davy, facts which could neither be evaded nor harmonized with the prevailing errors, were not without influence. That there was a general, though unconscious tendency toward a new philosophy of forces, in the early inquiries of the present century, is shown by the fact that various scientific men of different nations, and with no knowledge of each other's labors, gave expression to the same views at about the same time. Grove and Joule of England, Mayer of Germany, and Colding of Denmark, announced the general doctrine of the mutual relations of the forces, with more or less explication, about 1842, and Seguin of France, it is claimed, a little earlier. From this time the subject was closely pursued, and the names of Helmholtz, Holtzman, Clausius,* Faraday, Thompson, Rankine,† Tyndall, Carpenter, and others are intimately associated with its advancement. In this country Professors Henry ‡ and Leconte § have contributed to illustrate the organic phase of the doctrine.

I cannot here attempt an estimate of the respective shares which these men have had in constructing the new theories; the reader will gather various intimations upon this point from the succeeding essays. The foreign periodicals, both scientific and literary, show that the question is being thoroughly sifted, and materials accumulating for the future history of the subject. The paramount claims are, however, those of Joule, Mayer, and Grove.

* Clausius, Rudolph Julius Immanuel was born at Cöslin, Pommern, January 22, 1822. He became Professor of Philosophy and Physics in the Polytechnic School at Zurich in 1855, and then Professor of the Zurich University (1857). He was afterwards teacher of Physics and Artillery in the School of Berlin, and then private teacher of the University of that place.

† Rankine, William John Macquorn was born at Edinburgh, July 5, 1820. He is a civil engineer in Glasgow, a member of the Philosophical Society at that place, and of the Royal Society of London.

‡ See the article "Meteorology," in the Agricultural Report of the Patent Office, for 1857.

§ See the American Journal of Science for Nov. 1859.

According to the strict rule of science, that in all those cases where experimental proof is possible, he who first supplies it is the true discoverer, Dr. Joule must be assigned the foremost place among the modern investigators of the subject. He dealt with the whole question upon the basis of experiment. He labored with great perseverance and skill to determine the mechanical equivalent of heat—the corner-stone of the edifice; and in accomplishing this result in 1850, he may be said to have matured the work of Rumford, and finally established upon an experimental basis the great law of thermo-dynamics, to remain a demonstration of science forever.

Professor Grove has also worked out the subject in his own independent way. Combining original experimental investigations of great acuteness, with the philosophic employment of the general results of science, he was the first to give complete and systematic expression to the new views. His able work, which opens the present series, is an authoritative exposition, and an acknowledged classic upon the subject.

Again, the claims of Dr. Mayer to an eminent and enviable place among the pioneers of this great scientific movement, are unquestionable. There has evidently been, on the part of some English writers, an unworthy inclination to depreciate his merits, which has given rise to a sharp and searching controversy. The intellectual rights of the German philosopher have, however, been decisively vindicated by the chivalric pen of Prof. Tyndall; and it is to the public interest thus excited, that we are indebted for the translation of Mayer's papers, which appear in this volume. Mayer did not experiment to the extent of Joule and Grove, yet he well knew its importance, and made such investigations as his apparatus and the duties of a laborious profession would allow. Yet his views were not therefore mere ingenious and probable conjectures. Master of the results of modern science, and of the mathematical methods of dealing with them, possessing a broad philosophic grasp, and an extraordinary mental pertinacity, Dr. Mayer entered early upon the inquiry, and not only has he developed many of its prime applications in advance of any other thinker, but he has done his work under circumstances and in a manner which awakens the highest admiration for his genius.*

An eminent authority has remarked 'that these discoveries open a region which promises possessions richer than any hitherto granted to the intellect of man.' Involving as they do a revolution of fundamental ideas, their consequences must be as comprehensive as the range of human thought. A principle has been developed of all-pervading application, which brings the diverse and distant branches of knowledge into more intimate and harmonious alliance, and affords a profounder insight into the universal order. Not only is science itself deeply affected by the presentation of its questions, in new and suggestive lights, but its method is at once made universal. There is a crude notion in many minds, that it is the business of science to occupy itself merely with the study of matter. When, hitherto, it has pressed its inquiries into the higher

* Prof. Tyndall remarks: "Mayer probably had not the means of making experiments himself, but he ransacked the records of experimental science for his data, and thus conferred upon his writings a strength which mere speculation can never possess. From the extracts which I have given, the reader may infer his strong desire for quantitative accuracy, the clearness of his insight, and the firmness of his grasp. Regarding the recognition which will be ultimately accorded to Dr. Mayer, a shade of trouble or doubt has never crossed my mind. Individuals may seek to pull him down, but their efforts will be unavailing as long as such evidence of his genius exists, and as long as the general mind of humanity is influenced by considerations of justice and truth.

"The paucity of facts in Mayer's time has been urged as if it were a reproach to him; but it ought to be remembered that the quantity of fact necessary to a generalization is different for different minds. 'A word to the wise is sufficient for them,' and a single fact in some minds bears fruit that a hundred cannot produce in others. Mayer's data were comparatively scanty, but his genius went far to supply the lack of experiment, by enabling him to see clearly the bearing of such facts as he possessed. They enabled him to think out the law of conservation, and his conclusions received the stamp of certainty from the subsequent experimental labors of Mr. Joule. In reference to their comparative merits, I would say that as Seer and Generalizer, Mayer, in my opinion, stands first—*as experimental philosopher, Joule.*"

region of life, mind, society, history, and education, the traditional custodians of these subjects have bidden it keep within its limits and stick to *matter*. But science is not to be hampered by this narrow conception; its office is nothing less than to investigate the laws and universal relations of force, and its domain is therefore coextensive with the display of power. Indeed, as we know nothing of matter, except through its manifestation of forces, it is obvious that the study of matter itself is at last resolved into the study of forces. The establishment of a new philosophy of forces, therefore, by its vast extension of the scope and methods of science, constitutes a momentous event of intellectual progress.

The discussions of the present volume will make fully apparent the importance of the new doctrines in relation to physical science, but their higher implications are but partially unfolded. In the concluding article Dr. Carpenter has shown the applicability of the principle of correlation to vital phenomena. His argument is of interest, not only because of the facts and principles established, but as opening an inquiry which must lead to still larger results: for, if the principle be found operative in fundamental organic processes, it will undoubtedly be traced in those which are higher; if in the lower sphere of life, then throughout that sphere. If the forces are correlated in organic growth and nutrition, they must be in organic action; and thus human activity, in all its forms, is brought within the operation of the law. As a creature of organic nutrition, borrowing matter and force from the outward world; as a being of feeling and sensibility, of intellectual power and multiform activities, man must be regarded as amenable to the great law that forces are convertible and indestructible; and as psychology and sociology—the science of mind and the science of society—have to deal constantly with different phases and forms of human energy, the new principle must be of the profoundest import in relation to these great subjects.

The forces manifested in the living system are of the most varied and unlike character, mechanical, thermal, luminous, electric, chemical, nervous, sensory, emotional, and intellectual. That these forces are perfectly coördinated—that there is some definite relation among them which explains the marvellous dynamic unity of the living organism, does not admit of question. That this relation is of the same nature as that which is found to exist among the purely physical forces, and which is expressed by the term 'Correlation,' seems also abundantly evident. From the great complexity of the conditions, the same exactness will not, of course, be expected here as in the inorganic field, but this is one of the necessary limitations of all physiological and psychological inquiry; thus qualified the proofs of the correlation of the nervous and mental forces with the physical, are as clear and decisive as those for the physical forces alone.

If a current of electricity is passed through a small wire it produces heat, while if heat is applied to a certain combination of metals, it reproduces a current of electricity; these forces are, therefore, correlated. A current of electricity passed through a small portion of a motor or sensory nerve will excite the nerve-force in the remainder, while, on the other hand, as is shown in the case of the torpedo, the nerve-force may generate electricity. Nerve-force may produce heat, light, electricity, and, as we constantly experience, mechanical power, and these in their turn may also excite nerve-force. This form of energy is therefore clearly entitled to a place in the order of correlated agencies.

Again, if we take the highest form of mental action, viz.: will-power, we find that while it commands the movements of the system, it does not act directly upon the muscles, but upon the cerebral hemispheres of the brain. There is a dynamic chain of which voluntary power is but one link. The will is a power which excites nerve-force in the brain, which again excites mechanical power in the muscles. Will-power is therefore correlated with nerve-power in the same manner as the latter is with muscular power. Dr. Carpenter well observes: "It is difficult to see that the dynamical agency which we term will is more removed from nerve-force on the one hand than nerve-force is removed from motor force on the other. Each, in giving origin to the next, is itself expended or ceases to exist *as such*, and each bears, in its own intensity, a precise relation to that of its antecedent and its consequent." We have here only space briefly to trace the principle in its application to sensations, motions, and intellectual operations.

The physical agencies acting upon inanimate objects in the external world, change their form and state, and we regard these changes as transformed manifestations of the forces in action. A body is heated by hammering; the heat is but transmuted mechanical force; or a body is put in motion by heat, a certain quantity being transformed into mechanical effect, or motion of the mass. And so it is held that no force can arise except by the expenditure of a preëxisting force. Now, the living system is acted upon by the same agencies and under the same law. Impressions made upon the organs of sense give rise to sensations, and we have the same warrant in this, as in the former case, for regarding the effects as transformations of the forces in action. If the change of molecular state in a melted body represents the heat transformed in fusing it, so the sensation of warmth in a living body must represent the heat transformed in producing it. The impression on the retina, as well as that on the photographic tablet, results from the transmuted impulses of light. And thus impressions made from moment to moment on all our organs of sense, are directly correlated with external physical forces. This correlation, furthermore, is quantitative as well as qualitative. Not only does the light-force produce its peculiar sensations, but the intensity of these sensations corresponds with the intensity of the force; not only is atmospheric vibration transmuted into the sense of sound, but the energy of the vibration determines its loudness. And so in all other cases; the quantity of sensation depends upon the quantity of the force acting to produce it.

Moreover, sensations do not terminate in themselves, or come to nothing; they produce certain correlated and equivalent effects.

The feelings of light, heat, sound, odor, taste, pressure, are immediately followed by physiological effects, as secretion, muscular action, &c. Sensations increase the contractions of the heart, and it has been lately maintained that every sensation contracts the muscular fibres throughout the whole vascular system. The respiratory muscles also respond to sensations; the rate of breathing being increased by both pleasurable and painful nerve-impressions. The quantity of sensation, moreover, controls the quantity of emotion. Loud sounds produce violent starts, disagreeable tastes cause wry faces, and sharp pains give rise to violent struggles. Even when groans and cries are suppressed, the clenched hands and set teeth show that the muscular excitement is only taking another direction.

Between the emotions and bodily actions the correlation and equivalence are also equally clear. Moderate actions, like moderate sensations, excite the heart, the vascular system, and the glandular organs. As the emotions rise in strength, however, the various systems of muscles are thrown into action; and when they reach a certain pitch of intensity, violent convulsive movements ensue. Anger frowns and stamps; grief wrings its hands; joy dances and leaps—the amount of sensation determining the quantity of correlative movement.

Dr. Carpenter, in his Physiology, has brought forward numerous exemplifications of this principle of the conversion of emotion into movement, as seen in the common workings of human nature. Most persons have experienced the difficulty of sitting still under high excitement of the feelings, and also the relief afforded by walking or active exercise; while, on the other hand, repression of the movements protracts the emotional excitement. Many irascible persons get relief from their irritated feelings by a hearty explosion of oaths, others by a violent slamming of the door, or a prolonged fit of grumbling. Demonstrative persons habitually expend their feelings in action, while those who manifest them less retain them longer: hence the former are more weak and transient in their attachments than the latter, whose unexpended emotions become permanent elements of character. For the same reason, those who are loud and vehement in their lamentations seldom die of grief; while the deep-seated emotions of sorrow which others cannot work off in violent demonstrations, depress the organic functions, and often wear out the life.

The intellectual operations are also directly correlated with physical activities. As in the inorganic world we know nothing of forces except as exhibited by matter, so in the higher intellectual realm we know nothing of mind-force except through its material manifestations. Mental operations are dependent upon material changes in the nervous system; and it may now be regarded as a fundamental physiological principle, that "no idea or feeling can arise, save as the result of some physical force expended in producing it." The directness of this dependence is proved by the fact that any disturbance of the train of cerebral transformations disturbs mentality, while their arrest destroys it. And here, also, the correlation is quantitative. Other things being equal there is a relation between the size of the nerve apparatus and the amount of mental action of which it is capable. Again, it is dependent upon the vigor of the circulation; if this is arrested by the cessation of the heart's action, total unconsciousness results; if it is enfeebled, mental action is low; while if it is quickened, mentality rises, even to delirium, when the cerebral activity becomes excessive. Again, the rate of brain activity is dependent upon the special chemical ingredients of the blood, oxygen and carbon. Increase of oxygen augments cerebral action, while increase of carbonic acid depresses it. The degree of mentality is also dependent upon the phosphatic constituents of the nervous system. The proportion of phosphorus in the brain is smallest in infancy, idiocy, and old age, and greatest during the prime of life; while the quantity of alkaline phosphates excreted by the kidneys rises and falls with the variations of mental activity. The equivalence of physical agencies and mental effects is still further seen in the action of various substances, as alcohol, opium, hashish, nitrous oxide, etc., when absorbed into the blood. Within the limits of their peculiar action upon the nervous centres, the effect of each is strictly proportionate to the quantity taken. There is a constant ratio between the antecedents and consequents.

"How this metamorphosis takes place—how a force existing as motion, heat, or light, can become a mode of consciousness—how it is possible for aërial vibrations to generate the sensation we call sound, or for the forces liberated by chemical changes in the brain, to give rise to emotion, these are mysteries which it is impossible to fathom. But they are not profounder mysteries than the transformation of the physical forces into each other. They are not more completely beyond our comprehension than the natures of mind and matter. They have simply the same insolubility as all other ultimate questions. We can learn nothing more than that here is one of the uniformities in the order of phenomena."

The law of correlation being thus applicable to human energy as well as to the powers of nature, it must also apply to society, where we constantly witness the conversion of forces on a comprehensive scale. The powers of nature are transformed into the activities of society; water-power, wind-power, steam-power, and electrical-power are pressed into the social service, reducing human labor, multiplying resources, and carrying on numberless industrial processes: indeed, the conversion of these forces into social activities is one of the chief triumphs of civilization. The universal forces of heat and light are transformed by the vegetable kingdom into the vital energy of organic compounds, and then, as food, are again converted into human beings and human power. The very existence as well as the activity of society are obviously dependent upon the operations of vegetable growth. When that is abundant, population may become dense, and social activities multifarious and complicated, while a scanty vegetation entails sparse population and enfeebled social action. Any universal disturbance of the physical forces, as excessive rains or drouth, by reducing the harvest, is felt throughout the entire social organism. Where this effect is marked, and not counteracted by free communication with more fertile regions, the means of the community become restricted, business declines, manufactures are reduced, trade slackens, travel falls off, luxuries are diminished, education is neglected, marriages are fewer, and a thousand kindred results indicate decline of enterprise and depression of the social energies.

In a dynamical point of view there is a strict analogy between the individual and the social economies—the same law of force governs the development of both. In the case of the individual, the amount of energy which he possesses at any time is limited, and when consumed for one purpose it cannot of course be had for another. An undue demand in one direction involves a corresponding deficiency elsewhere. For example, excessive action of the digestive system exhausts the muscular and cerebral systems, while excessive action of the muscular system is at the expense of the cerebral and digestive organs; and again, excessive action of the brain depresses the digestive and muscular energies. If the fund of power in the growing constitutions of children is overdrawn in any special channel, as is often the case by excessive stimulation of the brain, the undue abstraction of energy from other portions of the system is sure to entail some form of physiological disaster. So with the social organism; its forces being limited, there is but a definite amount of power to be consumed in the various social activities. Its appropriation in one way makes impossible its employment in another, and it can only gain power to perform one function by the loss of it in other directions. This fact, that social force cannot be created by enactment, and that when dealing with the producing, distributing, and commercial activities of the community, legislation can do little more than interfere with their natural courses, deserves to be more thoroughly appreciated by the public.

But the law in question has yet higher bearings. More and more we are perceiving that the condition of humanity and the progress of civilization are direct resultants of the forces by which men are controlled. What we term the moral order of society, implies a strict regularity in the action of these forces. Modern statistics disclose a remarkable constancy in the moral activities manifested in communities of men. Crimes, and even the modes of crime, have been observed to occur with a uniformity which admits of their prediction. Each period may therefore be said to have its definite amount of morality and justice. It has been maintained, for instance, with good reason, that "the degree of liberty a people is capable of in any given age, is a fixed quantity, and that any artificial extension of it in one direction brings about an equivalent limitation in some other direction. French revolutions show scarcely any more respect for individual rights than the despotisms they supplant; and French electors use their freedom to put themselves again in slavery. So in those communities where State restraint is feeble, we may expect to find it supplemented by the sterner restraints of public opinion."

But society like the individual is progressive. Although at each stage of individual growth the forces of the organism, physiological, intellectual, and passional, have each a certain definite amount of strength, yet these ratios are constantly changing, and it is in this change that development essentially consists. So with society; the measured action of its forces gives rise to a fixed amount of morality and liberty in each age, but that amount increases with social evolution. The savage is one in whom certain classes of feelings and emotions predominate, and he becomes civilized just in proportion as these feelings are slowly replaced by others of a higher character. Yet the activities which determine human advancement are various. Not only must we regard the physiological forces, or those which pertain to man's physical organization and capacities, and the psychological, or those resulting from his intellectual and emotional constitution, but the influences of the external world, and those of the social state, are likewise to be considered. Man and society, therefore, as viewed by the eye of science, present a series of vast and complex dynamical problems, which are to be studied in the future in the light of the great law by which, we have reason to believe, all forms and phases of force are governed.

A further aspect of the subject remains still to be noticed. Mr. Herbert Spencer has the honor of crowning this sublime inquiry by showing that the law of the conservation, or as he prefers to term it the 'Persistence of Force,' as it is the underlying principle of all being, is also the fundamental truth of all philosophy. With masterly analytic skill he has shown that this principle of which the human mind has just become fully conscious, is itself the profoundest law of the human mind, the deepest foundation of consciousness. He has demonstrated that the law of the Persistence of Force, of which the most piercing intellects of past times had but partial and unsatisfying glimpses, and which the latest scientific research has disclosed as a great principle of nature, has a yet more transcendent character; is, in fact, an *à priori* truth of the highest order—a truth which is necessarily involved in our mental organization; which is broader than any possible induction, and of higher validity than any other truth whatever. This principle, which is at once the highest result of scientific investigation and metaphysical analysis, Mr. Spencer has made the basis of his new and comprehensive System of Philosophy; and in the first work of the series, entitled "First Principles," he has developed the doctrine in its broadest philosophic aspects. The lucid reasoning by which he reaches his conclusions cannot be presented here; a brief extract or two will, however, serve to indicate the important place assigned to the law by this acute and profound inquirer:

"We might, indeed, be certain, even in the absence of any such analysis as the foregoing, that there must exist some principle which, as being the basis of science, cannot be established by science. All reasoned out conclusions whatever must rest on some postulate. As before shown, we cannot go on merging derivative truths in these wider and wider truths from which they are derived, without reaching at last a widest truth which can be merged in no other, or derived from no other. And whoever contemplates the relation in which it stands to the truths of science in general, will see that this truth, transcending demonstration, is the Persistence of force." * * *

"Such, then, is the foundation of any possible system of positive knowledge. Deeper than demonstration—deeper even than definite cognition—deep as the very nature of mind, is the postulate at which we have arrived. Its authority transcends all others whatever; for not only is it given in the constitution of our own consciousness, but it is impossible to imagine a consciousness so constituted as not to give it. Thought, involving simply the establishment of relations, may be readily conceived to go on while yet these relations have not been organized into the abstracts we call space and time; and so there is a conceivable kind of consciousness which does not contain the truths commonly called *à priori*, involved in the organization of these forms of relations. But thought cannot be conceived to go on without some element between which its relations may be established; and so there is no conceivable kind of consciousness which does not imply continued existence as its datum. Consciousness without this or that particular form is possible; but consciousness without *contents* is impossible.

"The sole truth which transcends experience by underlying it, is thus the Persistence of force. This being the basis of experience, must be the basis of any scientific organization of experiences. To this an ultimate analysis brings us down; and on this a rational synthesis must be built up."

To the question, What then is the value of experimental investigations upon the subject, if the truth sought cannot be established by inductions from them? Mr. Spencer replies: "They are of value as disclosing the many particular implications which the general truth does not specify; they are of value as teaching us how much of one mode of force is the equivalent of so much of another mode; they are of value as determining under what conditions each metamorphosis occurs; and they are of value as leading us to inquire in what shape the remnant of force has escaped, when the apparent results are not equivalent to the cause." And it may be added, that it is to these investigations that we are indebted for the clear and comprehensive establishment of the principle as a law of physical nature; psychological analysis having only shown that it extends much further than it is the business of experimental science to go.

Thus the law characterized by Faraday as the highest in physical science which our faculties permit us to perceive, has a far more extended sway; it might well have been proclaimed the highest law of *all* science—the most far-reaching principle that adventuring reason has discovered in the universe. Its stupendous reach spans all orders of existence. Not only does it govern the movements of the heavenly bodies, but it presides over the genesis of the constellations; not only does it control those radiant floods of power which fill the eternal spaces, bathing, warming, illumining and vivifying our planet, but it rules the actions and relations of men, and regulates the march of terrestrial affairs. Nor is its dominion limited to physical phenomena; it prevails equally in the world of mind, controlling all the faculties and processes of thought and feeling. The star-suns of the remoter galaxies dart their radiations across the universe; and although the distances are so profound that hundreds of centuries may have been required to traverse them, the impulses of force enter the eye, and impressing an atomic change upon the nerve, give origin to the sense of sight. Star and nerve-tissue are parts of the same system—stellar and nervous forces are correlated. Nay more; sensation awakens thought and kindles emotion, so that this wondrous dynamic chain binds into living unity the realms of matter and mind through measureless amplitudes of space and time.

And if these high realities are but faint and fitful glimpses which science has obtained in the dim dawn of discovery, what must be the glories of the coming day? If indeed they are but 'pebbles' gathered from the shores of the great ocean of truth, what are the mysteries still hidden in the bosom of the mighty unexplored? And how far transcending all stretch of thought that Unknown and Infinite Cause of all to which the human spirit turns evermore in solemn and mysterious worship!

It remains only to observe, that so immense a step in the progress of our knowledge of natural agencies as the following pages disclose, cannot be without effect upon the intellectual culture of the age. To the adherents of that scholastic and verbal education which prefers words to things, and ancient to modern thought; which ignores the study of nature, and regards the progress of science with indifference or hostility, it matters little what views of the world are entertained, or what changes these views may undergo. But there is another, and happily an increasing class, who hold that it is the true destiny of mind to comprehend the vast order of existence in the midst of which it is placed, and that the faculties of man are divinely adapted to this sublime task; who see that the laws of nature must be understood before they can be obeyed, and that only through this understanding can man rise to the mastery of its powers, and bring himself into final harmony with his conditions. These will recognize that the discovery of new principles which expand, and elevate, and harmonize our views of the universe—which involve the workings of the mind itself, open a new chapter in philosophy, and touch the very foundations of knowledge, cannot be without a determining influence upon the future course and development of thought, and the spirit and methods of its acquisition.

THE CORRELATION OF PHYSICAL FORCES.

By W. R. GROVE, Q.C., M.A., F.R.S.

FIRST AMERICAN, FROM THE FOURTH ENGLISH EDITION.

William Robert Grove, an English lawyer and physicist, was born at Swansea, July 14, 1811. He graduated at Oxford in 1834, and during the next five years was Professor of Natural Philosophy at the London Institution. Professor Grove is a rare example of the ability which has achieved a distinguished eminence in different fields of effort. While pursuing with marked success the profession of an advocate, he has devoted his leisure to original scientific researches, and obtained a high distinction both as a discoverer and a philosophic writer upon scientific subjects. In 1852 he was made Queen's Counsel, and afterwards Vice-President of the Royal Society. He is the inventor of the powerful galvanic battery known by his name, and his chief researches have been in the field of electricity. Many of his experimental results are referred to in the following pages, which will also attest his high position among the founders of the new philosophy of forces.

PREFACE.

THE Phrase 'Correlation of Physical Forces' in the sense in which I have used it, having become recognized by a large number of scientific writers, it would produce confusion were I now to adopt another title. It would, perhaps, have been better if I had in the first instance used the term Co-relation, as the words 'correlate,' 'correlative,' had acquired a peculiar metaphysical sense somewhat differing from that which I attached to the substantive correlation. The passage in the text (p. 183) explains the meaning I have given to the term.

Twenty years having elapsed since I promulgated the views contained in this Essay, which were first advanced in a lecture at the London Institution in January 1842, and subsequently more fully developed in a course of lectures in 1843, I think it advisable to add a little to the Preface with reference to other labourers in the same field.

It has happened with this subject as with many others, that similar ideas have independently presented themselves to different minds about the same period. In May 1842 a paper was published by M. Mayer which I had not read when my last edition was published, and indeed only now know imperfectly by the *vivâ-voce* translation of a friend. It deduces very much the same conclusions to which I had been led, the author starting partly from *à priori* reasoning and partly from an experiment by which water was heated by agitation, and from another, which had, however, previously been made by Davy, viz. that ice can be melted by friction, though kept in a medium which is below the freezing point of water.

In 1843 a paper by Mr. Joule on the mechanical equivalent of heat appeared, which, though not in terms touching on the mutual and necessary dependence of all the Physical Forces, yet bears most importantly upon the doctrine.

While my third edition was going through the press I had the good fortune to make the acquaintance of M. Seguin, who informed me that his uncle, the eminent Montgolfier, had long entertained the idea that force was indestructible, though, with the exception of one sentence, in his paper on the hydraulic ram, and where he is apparently speaking of mechanical force, he has left nothing in print on the subject. Not so, however, M. Seguin himself, who in 1839, in a work on the 'Influence of Railroads,' has distinctly expressed his uncle's and his own views on the identity of heat and mechanical force, and has given a calculation of their equivalent relation, which is not far from the more recent numerical results of Mayer, Joule, and others.

Several of the great mathematicians of a much earlier period advocated the idea of what they termed the Conservation of Force, but although they considered that a body in motion would so continue for ever, unless arrested by the impact of another body, and, indeed, in the latter case, would, if elastic, still continue to move (though deflected from its course) with a force proportionate to its elasticity, yet with inelastic bodies the general, and, as far as I am aware, the universal belief was, that the motion was arrested and the force annihilated. Montgolfier went a step farther, and his hydraulic ram was to him a proof of the truth of his preconceived idea, that the shock or impact of bodies left the mechanical force undestroyed.

Previously, however, to the discoveries of the voltaic battery, electro-magnetism, thermo-electricity, and photography, it was impossible for any mind to perceive what, in the greater number of cases, became of the force which was apparently lost. The phenomena of heat, known from the earliest times, would have been a mode of accounting for the resulting force in many cases where motion was arrested, and we find Bacon announcing a theory that motion was the form, as he quaintly termed it, of heat. Rumford and Davy adopted this view, the former with a fair approximate attempt at numerical calculation, but no one of these philosophers seems to have connected it with the indestructibility of force. A passage in the writings of Dr. Roget, combating the theory that mere contact of dissimilar bodies was the source of voltaic electricity, philosophically supports his argument by the idea of non-creation of force.

As I have introduced into the later editions of my Essay abstracts of the different discoveries which I have found, since my first lectures, to bear upon the subject, I have been regarded by many rather as the historian of the progress made in this branch of thought than as one who has had anything to do with its initiation. Everyone is but a poor judge where he is himself interested, and I therefore write with diffidence, but it would be affecting an indifference which I do not feel if I did not state that I believe myself to have been the first who introduced this subject as a generalised system of philosophy, and continued to enforce it in my lectures and writings for many years, during which it met with the opposition usual and proper to novel ideas.

Avocations necessary to the well-being of others have prevented my following it up experimentally, to the extent that I once hoped; but I trust and believe that this Essay, imperfect though it be, has helped materially to impress on that portion of the public which devotes its attention rather to the philosophy of science than to what is now termed science, the truth of the thesis advocated.

To show that the work of to-day is not substantially different from the thoughts I first published on the subject, at a period when I knew little or nothing of what had been thought before, I venture to give a few extracts from the printed copy of my lecture of 1842:—

> Physical Science treats of Matter, and what I shall to-night term its *Affections;* namely, Attraction, Motion, Heat, Light, Electricity, Magnetism, Chemical-Affinity. When these re-act upon matter, they constitute Forces. The present tendency of theory seems to lead to the opinion that all these Affections are resolvable into one, namely, Motion; however, should the theories on these subjects be ultimately so effectually generalised as to become laws, they cannot avoid the necessity for retaining different names for these different Affections; or, as they would then be called, different modes of Motion. . . . .
>
> Œrsted proved that Electricity and Magnetism are two forces which act upon each other; not in straight lines, as all other known forces do, but in a rectangular direction: that is, that bodies invested with electricity, or the conduits of an electric-current, tend to place magnets at right angles to them; and, conversely, that magnets tend to place bodies conducting electricity at right angles to them. . . . .

The discovery of Œrsted, by which electricity was made a source of Magnetism, soon led philosophers to seek the converse effect; that is, to educe Electricity from a permanent magnet:—had these experimentalists succeeded in their expectations of making a stationary magnet a source of electric-currents, they would have realised the ancient dreams of perpetual motion, they would have converted statics into dynamics, they would have produced power without expenditure; in other words, they would have become creators. They failed, and Faraday saw their error; he proved that to obtain Electricity from Magnetism it was necessary to superadd to this latter, motion; that magnets while in motion induced electricity in contiguous conductors; and that the direction of such electric-currents was tangential to the polar direction of the magnet; that as Dynamic-electricity may be made the source of Magnetism and Motion, so Magnetism conjoined with Motion may be made the source of Electricity. Here originates the Science of Magneto-electricity, the true converse of Electro-magnetism; and thus between Electricity and Magnetism is shown to exist a reciprocity of force such that, considering either as the primary agent, the other becomes the re-agent; viewing one in the relation of cause, the other is the effect. . . . .

The Science of Thermo-Electricity connected heat with electricity, and proved these, like all other natural forces, to be capable of mutual reaction. . . . .

Voltaic action is Chemical action taking place at a distance or transferred through a chain of media; and the Daltonian equivalent numbers are the exponents of the amount of voltaic action for corresponding chemical substances. . . .

By regarding the quantity of electrical, as directly proportional to the efficient chemical action, and by experimentally tracing this principle, I have been fortunate enough to increase the power of the Voltaic-pile more than sixteen times, as compared with any combination previously known. . . . .

I am strongly disposed to consider that the facts of Catalysis depend upon voltaic action, to generate which three heterogeneous substances are always necessary. Induced by this belief I made some experiments on the subject, and succeeded in forming a voltaic combination by gaseous-oxygen, gaseous-hydrogen, and platinum; by which a galvanometer was deflected and water decomposed. . . . .

It appears to me that heat and light may be considered as affections; or, according to the Undulatory-theory, vibrations of matter itself, and not of a distinct etherial fluid permeating it: these vibrations would be propagated, just as sound is propagated by vibrations of wood or as waves by water. To my mind, all the consequences of the Undulatory-theory flow as easily from this, as from the hypothesis of a specific ether; to suppose which, namely, to suppose a fluid *sui generis*, and of extreme tenuity penetrating solid bodies, we must assume, first, the existence of the fluid itself; secondly, that bodies are without exception porous; thirdly, that these pores communicate; fourthly, that matter is limited in expansibility. None of these difficulties apply to the modification of this theory which I venture to propose; and no other difficulty applies to it which does not equally apply to the received hypothesis. With regard to the planetary spaces, the diminishing periods of comets is a strong argument for the existence of an universally-diffused matter: this has the function of resistance, and there appears to be no reason to divest it of the functions common to all matter, or superficially to appropriate it to certain affections. Again, the phenomena of transparency and opacity are, to my mind, more easily explicable by the former than by the latter theory; as resulting from a difference in the molecular arrangement of the matter affected. In regard to the effects of double-refraction and polarisation, the molecular gives at once a reason for the effects upon the one theory, while upon the other we must, in addition to previous assumptions, further assume a different elasticity of the ether in different directions within the doubly-refracting medium. The same theory is applicable to Electricity and Magnetism; my own experiments on the influence of the elastic intermedium on the voltaic-arc, and those of Faraday on electrical induction, furnish strong arguments in support of it. My inclination would lead me to detain you on this subject much longer than my judgment deems advisable: I therefore content myself with offering it to your consideration, and, should my avocations permit, I may at a future period more fully develope it. . . . .

Light, Heat, Electricity, Magnetism, Motion, and Chemical-affinity, are all convertible material affections; assuming either as the cause, one of the others will be the effect: thus heat may be said to produce electricity, electricity to produce heat; magnetism to produce electricity, electricity magnetism; and so of the rest. Cause and effect, therefore, in their abstract relation to these forces, are words solely of convenience: we are totally unacquainted with the ultimate generating power of each and all of them, and probably shall ever remain so; we can only ascertain the normæ of their action: we must humbly refer their causation to one omnipresent influence, and content ourselves with studying their effects and developing by experiment their mutual relations.

I have transposed the passages relating to voltaic action and catalysis, but I have not added a word to the above quotation, and, as far as I am now aware, the theory that the so-called imponderables are affections of ordinary matter, that they are resolvable into motion, that they are to be regarded in their action on matter as forces, and not as specific entities, and that they are capable of mutual reaction, thence alternately acting as cause and effect, had not at that time been publicly advanced.

My original Essays being a record of lectures, and being published by the managers of the Institution, I necessarily adhered to the form and matter which I had orally communicated. In preparing subsequent editions I found that, without destroying the identity of the work, I could not alter the style; although it would have been less difficult and more satisfactory to me to have done so, the work would not have been a republication; and I was for obvious reasons anxious to preserve as far as I could the original text, which, though added to, is but little altered.

The form of lectures has necessarily continued the use of the first person, and I would beg my readers not to attribute to me, from the modes of expression used, a dogmatism which is far from my thought. If my opinions are expressed broadly, it is that, if opinions are always hedged in by qualifications, the style becomes embarrassed and the meaning frequently unintelligible.

As a course of lectures can only be useful by inducing the auditor to consult works on the subject he hears treated, so the object of this Essay is more to induce a particular train of thought on the known facts of physical science than to enter with minute criticisms into each separate branch.

In one or two of the reviews of previous editions the general idea of the work was objected to. I believe, however, that will not now be the case; the mathematical labours of Mr. Thompson, Clausius, and others, though not suitable for insertion in an Essay such as this, have awakened an interest for many portions of the subject, which promises much for its future progress.

The short and irregular intervals which my profession permits me to devote to science so prevent the continuity of attention necessary for the proper evolution of a train of thought, that I certainly should not now have courage to publish for the first time such an Essay; and it is only the favour it has received from those whose opinions I highly value, and the, I trust pardonable, wish not to let some favourite thoughts of my youth lose all connection with my name, that have induced me to reprint it.

My scientific readers will, I hope, excuse the very short notices of certain branches of science which are introduced, as without them the work would be unintelligible to many for whom it is intended. I have endeavoured so to arrange my matter that each division should form an introduction to those which follow, and to assume no more preliminary knowledge to be possessed by my readers than would be expected from persons acquainted with the elements of physical science.

The notes contain references to the original memoirs in which the branches of science alluded to are to be found, as well as to those which bear on the main arguments; where these memoirs are numerous, or not easy of access, I have referred to treatises in which they are collated. To prevent the reader's attention being interrupted, I have in the notes referred to the pages of the text, instead of to interpolated letters.

CORRELATION

OF

PHYSICAL FORCES

I.—INTRODUCTORY REMARKS.

WHEN natural phenomena are for the first time observed, a tendency immediately developes itself to refer them to something previously known—to bring them within the range of acknowledged sequences. The mode of regarding new facts, which is most favourably received by the public, is that which refers them to recognised views—stamps them into the mould in which the mind has been already shaped. The new fact may be far removed from those to which it is referred, and may belong to a different order of analogies, but this cannot then be known, as its co-ordinates are wanting. It may be questionable whether the mind is not so moulded by past events that it is impossible to advance an entirely new view, but admitting such possibility, the new view, necessarily founded on insufficient data, is likely to be more incorrect and prejudicial than even a strained attempt to reconcile the new discovery with known facts.

The theory consequent upon new facts, whether it be a co-ordination of them with known ones, or the more difficult

1*

and dangerous attempt at remodelling the public ideas, is generally enunciated by the discoverers themselves of the facts, or by those to whose authority the world at the period of the discovery defers; others are not bold enough, or if they be so, are unheeded. The earliest theories thus enunciated obtain the firmest hold upon the public mind, for at such a time there is no power of testing, by a sufficient range of experience, the truth of the theory; it is accepted solely or mainly upon authority: there being no means of contradiction, its reception is, in the first instance, attended with some degree of doubt, but as the time in which it can fairly be investigated far exceeds that of any lives then in being, and as neither the individual nor the public mind will long tolerate a state of abeyance, a theory shortly becomes, for want of a better, admitted as an established truth: it is handed from father to son, and gradually takes its place in education. Succeeding generations, whose minds are thus formed to an established view, are much less likely to abandon it. They have adopted it in the first instance, upon authority, to them unquestionable, and subsequently to yield up their faith would involve a laborious remodelling of ideas, a task which the public as a body will and can rarely undertake, the frequent occurrence of which is indeed inconsistent with the very existence of man in a social state, as it would induce an anarchy of thought—a perpetuity of mental revolutions.

This necessity has its good; but the prejudicial effect upon the advance of science is, that by this means, theories the most immature frequently become the most permanent; for no theory can be more immature, none is likely to be so incorrect, as that which is formed at the first flush of a new discovery; and though time exalts the authority of those from whom it emanated, time can never give to the illustrious dead the means of analysing and correcting erroneous views which subsequent discoveries confer.

Take for instance the Ptolemaic System, which we may almost literally explain by the expression of Shakspeare: 'He that is giddy thinks the world turns round.' We now see the error of this system, because we have all an immediate opportunity of refuting it; but this identical error was received as a truth for centuries, because, when first promulgated, the means of refuting it were not at hand, and when the means of its refutation became attainable, mankind had been so educated to the supposed truth, that they rejected the proof of its fallacy.

I have premised the above for two reasons: first to obtain a fair hearing, by requesting as far as possible a dismissal from the mind of my readers of preconceived views by and in favour of which all are liable to be prejudiced; and secondly, to defend myself from the charge of undervaluing authority, or treating lightly the opinions of those to whom and to whose memory mankind looks with reverence. Properly to value authority, we should estimate it together with its means of information: if 'a dwarf on the shoulders of a giant can see further than the giant,' he is no less a dwarf in comparison with the giant.

The subject on which I am about to treat—viz., the relation of the affections of matter to each other and to matter—peculiarly demands an unprejudiced regard. The different aspects under which these agencies have been contemplated; the different views which have been taken of matter itself; the metaphysical subtleties to which these views unavoidably lead, if pursued beyond fair inductions from existing experience, present difficulties almost insurmountable.

The extent of claim which my views on this subject may have to originality has been stated in the Preface; they became strongly impressed upon my mind at a period when I was much engaged in experimental research, and were, as I then believed, and still believe, regarding them as a system, new: expressions in the works of different authors, bearing more or less on the subject, have subsequently been pointed out to me, some of which go back to a distant period. An attempt to analyse these in detail, and to trace how far I have been anticipated by others, would probably but little interest the reader, and in the course of it I should constantly have to make distinctions showing wherein I differed, and wherein I agreed with others. I might cite authorities which appear to me to oppose, and others which appear to coincide with certain of the views I have put forth; but this would interrupt the consecutive developement of my own ideas, and might render me liable to the charge of misconstruing those of others; I therefore think it better to avoid such discussion in the text; and in addition to the sketch given in the Preface, to furnish in the notes at the conclusion such references to different authors as bear upon the subjects treated of, which I have discovered, or which have been pointed out to me since the delivery of the lectures of which this essay is a record.

The more extended our research becomes, the more we find that knowledge is a thing of slow progression, that the very notions which appear to ourselves new, have arisen, though perhaps in a very indirect manner, from successive modifications of traditional opinions. Each word we utter, each thought we think, has in it the vestiges, is in itself the impress, of antecedent words and thoughts. As each material form, could we rightly read it, is a book, containing in itself the past history of the world; so, different though our philosophy may now appear to be from that of our progenitors, it is but theirs added to or subtracted from, transmitted drop by drop through the filter of antecedent, as ours will be through that of subsequent, ages.—The relic is to the past as is the germ to the future.

Though many valuable facts, and correct deductions from them, are to be found scattered amongst the voluminous works of the ancient philosophers; yet, giving them the credit which they pre-eminently deserve for having devoted their lives to purely intellectual pursuits, and for having thought, seldom frivolously, often profoundly, nothing can be more difficult than to seize and apprehend the ideas of those who reasoned from abstraction to abstraction—who, although, as we now believe, they must have depended upon observation for their first inductions, afterwards raised upon them such a complex superstructure of syllogistic deductions, that, without following the same paths, and tracing the same sinuosities which led them to their conclusions, such conclusions are to us unintelligible. To think as another thought, we must be placed in the same situation as he was placed: the errors of commentators generally arise from their reasoning upon the arguments of their text, either in blind obedience to its dicta, without considering the circumstances under which they were uttered, or in viewing the images presented to the original writer from a different point to that from which he viewed them. Experimental philosophy keeps in check the errors both of *à priori* reasoning and of commentators, and, at all events, prevents their becoming cumulative; though the theories or explanations of a fact be different, the fact remains the same. It is, moreover, itself the exponent of its discoverer's thought: the observation of known phenomena has led him to elicit from nature the new phenomena: and, though he may be wrong in his deductions from this after its discovery, the reasonings which conducted him to it are themselves valuable, and, having led from known to unknown truths, can seldom be uninstructive.

Very different views existed amongst the ancients as to the aims to be pursued by physical investigation, and as to the objects likely to be attained by it. I do not here mean the moral objects, such as the attainment of the *summum bonum*, &c.—but the acquisitions in knowledge which such investigations were likely to confer. Utility was one object in view, and this was to some extent attained by the progress made in astronomy and mechanics; Archimedes, for instance, seems to have constantly had this end in view; but, while pursuing natural knowledge for the sake of knowledge and the power which it brings with it, the greater number seemed to entertain an expectation of arriving at some ultimate goal, some point of knowledge, which would give them a mastery over the mysteries of nature, and would enable them to ascertain what was the most intimate structure of matter, and the causes of the changes it exhibits. Where they could not discover, they speculated. Leucippus, Democritus, and others, have given us their notions of the ultimate atoms of which matter was formed, and of the *modus agendi* of nature in the various transformations which matter undergoes.

The expectation of arriving at ultimate causes or essences continued long after the speculations of the ancients had been abandoned, and continues even to the present day to be a very general notion of the objects to be ultimately attained by physical science. Francis Bacon, the great remodeller of science, entertained this notion, and thought that, by experimentally testing natural phenomena, we should be enabled to trace them to certain primary essences or causes whence the various phenomena flow. These he speaks of under the scholastic name of 'forms'—a term derived from the ancient philosophy, but differently applied. He appears to have understood by 'form' the essence of quality—that in which, abstracting everything extraneous, a given quality consists, or that which, superinduced on any body, would give it its peculiar quality: thus the form of transparency, is that which constitutes transparency, or that by which, when discovered, transparency could be produced or superinduced. To take a specific example of what I may term the synthetic application of his philosophy:—'In gold there meet together yellowness, gravity, malleability, fixedness in the fire, a determinate way of solution, which are the simple natures in gold; for he who understands form, and the manner of superinducing this yellowness, gravity, ductility, fixedness, faculty of fusion, solution, &c., with their particular degrees and proportions, will consider how to join them together in some body, so that a transmutation into gold shall follow.'

On the other hand, the analytic method, or, 'the enquiry from what origin gold or any other metal or stone is generated from its first fluid matter or rudiments, up to a perfect mineral,' is to be perceived by what Bacon calls the latent process, or a search for 'what in every generation or transformation of bodies, flies off, what remains behind, what is added, what separated, &c.; also, in other alterations and motions, what gives motion, what governs it, and the like.' Bacon appears to have thought that qualities separate from the substances themselves were attainable, and if not capable of physical isolation, were at all events capable of physical transference and superinduction.

Subsequently to Bacon a belief has generally existed, and now to a great extent exists, in what are called secondary causes, or consequential steps, wherein one phenomenon is supposed necessarily to hang on another, until at last we arrive at an essential cause, subject immediately to the First Cause. This notion is generally prevalent both on the Continent and in this country: nothing is more familiar than the expression 'study the effects in order to arrive at the causes.'

Instead of regarding the proper object of physical science as a search after essential causes, I believe it ought to be, and must be, a search after facts and relations—that although the word Cause may be used in a secondary and concrete sense, as meaning antecedent forces, yet in an abstract sense it is totally inapplicable; we cannot predicate of any physical agency that it is abstractedly the cause of another; and if, for the sake of convenience, the language of secondary causation be permissible, it should be only with reference to the special phenomena referred to, as it can never be generalised.

The misuse, or rather varied use, of the term Cause, has

been a source of great confusion in physical theories, and philosophers are even now by no means agreed as to their conception of causation. The most generally received view of causation, that of Hume, refers it to invariable antecedence —i. e., we call that a cause which invariably precedes, that an effect which invariably succeeds. Many instances of invariable sequence might however be selected, which do not present the relation of cause and effect: thus as Reed observes, and Brown does not satisfactorily answer, day invariably precedes night and yet day is not the cause of night. The seed, again, precedes the plant, but is not the cause of it; so that when we study physical phenomena it becomes difficult to separate the idea of causation from that of force, and these have been regarded as identical by some philosophers. To take an example which will contrast these two views: if a floodgate be raised, the water flows out; in ordinary parlance, the water is said to flow *because* the floodgate is raised: the sequence is invariable; no floodgate, properly so called, can be raised without the water flowing out, and yet in another, and perhaps more strict, sense, it is the gravitation of the water which *causes* it to flow. But though we may truly say that, in this instance, gravitation causes the water to flow, we cannot in truth abstract the proposition, and say, generally, that gravitation is the cause of water flowing, as water may flow from other causes, gaseous elasticity, for instance, which will cause water to flow from a receiver full of air into one that is exhausted; gravitation may also, under certain circumstances, arrest instead of cause the flow of water.

Upon neither view, however, can we get at anything like abstract causation. If we regard causation as invariable sequence, we can find no case in which a given antecedent is the only antecedent to a given sequent: thus if water could flow from no other cause than the withdrawal of a floodgate, we might say abstractedly that this was the cause of water flowing. If, again, adopting the view which looks to causation as a force, we could say that water could be caused to flow only by gravitation, we might say abstractedly that gravitation was the cause of water flowing—but this we cannot say; and if we seek and examine any other example, we shall find that causation is only predicable of it in the particular case, and cannot be supported as an abstract proposition; yet this is constantly attempted. Nevertheless, in each *particular* case where we speak of Cause, we habitually refer to some antecedent power or force: we never see motion or any change in matter take effect without regarding it as produced by some previous change; and when we cannot trace it to its antecedent, we mentally refer it to one; but whether this habit be philosophically correct is by no means clear. In other words, it seems questionable, not only whether cause and effect are convertible terms with antecedence and sequence, but whether in fact cause does precede effect, whether force does precede the change in matter of which it is said to be the cause.

The actual priority of cause to effect has been doubted, and their simultaneity argued with much ability. As an instance of this argument it may be said, the attraction which causes iron to approach the magnet is simultaneous with and ever accompanies the movement of the iron; the movement is evidence of the co-existing cause or force, but there is no evidence of any interval in time between the one and the other. On this view time would cease to be a necessary element in causation; the idea of cause, except perhaps as referred to a primeval creation, would cease to exist; and the same arguments which apply to the simultaneity of cause with effect would apply to the simultaneity of Force with Motion. We could not, however, even if we adopted this view, dispense with the element of time in the sequence of phenomena; the effect being thus regarded as ever accompanied simultaneously by its appropriate cause, we should still refer it to some antecedent effect; and our reasoning as applied to the successive production of all natural changes would be the same.

Habit and the identification of thoughts with phenomena so compel the use of recognised terms, that we cannot avoid using the word cause even in the sense to which objection is taken; and if we struck it out of our vocabulary, our language, in speaking of successive changes, would be unintelligible to the present generation. The common error, if I am right in supposing it to be such, consists in the abstraction of cause, and in supposing in each case a general secondary cause—a something which is not the first cause, but which, if we examine it carefully, must have all the attributes of a first cause, and an existence independent of, and dominant over, matter.

The relations of electricity and magnetism afford us a very instructive example of the belief in secondary causation. Subsequent to the discovery by Oersted of electro-magnetism, and prior to that by Faraday of magneto-electricity, electricity and magnetism were believed by the highest authorities to stand in the relation of cause and effect—i. e. electricity was regarded as the cause, and magnetism as the effect; and where magnets existed without any apparent electrical currents to cause their magnetism, hypothetical currents were supposed, for the purpose of carrying out the causative view; but magnetism may now be said with equal truth to be the cause of electricity, and electrical currents may be referred to hypothetical magnetic lines: if therefore electricity cause magnetism, and magnetism cause electricity, why then electricity causes electricity, which becomes, so to speak, a *reductio ad absurdum* of the doctrine.

To take another instance, which may render these positions more intelligible. By heating bars of bismuth and antimony in contact, a current of electricity is produced; and if their extremities be united by a fine wire, the wire is heated. Now here the electricity in the metals is said to be caused by heat, and the heat in the wire to be caused by electricity, and in a concrete sense this is true; but can we thence say abstractedly that heat is the cause of electricity, or that electricity is the cause of heat? Certainly not; for if either be true, both must be so, and the effect then becomes the cause of the cause, or, in other words, a thing causes itself. Any other proposition on this subject will be found to involve similar difficulties, until, at length, the mind will become convinced that abstract secondary causation does not exist, and that a search after essential causes is vain.

The position which I seek to establish in this Essay is, that the various affections of matter which constitute the main objects of experimental physics, viz., heat, light, electricity, magnetism, chemical affinity, and motion, are all correlative, or have a reciprocal dependence; that neither, taken abstractedly, can be said to be the essential cause of the others, but that either may produce or be convertible into, any of the others: thus heat may mediately or immediately produce electricity, electricity may produce heat; and so of the rest, each merging itself as the force it produces becomes developed: and that the same must hold good of other forces, it being an irresistible inference from observed phenomena that a force cannot originate otherwise than by devolution from some pre-existing force or forces.

The term force, although used in very different senses by different authors, in its limited sense may be defined as that which produces or resists motion. Although strongly inclined to believe that the other affections of matter, which I have above named, are, and will ultimately be resolved into, modes of motion, many arguments for which will be given in subsequent parts of this Essay, it would be going too far, at present, to assume their identity with it; I therefore use the term force in reference to them, as meaning that active principle inseparable from matter which is supposed to induce its various changes.

The word force and the idea it aims at expressing might be objected to by the purely physical philosopher on similar grounds to those which apply to the word cause, as it represents a subtle mental conception, and not a sensuous perception or phenomenon. The objection would take something of this form. If the string of a bent bow be cut, the bow will straighten itself; we thence say there is an elastic *force* in the bow which straightens it; but if we applied our expressions to this experiment alone, the use of the term force would be superfluous, and would not add to our knowledge on the subject. All the information which our minds could get would be as sufficiently obtained from the expression, when the string is cut, the bow becomes straight, as from the expression, the bow becomes straight by its elastic force. Do we know more of the phenomena, viewed without reference to other phenomena, by saying it is produced by force? Certainly not. All we know or see is the effect; we do not see force—we see motion or moving matter.

If now we take a piece of caoutchouc and stretch it, when released it returns to its original length. Here, though the subject-matter is very different, we see some analogy in the effect or phenomenon to that of the strung bow. If again we suspend an apple by a string, cut the string, the apple falls. Here, though it is less striking, there is still an analogy to the strung bow and the caoutchouc.

Now when the word force is employed as comprehending these three different phenomena we find some use in the term, not by its explaining or rendering more intelligible the *modus agendi* of matter, but as conveying to the mind something which is alike in the three phenomena, however distinct they may be in other respects: the word becomes an abstract or generalised expression, and regarded in this light is of high utility. Although I have given only three examples, it is obvious that the term would equally apply to 300 or 3,000 examples.

But it will be said, the term force is used not as expressing the effect, but as that which produces the effect. This is true, and in this its ordinary sense I shall use it in these pages. But though the term has a potential meaning, to depart from which would render language unintelligible, we must guard against supposing that we know essentially more of the phenomena by saying they are produced by something, which something is only a word derived from the constancy and similarity of the phenomena we seek to explain by it. The relations of the phenomena to which the terms force or forces are applied give us real knowledge; these relations may be called relations of forces; our knowledge of them is not thereby lessened, and the convenience of expression is greatly increased, but the separate phenomena are not more intimately known; no further insight into why the apple falls is acquired by saying it is forced to fall, or it falls by the force of gravitation; by the latter expression we are enabled to relate it most usefully to other phenomena, but we still know no more of the particular phenomenon than that under certain circumstances the apple does fall.

In the above illustrations, force has been treated as the producer of motion, in which case the evidence of the force is the motion produced; thus we estimate the force used to project a cannon ball in terms of the mass of matter, and the velocity with which it is projected. The evidence of force when the term is applied to resistance to motion is of a somewhat different character; the matter resisting is molecularly affected, and has its structure more or less changed; thus a strip of caoutchouc to which a weight is suspended is elongated, and its molecules are displaced as compared with their position when unaffected by the gravitating force. So a piece of glass bent by an appended weight has its whole structure changed; this internal change is made evident by transmitting through it a beam of polarised light: a relation thus becomes established between the molecular state of bodies and the external forces or motion of masses. Every particle of the caoutchouc or glass must be acting and contributing to resist or arrest the motion of the mass of matter appended to it.

It is difficult, in such cases, not to recognise a reality in force. We need some word to express this state of tension; we know that it produces an effect, though the effect be negative in character: although in this effort of inanimate matter we can no more trace the mode of action to its ultimate elements than we can follow out the connection of our own muscles with the volition which calls them into action, we are experimentally convinced that matter changes its state by the agency of other matter, and this agency we call force.

In placing the weight on the glass, we have moved the former to an extent equivalent to that which it would again describe if the resistance were removed, and this motion of the mass becomes an exponent or measure of the force exerted on the glass; while this is in the state of tension, the force is ever existing, capable of reproducing the original motion, and while in a state of abeyance as to actual motion, it is really acting on the glass. The motion is suspended, but the force is not annihilated.

But it may be objected, if tension or static force be thus motion in abeyance, there is at all times a large amount of dynamical action subtracted from the universe. Every stone upon a hill, every spring that is bent, and has required force to upraise or bend it, has for a time, and possibly for ever, withdrawn this force, and annihilated it. Not so; what takes place when we raise a weight and leave it at the point to which it has been elevated? we have changed the centre of gravity of the earth, and consequently the earth's position with reference to the sun, planets, and stars; the effort we have made pervades and shakes the universe; nor can we present to the mind any exercise of force, which is thus not permanent in its dynamical effects. If, instead of one weight being raised, we raise two weights, each placed at a point diametrically opposite the other, it would be said, here you have compensation, a balance, no change in the centre of gravity of the earth; but we have increased the mean diameter of the earth, and a perturbation of our planet, and of all other celestial bodies necessarily ensues.

The force may be said to be in abeyance with reference to the effect it would have produced, if not arrested, or placed in a state of tension; but in the act of imposing this state, the relations of equilibrium with other bodies have been changed, and these move in their turn, so that motion of the same amount would seem to be ever affecting matter conceived in its totality.

Press the hands violently together; the first notion may be that this is power locked up, and that no change ensues. Not so; the blood courses more quickly, respiration is accelerated, changes which we may not be able to trace, take place in the muscles and nerves, transpiration is increased; we have given off force in various ways, and must, if the effort be prolonged, replenish our sources of power, by fresh chemical action in the stomach.

In books which treat of statics and dynamics, it is common and perhaps necessary to isolate the subjects of consideration; to suppose, for instance, two bodies gravitating, and to ignore the rest of the universe. But no such isolation exists in reality, nor could we predict the result if it did exist. Would two bodies gravitate towards each other in empty space, if space can be empty? the notion that they would is founded on the theory of attraction, which Newton himself repudiated, further than as a convenient means of regarding the subject. For purposes of instruction or argument it may be convenient to assume isolated matter: many conclusions so arrived at may be true, but many will be erroneous.

If, in producing effects of tension or of static force, the effort made pervades the universe, it may be said, when the bent spring is freed, when the raised weight falls, a converse series of motions must be effected, and this theory would lead to a mere reciprocation, which would be equally unproductive of permanent change with the annihilation of force. If raising the weight has changed the centre of gravity of the earth, and thence of the universe, the fall of the weight, it will be said, restores the original centre of gravity, and everything comes back to its original status. In this argument we again, in thought, isolate our experiment; we neglect surrounding circumstances. Between the time of the raising and falling of the weight, be the interval never so small, nay, more, during the rising and during the fall, the earth has been going on revolving round its axis and round the sun, to say nothing of other changes, such as temperature, cosmical magnetism, &c., which we may call accidental, but which, if we knew all, would probably be found to be as necessary and as reducible to law as the motion of the earth. A change having taken place, the fall of the weight does not bring back the *status quo*, but other changes supervene, and so on. Nothing repeats itself, because nothing can be placed again in the same condition: the past is irrevocable.

II.—MOTION.

MOTION—which has been taken as the main exponent of force in the above examples—is the most obvious, the most distinctly conceived of all the affections of matter. Visible motion, or relative change of position in space, is a phenomenon so obvious to simple apprehension, that to attempt to define it would be to render it more obscure; but with motion, as with all physical appearances, there are certain vanishing gradations or undefined limits, at which the obvious mode of action fades away; to detect the continuing existence of the phenomena we are obliged to have recourse to other than ordinary methods of investigation, and we frequently apply other and different names to the effects so recognised.

Thus sound is motion; and although in the earlier periods of philosophy the identity of sound and motion was not traced out, and they were considered distinct affections of matter—indeed, at the close of the last century a theory was advanced that sound was transmitted by the vibrations of an ether—we now so readily resolve sound into motion, that to those who are familiar with acoustics, the phenomena of sound immediately present to the mind the idea of motion, i. e. motion of ordinary matter.

Again, with regard to light: no doubt now exists that light moves or is accompanied by motion. Here the phe-

2

nomena of motion are not made evident by the ordinary sensuous perception, as for instance the motion of a visibly moving projectile would be, but by an inverse deduction from known relations of motion to time and space: as all observation teaches us that bodies in moving from one point in space to another occupy time, we conclude that, wherever a continuing phenomenon is rendered evident in two different points of space at different times, there is motion, though we cannot see the progression. A similar deduction convinces us of the motion of electricity.

As we in common parlance speak of sound moving, although sound is motion, it requires no great stretch of imagination to conceive light and electricity as motions, and not as things moving. If one end of a long bar of metal be struck, a sound is soon perceptible at the other end. This we now know to be a vibration of the bar; sound is but a word expressive of the mode of motion impressed on the bar; so one end of a column of air or glass subjected to a luminous impulse gives a perceptible effect of light at the other end: this can equally be conceived to be a vibration or transmitted motion of particles in the transparent column: this question will, however, be further discussed hereafter; for the present we will confine ourselves to motion within the limits to which the term is usually restricted.

With the perceptible phenomena of motion the mental conception has been invariably associated to which I have before alluded, and to which the term force is given—the which conception, when we analyse it, refers us to some antecedent motion. If we except the production of motion by heat, light, &c., which will be considered in the sequel, when we see a body moving we look to motion having been communicated to it by matter which has previously moved.

Of absolute rest Nature gives us no evidence: all matter, as far as we can ascertain, is ever in movement, not merely in masses, as with the planetary spheres, but also molecularly, or throughout its most intimate structure: thus every alteration of temperature produces a molecular change throughout the whole substance heated or cooled; slow chemical or electrical actions, actions of light or invisible radiant forces, are always at play, so that as a fact we cannot predicate of any portion of matter that it is absolutely at rest. Supposing, however, that motion is not an indispensable function of matter, but that matter can be at rest, matter at rest would never of itself cease to be at rest; it would not move unless impelled to such motion by some other moving body, or body which has moved. This proposition applies not merely to impulsive motion, as when a ball at rest is struck by a moving body, or pressed by a spring which has previously been moved, but to motion caused by attractions such as magnetism or gravitation. Suppose a piece of iron at rest in contact with a magnet at rest; if it be desired to move the iron by the attraction of the magnet, the magnet or the iron must first be moved; so before a body falls it must first be raised. A body at rest would therefore continue so for ever, and a body once in motion would continue so for ever, in the same direction and with the same velocity, unless impeded by some other body, or affected by some other force than that which originally impelled it. These propositions may seem somewhat arbitrary, and it has been doubted whether they are necessary truths; they have for a long time been received as axioms, and there can at all events be no harm in accepting them as postulates. It is however very generally believed that if the visible or palpable motion of one body be arrested by impact on another body, the motion ceases, and the force which produced it is annihilated.

Now the view which I venture to submit is, that force cannot be annihilated, but is merely subdivided or altered in direction or character. First, as to direction. Wave your hand: the motion, which has apparently ceased, is taken up by the air, from the air by the walls of the room, &c., and so by direct and reacting waves, continually comminuted, but never destroyed. It is true that, at a certain point, we lose all means of detecting the motion, from its minute subdivision, which defies our most delicate means of appreciation, but we can indefinitely extend our power of detecting it according as we confine its direction, or increase the delicacy of our examination. Thus, if the hand be moved in unconfined air, the motion of the air would not be sensible to a person at a few feet distance; but if a piston of the same extent of surface as the hand be moved with the same rapidity in a tube, the blast of air may be distinctly felt at several yards distance. There is no greater absolute amount of motion in the air in the second than in the first case, but its direction is restrained, so to make the means of detection more facile. By carrying on this restraint, as in the air-gun, we get a power of detecting the motion, and of moving other bodies at far greater distances. The puff of air which would in the air-gun project a bullet a quarter of a mile, if allowed to escape without its direction being restrained, as by the bursting of a bladder, would not be perceptible at a yard distance, though the same absolute amount of motion be impressed on the surrounding air.

It may, however, be asked, what becomes of force when motion is arrested or impeded by the counter-motion of another body? This is generally believed to produce rest, or entire destruction of motion, and consequent annihilation of force: so indeed it may, as regards the motion of the masses, but a new force, or new character of force, now ensues, the exponent of which, instead of visible motion, is heat. I venture to regard the heat which results from friction or percussion as a continuation of the force which was previously associated with the moving body, and which, when this impinges on another body, ceasing to exist as gross, palpable motion, continues to exist as heat.

Thus, let two bodies, A and B, be supposed to move in opposite directions (putting for the moment out of question all resistance, such as that of the air, &c.), if they pass each other without contact each will move on for ever in its respective direction with the same velocity, but if they touch each other the velocity of the movement of each is reduced, and each becomes heated: if this contact be slight, or such as to occasion but a slight diminution of their velocity, as when the surfaces of the bodies are oiled, then the heat is slight; but if the contact be such as to occasion a great diminution of motion, as in percussion, or as when the surfaces are roughened, then the heat is great, so that in all cases the resulting heat is proportionate to the diminished velocity. Where, instead of resisting and consequently impeding the motion of the body A, the body B gives way, or itself takes up the motion originally communicated to A, then we have less heat in proportion to the motion of the body B, for here the operation of the force continues in the form of palpable motion: thus the heat resulting from friction in the axle of a wheel is lessened by surrounding it by rollers; these take up the primary motion of the axle, and the less, by this means, the initial motion is impeded, the less is the resulting heat. Again, if a body move in a fluid, although some heat is produced, the heat is apparently trifling, because the particles of the fluid themselves move, and continue the motion originally communicated to the moving body: for every portion of motion communicated to them this loses an equivalent, and where both lose, then an equivalent of heat results.

As the converse of this proposition, it should follow that the more rigid the bodies impinging on each other the greater should be the amount of heat developed by friction, and so we find it. Flint, steel, hard stones, glass, and metals, are those bodies which give the greatest amount of heat from friction or percussion; while water, oil, &c., give little or no heat, and from the ready mobility of their particles lessen its developement when interposed between rigid moving bodies. Thus, if we oil the axles of wheels, we have more rapid motion of the bodies themselves, but less heat; if we increase the resistance to motion, as by roughening the points of contact, so that each particle strikes against and impedes the motion of others, then we have diminished motion, but increased heat; or if the bodies be smooth, but instead of sliding past each other be pressed closely together and then rubbed, we shall in many cases evolve more heat than by the roughened bodies, as we get a greater number of particles in contact and a greater resistance to the initial motion. I cannot present to my mind any case of heat resulting from friction which is not explicable by this view: friction, according to it, is simply impeded motion. The greater the impediment, the more force is required to overcome it, and the greater is the resulting heat; this resulting heat being a continuation of indestructible force, capable, as we shall presently see, of reproducing palpable motion, or motion of definite masses.

Whatever be the nature of the bodies, rough or smooth, solid or liquid, provided there be the same initial force, and the whole motion be ultimately arrested, there should be the same amount of heat developed, though where the motion is carried on through a great number of points of matter we do not so sensibly perceive the resulting heat from its greater dissipation. The friction of fluids produces heat, an effect first noticed I believe by Mayer. The total heat produced by the friction of fluids should, therefore, it will be said, be equal to that produced by the friction of solids; for although each particle produces little heat, the motion being readily taken up by the neighbouring particles, yet by the time the whole mass has attained a state of rest there has been the same impeding of the initial motion as by the friction of solids if produced by the same initial force. If the heat be viewed in the aggregate, and allowance be made for the specific thermal capacity of the substances employed, it probably is the same, though apparently less; the heat in the case of solids being manifested at certain defined points, while in that of fluids it is dissipated, both the time and space during and through which the motion is propagated differ in the two cases, so that the heat in the latter case is more readily carried off by surrounding bodies.

If the body be elastic, and by its reaction the motion impressed on it by the initial force be continued, then the heat is proportionately less; and were a substance perfectly elastic, and no resistance opposed to it by the air or other matter, then the movement once impressed would be perpetual, and no heat would result. A ball of caoutchouc bandied about for many minutes between a racket and a wall is not perceptibly heated, while a leaden bullet projected by a gun against a wall is rendered so hot as to be intolerable to the touch: in the former case, the motion of the mass is continued by the reaction due to its elasticity; in the latter, the motion of the mass is extinguished, and heat ensues.

A pendulum started in the exhausted receiver of an air-pump continues its oscillation for hours or even days; the friction at its point of suspension and the resistance of the air is minimised, and the heat is imperceptible, but these trifling resistances in the end arrest the motion of the mass, the one giving it out as heat, the other conveying the force to the receiver, and thence to surrounding bodies. Similar reasoning may be applied to the oscillation of a coiled spring and balance wheel.

To wind up a clock a certain amount of force is expended by the arm; this force is given back by the descent of the weight, the wheels move, the pendulum is kept oscillating, heat is generated at each point of friction, and the surrounding air is set in motion, a part of which is made obvious to us by the ticking sound. But it will be said, if instead of allowing the weight to act upon the machinery, the cord by which it is suspended be cut, the weight drops and the force is at an end. By no means, for in this case the house is shaken by the concussion, and thus the force and motion are continued, while in the former case the weight reaches the ground quietly, and no evidence of force or motion is manifested by its impact, the whole having been previously dissipated.

If the initial motion, instead of being arrested by the impact of other bodies, as in friction or percussion, is impeded by confinement or compression, as where the dilatation of a gas is prevented by mechanical means, heat equally results: thus if a piston is used to compress air in a closed vessel, the compressed air and, from it, the sides of the vessel will be heated: the air being unable to take up and carry on the original motion communicates molecular motion or expansion to all bodies in contact with it; and, conversely, if we expand air by mechanical motion, as by withdrawing the piston, cold is produced. So when a solid has its particles compressed or brought nearer together, as when a bar of iron is hammered, heat is produced beyond that which is due to percussion alone. In this latter case we cannot very easily effect the converse result, or produce cold by the mechanical dilatation of a solid, though the phenomena of solution, where the particles of a solid are detached from each other, or drawn more widely asunder, give us an approximation to it: in the case of solution cold is produced.

We are from a very extensive range of observation and experiment entitled to conclude that, with some curious exceptions to be presently noticed, whenever a body is compressed or brought into smaller dimensions it is heated, i. e. it expands neighbouring substances. Whenever it is dilated or increased in volume it is cooled, or contracts neighbouring substances.

Mr. Joule has made a great number of experiments for the purpose of ascertaining what quantity of heat is produced by a given mechanical action. His mode of experimenting is as follows. An apparatus formed of floats or paddles of brass or iron is made to rotate in a bath of water or mercury. The power which gives rise to this rotation is a weight raised like a clock-weight to a certain height; this by acting during its fall on a spindle and pulley communicates motion to the paddle-wheel, the water or mercury serving as a friction medium and calorimeter; and the heat is measured by a delicate mercurial thermometer. The results of his experiments he considers prove that a fall of 772 lbs. through a space of one foot is able to raise the temperature of one pound of water through one degree of Fahrenheit's thermometer. Mr. Joule's experiments are of extreme delicacy—he tabulates to the thousandth part of a degree of Fahrenheit, and a large number of his thermometric data are comprehended within the limits of a single degree. Other experimenters have given very different numerical results, but the general opinion seems to be that the numbers given by Mr. Joule are the nearest approximation to the truth yet obtained.

Hitherto I have taken no distinction as to the physical character of the bodies impinging on each other; but Nature gives us a remarkable difference in the character or mode of the force eliminated by friction, accordingly as the bodies which impinge are homogeneous or heterogeneous: if the former, heat alone is produced; if the latter, electricity.

We find, indeed, instances given by authors, of electricity resulting from the friction of homogeneous bodies; but, as I stated in my original Lectures, I have not found such facts confirmed by my own experiments, and this conclusion has been corroborated by some experiments of Professor Erman, communicated to the meeting of the British Association in the year 1845, in which he found that no electricity resulted from the friction of perfectly homogeneous substances; as, for instance, the ends of a broken bar. Such experiments as these will, indeed, be seldom free from slight electrical currents, on account of the practical difficulty of fulfilling the condition of perfect homogeneity in the substances themselves, their size, their temperature, &c.; but the effects produced are very trifling and vary in direction, and the resultant effect is nought. Indeed, it would be difficult to conceive the contrary. How could we possibly image to the mind or describe the direction of a current from the same body to the same body, or give instructions for a repetition of the experiment? It would be unintelligible to say that in rubbing to and fro two pieces of bismuth, iron, or glass, a current of electricity circulated from bismuth to bismuth, or from iron to iron, or from glass to glass; for the question immediately occurs—from which bismuth to which does it circulate? And should this question be answered by calling one piece A, and the other B, this would only apply to the particular specimens employed, the distinctive appellation denoting a distinction in fact, as otherwise A could be substituted for B, and the bar to which the positive electricity flowed would in turn become the bar to which the negative electricity flowed. We may say that it circulates from rough glass to smooth, from cast iron to wrought, for here there is not homogeneity. It is moreover conceivable, that when the motion is continuous in a definite direction, electricity may result from the friction of homogeneous bodies. If A and B rub against each other, revolving in opposite directions, concentric currents of positive and negative electricity may be conceived circulating within the metals, and be described by reference to the direction of their motion; this indeed would be a different phenomenon from those we have been considering; but without some distinction between the two substances in quality or direction, the electrical effects are indescribable, if not inconceivable.

When, however, homogeneous bodies are fractured or

even rubbed together, phenomena are observed to which the term electricity is applied; a flash or line of light appears at the point of friction which by some is called electrical, by others phosphorescent.

I have myself observed a remarkable case of the kind in the caoutchouc fabric now commonly used for waterproof clothing: if two folds of this substance be allowed to cohere so as partly to unite and present a difficulty of separation, then, on stripping the one from the other, or tearing them asunder, a line of light will follow the line of separation.

If this class of phenomena be electrical, it is electricity determined as it is generated; there is no dual character impressed on the matter acting, the flash is electrical as a spark from the percussion of flint is electrical, or as the slow combustion of phosphorus, or any other case of the development of heat and light. It seems to be better to class this phenomenon under the categories of heat and light than under that of electricity, the latter word being retained for those cases where a dual or polar character of force is manifested. In experiments which have been made by the friction of similar substances where the one appears positively and the other negatively electrical, there will be found some difference in the mode of rubbing by which the molecular state of the bodies is in all probability changed, making one a dissimilar substance from the other; thus it is said by Bergmann, that when two pieces of glass are rubbed so that all the parts of one pass over one part of the other, the former is positive and the latter negative. It is obvious that in this case the rubbing in one is confined to a line, and that must be more altered in molecular structure at the line of friction than the one where the friction is spread over the whole surface: so if a ribbon be drawn transversely over another ribbon, the substances are not, *qua* the rubbing action, identical; so again, in the rupture of crystals, we are dealing with substances having a polar arrangement of particles—the surfaces of the fragments cannot be assumed to be molecularly identical.

The developement of electricity by the common electrical machine arises, as far as I can understand it, from the separation or rupture of contiguity between dissimilar bodies; a metallic surface, the amalgam of the cushion, is in contact with glass; these two bodies act upon each other by the force of cohesion; and when, by an external mechanical force, this is ruptured, as it is at each moment of the motion of the glass plate or cylinder, electricity is developed in each; were they similar bodies, heat only would be developed.

According to the experiments of Mr. Sullivan electricity may be produced by vibration alone if the substance vibrating be composed either of dissimilar metals, as a wire partly of iron and partly of brass caused to emit a musical sound; or of the same metal, if its parts be not homogeneous, as a piece of iron, one portion of which is hard and crystallised and the other soft and fibrous; the current resulting appears to be due to the vibration, and not to heat engendered, as it ceases immediately with the vibration.

We may say, then, that in our present state of knowledge, where the mutually impinging bodies are homogeneous, heat and not electricity is the result of friction and percussion; where the bodies impinging are heterogeneous, we may safely state that electricity is always produced by friction or percussion, although heat in a greater or less degree accompanies it; but when we come to the question of ratio in which frictional electricity is produced, as determined by the different characters of the substances employed, we find very complex results. Bodies may differ in so many particulars which influence more or less the developement of electricity, such as their chemical constitution, the state of their surfaces, their state of aggregation, their transparency or opacity, their power of conducting electricity, &c., that the *normæ* of their action are very difficult of attainment. As a general rule, it may be said that the developement of electricity is greater when the substances employed are broadly distinct in their physical and chemical qualities, and more particularly in their conducting powers; but up to the present time the laws governing such developement have not been even approximately determined.

I have said, in reference to the various forces or affections of matter, that either of them may, *mediately* or *immediately*, produce the others; and this is all I can venture to predicate of them in the present state of science; but after much consideration I incline strongly to the opinion that science is rapidly progressing towards the establishment of immediate or direct relations between all these forces. Where at present no immediate relation is established between any of them, electricity generally forms the intervening link or middle term.

Motion, then, will directly produce *heat* and *electricity*, and electricity, being produced by it, will produce *magnetism* —a force which is always developed by electrical currents at right angles to the direction of those currents, as will be subsequently more fully explained. *Light* also is readily produced by motion, either directly, as when accompanying the heat of friction, or mediately, by electricity resulting from motion; as in the electrical spark, which has most of the attributes of solar light, differing from it only in those respects in which light differs when emanating from different sources or seen through different media; for instance, in the position of the fixed lines in the spectrum or in the ratios of the spaces occupied by rays of different refrangibility. In the decompositions and compositions which the terminal points proceeding from the conductors of an electrical machine develope when immersed in different chemical media, we get the production of *chemical affinity* by electricity, of which motion is the initial source. Lastly, *motion* may be again reproduced by the forces which have emanated from motion; thus, the divergence of the electrometer, the revolution of the electrical wheel, the deflection of the magnetic needle, are, when resulting from frictional electricity, palpable movements reproduced by the intermediate modes of force, which have themselves been originated by motion.

III.—HEAT.

IF we now take HEAT as our starting point, we shall find that the other modes of force may be readily produced by it. To take motion first: this is so generally, I think I may say invariably, the immediate effect of heat, that we may almost, if not entirely, resolve heat into motion, and view it as a mechanically repulsive force, a force antagonist to attraction of cohesion or aggregation, and tending to *move* the particles of all bodies, or to separate them from each other.

It may be well here to premise, that in using the terms 'particles' or 'molecules,' which will be frequently employed in this Essay, I do not use them in the sense of the atomist, or mean to assert that matter consists of indivisible particles or atoms. The words will be used for the necessary purpose of contradistinguishing the action of the indefinitely minute physical elements of matter from that of masses having a sensible magnitude, much in the same way as the term 'lines' or 'points' may be used, and with advantage in an abstract sense; though there does not exist, in fact, a thing which has length and breadth without thickness, and though a thing without parts or dimensions is nothing.

If we put aside the sensation which heat produces in our own bodies, and regard heat simply as to its effects upon inorganic matter, we find that, with a very few exceptions, which I shall presently notice, the effects of what is called heat are simply an expansion of the matter acted upon, and that the matter so expanded has the power by its own contraction of communicating expansion to all bodies in contiguity with it. Thus, if the body be a solid, for instance, iron, a liquid, say water, or a gas, say atmospheric air—each of these, when heated, is expanded in every direction; in the two former cases, by increasing the heat to a certain point, we change the physical character of the substance, the solid becomes a liquid, and the liquid becomes a gas; these, however, are still expansions, particularly the latter, when, at a certain period, the expansion becomes rapidly and indefinitely greater. But what is, in fact, commonly done in order to heat a substance, or to increase the heat of a substance? it is merely approximated to some other heated, that is, to some other expanded substance, which latter is cooled or contracted as the former expands. Let us now divest the mind of the impression that heat is in itself anything substantive, and suppose that these phenomena are regarded for the first time, and without any preconceived notions on the subject; let us introduce no hypothesis, but merely express as simply as we can the facts of which we have become cognisant; to what do they amount? to this, that matter has pertaining to it a molecular repulsive power, a power of dilatation, which is communicable by contiguity or proximity.

Heat thus viewed, is motion, and this molecular motion we may readily change into the motion of masses, or motion in its most ordinary and palpable form: for example, in the steam engine, the piston and all its concomitant masses of matter are moved by the molecular dilatation of the vapour of water.

To produce continuous motion there must be an alternate action of heat and cold; a given portion of air, for instance, heated beyond the temperature of the circumambient air, is expanded. If now it be made to act on a movable piston, it moves this to a point at which the tension or elastic force of the confined air equals that of the surrounding air. If the confined air be kept at this point, the piston would remain stationary; but if it be cooled, the external air exercising then a greater relative degree of pressure, the piston returns towards its original position; just as it will be seen, when we come to the magnetic force, that a magnet placed in a particular position produces motion in iron near it, but to make this motion continuous, or to obtain an available mechanical power, the magnet must be demagnetised, or a stable equilibrium is obtained.

In the case of the piston moved by heated air the motion of the mass becomes the exponent of the amount of heat—i. e. of the expansion or separation of the molecules; nor do we, by any of our ordinary methods, test heat in any other way than by its purely dynamical action. The various modifications of the thermometer and pyrometer are all measurers of heat by motion: in these instruments liquid or solid bodies are expanded and elongated, i. e. moved in a definite direction, and, either by their own visible motion, or by the motion of an attached index, communicate to our senses the amount of the force by which they moved. There are, indeed, some delicate experiments which tend to prove that a repulsive action between separate masses is produced by heat. Fresnel found that mobile bodies heated in an exhausted receiver repelled each other to sensible distances; and Baden Powell found that the coloured rings usually called Newton's rings change their breadth and position, when the glasses between which they appear are heated, in a manner which showed that the glasses repelled each other. M. Faye's theory of comets is based on some such repellent force. There is, however, some difficulty in presenting these phenomena to the mind in the same aspect as the molecular repulsive action of heat.

The phenomena of what is termed latent heat have been

generally considered as strongly in favour of that view which regards heat either as actual matter, or, at all events, as a substantive entity, and not a motion or affection of ordinary matter.

The hypothesis of latent matter is, I venture with diffidence to think, a dangerous one—it is something like the old principle of Phlogiston, it is not tangible, visible, audible; it is, in fact, a mere subtle mental conception, and ought, I submit, only to be received on the ground of absolute necessity, the more so as these subtleties are apt to be carried on to other natural phenomena, and so they add to the hypothetical scaffolding which is seldom requisite, and should be sparingly used, even in the early stages of discovery. As an instance, I think a striking one, of the injurious effects of this, I will mention the analogous doctrine of 'invisible light;' and I do this, meaning no disrespect to its distinguished author, any more than in discussing the doctrine of latent heat, I can be supposed, in the slightest degree, to aim at detracting from the merits of the illustrious investigators of the facts which that doctrine seeks to explain. Is not 'invisible light,' a contradiction in terms? has not light ever been regarded as that agent which affects our visual organs? Invisible light, then, is darkness, and if it exist, then is darkness light. I know it may be said, that one eye can detect light where another cannot; that a cat may see where a man cannot; that an insect may see where a cat cannot; but then it is not invisible light to those who see it: the light, or rather the object seen by the cat, may be invisible to the man, but it is visible to the cat, and, therefore, cannot abstractedly be said to be invisible. If we go further, and find an agent which affects certain substances similarly to light, but does not, as far as we are aware, affect the visual organs of any animal, then is it not an erroneous nomenclature which calls such an agent light? There are many cases in which a deviation from the once accepted meaning of words has so gradually entered into common usage as to be unavoidable, but I venture to think that additions to such cases should as far as possible be avoided, as injurious to that precision of language which is one of the safest guards to knowledge, and from the absence of which physical science has materially suffered.

Let us now shortly examine the question of latent heat, and see whether the phenomena cannot be as well, if not more satisfactorily, explained without the hypothesis of latent matter, an idea presenting many similar difficulties to that of invisible light, though more sanctioned by usage. Latent heat is supposed to be the matter of heat, associated, in a masked or dormant state, with ordinary matter, not capable of being detected by any test so long as the matter with which it is associated remains in the same physical state, but communicated to or absorbed from other bodies, when the matter with which it is associated changes its state. To take a common example: a pound or given weight of water at 172°, mixed with an equal weight of water at 32°, will acquire a mean temperature, or 102°; while water at 172°, mixed with an equal weight of ice at 32°, will be reduced to 32°. By the theory of latent heat this phenomenon is thus explained:—In the first case, that of the mixture of water with water, both the bodies being in the same physical state, no latent heat is rendered sensible, or sensible heat latent; but in the second, the ice changing its condition from the solid to the liquid state abstracts from the liquid as much heat as it requires to maintain it in the liquid state, which it renders latent, or retains associated with itself, so long as it remains liquid, but of which heat no evidence can be afforded by any thermoscopic test.

I believe this and similar phenomena, where heat is connected with a change of state, may be explained and distinctly comprehended without recourse to the conception of latent heat, though it requires some effort of the mind to divest itself of this idea, and to view the phenomena simply in their dynamical relations. To assist us in so viewing them, let us first parallel with purely mechanical actions, certain simple effects of heat, where change of state (I mean such change as from the solid to the liquid, or liquid to the gaseous state) is not concerned. Thus, place within a receiver a bladder, and heat the air within to a higher temperature than that without it, the bladder expands; so, force the air mechanically into it by the air-pump, the bladder expands; cool the air on the outside, or remove its pressure mechanically by an exhausting pump, the bladder also expands; conversely, increase the external repellent force, either by heat or mechanical pressure, and the bladder contracts. In the mechanical effects, the force which produced the distension is derived from, and at the expense of, the mechanical power employed, as from muscular force, from gravitation, from the reacting elasticity of springs, or any similar force by which the air-pump may be worked. In the heating effects, the force is derived from the chemical action in the lamp or source of heat employed.

Let us next consider the experiment so arranged that the force, which produces expansion in the one case, produces a correlative contraction in the other: thus, if two bladders, with a connecting neck between them, be half-filled with air, as the one is made to contract by pressure the other will dilate, and vice versâ; so a bladder partly filled with cold air, and contained within another filled with hot air, expands, while the space between the bladders contracts, exhibiting a mere transfer of the same amount of repulsive force, the mobility of the particles, or their mutual attraction, being the same in each body; in other words, the repulsive force acts in the direction of least resistance until equilibrium is produced; it then becomes a static or balanced, instead of a dynamic or motive force.

Let us now consider the case where a solid is to be

changed to a liquid, or a liquid to a gas; here a much greater amount of heat or repulsive force is required, on account of the cohesion of the particles to be separated. In order to separate the particles of the solid, precisely as much force must be parted with by the warmer liquid body as keeps an equal quantity of it in its liquid state; it is, indeed, only with a more striking line of demarcation, the case of the hot and cold bladder—a part of the repellent power of the hot particles is transferred to the cold particles, and separates them in their turn, but the antagonist force of cohesion or aggregation necessary to be overcome, being in this case much stronger, requires and exhausts an exactly proportionate amount of repellent force mechanically to overcome it; hence the different effect on a body such as the common thermometer, the expanding liquid of which does not undergo a similar change of state. Thus, in the example above given, of the mixture of cold with hot water, the hot and cold water and the mercury of the thermometer being all in a liquid state before, and remaining so after contact, the resulting temperature is an exact mean; the hot water contracts to a certain extent, the cold water expands to the same extent, and the thermometer either sinks or rises the same number of degrees, accordingly as it had been previously immersed in the cold or in the hot solution, its mercury gaining or losing an equivalent of repellent force. In the second instance, viz. the mixture of ice with hot water, the substance we use as an indicator, i. e. mercury, does not undergo the same physical change as those whose relations of volume we are examining. The force—viewing heat simply as mechanical force—which is employed in loosening or tearing asunder the particles of the solid ice, is abstracted from the liquid water, and from the liquid mercury of the thermometer, and in proportion as this force meets with a greater resistance in separating the particles of a solid than of a liquid, so the bodies which yield the force suffer proportionately a greater contraction.

If we compare the action of heat on the two substances, water and mercury, alone, and throw out of our consideration the ice, we shall be able to apply the same view: thus, if a given source of heat be applied to water containing a mercurial thermometer, both the water and mercury gradually expand, but in different degrees; at a certain point the attractive force of the molecules of the water is so far overcome that the water becomes vapour. At this point, the heat or force, meeting with much less resistance from the attraction of the particles of steam than from those of the mercury, expends itself upon the former; the mercury does not further expand, or expands in an infinitesimally small degree, and the steam expands greatly. As soon as this arrives at a point where circumambient pressure causes its resistance to further expansion to be equal to the resistance to expansion in the mercury of the thermometer, the latter again rises, and so both go on expanding in an inverse ratio to their molecular attractive force. If the circumambient pressure be increased, as by confining the water at the commencement of the experiment within a less expansible body than itself, such as a metallic chamber, then the mercury of the thermometer continues to rise; and if the experiment were continued, the water being confined and not the mercury, until we have arrived at a degree of repulsive force which is able to overcome the cohesive power of the mercury, so that this expands into vapour, then we get the converse effect; the force expends itself upon the mercury, which expands indefinitely, as the water did in the first case, and the water does not expand at all.

Another very usual mode of regarding the subject may embarras at first sight, but a little consideration will show that it is explicable by the same doctrine. Water which has ice floating in it will give, when measured by the thermometer, the same temperature as the ice; i. e. both the water and ice contract the mercury of the thermometer to the point conventionally marked as 32°. It may be said, how is this reconcileable with the dynamical doctrine, for, according to that, the solid should take from the mercury of the thermometer more repulsive power than the liquid; consequently, the ice should contract the mercury more than the water?

My answer is, that in the proposition as thus stated, the quantities of the water, ice, and mercury are not taken into consideration, and hence a necessary dynamical element is neglected: if the element of quantity be included, this objection will not apply. Let the thermometer, for instance, contain 13 oz. of mercury, and stand at 100°; if placed in contact with an unlimited quantity of ice at 32°, the mercury will sink to 32°. If the same thermometer be immersed in an unlimited quantity of water at 32°, the mercury sinks also to 32°; not absolutely, perhaps, because, however great the quantity of water or ice, it will be somewhat raised in temperature by the warmer mercury. This elevation of temperature above 32° will be smaller in proportion as the quantity of water or ice is larger than the quantity of mercury; and, as we know of no intermediate state between ice and water, the contact of a thermometer at a temperature above the freezing point with any quantity of ice exactly at the freezing point would, theoretically speaking, liquefy the whole, provided it had sufficient time; for as every portion of that ice would in time have its temperature raised by the contact of the warmer body, and as any elevation of temperature above the freezing point liquefies ice, every portion should be liquefied. Practically speaking, however, in both cases, that of the water and of the ice, when the quantity is indefinitely great the thermometer falls to 32°.

Now place the same thermometer at 100°, successively in one oz. of water at 32°, and in one of ice at 32°; we shall find in the former case it will be lowered only to 54°, and in the latter to 32°; apply to this the doctrine of repulsive force, and we get a satisfactory explanation.

In the first case, the quantities both of ice and water being indefinitely great in respect to the mercury, each reduces it to its own temperature, viz. 32°, and the ice cannot reduce the mercury below 32°, because it would receive back repulsive power from the newly formed water, and this would become ice; in the second case, where the quantities are limited, the mercury does lose more repulsive power by the ice than by the water, and the observations made in reference to the first illustration apply.

The above doctrine is beautifully instanced in the experiment of Thilorier, by which carbonic acid is solidified. Carbonic acid gas, retained in a strong vessel under great pressure, is allowed to escape from a small orifice; the sudden expansion requires so great a supply of force, that in furnishing the demands of the expanding gas certain other portions of the gas contract to such an extent as to solidify: thus, we have reciprocal expansion and contraction going on in one and the same substance, the time being too limited for the whole to assume a uniform temperature, or in other words, a uniform extent of expansion.

It has been observed with reference to heat thus viewed, that it would be as correct to say, that heat is absorbed, or cold produced by motion, as that heat is produced by it. This difficulty ceases when the mind has been accustomed to regard heat and cold as themselves, motion; i. e. as correlative expansions and contractions, each being evidenced by relation, and being inconceivable as an abstraction.

For instance, if the piston of an air-pump be drawn down by a weight, cold is produced in the receiver. It may be here said that a mechanical force, and the motion consequent upon it, produces cold; but heat is produced on the opposite side of the piston, if a receiver be adapted so as to retain the compressed air. Assuming them to equivalise each other, the force of the falling weight would be expressed by the heat of friction of the piston against its tube, and by the tension or power of reaction of the compressed against the dilated air. If the heat due to compression be made to perform mechanical work, it would *pro tanto* be consumed, and could not restore the temperatúre to the dilated air; but if it perform no work, no heat is lost. Mr. Joule has experimentally proved this proposition.

In commencing the subject of heat, I asked my reader to put out of consideration the sensations which heat produces in our own bodies; I did this because these sensations are likely to deceive, and have deceived many as to the nature of heat. These sensations are themselves occasioned by similar expansions to those which we have been considering; the liquids of the body are expanded, i. e. rendered less viscid by heat, and from their more ready flow, we obtain the sensation of agreeable warmth. By a greater degree of heat, their expansion becomes too great, giving rise to a sense of pain, and, if pushed to extremity, as with the heat which produces a burn, the liquids of the body are dissipated in vapour, and an injury or destruction of the organic structure takes place. A similar though converse effect may be produced by intense cold; the application of frozen mercury to the animal body produces a burn similar to that produced by great heat, and accompanied with a similar sensation.

Doubtless other actions than those above mentioned interfere in producing the sensations of heat and cold; but I think it will be seen that these will not affect the arguments as to the nature of heat. The phenomenal effects will be found unaltered: heat will still be found to be expansion, cold to be contraction; and the expansion and contraction are, as with the two bladders of air, correlative—i. e. we cannot expand one body, A, without contracting some other body, B; we cannot contract A without expanding B, assuming that we view the bodies with relation to heat alone, and suppose no other force to be manifested.

I have said that there are few exceptions as to heat being

always manifested by an expansion of matter. One class of these exceptions is only apparent: moist clay, animal or vegetable fibre, and other substances of a mixed nature, which contain matter of different characters, some of which is more and some less volatile, i. e. expansible, are contracted on the application of heat; this arises from the more volatile matter being dissipated in the form of vapour or gas; and the interstices of the less volatile being thus emptied, the latter contracts by its own cohesive attraction, giving thus a prima facie appearance of contraction by heat. The pyrometer of Wedgwood is explicable on this principle.

The second class of exceptions, though much more limited in extent, is less easily explained. Water, fused bismuth, and probably some other substances (though the fact as to them is not clearly established), expand as they approach very near to the freezing or solidifying point. The most probable explanation of these exceptions is, that at the point of maximum density the molecules of these bodies assume a polar or crystalline condition; that by the particles being thus arranged in linear directions like chevaux de frise, interstitial spaces are left, containing matter of less density, so that the specific density of the whole mass is diminished.

Some recent experiments of Dr. Tyndall on the physical properties of ice seem to favour this view. When a sunbeam, concentrated by a lens, is allowed to fall on a piece of apparently homogeneous ice the path of the rays is instantly studded with numerous luminous spots like minute air bubbles, and the planes of freezing are made manifest by these and by small fissures. Stars or flower-like figures of six petals appear parallel to the planes of freezing, and seemingly spreading out from a central bubble. These flowers are formed of water. When the ice is melted in warm water no air is given off from the bubbles, so they seem to be vacuous; it is, however, possible that extremely minute particles of air sufficient to form foci for the melting points of ice might be dissolved by the water as soon as they came in contact with it. Be this as it may, the existence of these points throughout the ice, where it gives way to the heat of the solar beam, if it does not prove actual vacuous or aeriform spaces to exist in ice, proves that it is not homogeneous, that its structure is probably definitely crystalline, and that the matter composing it is in different degrees of aggregation, so that its mean specific gravity might well be less than that of water.

We cannot examine piecemeal the ultimate structure of matter, but in addition to the fact that the bodies which evince this peculiarity are bodies which, when solidified, exhibit a very marked crystalline character, there are experiments which show that water between the point of maximum density and its point of solidification polarises light circularly; showing, if these experiments be correct, a structural alteration in water, and one analogous to that possessed by certain crystalline solids, and to that possessed by water itself, where it is forcibly made to assume a polarised condition by the influence of magnetism.

The accuracy of these results has, however, been doubted, and the experiments have not succeeded when repeated by very experienced hands. Whether this be so or not, and whether the above explanation of the exception to the otherwise invariable effect of expansion by heat be or be not regarded as admissible, must be left to the judgment of each individual who thinks upon the subject; at all events, no theory of heat yet proposed removes the difficulty, and therefore it equally opposes every other view of the phenomena of heat, as it does that which I have here considered, and which regards heat as communicable expansive force.

As certain bodies expand in freezing, and indeed, under some circumstances, before they arrive at the temperature at which they solidify, we get the apparent anomaly that the motion or mechanical force generated by heat or change of temperature is reversed in direction when we arrive at the point of change from the solid to the liquid state. Thus a piece of ice at the temperature of Zero, Fahrenheit, would expand by heat, and produce a mechanical force by such expansion until it arrives at 32°; but then by an increment of heat it contracts, and if the first expansion had moved a piston upwards, the subsequent contraction would bring it back to a certain extent, or move it downwards, an apparent negation of the force of heat.

Again with water above 40°, i. e, above its point of maximum density, a progressive increment of cold or decrement of heat would produce contraction to a certain point, and then expansion or a mechanical force in an opposite direction. Thus not only heat or the expansive force given to other bodies by a body cooling would be given out by water freezing, but also the force due to the converse expansion in the body itself, and force would thus seem to be got out of nothing: but if water in a confined space be gradually cooled, the expansion attendant on its cooling as it approaches the freezing point would occasion pressure amongst its particles, and thence tend to antagonise the force of dilatation produced in them by cooling, or to resist their tendency to freeze; or in other words, the pressure would tend to liquefaction, and conversely to the usual effect of pressure, produce cold instead of heat, and thus neutralise some of the heat yielded by the cooling body. Hence we find that it requires a lower temperature to freeze water under pressure than when exempt from it, or that the freezing point is lowered as the pressure increases for bodies which expand in freezing—an effect first predicted by Mr. J. Thompson, and experimentally verified by Mr. W. Thompson; while as shown by M. Bunsen, the converse effect takes place with bodies which contract in freezing. Here the pressure cooperates with the effects of cold, both tending to approximate the particles, and such substances solidify at a higher temperature in proportion as the pressure is greater; so that we might expect a body of this class, which under the ordinary pressure of the air is at a temperature just above its freezing point, to solidify by being submitted to pressure alone, the temperature being kept constant.

A similar class of exception to the general effect of heat in expanding bodies is presented by vulcanised caoutchouc. This has been observed by Mr. Gough, and, indeed, was pointed out to me many years ago by Mr. Brockedon to be heated when stretched, and cooled when unstretched.

Mr. Joule finds that its specific gravity is lower when stretched than when unstretched, and that when heated in its stretched state it shortens, presenting in this particular condition a similar series of converse relations to those which are presented by water near or at its freezing point.

With the exception of this class of phenomena, which offer difficulties to any theory which has been proposed, the general phenomena of heat may, I believe, be explained upon a purely dynamical view, and more satisfactorily than by having recourse to the hypothesis of latent matter. Many, however, of the phenomena of heat are involved in much mystery, particularly those connected with specific heat or that relative proportion of heat which equal weights of different bodies require to raise them from a given temperature to another given temperature, which appear to depend in some way hitherto inexplicable upon the molecular constitution of different bodies.

The view of heat which I have taken, viz. to regard it simply as a communicable molecular repulsive force, is supported by many of the phenomena to which the term specific or relative heat is applied; for example, bodies as they increase in temperature increase in specific heat. The ratio of this increase in specific heat is greater with solids than with liquids, although the latter are more dilatable; an effect probably depending upon the commencement of fusion. Again, those metals whose rate of expansion increases most rapidly when they are heated, increase most in specific heat; and their specific heat is reduced by percussion, which, by approximating their particles, makes them specifically more dense. When, however, we examine substances of very different physical characters, we find that their specific heats have no relation to their density or rate of expansion by heat; their differences of specific heat must depend upon their intimate molecular constitution in a manner accounted for (as far as I am aware) by no theory of heat hitherto proposed.

In the greater number, probably in all solids and liquids, the expansion by heat is relatively greater as the temperature is higher; or, preserving the view of expansion and contraction, if two equal portions of the same substance be juxtaposed at different temperatures, the hotter portion will contract a little more than the colder will expand; from this fact, viz. that the coefficient of expansion increases in a given body with the temperature, and from other considerations, Dr. Wood has argued, with much apparent reason, that the nearer the particles of bodies are to each other, the less they require to move to produce a given expansion or contraction in those of another body. His mode of reasoning, if I rightly conceive it, may be concisely put as follows:—

As bodies contract by cold, it is clear that, in a given body, the lower the temperature the nearer are the particles; and, as the coefficient of expansion increases with the temperature, the lower the temperature of the substance be, the less the particles require to move, or approach to or recede from each other, so as to compensate the correlative recession or approach of the particles in a hotter portion of the same substance, that is, in another portion of the same substance in which the particles are more distant from each other. The amount of approximation or recession of the particles of a body, in other words, its change of bulk by a given change of temperature, being thus in a given substance an index of the relative proximity of its particles, may it not be so of all bodies? The proposition is very ingeniously argued by Dr. Wood, but the argument is based upon certain hypotheses as to the sizes and distances of atoms, which must be admitted as postulates by those who adopt his conclusions. Dr. Wood seeks by means of this theory to explain the heat produced by chemical combination, and I shall endeavour to give a sketch of his mode of reasoning when I arrive at that part of my subject.

Although the comparative effects of specific heat may not be satisfactorily explicable by any known theory, the absolute effect of heat upon each separate substance is simply expansion, but when bodies differing in their physical characters are used, the rate of expansion varies, if measured by the correlative contractions exhibited by the substances producing it. Though I am obliged, in order to be intelligible, to talk of heat as an entity, and of its conduction, radiation, &c., yet these expressions are, in fact, inconsistent with the dynamic theory which regards heat as motion and nothing else; thus conduction would be simply a progressive dilatation or motion of the particles of the conducting substance, radiation an undulation or motion of the particles of the medium through which the heat is said to be transmitted, &c.; and it is a strong argument in favour of this theory, that for every diversity in the physical character of bodies, and for every change in the structure and arrangement of particles of the same body, a change is apparent in the thermal effects. Thus gold conducts heat, or transmits the motion called heat, more readily than copper, copper than iron, iron than lead, and lead than porcelain, &c.

So when the structure of a substance is not homogeneous, we have a change in the conduction of different parts dependent upon the structure. This is beautifully shown with bodies whose structure is symmetrically arranged, as in crystals. Senarmont has shown that crystals conduct heat differently in different directions with reference to the axis of symmetry, but definitely in definite directions. His mode of experimenting is as follows:—A plate of the crystal is cut in a direction, for one set of experiments parallel, and for another at right angles to the axis; a tube of platinum is inserted through the centre of the plate, and bent at one extremity, so as to be capable of being heated by a lamp without the heat which radiates from the lamp affecting the crystal; the surfaces or bases of the plate of crystal are covered with wax. When the platinum is heated, the direction of the heat conducted by the crystal is made known by the melting of the wax, and a curved line is visible at the juncture of the solid and liquid wax. This curve, with homogeneous substances, as glass or zinc, is a circle; it is also a circle on plates of calc spar cut perpendicular to the axis of symmetry; but on plates cut parallel to the axis of symmetry, and having their plane perpendicular to one of the faces of the primitive rhombohedron, the curves are well-defined ellipses, having their longer axes in the direction of the axis of symmetry, showing that this axis is a direction of greater conductibility. From experiments of this character the inference is drawn, that 'in media constituted like crystals of the rhombohedral system, the conducting power varies in such a manner, that, supposing a centre of heat to exist within them, and the medium to be indefinitely extended in all directions, the isothermal surfaces are concentric ellipsoids of revolution round the axis of symmetry, or at least surfaces differing but little therefrom.'

Knoblauch has further shown, that radiant heat is absorbed in different degrees, according as its direction is parallel or perpendicular to the axis of a crystal.

If we select a substance of a different but also of a definite structure, such as wood, we find that heat progresses through it with more or less rapidity, according to its direction with reference to the fibre of the wood: thus Decandolle and De la Rive found that the conduction was better in a direction parallel to the fibre than in one transverse to it; and Dr. Tyndall has added the fact, that the conduction is better in a direction transverse to the fibres and layers of the wood than when transverse to the fibre but parallel to the layers, though in both these directions the conduction is inferior to that following the direction of the fibre. Thus, in the three possible directions in which the structure of wood may be contemplated, we have three different degrees of progression for heat.

In the above examples we see, as we shall see farther on with reference to all the so-called imponderables, that the phenomena depend upon the molecular structure of the matter affected; and although these facts are not absolutely inconsistent with the theory which supposes them to be fluids or entities, it will, I think, be found to be far more consistent with that which views them as motion. Heat, which we are at present considering, cannot be insulated: we cannot remove the heat from a substance and retain it as heat; we can only transmit it to another substance, either as heat or as some other mode of force. We only know certain changes of matter, for which changes heat is a generic name; the *thing* heat is unknown.

Heat having been shown to be a force capable of producing *motion*, and motion to be capable of producing the other modes of force, it necessarily follows that heat is capable, mediately, of producing them; I will, therefore, content myself with enquiring how far heat is capable of immediately producing the other modes of force. It will immediately produce *electricity*, as shown in the beautiful experiments of Seebeck, one of which I have already cited, which experiments proved, that when dissimilar metals are made to touch, or are soldered together and heated at the point of contact, a current of electricity flows through the metals having a definite direction according to the metals employed, which current continues as long as an increasing temperature is gradually pervading the metals, ceases when the temperature is stationary, and flows in the contrary direction with the decrement of temperature.

Another class of phenomena which have been generally attributed to the effects of radiant heat, and to which, from this belief, the term thermography has been applied, may also, in their turn, be made to exhibit electrical effects—effects here of Franklinic or static electricity, as Seebeck's experiments showed effects of voltaic or dynamic electricity.

If polished discs of dissimilar metals—say, zinc and copper—be brought into close proximity, and kept there for some time, and either of them has irregularities upon its surface, a superficial outline of these irregularities is traceable upon the other disc, and vice versâ. Many theories have been framed to account for this phenomenon, but whether it be due or not to thermic radiations, the relative temperature of the discs, their relative capacities and conducting and radiating powers for heat, undoubtedly influence the phenomena.

Now, if two such discs in close proximity be connected with a delicate electroscope, and then suddenly separated, the electroscope is affected, showing that the reciprocal radiation from surface to surface has produced electrical force. I cite this experiment in treating of heat as an initial force, because at present the probabilities are in favour of thermic radiation producing the phenomenon. The origin of these so-called thermographic effects is, however, a question open to much doubt, and needs much further experiment. When I first published the experiment which showed that the mere approximation of metallic discs would give rise to electrical effects, I mentioned that I considered the fact of the superficial change upon the surface of metals in proximity, and, *à fortiori*, in contact, would explain the developement of electricity in Volta's original contact experiment, without having recourse to the contact theory, i. e. a theory which supposes a force to be produced by mere contact of dissimilar metals without any molecular or chemical change. I have seen nothing to alter this view. Mr. Gassiot has repeated and verified my experiment with more delicate apparatus and under more unexceptionable circumstances; and without saying that radiant heat is the initial force in this case, we have evidence, by the superficial change which takes place in bodies closely approximated, that some molecular change is taking place, some force is called into action by their proximity, which produces changes in matter as it expends, or rather transmits itself; and, therefore, is not a force without molecular change, as the supposed contact force would be. The force in this, as in all other cases, is not created, but developed by the action of matter on matter, and not annihilated, as it is shown by this experiment to be convertible into another mode of force.

To say that heat will produce *light*, is to assert a fact apparently familiar to every one, but there may be some reason to doubt whether the expression to produce light is correct in this particular application; the relation between heat and light is not analogous to the correlation between these and the other four affections of matter. Heat and light appear to be rather modifications of the same force than distinct forces mutually dependent. The modes of action of radiant heat and of light are so similar, both being subject to the same laws of reflection, refraction, and double refraction, and polarisation, that their difference appears to exist more in the manner in which they affect our senses than in our mental conception of them.

The experiments of Melloni, which have mainly contributed to demonstrate this close analogy of heat and light, afford a beautiful instance of the assistance which the progress of one branch of physical science renders to that of another The discoveries of Oersted and Seebeck led to the construction of an instrument for measuring temperature, incomparably more delicate than any previously known. To distinguish it from the ordinary thermometer, this instrument is called the *thermomultiplier*. It consists of a series of small bars of bismuth and antimony, forming one zigzag chain of alternations arranged parallel to each other, in the shape of a cylinder or prism; so that the points of junction, which are soldered, shall be all exposed at the bases of the cylinder: the two extremities of this series are united to a galvanometer—that is, a flat coil of wire surrounding a freely-suspended magnetic needle, the direction of which is parallel to the convolutions of the wire. When radiant heat impinges upon the soldered ends of the multiplier, a thermo-electric current is induced in each pair; and, as all these currents tend to circulate in the same direction, the energy of the whole is increased by the cooperating forces: this current, traversing the helix of the galvanometer, deflects the needle from parallelism by virtue of the electro-magnetic tangential force, and the degree of this deflection serves as the index of the temperature.

Bodies examined by these means show a remarkable difference between their transcalescence, or power of transmitting heat, and their transparency: thus, perfectly transparent alum arrests more heat than quartz so dark coloured as to be opaque; and alum coupled with green glass Melloni found was capable of transmitting a beam of brilliant light, while, with the most delicate thermoscope, he could detect no indications of transmitted heat: on the other hand, rock-salt, the most transcalescent body known, may be covered with soot until perfectly opaque, and yet be found capable of transmitting a considerable quantity of heat. Radiant heat, when transmitted through a prism of rock-salt, is found to be unequally refracted, as is the case with light; and the rays of heat thus elongated into what is, for the sake of analogy, called a spectrum, are found to possess similar properties to the primary or coloured rays of light. Thus rock-salt is to heat what colourless glass is to light; it transmits heat of all degrees of refrangibility: alum is to heat as red glass to light; it transmits the least, and stops the most refrangible rays; and rock-salt covered with soot represents blue glass, transmitting the most, and stopping the least refrangible rays.

Certain bodies, again, reflect heat of different refrangibility: thus paper, snow, and lime, although perfectly white—that is, reflecting light of all degrees of refrangibility, reflect heat only of certain degrees; while metals, which are coloured bodies—that is, bodies which reflect light only of certain degrees of refrangibility—reflect heat of all degrees. Radiant heat incident upon substances which doubly refract light is doubly refracted; and the emergent rays are polarised in planes at right angles to each other, as is the case with light.

The relation of radiation to absorption also holds good with light as with heat: with the latter it has been long known that the radiating power of different substances is directly proportional to their absorptive and inverse to their reflective power; or rather, that the sum of the heat radiated and reflected is a constant quantity. So, as has been shown by Mr. Balfour Stewart, the absorption bears the same relation to radiation for heat as to quality as well as quantity.

Light presents us with similar relations. Coloured glass, when heated so as to be luminous, emits the same light which at ordinary temperatures it absorbs: thus red glass gives out or radiates a greenish light, and green glass a red tint.

The flame of substances containing sodium yields a yellow light of such purity that other colours exposed to it appear black—a phenomenon shown by the familiar experiment of exposing a picture of bright colours, other than yellow, to the flame of spirits of wine with which common salt is mixed: the picture loses its colours, and appears to be black and white. When the prismatic spectrum of such a flame is examined, it is found to exhibit two bright yellow lines at a certain fixed position. If a source of light be employed which gives no lines in its spectrum, and this, being at a higher temperature, be made to pass through the sodium flame, two dark lines will appear in the spectrum precisely coincident in position with the yellow lines which were given by the sodium flame itself. The same relation of absorption to radiation is therefore shown here: the substance absorbs that light which it yields when it is itself the source of light. The same is true of other substances, the spectra of which exhibit respectively lines of peculiar colour and position. Now, the solar prismatic spectrum is traversed by a great number of dark lines; and Kirchoff has deduced from considerations such as those which I have shortly stated, that these dark lines in the solar spectrum are due to metals existing in an atmosphere around the sun, which absorb the light from a central incandescent nucleus, each metal absorbing that light which would appear as a bright line or lines in its own spectrum.

By comparing the position of the bright lines in the spectra of metals with that of the dark lines in the solar spectrum, several of them are found to be in identically the same place: hence it is inferred, and the inference seems reasonable, that the metals which show luminous lines in their spectra, identical in position with dark lines in the solar spectrum, exist in the sun, and are diffused in a gaseous state in its atmosphere. It does not seem to me necessary to this conclusion to assume that the sun is a solid mass of incandescent matter: it may well be that what we term the photosphere or luminous envelope of the sun has surrounding it a more diffuse atmosphere containing vaporised metals, and that the mass of the sun itself may be in a different state, and not necessarily at an incandescent temperature; indeed, the protuberances and red light seen at the period of total eclipses afford some evidence of an atmosphere exterior to the photosphere. It would, however, be out of place here to speculate on these subjects: the point which concerns us is the analogies of heat and light, which these discoveries illustrate. Kirchoff has carried the analogy farther by showing that a plate of tourmaline absorbs the polarised ray which when heated it radiates. Thus, the phenomena of light are imitated closely by those of radiant heat; and the same theory which is considered most plausibly to account for the phenomena of the one, will necessarily be applied to the other agent, and in each case molecular change is accompanied by a change in the phenomenal effects.

In certain cases heat appears to become partially converted into light, by changing the matter affected by heat: thus gas may be heated to a very high point without producing light, or producing it to a very slight degree; but the introduction of solid matter—for instance, the metal platinum into the highly-heated gas—instantly exhibits light. Whether the heat is converted into light, or whether it is concentrated and increased in intensity by the solid matter so as to become visible, may be open to some doubt: the fact of solid matter, when ignited by the oxyhydrogen jet decomposing water, as will be presently explained, would seem to indicate that the heat was rendered more intense by condensation in the solid matter, as water is in this case decomposed by a heated body, which body has itself been heated by the combining elements of water. The apparent effect, however, of the introduction of solid incombustible matter into heated gas, is a conversion of heat into light.

There is another method by which heat would probably

be made to produce luminous effects, though I am not aware that the experiment has ever been made.

If we concentrate into a focus by a large lens a dim light, we increase the intensity of the light. Now if a heated body be taken, which, to the unassisted eye, has just ceased to be visible, it seems probable that by collecting and condensing by a lens the different rays which have so ceased to be visible, light would reappear at the focus. The experiment is, for reasons obvious to those acquainted with optics, a difficult one, and, to be conclusive, should be made on a large scale, and with a very perfect lens of large diameter and short focus. I have obtained an approximation to the result in the following manner:—In a dark room a platinum wire is brought just to the point of visible ignition by a constant voltaic battery; it is then viewed, at a short distance, through an opera-glass of large aperture applied to one eye, the other being kept open. The wire will be distinctly visible to that eye which regards it through the opera-glass, and at the same time totally invisible to the other and naked eye. It may be said with some justice that such experiments prove little more than the fact already known, viz. that by increasing the intensity of heat, light is produced: they however exhibit this effect in a more striking form, as bearing on the relations of heat and light.

With regard to *chemical affinity* and *magnetism*, perhaps the only method by which in strictness the force of heat may be said to produce them is through the medium of electricity, the thermo-electrical current, produced, as before described, by heating dissimilar metals, being capable of deflecting the magnet, of magnetising iron, and exhibiting the other magnetic effects, and also of forming and decomposing chemical compounds, and this in proportion to the progression of heat: this has not, indeed, as yet been proved to bear a measurable quantitative relation to the other forces thus produced by it, because so little of the heat is utilised or converted into electricity, much being dissipated, without change, in the form of heat.

Heat, however, directly affects and modifies both the magnet and chemical compounds; the union of certain chemical substances is induced by heat, as, for instance, the formation of water by the union of oxygen and hydrogen gases: in other cases this union is facilitated by heat, and in many instances, as in ammonia and its salts, it is weakened or antagonised. In many of these cases, however, the force of heat seems more a determining than a producing influence; yet to be this, it must have an immediate relation with the force whose reaction it determines: thus, although gunpowder, touched with an ignited wire, subsequently carries on its own combustion or chemical combination, independently of the original source of heat, yet the chemical affinities of the first portion touched must be exalted by, and at the cost of, the heat of the wire; for to disturb even an unstable equilibrium requires a force in direct relation with those which maintain equilibrium.

Since the first edition of this essay was published, I have communicated to the Royal Society some experiments by which an important exception to the general effect of heat on chemical affinity is removed, and the results of which induce a hope that a generalised relation will ultimately be established between heat, chemical affinity, and physical attraction. I find that if a substance capable of supporting an intense heat, and incapable of being acted upon by water or either of its elements—such, for instance, as platinum, or iridium—be raised to a high point of ignition and then immersed in water, bubbles of permanent gas ascend from it, which on examination are found to consist of mixed oxygen and hydrogen in the proportions in which they form water. The temperature at which this is effected is, according to Dr. Robinson, who has since written a valuable paper on the subject, = 2386°. Now, when mixed oxygen and hydrogen are exposed to a temperature of about 800°, they combine and form water; heat therefore appears to act differently upon these elements according to its intensity, in one case producing composition, in the other decomposition. No satisfactory means of reconciling this apparent anomaly have been pointed out: the best approximation to a theory which I can frame is by assuming that the constituent molecules of water are, below a certain temperature, in a state of stable equilibrium; that the molecules of mixed or oxyhydrogen gas are, above a certain temperature, also in a state of stable equilibrium, but of an opposite character; while below this latter temperature the molecules of mixed gas are in a state of unstable equilibrium, somewhat similar to that of the fulminates or similar bodies, in which a slight derangement subverts the nicely-balanced forces.

If, for instance, we suppose four molecules, A, B, C, D, to be in a balanced state of equilibrium between attracting and repelling forces, the application of a repulsive force between B and C, though it may still farther separate B and C, will approximate B to A and C to D, and may bring them respectively within the range of attractive force; or, supposing the repulsive force to be in the centre of an indefinite sphere of particles, all these, excepting those immediately acted on by the force, will be approximated, and having from attraction assumed a state of stable equilibrium, they will retain this, because the repulsive force divided by the mass is not capable of overcoming it. But if the repulsive force be increased in quantity and of sufficient intensity, then the attractive force of all the molecules may be overcome, and decomposition ensue. Thus, water or steam below a certain temperature, and mixed gas above a certain temperature, may be supposed to be in a state of stable equilibrium, whilst below this limiting temperature, the equilibrium of oxyhydrogen gas is unstable.

This, it must be confessed, is but a crude mode of explaining the phenomena, and requires the assumption, that the particles of a gas exercise an attraction for each other as do the particles of a solid, though different in degree, perhaps in kind. Whether this be so or not, there can be no doubt that both gases and solids expand or contract according to the inverse contraction or expansion of other neighbouring bodies, and so far resemble each other in their relations to heat and cold. The extent to which such expansion or contraction can be carried, seems to be limited only by the correlative state of other bodies; these again, by others, and so on, as far as we may judge, throughout the universe.

Adopting the explanation above given of the decomposition of water by heat, heat would have the same relation to chemical affinity as it has to physical attraction; its immediate tendency is antagonistic to both, and it is only by a secondary action that chemical affinity is apparently promoted by heat. This view would explain how heat may promote changes of the equilibrium of chemical affinity among mixed compound substances, by decomposing certain compounds and separating elementary constituents whose affinity is greater, when they are brought within the sphere of attraction for the substance with which they are mixed, than for those with which they were originally chemically united: thus an intense heat being applied to a mixture of chlorine and the vapour of water, occasions the production of muriatic acid, liberating oxygen.

Carrying out this view, it would appear that a sufficient intensity of heat might yield indefinite powers of decomposition; and there seems some probability of bodies now supposed to be elementary, being decomposed or resolved into further elements by the application of heat of sufficient intensity; or, reasoning conversely, it may fairly be anticipated that bodies, which will not enter into combination at a certain temperature, will enter into combination if their temperature be lowered, and that thus new compounds may be formed by a proper disposition of their constituents when exposed to an extremely low temperature, and the more so if compression be also employed.

In considering the effect of heat as a mechanical force, it would be expected, *à priori*, and independently of any theory of heat which may be adopted, that a given amount of heat acting on a given material must produce a given amount of motive power; and the next question which occurs to the mind is, whether the same amount of heat would produce the same amount of mechanical power, whatever be the material acted on or affected by the heat. I will endeavour to reason this out on the view of heat which I have advocated. Heat has been considered in this essay as itself motion or mechanical power, and quantity of heat as measured by motion. Thus, if by a given contraction of a body (say mercury) air within a cylinder having a moveable piston be expanded, the piston moves, and in this case the expansion or motion of the material (say iron) of the cylinder itself and of the air surrounding it is commonly neglected. As the air dilates it becomes colder; in other words, by undergoing expansion itself, it loses its power of making neighbouring bodies expand; but if the piston be forcibly kept down, the expansive power due to the mercury continues to communicate itself to the iron and to the surrounding air, which become hotter than they would if the piston had given way.

Now, in the above case, if the air be confined and its volume unchanged, will the expansion of the iron, assuming that it can be utilised, produce an exactly equivalent mechanical effect to that which the expansion of the air would produce if the heat be entirely confined to it?

Assuming that (with the exception of bodies which expand in freezing, where, through a limited range of temperature, the converse effects obtain) whenever a body is compressed it is heated, i. e. it expands neighbouring substances; whenever it is dilated or increased in volume it is cooled, i. e.

it contracts neighbouring substances—the conclusion appears to me inevitable that the mechanical power produced by heat will be definite, or the same for a given amount and intensity of heat, whatever be the substance acted on.

Thus, let A be a definite source of heat, say a pound of mercury at the temperature of 400°; let B be another equal and similar source of heat: suppose A be employed to raise a piston by the dilatation of air, and B to raise another piston by the dilatation of the vapour of water. Imagine the pistons attached to a beam, so that they oppose each other's action, and thus represent a sort of calorific balance. If A being applied to air could conquer B, which is applied to water, it would depress or throw back the piston of the latter, and, by compressing the vapour, occasion an increase of temperature; this, in its turn, would raise the temperature of the source of heat, so that we should have the anomaly that a pound of mercury at 400° could heat another pound of mercury at 400° to 401°, or to some point higher than its original temperature, and this without any adventitious aid: it will be obvious that this is impossible, at least contradictory to the whole range of our experience.

The above experiment is ideal, and stated for the object of giving a more precise form to the reasoning; to bring the idea more prominently into relief, all statements as to quantities, specific heats, &c., so as to yield comparative results for given materials, are omitted. The argument may be thus stated in another form, viz. that by no mechanical appliance or difference of material acted on can a given source of heat be made to produce more heat than it originally possessed; and that, if all be converted into mechanical power, an excess cannot be supposed, for that could be converted into a surplus of heat, and be a creation of force; and a deficit cannot be supposed, for that would be annihilation of force. I cannot, however, see how the theoretical conception could be verified by experiment; the enormous weights and the complex mechanical contrivances requisite to give the measure of power yielded by matter in its less dilatable forms, would be far beyond our present experimental resources. It would also be difficult to prevent the interference of molecular attractions, inertia, &c., the overcoming of which expends a part of the mechanical power generated, but which could hardly be made to appear in the result. We could not, for instance, practically realise the above conception by the construction of a machine which should act by the expansion and contraction of a bar of iron, and produce a power equal to that of a steam engine, supplied with an equal quantity of heat.

Carnot, who wrote in 1824 an essay on the motive power of heat, regarded the mechanical power produced by heat as resulting from a transfer of heat from one point to another, without any ultimate loss of heat. Thus, in the action of an ordinary steam engine, the heat from the furnace having expanded the water of the boiler and raised the piston, a mechanical motion is produced; but this cannot be continued without the removal of the heat, or the contraction of the expanded water. This is done by the condenser, and the piston descends. But then we have apparently transferred the heat from the furnace to the condenser, and in the transfer effected mechanical motion.

Should the mechanical motion produced by heat be considered as the effect of a simple transference of heat from one point to another, or as the result of a conversion of heat into the mechanical force of which this motion is the result? This question leads to the following: does the heat which generates the mechanical power return to the thermal machine as heat, or is it conveyed away by the work performed?

If a definite quantity of air be heated it is expanded, and by its expansion it cools or loses some of its power of communicating heat to neighbouring bodies. That which we should have called heat if the expansion of the air had been prevented, we call mechanical effect, or may view as converted into mechanical effect ceasing to be heat; but, throwing out of the question nervous sensation, this expansion or mechanical effect is all the evidence we have of heat, for if the air is allowed to expand freely, this expansion becomes the index of the heat; if the air be confined, the expansion of the matter of the vessel confining it, or of the mercury of a thermometer in contact with it, &c., are the indices of the heat.

If, again, the air which has been expanded be, by mechanical pressure or by other means, restored to its original bulk, it is capable of heating or expanding other substances to a degree to which it would not be equal, if it had remained in its expanded state. To produce continuous motion, or the up and down stroke of a piston, we must heat and cool, just as with a magnetic machine we must magnetise and demagnetise in order to produce a continuous mechanical effect; and although, from the impossibility of insulating heat, some heat is apparently lost in the process, the result may be said to be effected by the transfer of heat from the hot to the cold body, from the furnace to the condenser. But we may equally well say that the heat has been converted into mechanical force, and the mechanical force back into heat; the effects are always correlative, as are the mechanical effects of an air pump, with which, as we dilate the air on one side, we condense it on the other; and as we cannot dilate without the reciprocal condensation, so we cannot heat without the reciprocal cooling, or vice versâ.

Hitherto the resistances of the piston or of any superimposed weight have been thrown out of consideration, or, what amounts to the same thing, it has been assumed that the weight raised by the piston has descended with it. The heat has not merely been employed in dilating the air or vapour, but in raising the piston with its weight. If, as the vapour is cooled, the weight be permitted to descend, its mechanical force restores the heat lost by the dilatation; but in this case no part of the power can be abstracted so as to be employed for any practical purpose: this question then follows, what takes place with regard to the initial heat, if, after the ascent of the piston, the weight be removed so as not to help the piston in its descent, but to fall upon a lever or produce some extraneous mechanical effect?

To answer this question, let us suppose a weight to rest on a piston which confines air at a definite temperature, say for example 50°, in a cylinder, the whole being assumed to be absolutely non-conducting for heat. A part of the heat of this confined air will be due to the pressure, since, as we have seen, compression of an elastic fluid produces heat.

Suppose, now, the confined air to be heated to 70°, the piston with its superincumbent weight will ascend, and the temperature, in consequence of the dilatation of the air, will be somewhat lowered, say to 69° (we will assume, for the sake of simplicity, that the heat engendered by the friction of the piston compensates the force lost by friction).

The piston having reached its maximum of elevation, let a cold body or condenser take away 20° from the temperature of the confined air; the piston will now descend, and by the compression which the weight on it produces, will restore the 1° lost by dilatation, and when the piston reaches its original position the temperature of the air will be restored to 50°. Suppose this experiment repeated up to the rise of the piston; but when the piston is at its full elevation, and the cold body applied, let the weight be removed, so as drop upon a wheel, or to be used for other mechanical purposes. The descending piston will not now reach its original point without more heat being abstracted; in consequence of the removal of the weight, there will not be the same force to restore the 1°, and the temperature will be 49°, or some fraction short of the original 50°. If this were otherwise, then, as the weight in falling may be made to produce heat by friction, we should have more heat than at first, or a creation of heat out of nothing—in other words, perpetual motion.

Let us now assume that this 20° supplied in the first instance was yielded by a body at 90°, of such size and material that its total capacity for heat is equal to that of the mass of confined air: this body would be reduced in temperature to 70°, in other words, our furnace would have lost 20° of heat. Let the cold body of the same size and material, used as a condenser, be at 30°. In the first experiment, the body at 30° would bring back the piston to its original point; but in the second experiment, or that where the weight has been removed, the body at 30° would not suffice to restore the piston: to effect this, the cold body or condenser must be at a lower temperature.

The question in Carnot's theory, which is not experimentally resolved, and which presents extreme experimental difficulty, is the following: Granted that a piston with a superimposed weight be raised by the thermic expansion of confined gas or vapour below it; if the elastic medium be restored to its original temperature by cooling, the weight in depressing the piston will restore that portion of the heat which has been lost by the expansion, and by the mechanical effect consequent thereon; but if the weight be removed when at its maximum of elevation, and the piston be brought back to its starting point by a necessarily cooler body than could restore it if the weight were not removed, would the return of the piston now restore the heat which had been lost by the dilatation, or, in other words, would pulling the piston down by cold restore the heat equally with the pressing it down by mechanical force? The argument from the impossibility of perpetual motion would say no, for if all the heat were restored, the mechanical effect produced by the fall of the weight, or the heating effect which might be made to result from this mechanical power, would be got from nothing.

Then follows another question, viz. whether, where an external or derived mechanical effect has been obtained, would the return of the piston, effected without the weight or external force to assist it, but solely by the colder body, give to this latter the same number of thermometric degrees as had been lost by the hot body in the first instance? Suppose, for instance, the cold body in our experiment to be at 20° instead of 30°, would this body gain 20°, and then reach the temperature of 40° when the piston is brought back, or would its temperature be higher or lower than 40°? The argument from the impossibility of perpetual motion does not apply here, for it does not necessarily follow that 20°, on the thermometric scale from 20° to 40°, represents an equal amount of force to 20° on the scale from 70° to 90°, and therefore it is quite conceivable that we may lose 20° from the furnace, and gain 20° in the condenser, and yet have obtained a certain amount of derived mechanical power. It will also follow, upon a consideration of the above imaginary experiments, that the greater the mechanical power required, the greater should be the difference between the temperature of the furnace and that of the condenser; but the exact relation in temperature between these, for a given mechanical effect, has not, as far as I am aware, been satisfactorily established by experiment, though it has been shown that steam at high pressure produces, comparatively, a greater mechanical effect for the same number of degrees than steam at low pressure.

Carnot, assuming the number of degrees of temperature to be restored, but at a lower point of the thermometric scale, termed this the fall (*chute*) of caloric. The mechanical effect of heat, on this view, may be likened to that of a series of cascades on water-wheels. The highest cascade turns a wheel, and produces a given mechanical effect; the water which has produced this cannot again effect it at the same level without being carried back to its original elevation, i. e.

without an extra force being employed equivalent to, or rather a fraction more than the force of the descending water; but though its power is spent with reference to the first wheel, the same water may, by falling over a new precipice upon a second wheel, again reproduce the same mechanical effect (strictly speaking, rather more, for it has approximated the centre of gravity), and so on, until no lower fall can be attained. So with heat: it involves no necessity of assuming perpetual motion to suppose that, after a given mechanical effect, produced by a certain loss of heat, the number of degrees lost from the original temperature may be restored to the condenser, but at a lower point of the thermometric scale.

If work has been done, i. e. if force has been parted with, the original temperature itself cannot be restored, but there is no *à priori* impossibility in the same number of degrees of heat as have been converted into work being conveyed to a condensing body so cold that, when it receives this heat, it will still be below the original temperature to which the work-producing heat was added.

In the theory of the steam-engine, this subject possesses a great practical interest. Watt supposed that a given weight of water required the same quantity of what is termed total heat (that is, the sensible added to the latent heat) to keep it in the state of vapour, whatever was the pressure to which it was subjected, and, consequently, however its expansive force varied. Clement Desormes was also supposed to have experimentally verified this law. If this were so, vapour raising a piston with a weight attached would produce mechanical power; and yet, the same heat existing as at first, there would be no expenditure of the initial force; and if we suppose that the heat in the condenser was the real representative of the original heat, we should get perpetual motion. Southern supposed that the latent heat was constant, and that the heat of vapour under pressure increased as the sensible heat. M. Despretz, in 1832, made some experiments, which led him to the conclusion that the increase was not in the same ratio as the sensible heat, but that yet there was an increase; a result confirmed and verified with great accuracy by M. Regnault, in some recent and elaborate researches. What seems to have occasioned the error in Watt and Clement Desormes' experiments was, the idea involved in the term latent heat; by which, supposing the phenomenon of the disappearance of sensible heat to be due to the absorption of a material substance, that substance, 'caloric,' was thought to be restored when the vapour was condensed by water, even though the water was not subjected to pressure; but to estimate the total heat of vapour under pressure the vapour should be condensed while subjected to the same pressure as that under which it is generated, as was done in M. Despretz and M. Regnault's experiments.

M. Seguin, in 1839, controverted the position that derived power could be got by the mere transfer of heat, and by calculation from certain known data, such as the law of Mariotte, viz. that the elastic force of gases and vapours increased directly with the pressure; and assuming that for vapour between 100° and 150° centigrade, each degree of elevation of temperature was produced by a thermal unit, he deduced the equivalent of mechanical work capable of being performed by a given decrement of heat; and thus concluded that, for ordinary pressures, about one gramme of water losing one degree centigrade would produce a force capable of raising a weight of 500 grammes through a space of one mètre: this estimate is a little beyond that given by the converse experiments of Mr. Joule, already stated, in which the heat produced by a given amount of mechanical action is estimated. I am not aware that the amount of mechanical work which is produced by a given quantity of heat has been directly established by experiment, though some approximative results in particular cases have been given. Theoretically it should be the same—that is to say, if a fall of 772 lbs. through a space of one foot will raise the temperature of 1 lb. of water through one degree of Fahrenheit, then the fall in the temperature of 1 lb. of water through one degree of Fahrenheit should be able to raise 772 lbs. through a space of one foot. The calculations of M. Seguin are not far from this, but since the elaborate experiments of M. Regnault he has expressed some doubt of the correctness of his former estimate, as by these experiments it appears that, within certain limits, for elevating the temperature of compressed vapour by one degree, no more than about three-tenths of a degree of total heat is required; consequently, the equivalent multiplied in this ratio would be 1,666 grammes, instead of 500. Other investigators have given numbers more or less discordant; so that, without giving any opinion on their different results, this question may be considered at present far from settled. M. Regnault himself does not give the law by which the ratio of heat varies with reference to the pressure, and is still believed to be engaged in researches on the subject—one involving questions of which experiments on the mechanical effects of elastic fluids seem to offer the most promising means of solution.

I have endeavoured to give a proof (by showing the anomaly to which the contrary conclusion would lead) that, whatever amount of mechanical power is produced by one mode of application of heat, the same should, in theory, be equally produced by any other mode. But in practice the difference is immense; and therefore it becomes a question of great interest practically to ascertain what is the most convenient medium on which to apply the heat employed, and the best machinery for economising it. One great problem to be solved is the saving of the heat which the steam in ordinary engines, after having done its work, carries into the condenser, or, in the high-pressure engine, into the air. It is argued you have a large amount of fuel consumed to raise water to the boiling point, at which its efficiency as a motive agent commences. After it has done a small portion of work, and while it still retains a very large portion of the heat originally communicated to it, you reject it, and have to start again with a fresh portion of steam which has similarly exhausted fuel—in other words, you throw away all, and more than all the heat which has been employed in raising the water to the boiling point. Various plans have been devised to remedy this. Using again the warm water of the condenser to feed the boiler regains a part, but a very small part, of the heat. Employing the steam first for a high pressure, and then before its rejection or condensation using it for a low pressure, cylinder, is a second mode; a third is to use the steam, after it has done its work on the piston, as a source of heat or second furnace, to boil ether, or some liquid which evaporates at a lower temperature than water. These plans have certain advantages; but the complexity of apparatus, the danger from combustion of ether, and other reasons, have hitherto precluded their general adoption. Under the term regenerating engine various ingenious combinations have lately been suggested, and some experimental engines tried, with what success it is perhaps too early at present to pronounce an opinion. The fundamental notion on which this class of engine is based is that the vapour or air, when it has performed a certain amount of work, as by raising a piston, should, instead of being condensed or blown off, be retained and again heated to its original high temperature, and then used *de novo;* or that it should impart its heat to some other substance, and the latter in turn impart it to the fresh vapour about to act. The latter plan has been proposed by Mr. Ericsson: he passes the air which has done its work through layers of wire gauze, which are heated by the rejected air, and through which the next charge of air is made to pass. M. Seguin and Mr. Siemens have constructed machines upon the former principle, which are said to have given good experimental results. There is, however, a theoretical difficulty in all these, not affecting their capability of acting, but affecting the question of economy, which it does not seem easy to escape from. Whether the heated air or vapour be retained, or whether it yield its heat to a metallic or other substance, this heat must exercise its usual repulsive force, and this must re-act either against the returning piston or against the incoming vapour, and require a greater pressure in that to neutralise it. Vapour raising a piston and producing mechanical force effects this with decreasing power in proportion as the piston is moved. At a certain point the piston is arrested, or the stroke, as it is termed, is completed, but there is still compressed vapour in the cylinder capable of doing work, but so little that it is, and must in practice be neglected; if this compressed vapour be retained, the piston cannot be depressed without an extra force capable of over coming the resistance of this, so to speak, semi-compressed vapour, in addition to that which is requisite to produce the normal work of the machine; and in whatever way the residual force be retained, it must either be antagonised at a loss of power for the initial force, or at most can only yield the more feeble power which it would have originally given if it had been allowed to act for a longer stroke on the piston. It may be that a portion of this residual force may be economised; indeed, this is done when the boiler is charged with warm water from the condenser, instead of with cold water; but some, indeed a notable loss, seems inevitable.

Without farther discussing the various inventions and theories on this subject, which are daily receiving increased development, it may be well to point out how far nature distances art in its present state. According to some careful estimates, the most economical of our furnaces consume from ten to twenty times as much fuel to produce the same quantity of heat as an animal produces; and Matteucci found that, from a given consumption of zinc in a voltaic battery, a far greater mechanical effect could be produced by making it act on the limbs of a recently-killed frog, notwithstanding the manifold defects of such an arrangement and its inferiority to the action of the living animal, than when the same battery was made to produce mechanical power, by acting on an electro-magnetic or other artificial motor apparatus. The ratio in his experiments was nearly six to one. Thus in all our artificial combinations we can but apply natural forces, and with far inferior mechanism to that which is perceptible in the economy of nature.

> Nature is made better by no mean;
> But nature makes that mean; so o'er that art,
> Which you say adds to nature, is an art
> That nature makes.

A speculation has been thrown out by Mr. Thompson, that, as a certain amount of heat results from mechanical action, chemical action, &c., and this heat is radiated into space, there must be a gradual diminution of temperature for the earth, by which expenditure, however slow, being continuous, it would ultimately be cooled to a degree incompatible with the existence of animal and vegetable life—in short, that the earth and the planets of our system are parting with more heat than they receive, and are therefore progressively cooling. Geological researches support to some extent this view, as they show that the climate of many portions of the terrestrial surface was at remote periods hotter than at the present time: the animals whose fossilised remains are found in ancient strata have their organism adapted to what we should now term a hot climate. There are, however, so many circumstances of difficulty attending cosmical speculations, that but little reliance can be placed upon the most profound. We know not the original source of terrestrial heat; still less that of the solar heat; we know not whether or not systems of planets may be so constituted as to communicate forces, *inter se*, so that forces which have hitherto escaped detection may be in a continuous or recurring state of inter change.

The movements produced by mutual gravitation may be the means of calling into existence molecular forces within the substances of the planets themselves. As neither from observation, nor from deduction, can we fix or conjecture any boundary to the universe of stellar orbs, as each advance in telescopic power gives us a new shell, so to speak, of stars, we may regard our globe, in the limit, as surrounded by a sphere of matter radiating heat, light, and possibly other, forces.

Such stellar radiations would not, from the evidence we have at present, appear sufficient to supply the loss of heat by terrestrial radiations; but it is quite conceivable that the whole solar system may pass through portions of space having different temperatures, as was suggested, I believe, by Poisson; that as we have a terrestrial summer and winter, so there may be a solar or systematic summer and winter, in which case the heat lost during the latter period might be restored during the former. The amount of the radiations of the celestial bodies may again, from changes in their positions, vary through epochs which are of enormous duration as regards the existence of the human species.

The views of Mr. Thompson differ from those of Laplace, recently enforced by M. Babinet, which suppose the planets to have been formed by a gradual condensation of nebulous matter. A modification of this view might, perhaps, be suggested, viz. that worlds or systems, instead of being created as wholes at definite periods, are gradually changing by atmospheric additions or subtractions, or by accretions or diminutions arising from nebulous substance or from meteoric bodies, so that no star or planet could at any time be said to be created or destroyed, or to be in a state of absolute stability, but that some may be increasing, others dwindling away, and so throughout the universe, in the past as in the future. When, however, questions relating to cosmogony, or to the beginning or end of worlds, are contemplated from a physical point of view, the period of time over which our experience, in its most enlarged sense, extends, is so indefinitely minute with reference to that which must be required for any notable change, even in our own planet, that a variety of theories may be framed equally incapable of proof or of disproof. We have no means of ascertaining whether many changes, which endure in the same direction for a term beyond the range of human experience, are really continuous or only secular variations, which may be compensated for at periods far beyond our ken, so that in such cases the question of comparative stability or change can at best be only answered as to a term which, though enormous with referference to our computations, sinks into nothing with reference to cosmical time, if cosmical time be not eternity. Subjects such as these, though of a kind on which the mind delights to speculate, appear, with reference to any hope of attaining reliable knowledge, far beyond the reach of any present or immediately prospective capacity of man.

IV. ELECTRICITY.

ELECTRICITY is that affection of matter or mode of force which most distinctly and beautifully relates other modes of force, and exhibits, to a great extent in a quantitative form, its own relation with them, and their reciprocal relations with it and with each other. From the manner in which the peculiar force called electricity is seemingly transmitted through certain bodies, such as metallic wires, the term *current* is commonly used to denote its apparent progress. It is very difficult to present to the mind any theory which will give a definite conception of its *modus agendi:* the early theories regard its phenomena as produced either by a single fluid idio-repulsive, but attractive of all matter, or else as produced by two fluids, each idio-repulsive but attractive of the other. No substantive theory has been proposed other than these two; but although this is the case, I think I shall not be unsupported by many who have attentively studied electrical phenomena, in viewing them as resulting, not from the action of a fluid or fluids, but as a molecular polarisation of ordinary matter, or as matter acting by attraction and repulsion in a definite direction. Thus, the transmission of the voltaic current in liquids is viewed by Grotthus as a series of chemical affinities acting in a definite direction: for instance, in the electrolysis of water, i. e. its decomposition when placed between the poles or electrodes of a voltaic battery, a molecule of oxygen is supposed to be displaced by the exalted attraction of the neighbouring electrode; the hydrogen liberated by this displacement unites with the oxygen of the contiguous molecule of water; this in turn liberates its hydrogen, and so on; the current being nothing else than this molecular transmission of chemical affinity.

There is strong reason for believing that, with some exceptions, such as fused metals, liquids do not conduct electricity without undergoing decomposition; for even in those extreme cases where a trifling effect of conduction is apparently produced without the usual elimination of substances at the electrodes, the latter when detached from the circuit show, by the counter-current which they are capable of producing when immersed in a fresh liquid, that their superficial state has been changed, doubtless by the determination to the surfaces of minute layers of substances having opposite chemical characters. The question whether or not a minute conduction in liquids can take place unaccompanied by chemical action, has however been much agitated, and may be regarded as *inter apices* of the science.

Assuming for the moment electrolysis to be the only known electrical phenomenon, electricity would appear to consist in transmitted chemical action. All the evidence we have is, that a certain affection of matter or chemical change takes place at certain distant points of space, the change at one point having a definite relation to the change at the other, and being capable of manifestation at any intermediate points.

If, now, the electrical effect called induction be examined, the phenomena will be found equally opposed to the theory of a fluid, and consistent with that of molecular polarisation. When an electrified conductor is brought near another which is not electrified, the latter becomes electrified by influence or induction, as it is termed, the nearest parts of each of these two bodies exhibiting states of electricity of the contrary denominations. Until this subject was investigated by Faraday, the intervening non-conducting body or dielectric was supposed to be purely negative, and the effect was attributed to the repulsion at a distance of the electrical fluid. Faraday showed that these effects differed greatly according to the dielectric that was interposed. Thus they were more exalted with sulphur than with shellac; more with shellac than with glass, &c. Matteucci, though differing from Faraday as to the explanation he gave, added some experiments which prove that the intervening dielectric is molecularly polarised. Thus a number of thin plates of mica are superposed like a pack of cards; metallic plates are applied to the outer facings, and one of them electrified, so that the apparatus is charged like a Leyden phial. Upon separating the plates with insulating handles, each plate is separately electrified, one side of it being positive and the other negative, showing very neatly and decisively a polarisation throughout the intervening substances by the effect of induction.

Indeed, chemical action or electrolysis may, as I have shown, be transmitted by induction across a dielectric substance, such as glass, but apparently only while the glass is being charged with electricity. A wire passing through and hermetically sealed into a glass tube, a short portion only projecting, is made to dip into water contained in a Florence flask; the flask is immersed in water to an equal depth with that within it; the wire and another similar wire dipping into the outer water are made to communicate metallically with the powerful electrical machine known as Rhumkorf's coil; bubbles of gas instantly ascend from the exposed portions of the wires, but cease after a certain time, and are renewed when, after an interval of separation, the coil is again connected with the wires.

The following interesting experiment by Mr. Karsten goes a step farther in corroboration of the molecular changes consequent upon electrisation: A coin is placed on a pack of thin plates of glass, and then electrified. On removing the coin and breathing on the glass plate, an impression of the coin is perceptible; this shows a certain molecular change on the surface of the glass opposed to the plate, or of the vapours condensed on such surface. This effect might, and has been interpreted as arising from a film of greasy deposit, supposed to exist on the plate; the impressions, however, have been proved to penetrate to certain depths below the surface, and not to be removed by polishing.

The following experiment, however, goes farther: On separating carefully the glass plates, images of the coin can be developed on each of the surfaces, showing that the molecular change has been transmitted through the substance of the glass; and we may thence reasonably suppose that a piece of glass, or other dielectric body, if it could be split up while under the influence of electric induction, would exhibit some molecular change at each side of each lamina, however minutely subdivided. I have succeeded in farther extending this experiment, and in permanently fixing the images thus produced by electricity. Between two carefully-cleaned glass plates is placed a word or device cut out of paper or tinfoil; sheets of tinfoil a little smaller than the glass plates are placed on the outside of each plate, and these coatings are brought into contact with the terminals of Rhumkorf's coil. After electrisation for a few seconds, the glasses are separated, and their interior surfaces exposed to the vapour of hydrofluoric acid, which acts chemically on glass; the portions of the glass not protected by the paper device are corroded, while those so protected are untouched or less affected by the acid, so that a permanent etching is thus produced, which nothing but disintegration of the glass will efface.

Some further experiments of mine on this subject bring out in a still more striking manner these curious molecular changes. One of the plates of glass having been electrified in the manner just mentioned, is coated, on the side impressed with the invisible electrical image, with a film of iodised collodion in the manner usually adopted for photographic purposes; it is then in a dark room immersed in a solution of nitrate of silver; then exposed to diffuse light for a few seconds. On pouring over the collodion the usual solution of pyrogallic acid, the invisible electrical image is brought out as a dark device on a light ground, and can be permanently fixed by hyposulphite of soda. The point worthy of observation in this experiment is, that this permanent image exists in the collodion film, which can be stripped off the glass, dried, and placed on any other surface, so that the molecular change consequent on electrisation has communicated, by contact or close proximity, a change to the film of collodion corresponding in form with that on the glass, but being undoubtedly of a chemical nature. Electricity has, moreover, in this experiment so modified the surface of glass, that it can, in its turn, modify the structure of another substance so as to alter the relation of the latter to light. It would require a curious complication of hypothetic fluids to explain this; but if electricity and light be supposed to be affections of ordinary ponderable matter, the difficulty is only one of detail.

If, again, we examine the electricity of the atmosphere, when, as is usually the case, it is positive with respect to that of the earth, we find that each successive stratum is positive to those below it and negative to those above it; and the converse is the case when the electricity of the atmosphere is negative with respect to that of the earth.

If another electrical phenomenon be selected, another sort of change will be found to have taken place. The electric spark, the brush, and similar phenomena, the old theories regarded as actual emanations of the matter or fluid, Electricity; I venture to regard them as produced by an emission of the material itself from whence they issue, and a molecular action of the gas, or intermedium, through or across which they are transmitted.

The colour of the electric spark, or of the voltaic arc (i. e. the flame which plays between the terminal points of a powerful voltaic battery), is dependent upon the substance of the metal, subject to certain modifications of the intermedium: thus, the electric spark or arc from zinc is blue; from silver, green; from iron, red and scintillating; precisely the colours afforded by these metals in their ordinary combustion. A portion of the metal is also found to be actually transmitted with every electric or voltaic discharge: in the latter case, indeed, where the quantity of matter acted upon is greater than in the former, the metallic particles emitted by the electrodes or terminals can be readily collected, tested, or even weighed. It would thus appear that the electrical discharge arises, at least in part, from an actual repulsion and severance of the electrified matter itself, which flies off at the points of least resistance.

A careful examination of the phenomena attending the electric spark or the voltaic arc, which latter is the electric disruptive discharge acting on greater portions of matter, tends to modify considerably our previous idea of the nature of the electric force as a producer of ignition and combustion. The voltaic arc is perhaps, strictly speaking, neither ignition nor combustion. It is not simply ignition; because the matter of the terminals is not merely brought to a state of incandescence, but is physically separated and partially transferred from one electrode to another, much of it being dissipated in a vaporous state. It is not combustion; for the phenomena will take place independently of atmospheric air, oxygen gas, or any of the bodies usually called supporters of combustion, combustion being in fact chemical union attended with heat and light. In the voltaic arc we may have no chemical union; for if the experiment be performed in an exhausted receiver, or in nitrogen, the substance forming the electrodes is condensed, and precipitated upon the interior of the vessel in, chemically speaking, an unaltered state. Thus, to take a very striking example, if the voltaic discharge be taken between zinc terminals in an exhausted receiver, a fine black powder of zinc is deposited on the sides of the receiver; this can be collected, and takes fire readily in the air by being touched with a match, or ignited wire, instantly burning into white oxide of zinc. To an ordinary observer, the zinc would appear to be burned twice—first in the receiver, where the phenomenon presents all the appearance of combustion, and secondly in the real combustion in air. With iron the experiment is equally instructive. Iron is volatilised by the voltaic arc in nitrogen or in an exhausted receiver; and when a scarcely perceptible film has lined the receiver, this is washed with an acid, which then gives, with ferrocyanide of potassium, the prussian-blue precipitate. In this case we *readily* distil iron, a metal by ordinary means *fusible* only at a very high temperature.

Another strong evidence that the voltaic discharge consists of the material itself of which the terminals are composed, is the peculiar rotation which is observed in the light when iron is employed, the magnetic character of this metal causing its molecules to rotate by the influence of the voltaic current.

If we increase the number of reduplications in a voltaic series, we increase the length of the arc, and also increase its intensity or power of overcoming resistance. With a battery consisting of a limited number, say 100 reduplications, the discharge will not pass from one terminal to the other without first bringing them into contact, but if we increase the number of cells to 400 or 500, the discharge will pass from one terminal to the other before they are brought into contact. The difference between what is called Franklinic electricity, or that produced by an ordinary electrical machine, and voltaic electricity, or that produced by the ordinary voltaic battery, is that the former is of much greater intensity than the latter, or has a greater power of overcoming resistance, but acts upon a much smaller quantity of matter. If, then, a voltaic battery be formed with a view to increase the intensity and lessen the quantity, the character of the electrical phenomena approximate those of the electrical machine. In order to effect this, the sizes of the plates of the battery and thence the quantity of matter acted on in each cell, must be reduced, but the number of reduplications increased. Thus if in a battery of 100 pairs of plates each plate be divided, and the battery be arranged so as to form 200 pairs, each being half the original size, the quantitative effects are diminished, and the effects of intensity increased. By carrying on this sub-division, diminishing the sizes and increasing the number, as is the case in the voltaic piles of Deluc and Zamboni, effects are ultimately produced similar to those of Franklinic electricity, and we thus gradually pass from the voltaic arc to the spark or electric discharge.

This discharge, as I have already stated, has a colour depending in part upon the nature of the terminals employed. If these terminals be highly polished, a spot will be observed, even in the case of a small electric spark, at the points from which the discharge emanates. The matter of the terminals is itself affected; and a transmission of this matter across the intervening space is detected by the deposition of minute quantities of the metal or substance composing the one, upon the other terminal.

If the gas or elastic medium between the terminals be changed, a change takes place in the length or colour of the discharge, showing an affection of the intervening matter. If the gas be rarefied, the discharge gradually changes with the degree of rarefaction, from a spark to a luminous glow or diffuse light, differing in colour in different gases, and capable of extending to a much greater distance than when it takes place in air of the ordinary density. Thus, in highly attenuated air a discharge may be made to pass across six or seven feet of space, while in air of the ordinary density it would not pass across an inch. An observer regarding the beautiful phenomena exhibited by this electric discharge in attenuated gas, which, from some degree of similarity in appearance to the Aurora Borealis, has been called the electric Aurora, would have some difficulty in believing such effects could be due to an action of ordinary matter. The amount of gas present is extremely small; and the terminals, to a cursory examination, show no change after long experimenting. It is therefore not to be wondered at that the first observers of this and similar phenomena, regarded electricity as in itself something—as a specific existence or fluid. Even in this extreme case, however, upon a more careful examination we shall find that a change does take place, both as regards the gas and as regards the terminals. Let one of these consist of a highly-polished metal—a silver plate is one of the best materials for the purpose—and let the discharges in attenuated atmospheric air take place from a point, say a common sewing needle, to the surface of the polished silver plate; it will be found that this is gradually changed in appearance opposite the point—it is oxidated, and gradually more and more corroded as the discharge is continued.

If now the gas be changed, and highly-rarefied hydrogen be substituted for the rarefied air, all other things remaining the same, upon passing the discharges as before the oxide will be cleared off the plate, and the polish to a great extent restored—not entirely, because the silver has been disintegrated by the oxidation—and the portion which has been affected by the discharge will present a somewhat different appearance from the remainder of the plate.

A question will probably here occur to the reader:—What will be the effect if there be not an oxidating medium present, and the experiment be first performed in a rarefied gas, which possesses no power of chemically acting on the plate?

In this case there will still be a molecular change or disintegration of the plate; the portion of it acted on by the discharge will present a different appearance from that which is beyond its reach, and a whitish film, somewhat similar to that seen on the mercurialised portions of a daguerreotype, will gradually appear on the portion of the plate affected by the discharge. If the gas be a compound, as carbonic oxide, or a mixture, as oxygen and hydrogen, and consequently contain elements capable of producing oxidation and reduction, then the effect upon the plate will depend upon whether it be positive or negative; in the former case it will be oxidated, in the latter the oxide, if existing, will be reduced. This effect will also take place in atmospheric air, if it be highly rarefied, and can hardly be explained otherwise than by a molecular polarisation of the compound gas. If, again, the metal be reduced to a small point, and be of such material that the gas cannot act chemically upon it, it can yet be shown to be disintegrated by the electric spark. Thus, let a fine platinum wire be hermetically sealed in a glass tube, and the extremity of the tube and the wire ground to a flat surface, so as to expose a section only of the wire; after taking the discharge from this for some time, it will be found that the platinum wire is worn away, and that its termination is sensibly below the level of the glass. If the discharges from such a platinum wire be taken in gas contained in a narrow tube, a cloud or film consisting of a deposit of platinum will be seen on the part of the tube surrounding the point.

Another curious effect which, in addition to the above, I have detected in the electrical discharge in attenuated media, is that when passing between terminals of a certain form, as from a wire placed at right angles to a polished plate, the discharge possesses certain phases or fits of an alternate character, so that, instead of impressing an uniform mark on a polished plate, a series of concentric rings is formed.

Priestley observed that, after the discharge of a Leyden

battery, rings consisting of fused globules of metal were formed on the terminal plates; in my experiments made in attenuated media, alternate rings of oxidation and deoxidation are formed. Thus, if the plate be polished, coloured rings of oxide will alternate with rings of polished or unoxidated surface; and if the plate be previously coated with an uniform film of oxide, the oxide will be removed in concentric spaces, and increased in the alternate ones, showing a lateral alternation of positive and negative electricity, or electricity of opposite character in the same discharge.

It would be hasty to assert that in no case can the electrical disruptive discharge take place without the terminals being affected. I have, however, seen no instance of such a result where the discharge has been sufficiently prolonged, and the terminals in such a state as could be expected to render manifest slight changes.

The next question which would occur in following out the enquiry which has been indicated, would probably be, What is the action upon the gas itself? is this changed in any manner?

In answer to this, it must be admitted that, in the present state of experimental knowledge on this subject, certain gases only appear to leave permanent traces of their having been changed by the discharge, while others, if affected by it, which, as will be presently seen, there are reasons to believe they are, return to their normal state immediately after the discharge.

In the former class we may place many compound gases, as ammonia, olefiant gas, protoxide of nitrogen, deutoxide of nitrogen, and others, which are decomposed by the action of the discharge. Mixed gases are also chemically combined: for instance, oxygen and hydrogen unite and form water; common air gives nitric acid; chlorine and aqueous vapour give oxygen, the chlorine uniting with the hydrogen of the water.

But, further than this, in the case of certain elementary gases a permanent change is effected by the electrical discharge. Thus, oxygen submitted to the discharge is partially changed into the substance now considered to be an allotropic condition of oxygen; and there is reason to believe that when the change takes place, there is a definite polar condition of the gas, and that definite portions of it are affected —that in a certain sense one portion of the oxygen bears temporarily to the other the relation which hydrogen ordinarily does to oxygen.

If the discharge be passed through the vapour of phosphorus in the vacuum of a good air-pump, a deposit of allotropic phosphorus soon coats the interior of the receiver, showing an analogous change to that produced in oxygen; and in this case a series of transverse bands or stratifications appears in the discharge, showing a most striking alteration in its physical character, dependent on the medium across which it is transmitted. These effects were first observed by me in the year 1852. They have since been much examined by continental philosophers, and much extended by Mr. Gassiot; but no satisfactory *rationale* of them has yet been given.

There are many gases which either do not show any permanent change, or (which is more probably the case) the changes produced in them by the electrical discharge have not yet been detected. Even with these gases, however, the difference of colour, of length, or of the different position of a certain dark space or spaces which appear in the discharge, show that the discharge differs for different media. We never find that the discharge has itself added to or subtracted from the total weight of the substances acted on: we find no evidence of a fluid but the visible phenomena themselves; and those we may account for by the change which takes place in the matter affected.

I have here, as elsewhere, used words of common acceptation, such as 'matter affected by the discharge,' &c., though upon the view I am suggesting, the discharge is itself this affection of matter: and the writing these passages affords, to me at least, a striking instance of how much ideas are bound up in words, when, to express a view differing from the received one, words involving the received one are necessarily used.

Passing now to the effect of the transmission of electricity by the class of the best conducting bodies, such as the metals and carbon, here, though we cannot at present give the exact character of the motion impressed upon the particles, there are yet many experiments which show that a change takes place in such substances when they are affected by electricity.

Let discharges from a Leyden jar or battery be passed through a platinum wire, too thick to be fused by the discharges, and free from constraint, it will be found that the wire is shortened; it has undergone a molecular change, and apparently been acted on by a force tranverse to its length. If the discharges be continued, it gradually gathers up in small irregular bends or convolutions. So with voltaic electricity: place a platinum wire in a trough of porcelain, so that when fused it shall retain its position as a wire, and then ignite it by a voltaic battery. As it reaches the point of fusion it will snap asunder, showing a contraction in length, and consequently a distension or increase in its transverse dimensions. Perform the same experiment with a lead wire, which can be more readily kept in a state of fusion, and follow it, as it contracts, by the terminal wires of the battery; it will be seen to gather up in nodules, which press on each other like a string of beads of a soft material which have been longitudinally compressed.

As we increase the thickness of the wires in these experiments with reference to the electrical force employed, we lessen the perceptible effect: but even in this case we shall be enabled safely to infer that some molecular change accompanies the transmission of electricity: the wires are heated in a degree decreasing as their thickness increases—but by increasing the delicacy of our tests as the heating effects decrease in intensity, we may indefinitely detect the augmentation of temperature accompanying the passage of electricity—and wherever there is augmentation of temperature there must be expansion or change of position of the molecules.

Again, it has been observed that wires which have for a long time transmitted electricity, such as those which have served as conductors for atmospheric electricity, have their texture changed, and are rendered brittle. In this observation, however, though made by a skillful electrician, M. Peltier, the effects of exposure to the atmosphere, to changes of temperature, &c., have not been sufficiently eliminated to render it worthy of entire confidence. There are, however, other experiments which show that the elasticity of metals is changed by the passage through them of the electric current.

Thus M. Wertheim has, from an elaborate series of experiments, arrived at the conclusion that there is a temporary diminution in the coefficient of elasticity in wires while they are transmitting the electric current, which is independent of the heating effect of the current.

M. Dufour has made a considerable number of experiments with the view of ascertaining if any permanent change in metals is effected by electrisation. He arrives at the curious result that in a copper wire through which a feeble voltaic current has passed for several days, a notable diminution in tenacity takes place; while, in an iron wire, the tenacity is increased; and that these effects were more perceptible when the wires had been electrised for a long time (nineteen days) than for a short time (four days). The copper wire was, in his experiment, not perfectly pure; so that the effect, or a portion of it, might be due to the state of alloy: in the case of iron, the magnetic character of the metal would probably modify the effects, and might account for the opposite character of the results with these two metals.

Matteucci has made experiments on the conduction of electricity by bismuth in directions parallel or transverse to the planes of principal cleavage, and he finds that bismuth conducts electricity and heat better in the direction of the cleavage planes than in that transverse to them.

Many other experiments have been made both on the production of thermo-electric currents by two portions of the same crystalline metal, but with the planes of crystallization arranged in different directions relatively to each other, and also on the differences in conduction of heat and electricity according to the direction in which they are transmitted with reference to the planes of crystallization.

It is found, moreover, that the slightest difference in homogeneity in the same metal enables it when heated to produce a thermo-electric current, and that metals in a state of fusion, in which state they may be presumed to be homogeneous throughout, give no thermo-electric current: thus, hot in contact with cold mercury has been shown by Matteucci to give no thermo-electric current, and the same is the case with portions of fused bismuth unequally heated.

The fact that the molecular structure or arrangement of a body influences—indeed I may say determines—its conducting power, is by no means explained by the theory of a fluid; but if electricity be only a transmission of force or motion, the influence of the molecular state is just what would be expected. Carbon, in a transparent crystalline state, as diamond, is as perfect a non-conductor as we know; while in an opaque amorphous state, as graphite or charcoal, it is one of the best conductors: thus, in the one state, it transmits light and stops electricity, in the other it transmits electricity and stops light.

It is a circumstance worthy of remark, that the arrangement of molecules, which renders a solid body capable of transmitting light, is most unfavourable to its transmission of electricity, transparent solids being very imperfect conductors of electricity; so all gases readily transmit light, but are amongst the worst conductors of electricity, if, indeed, properly speaking, they can be said to conduct at all.

The conduction of electricity by different classes of bodies has been generally regarded as a question of degree: thus metals were viewed as perfect conductors, charcoal less so, water and other liquids as imperfect conductors, &c. But, in fact, though between one metal and another the mode of transmission may be the same and the difference one of degree, a different molecular effect obtains, when we contrast metals with electrolytic liquids and these with gases.

Attenuated gases may be, in one sense, regarded as non-conductors, in another, as conductors; thus if gold-leaves be made to diverge, by electrical repulsion, in air at ordinary pressure, they in a short time collapse; while in highly-rarefied air, or what is commonly termed a vacuum, they remain divergent for days; and yet electricity of a certain degree of tension passes readily across attenuated air, and with difficulty across air of ordinary density.

Again, where the electrical terminals are brought to a state of visible ignition, there are symptoms of the transmission of electricity of low tension across gases; but no such effects have been detected at lower temperatures. All this presents a strong argument in favour of the transmission of electricity across gases being effected by the disruptive discharge, and not by a conduction similar to that which takes place with metals or with electrolytes.

The ordinary attractions and repulsions of electrified bodies present no more difficulty when regarded as being produced by a change in the state or relations of the matter affected, than do the attractions of the earth by the sun, or of a leaden ball by the earth; the hypothesis of a fluid is not considered necessary for the latter, and need not be so for the former class of phenomena. How the phenomena are produced to which the term attraction is applied is still a mystery. Newton, speaking of it, says, 'What I call attraction may be performed by impulse, or by some other means unknown to me. I use that word here to signify only in general any force by which bodies tend towards one another, whatsoever be the cause.' If we suppose a fluid to act in attractions and repulsions, the imponderable fluid must drag or push the matter with it: thus when we feel a stream of air rushing from an electrified metallic point, each molecule of air contiguous to the point being repelled, another takes its place, which is in its turn repelled:—how does a hypothetic fluid assist us here? If we say the electrical fluid repels itself, or the same electricity repels itself, we must go farther and assert, that it not only repels itself, but either communicates its repulsive force to the particles of the air, or carries with it the particle of air in its passage. Is it not more easy to assume that the particle of air is in such a state that the ordinary forces which keep it in equilibrium are disturbed by the electrical force, or force in a definite direction communicated to it, and that thus each particle in turn recedes from the point? As this latter force is increased, not only does the particle of air which was contiguous to the metallic point recede, but the cohesion of the extreme particles of metal may be overcome to such an extent that these are detached, and the brush or spark may consist wholly or in part of minute particles of the metal itself thrown off. Of this there is some evidence, though the point can hardly be considered as proved. A similar effect undoubtedly takes place with voltaic electricity, acting upon a terminal immersed in a liquid; thus if metallic terminals of a powerful voltaic battery be immersed in water, metal, or the oxide of metal, is forcibly detached, producing great heat at the point of disruption.

If we apply ourselves to the effect of electricity in the

animal economy, we find that the first rationale given of the convulsive effect produced by transmission through the living or recently killed animal was, that electricity itself, something substantive, passed rapidly through the body, and gave rise to the contractions; step by step we are now arriving at the conviction that consecutive particles of the nerves and muscles are affected. Thus the contractions which the prepared leg of a frog undergoes at the moment it is submitted to a voltaic current, cease after a time if the current be continued, and are renewed on breaking the circuit, i. e. at the moment when the current ceases to traverse it. The excitability of a nerve, moreover, or its power of producing muscular contraction, is weakened or destroyed by the transmission of electricity in one direction, while the excitability is increased by the transmission of electricity in the opposite direction; showing that the fibre or matter itself of the nerve is changed by electrisation, and changed in a manner bearing a direct relation to the other effects produced by electricity.

Portions of muscle and of nerve present different electrical states with reference to other portions of the same muscle or nerve; thus the external part of a muscle bears the same relation to the internal part as platinum does to zinc in the voltaic battery; and delicate galvanoscopes will show electrical effects when interposed in a conducting circuit connecting the surface of a nerve with its interior portions. Matteucci has proved that a species of voltaic pile may be formed by a series of slices of muscle, so arranged that the external part of one slice may touch the internal part of the next, and so on.

Lastly, the magnetic effects produced by electricity also show a change in the molecular state of the magnetic substance affected; as we shall see when the subject of magnetism is discussed.

I have taken in succession all the known classes of electrical phenomena; and, as far as I am aware, there is not an electrical effect, where, if a close investigation be instituted, and the materials chosen in a state for exhibiting minute changes, evidence of molecular change will not be detected; thus, excepting those cases where infinitesimally small quantities of matter are acted on, and our means of detection fail, electrical effects are known to us only as changes of ordinary matter. It seems to me as easy to imagine these changes to be effected by a force acting in definite directions, as by a fluid which has no independent or sensible existence, and which, it must be assumed, is associated with, or exerts a force acting upon ordinary matter, or matter of a different order from the supposed fluid. As the idea of the hypothetic fluid is pursued, it gradually vanishes, and resolves itself into the idea of force. The hypothesis of matter without weight presents in itself, as I believe, fatal objections to the theories of electrical *fluids*, which are entirely removed by viewing electricity as force, and not as matter.

If it be said that the effects we have been considering may still be produced by a fluid, and that this fluid acts upon ordinary matter in certain cases, polarising the matter affected or arranging its particles in a definite direction, whilst in others, by its attractive or repulsive force, it carries with it portions of matter; yet, if the fluid in itself be incapable of recognition by any test, if it be only evidenced by the changes which it operates in ponderable matter, the words fluid and force become identical in meaning; we may as well say that the attraction of gravitation or weight is occasioned by a fluid, as that electrical changes are so.

When, as is constantly done in common parlance, a house is said to be *struck*, windows *broken*, metals *fused* or *dissipated* by the electrical *fluid*, are not the expressions used such as, if not sanctioned by habit, would seem absurd? In all the cases of injury done by lightning there is no fluid perceptible; the so-called sulphurous odour is either ozone developed by the action of electricity on atmospheric air, or the vapour of some substance dissipated by the discharge; on the other hand, it seems more consonant with experience to regard these effects as produced by force, as we have analogous effects produced by admitted forces, in cases where no one would invoke the aid of a hypothetic fluid for explanation. For instance, glasses may be broken by electrical discharges; so may they by sonorous vibrations. Metals electrified or magnetised will emit a sound; so they will if struck, or if a musical note with which they can vibrate in unison be sounded near to them.

Even chemical decomposition, in cases of feeble affinity, may be produced by purely mechanical effects. A number of instances of this have been collected by M. Becquerel; and substances whose constituents are held together by feeble affinities, such as iodide of nitrogen and similar compounds, are decomposed by the vibration occasioned by sound.

If, instead of being regarded as a fluid or imponderable matter *sui generis*, electricity be regarded as the motion of an ether, equal difficulties are encountered. Assuming ether to pervade the pores of all bodies, is the ether a conductor or non-conductor? If the latter—that is, if the ether be incapable of transmitting the electrical wave—the ethereal hypothesis of electricity necessarily falls; but if the motion of the ether constitute what we call conduction of electricity, then the more porous bodies, or those most permeable by the ether, should be the best conductors. But this is not the case. If, again, the metal and the air surrounding it are both pervaded by ether, why should the electrical wave affect the ether in the metal, and not stir that in the gas? To support an ethereal hypothesis of electricity, many additional and hardly reconcilable hypotheses must be imported.

The fracture and comminution of a non-conducting body, the fusion or dispersion of a metallic wire by the electrical discharge, are effects equally difficult to conceive upon the hypothesis of an ethereal vibration, as upon that of a fluid, but are necessary results of the sudden subversion of molecular polarisation, or of a sudden or irregular vibratory movement of the matter itself. We see similar effects produced by sonorous vibrations, which might be called conduction and non-conduction of sound. One body transmits sound easily, another stops or deadens it, as it is termed—i. e. disperses the vibrations, instead of continuing them in the same direction as the primary impulse; and solid bodies may, as has been above observed, be shivered by sudden impulses of sound in those cases where all the parts of the body cannot uniformly carry on the undulatory motion.

The progressive stages in the History of Physical Philosophy will account in a great measure for the adoption by the early electricians of the theories of fluids.

The ancients, when they witnessed a natural phenomenon, removed from ordinary analogies, and unexplained by any mechanical action known to them, referred it to a soul, a spiritual or preternatural power: thus amber and the magnet were supposed by Thales to have a soul; the functions of digestion, assimilation, &c., were supposed by Paracelsus to be effected by a spirit (the Archæus). Air and gases were also at first deemed spiritual, but subsequently became invested with a more material character; and the word gas, from *geist*, a ghost or spirit, affords us an instance of the gradual transmission of a spiritual into a physical conception.

The establishment by Torricelli of the ponderable character of air and gas, showed that substances which had been deemed spiritual and essentially different from ponderable matter were possessed of its attributes. A less superstitious mode of reasoning ensued, and now aëriform fluids were shown to be analogous in many of their actions to liquids or known fluids. A belief in the existence of other fluids, differing from air as this differed from water, grew up, and when a new phenomenon presented itself, recourse was had to a hypothetic fluid for explaining the phenomenon and connecting it with others; the mind once possessed of the idea of a fluid, soon invested it with the necessary powers and properties, and grafted upon it a luxurious vegetation of imaginary offshoots.

In what I am here throwing out, I wish to guard myself from being supposed to state that the theory, historically viewed, followed exactly the dates of the discoveries which were effectual in changing its character; sometimes a discovery precedes, at other times it succeeds to a change in the general course of thought; sometimes, and perhaps most frequently, it does both—i. e. the discovery is the result of a tendency of the age and of the continually improved methods of observation, and when made, it strengthens and extends the views which have led to it. I think the phases of thought which physical philosophers have gone through, will be found generally such as I have indicated, and that the gradual accumulation of discoveries which has taken place during the more recent periods, by showing what effects can be produced by dynamical causes alone, is rapidly tending to a general dynamical theory into which that of the imponderable fluids promises ultimately to merge.

Commencing with electricity as an initiating force, we get *motion* directly produced by it in various forms; for instance, in the attraction and repulsion of bodies, evidenced by mobile electrometers, such as that of Cuthbertson, where large masses are acted on; the rotation of the fly-wheel, another form of electrical repulsion, and the deflection of the galvanometer needle, are also modes of palpable, visible motion.

It would follow, from the reasoning in this essay, that when electricity performs any mechanical work which does not return to the machine, electrical power is lost. It would be unsuitable to the scope of this work to give the mathematical labours of M. Clausius and others here; but the following experiment, which I devised for making the result evident to an audience at the Royal Institution, will form a useful illustration:—A Leyden jar, of one square foot coated surface, has its interior connected with a Cuthbertson's electrometer, between which and the outer coating of the jar are a pair of discharging balls fixed at a certain distance (about half an inch apart). Between the Leyden jar and the prime conductor is inserted a small unit jar of nine inches surface, the knobs of which are 0·2 inch apart.

The balance of the electrometer is now fixed by a stiff wire inserted between the attracting knobs, and the Leyden jar charged by discharges from the unit jar. After a certain number of these, say twenty, the discharge of the large jar takes place across the half-inch interval. This may be viewed as the expression of electrical power received from the unit jar. The experiment is now repeated, the wire between the balls having been removed, and therefore the 'tip,' or the raising of the weight, is performed by the electrical repulsion and attraction of the two pairs of balls. At twenty discharges of the unit jar the balance is subverted, and one attracting knob drops upon the other; but *no discharge takes place*, showing that some electricity has been lost or converted into the mechanical power which raised the balance.

By another mode of expression, the electricity may be supposed to be masked or analogous to latent heat, and it would be restored if the ball were brought back without discharge by extraneous force. If the discharge or other electrical effects were the same in both cases, then, since the raising of the ball or weight is an extra mechanical effort, and since the weight is capable by its fall of producing electricity, heat, or other force, it would seem that force could be got out of nothing, or perpetual motion obtained.

The above experiment is suggestive of others of a similar character, which may be indefinitely varied. Thus I have found that two balls made to diverge by electricity do not give to an electrometer the same amount of electricity as they do if, whilst similarly electrified, they are kept forcibly together. This experiment is the converse of the former one. There is an advantage in electrical experiments of this class as compared with those on heat, viz. that though there is no perfect insulation for electricity, yet our means of insulation are immeasurably superior to any attainable for heat.

Electricity directly produces *heat*, as shown in the ignited wire, the electric spark, and the voltaic arc: in the latter the most intense heat with which we are acquainted—so intense, indeed, that it cannot be measured, as every sort of matter is dissipated by it.

In the phenomenon of electrical ignition, as shown by a heated conjunctive wire, the relation of force and resistance, and the correlative character of the two forces, electricity and heat, are strikingly demonstrated. Let a thin wire of platinum join the terminals of a voltaic battery of suitable power, the wire will be ignited, and a certain amount of chemical action will take place in the cells of the battery—a definite quantity of zinc being dissolved and of hydrogen eliminated in a given time. If now the platinum wire be immersed in water, the heat will, from the circulating currents of the liquid, be more rapidly dissipated, and we shall instantly find that the chemical action in the battery will be increased, more zinc will be dissolved, and more hydrogen eliminated for the same time; the heat being conveyed away by the water, more chemical action is required to generate it, just as more fuel is required in proportion as evaporation is more rapid.

Reverse the experiment, and instead of placing the wire in water, place it in the flame of a spirit lamp, so that the force of heat meets with greater resistance to its dissipation. We now find that the chemical action is less than in the first or normal experiment. If the wire be placed in other different gaseous or liquid media, we shall find that the chemical action of the battery will be proportioned to the facility with which the heat is circulated or radiated by these media, and we thus establish an alternating reciprocity of action between these two forces: a similar reciprocity may be established between electricity and motion, magnetism and motion, and so of other forces. If it cannot be realised with all, it is probably because we have not yet eliminated interfering actions. If we carefully think over the matter, we shall, unless I am much mistaken, arrive at the conclusion that it cannot be otherwise, unless it be supposed that a force can arise from nothing—can exist without antecedent force.

In the phenomenon of the voltaic arc, the electric spark, &c., to which I have already adverted, electricity directly produces *light* of the greatest known intensity. It directly produces *magnetism*, as shown by Oersted, who first distinctly proved the connection between electricity and magnetism. These two forces act upon each other, not in straight lines, as all other known forces do, but in a rectangular direction; that is, bodies affected by dynamic electricity, or the conduits of an electric current, tend to place magnets at right angles to them; and, conversely, magnets tend to place bodies conducting electricity at right angles to them. Thus an electric current appears to have a magnetic action, in a direction cutting its own at right angles; or, supposing its section to be a circle, tangential to it: if, then, we reverse the position, and make the electric current form a series of tangents to an imaginary cylinder, this cylinder should be a magnet. This is effected in practice by coiling a wire as a helix or spiral, and this, when conducting an electrical current, is to all intents and purposes a magnet. A soft iron core placed within such a helix has the property of concentrating its power, and then we can, by connection or disconnection with the source of electricity, instantly make or unmake a most powerful magnet.

We may figure to the mind electrified and magnetised

matter, as lines of which the extremities repel each other in a definite direction; thus, if a line A B represent a wire affected by electricity, and superposed on C D a wire affected by magnetism, the extreme points A and B will be repelled to the farthest distances from the points C and D, and the line A B be at right angles to the line C D; and so, if the lines be subdivided to any extent, each will have two extremities or poles repulsive of those of the other. If the line of matter affected by electricity be a liquid, and consequently have entire mobility of particles, a continuous movement will be produced by magnetism, each particle successively tending, as it were, to fly off at a tangent from the magnet: thus, place a flat dish containing acidulated water on the poles of a powerful magnet, immerse the terminals of a voltaic battery in the liquid just above the magnetic poles, so that the lines of electricity and of magnetism coincide; the water will now assume a movement at right angles to this line, flowing continously, as if blown by an equatorial wind, which may be made east or west with reference to the magnetic poles by altering the direction of the electrical current: a similar effect may be produced with mercury. These cases afford an additional argument to those previously mentioned of the particles of matter being affected by the forces of electricity and magnetism in a way irreconcilable with the fluid or ethereal hypothesis.

The representation of transverse direction by magnetism and electricity appears to have led Coleridge to parallel it by the transverse expansion of matter, or length and breadth, though he injured the parallel by adding galvanism as depth: whether a third force exists which may bear this relation to electricity and magnetism is a question upon which we have no evidence.

The ratio which the attractive magnetic force produced bears to the electric current producing it has been investigated by many experimentalists and mathematicians. The data are so numerous and so variable, that it is difficult to arrive at definite results. Thus the relative size of the coil and the iron, the temper or degree of hardness of the latter, its shape, or the proportions of length to diameter, the number of coils surrounding it, the conducting power of the metal of which the coils are formed, the size of the keeper or iron in which magnetism is induced, the degree of constancy of the battery, &c., complicate the experiments.

The most trustworthy general relation which has been ascertained is, that the magnetic attraction is as the square of the electric force; a result due to the researches of Lenz and Jacobi, and also of Sir W. S. Harris.

Lastly, electricity produces *chemical affinity*; and by its agency we are enabled to obtain effects of analysis or synthesis with which ordinary chemistry does not furnish us. Of these effects we have examples in the brilliant discoveries, by Davy, of the alkaline metals, and in the peculiar crystalline compounds made known by Crosse and Becquerel.

V.—LIGHT.

IN entering on the subject of LIGHT, it will be well to describe briefly, and in a manner as far as may be independent of theory, the effects to which the term polarisation has been applied.

When light is reflected from the surface of water, glass, or many other media, it undergoes a change which disables it from being again similarly reflected in a direction at right angles to that at which it has been originally reflected. Light so affected is said to be polarised; it will always be capable of being reflected in planes parallel to the plane in which it has been first reflected, but incapable of being reflected in planes at right angles to that plane. At planes having a direction intermediate between the original plane of reflection, and a plane at right angles to it, the light will be capable of being partially reflected, and more or less so according as the direction of the second plane of reflection is more or less coincident with the original plane. Light, again, when passed through a crystal of Iceland spar, is what is termed doubly refracted, i. e. split into two divisions or beams, each having half the luminosity of the original incident light; each of these beams is polarised in planes at right angles to each other; and if they be intercepted by the mineral tourmaline, one of them is absorbed, so that only one polarised beam emerges. Similar effects may be produced by certain other reflections or refractions. A ray of light once polarised in a certain plane continues so affected throughout its whole subsequent course; and at any indefinite distance from the point where it originally underwent the change, the direction of the plane will be the same, provided the media through which it is transmitted be air, water, or certain other transparent substances which need not be enumerated. If, however, the polarised ray, instead of passing through water, be made to pass through oil of turpentine, the definite direction in which it is polarised will be found to be changed; and the change of direction will be greater according to the length of the column of interposed liquid. Instead of being an uniform plane, it will have a curvilinear direction, similar to that which a strip of card would have if forced along two opposite grooves of a rifle-barrel. This curious effect is produced in different degrees by different media. The direction also varies; the rotation, as it is termed, being sometimes to the right hand and sometimes to the left, according to the peculiar molecular character of the medium through which the polarised ray is transmitted.

Light is, perhaps, that mode of force the reciprocal relations of which with the others have been the least traced out. Until the discoveries of Niepce, Daguerre, and Talbot, very little could be definitely predicated of the action of light in producing other modes of force. Certain chemical compounds, among which stand pre-eminent the salts of silver, have the property of suffering decomposition when exposed to light. If, for instance, recently formed chloride of silver be submitted to luminous rays, a partial decomposition ensues; the chlorine is separated and expelled by the action of light, and the silver is precipitated. By this decomposition the colour of the substance changes from white to blue. If now, paper be impregnated with chloride of silver, which can be done by a simple chemical process, then partially covered with an opaque substance, a leaf for example, and exposed to a strong light, the chloride will be decomposed in all those parts of the paper where the light is *not* intercepted, and we shall have, by the action of light, a white image of the leaf on a purple ground. If similar paper be placed in the focus of a lens in a camera-obscura, the objects there depicted will decompose the chloride, just in the proportion in which they are luminous; and thus, as the most luminous parts of the image will most darken the chloride, we shall have a picture of the objects with reversed lights and shadows. The picture thus produced would not be permanent, as subsequent exposure would darken the light portion of the picture: to fix it, the paper must be immersed in a solution which has the property of dissolving chloride of silver, but not metallic silver. Iodide of potassium will effect this; and the paper being washed and dried will then preserve a permanent image of the depicted objects. This was the first and simple process of Mr. Talbot; but it is defective as to the purposes aimed at, in many points. First, it is not sufficiently sensitive, requiring a strong light and a long time to produce an image; secondly, the lights and shadows are reversed; and thirdly, the coarse structure of the finest paper does not admit of the delicate traces of objects being distinctly impressed. These defects have been to a great extent remedied by a process subsequently discovered by Mr. Talbot, and which bears his name, and which has led to the collodion process, and others unnecessary to be detailed here.

The photographs of M. Daguerre, with which all are now familiar, are produced by holding a plate of highly-polished silver over iodine. A thin film of iodide of silver is thus formed on the surface of the metal; and when these iodized plates are exposed in the camera, a chemical alteration takes place. The portions of the plate on which the light has impinged part with some of the iodine, or are otherwise changed —for the theory is somewhat doubtful—soas to be capable of ready amalgamation. When, therefore, the plate is placed over the vapour of heated mercury, the mercury attaches itself to the portions affected by light, and gives them a white frosted appearance; the intermediate tints are less affected, and those parts where no light has fallen, by retaining their original polish, appear dark; the iodide of silver is then washed off by hyposulphite of soda, which has the property of dissolving it, and there remains a picture in which the lights and shadows are as in nature, and the molecular uniformity of the metallic surface enables the most microscopic details to be depicted with perfect accuracy. By using chloride of iodine, or bromide of iodine, instead of iodine, the equilibrium of chemical forces is rendered still more unstable, so that images may be taken in an indefinitely short period—a period practically instantaneous.

It would be foreign to the object of this essay to enter upon the many beautiful details into which the science of photography has branched out, and the many valuable discoveries and practical applications to which it has led. The short statement I have given above is perhaps superfluous, as, though they were new and surprising at the period when these Lectures were delivered, photographic processes have now become familiar, not only to the cultivator of science, but to the artist and amateur; the important point for consideration here is that light will chemically or molecularly affect matter. Not only will the particular compounds above selected as instances be changed by the action of light; but a vast number of substances, both elementary and compound, are notably affected by this agent, even those apparently the most unalterable in character, such as metals: so numerous, indeed, are the substances affected, that it has been supposed, not without reason, that matter of every description is altered by exposure to light.

The permanent impression stamped on the molecules of matter by light can be made to repeat itself by the same agency, but always with decreasing force. Thus a photograph placed opposite a camera containing a sensitive plate will be reproduced, but if the size of the image be equal to the picture, the second picture will be fainter than the first, and so on. Thus again, a photograph taken on a dull day cannot, by being placed in bright sunshine be made to reproduce a second photograph of the same size and more distinctly marked than itself; I at least have never succeeded in such reproduction, and I am not aware that others have: the image loses in intensity as light itself does by each transmission. The surface of the metal or paper may give a brighter image from its being exposed to a more intense light, but the photographic details are limited to the intensity of the first impression, or rather to something short of this. A question of theoretical interest arises from the consideration of these reproduced photographs. We know that the luminosity of the image at the focus of a telescope is limited by the area of the object-glass. The image of any given object cannot be intensified by throwing upon it extraneous light; it is indeed diminished in intensity, and when for certain purposes astronomers illuminate the fields of their telescopes, they are obliged to be contented with a loss of intensity in the telescopic image.

Now, let us suppose that the minutest details in the image of an object seen in a given telescope, and with a given power, are noted; that then a photographic plate is placed in the focus of the same telescope so as to obtain a permanent impression of the image which has been viewed by the eye-glass. Could the observer, by throwing a beam of condensed light upon the photograph, enable himself to bring out fresh details? or in other words, could he use with advantage a higher power applied to the illuminated photograph?

It is, perhaps, hardly safe to answer *a priori* this question; but the experiment of reproducing photographs would seem to show that more than the initial light cannot be got, and that we cannot expect to increase telescopic power by photography, though we may render observations more convenient; may by its means fix images seen on rare and favourable occasions, and may preserve permanent and infallible records of the past state of astronomical objects.

The effect of light on chemical compounds affords us a striking instance of the extent to which a force, ever active, may be ignored through successive ages of philosophy. If we suppose the walls of a large room covered with photographic apparatus, the small amount of light reflected from the face of a person situated in its centre would simultaneously imprint his portrait on a multitude of recipient surfaces. Were the cameras absent, but the room coated with photographic paper, a change would equally take place in every portion of it, though not a reproduction of form and figure. As other substances not commonly called photographic are known to be affected by light, the list of which might be indefinitely extended, it becomes a curious object of contemplation to consider how far light is daily operating changes in ponderable matter—how far a force, for a long time recognised only in its visual effects, may be constantly producing changes in the earth and atmosphere, in addition to the changes it produces in organised structures which are now beginning to be extensively studied. Thus every portion of light may be supposed to write its own history by a change more or less permanent in ponderable matter.

The late Mr. George Stephenson had a favourite idea, which would now be recognised as more philosophical than it was in his day, viz. that the light, which we nightly obtain from coal or other fuel, was a reproduction of that which had at one time been absorbed by vegetable structures from the sun. The conviction that the transient gleam leaves its permanent impress on the world's history, also leads the mind to ponder over the many possible agencies of which we of the present day may be as ignorant as the ancients were of the chemical action of light.

I have used the term light, and affected by light, in speaking of photographic effects; but, though the phenomena derived their name from light, it has been doubted by many competent investigators whether the phenomena of photography are not mainly dependent upon a separate agent accompanying light, rather than upon light itself. It is, indeed, difficult not to believe that a picture, taken in the focus of a camera-obscura, and which represents to the eye all the gradations of light and shade shown by the original luminous image, is not an effect of light; certain it is, however, that the different coloured rays exercise different actions upon various chemical compounds, and that the effects on many, perhaps on most of them, are not proportionate in intensity to the effects upon the visual organs. Those effects, however, appear to be more of degree than of specific difference; and, without pronouncing myself positively upon the question, hitherto so little examined, I think it will be safer to regard the action on photographic compounds as resulting from a function of light. So viewing it, we get light as an initiating force, capable of producing, mediately or immediately, the other modes of force. Thus, it immediately produces chemical action; and having this, we at once acquire a means of producing the others. At my Lectures in 1843, I showed an experiment by which the production of all the other modes of force by light is exhibited: I may here shortly describe it. A prepared daguerreotype plate is enclosed in a box filled with water, having a glass front with a shutter over it. Between this glass and the plate is a gridiron of silver wire; the plate is connected with one extremity of a galvanometer coil, and the gridiron of wire with one extremity of a Breguet's helix—an elegant instrument, formed by a coil of two metals, the unequal expansion of which indicates slight changes in temperature—the other extremities of the galvanometer and helix are connected by a wire, and the needles brought to zero. As soon as a beam of either daylight or the oxyhydrogen light is, by raising the shutter, permitted to impinge upon the plate, the needles are deflected. Thus, light being the initiating force, we get *chemical action* on the plate, *electricity* circulating through the wires, *magnetism* in the coil, *heat* in the helix, and *motion* in the needles.

If two plates of platinum be placed in acidulated water, and connected with a delicate galvanometer, the needle of this is always deflected, a result due to films of gas or other matter on the surface of the platinum, which no cleaning can remove. If, after the needle has returned to zero, which will not be the case for some hours or even days, one of the platinum surfaces be exposed to light, a fresh deflection of the needle takes place, due, as far as I have been able to resolve it, to an augmentation of the chemical action which had occasioned the original deflection, for the deviation is in the same direction. If, instead of white light, coloured light be permitted to impinge on the plate, the deviation is greater with blue than with red or yellow light, showing, in addition to other tests, that the effect is not due to the heat of the sun's rays, as the calorific effects of light are greater with red than with blue light, while the chemical effects are the inverse.

There are other apparently more direct agencies of light in producing electricity and magnetism, such as those observed by Morichini and others, as well as its effects upon crystallization; but these results have hitherto been of so indefinite a character, that they can only be regarded as presenting fields for experiment, and not as proving the relations of light to the other forces.

Light would seem directly to produce heat in the phenomena of what is termed absorption of light: in these we find that heat is developed in some proportion to the disappearance of light. To take the old experiment of placing a series of different coloured pieces of cloth upon snow exposed to sunshine, the black cloth absorbing the most light, and developing the most heat, sinks more deeply in the snow than any others; the other colours or shades of colour sink the more deeply in proportion as they absorb or cause to disappear the more light, until we come to the white cloth, which remains upon the surface. The heating powers of different colours are, however, not by any means in exact proportion to the intensity of their light as affecting the visual organs. Thus red light, when produced by refraction from a prism of glass, produces greater heating effect than yellow light in the phenomena of absorption, as has been observed by Sir W. Herschel. The red rays appear, however, to produce a dynamic effect greater than any of the others; thus they penetrate water to a greater depth than the other colours; but, according to Dr. Seebeck, we get a further anomaly, viz. that when light is refracted by a prism of water the yellow rays produce the greater heating effect. The subject, therefore, requires much more experiment before we can ascertain the rationale of the action of the forces of light and heat in this class of phenomena.

In a former edition of this Essay, I suggested the following experiment on this subject:—Let a beam of light be passed through two plates of tourmaline, or similar substance, and the temperature of the second plate, or that on which the light last impinges, be examined by a delicate thermoscope, first when it is in a position to transmit the polarised beam coming from the first plate, and secondly when it has been turned round through an arc of 90°, and the polarised beam is absorbed. I expected that, if the experiment were carefully performed, the temperature of the second plate would be more raised in the second case than in the first, and that it might afford interesting results when tried with light of different colours. I met with difficulties in procuring a suitable apparatus, and was endeavouring to overcome them when I found that Knoblauch had, to some extent, realised this result. He finds that, when a solar beam, polarised in a certain plane, is transmitted perpendicularly to the axis of a crystal of brown quartz or tourmaline, the heat is transmitted in a smaller proportion than when the beam passes along the direction of the axis of the crystal.

It is generally—as far as I am aware, universally—true that, while light continues as light, even though reflected or transmitted by different media, little or no heat is developed: and, as far as we can judge, it would appear that, if a medium were perfectly transparent, or if a surface perfectly reflected light, not the slightest heating effect would take place; but, wherever light is absorbed, then heat takes its place, affording us apparently an instance of the conversion of light into heat, and of the fact that the force of light is not, in fact, absorbed or annihilated, but merely changed in character, becoming in this instance converted into heat by impinging on solid matter, as in the instance mentioned in treating of heat, this force was shown to be converted into light by impinging on solid matter. As, however, I have before observed, this correlation of light and heat is not so distinct, as with the other affections of matter. One experiment, indeed, of Melloni, already mentioned, would seem to show that light may exist in a condition in which it does not produce heat, which our instruments are able to detect; but some doubt has recently been thrown on the accuracy of this experiment; probably the substances themselves through which the light is transmitted would be found to have been heated.

The recipient body, or that upon which light impinges, seems to exercise as important an influence on our perceptions of light as the emittent body, or that from which the light first proceeds. The recent experiments of Sir John Herschel and Mr. Stokes show that radiant impulses, which, falling on certain bodies, give no effect of light, become luminous when falling on other bodies.

Thus, let ordinary solar light be refracted by a prism (the best material for which is quartz), and the spectrum received on a sheet of paper, or of white porcelain; looking on the paper, the eye detects no light beyond the extreme violet rays. If, therefore, an opaque body be interposed so as just to cut off the whole visible spectrum, the paper would be dark or invisible, with the exception of some slight illumination from light reflected by the air and surrounding bodies. Substitute for that portion of the paper which was beyond the visible spectrum a piece of glass tinged by the oxide of uranium, and the glass is perfectly visible ; so with a bottle of sulphate of quinine, or of the juice of horse-chestnuts, or even paper soaked in these latter solutions. Other substances exhibit this effect in different degrees ; and among the substances which have hitherto been considered perfectly analogous as to their appearance when illuminated, notable differences are discovered. Thus it appears that emanations which give no impression of light to the eye, when impinging on certain bodies, become luminous when impinging on others. We might imagine a room so constructed that such emanations alone are permitted to enter it, which would be dark or light according to the substance with which the walls were coated, though in full daylight the respective coatings of the walls would appear equally white ; or, without altering the coating of the walls, the room exposed to one class of rays, might be rendered dark by windows which would be transparent to another class.

If, instead of solar light, the electrical light be employed for similar experiments, an equally striking effect can actually be produced. A design, drawn on white paper with a solution of sulphate of quinine and tartaric acid, is invisible by ordinary light, but appears with beautiful distinctness when illuminated by the electric light. Thus, in pronouncing upon a luminous effect, regard must be had to the recipient as well as to the emittent body. That which is, or becomes, light when it falls upon one body is not light when it falls upon another. Probably the retinæ of the eyes of different persons differ to some extent in a similar manner ; and the same substance, illuminated by the same spectrum, may present different appearances to different persons, the spectrum appearing more elongated to the one than to the other, so that what is light to the one is darkness to the other. A dependence on the recipient body may also, to a great extent, be predicated of heat. Let two vessels of water, the contents of the one clear and transparent, of the other tinged by some colouring matter, be suspended in a summer's sun; in a very short time a notable difference of temperature will be observed, the coloured having become much hotter than the clear liquid. If the first vessel be placed at a considerable distance from the surface of the earth, and the second near the surface, the difference is still more considerable. Carrying on this experiment, and suspending the first over the top of a high mountain, and the second in a valley, we may obtain so great a difference of temperature, that animals whose organization is suited for the one temperature could not live in the other, and yet both are exposed to the same luminous rays at the same time, and substantially at the same distance from the emittent body—the substance nearer the sun is in fact colder than the more remote. So, with regard to the medium transmitting the influence: a green-house may have its temperature considerably varied by changing the glass of which its roof is made.

These effects have an important bearing on certain cosmical questions which have lately been much discussed, and should induce the greatest caution in forming opinions on such subjects as light and heat on the sun's surface, the temperature of the planets, &c. This may depend as much upon their physical constitution as upon their distance from the sun. Indeed, the planet Mars gives us a highly probable argument for this; for, notwithstanding that it is half as far again from the sun as the earth is, the increase of the white tracts at its poles during its winter, and their diminution during its summer, show that the temperature of the surface of this planet oscillates about that of the freezing point of water, as do the analogous zones of our planet. It is true, in this we assume that the substance thus changing its state is water, but, considering the many close analogies of this planet with the earth, and the identity in appearance of these very effects with what takes place on the earth, it seems a highly probable assumption.

So it by no means necessarily follows, that because Venus is nearer to the sun than the earth, that planet is hotter than our globe. The force emitted by the sun may take a different character at the surface of each different planet, and require different organisms or senses for its appreciation. Myriads of organised beings may exist imperceptible to our vision, even if we were among them; and we might be also imperceptible to them!

However vain it may be, in the present state of science, to speculate upon such existences, it is equally vain to assume identity or close approximations to our own forms in those beings which may people other worlds. From analogical reasoning, or from final causation, if that be admitted, we may feel convinced that the gorgeous globes of the universe are not unpeopled deserts; but whether the denizens of other worlds are more or less powerful, more or less intelligent, whether they have attributes of a higher or lower class than ourselves, is at present an utterly hopeless guessing.

Specific gravity and intelligence have no necessary connexion. On our own planet five senses, and a mean density equal to that of water, are not invariably associated with intellectual or moral greatness, and the many arguments which have been used to prove that suns and planets other than the earth are uninhabited, or not inhabited by intellectual beings, might, *mutatis mutandis*, equally be used by the denizens of a sun or planet to prove that this world was uninhabited.

Men are too apt, because they are men, because their existence is the one thing of all importance to themselves, to frame schemes of the universe as though it was formed for man alone: painted by an artist of the sun, a man might not represent so prominent an object of creation as he does when represented by his own pencil.

Light was regarded, by what was termed the corpuscular theory, as being in itself matter or a specific fluid emanating from luminous bodies, and producing the effects of sensation by impinging on the retina. This theory gave way to the undulatory one, which is generally adopted in the present day, and which regards light as resulting from the undulation of a specific fluid to which the name of ether has been given, which hypothetic fluid is supposed to pervade the universe, and to penetrate the pores of all bodies.

In a Lecture delivered in January 1842, when I first publicly advanced the views advocated in this Essay, I stated that it appeared to me more consistent with known facts to regard light as resulting from a vibration or motion of the molecules of matter itself, rather than from a specific ether pervading it; jnst as sound is propagated by the vibrations of wood, or as waves are by water. I am not here speaking of the character of the vibrations of light, sound, or water, which are doubtless very different from each other, but am only comparing them so far as they illustrate the propagation of force by motion in the matter itself.

I was not aware, at the time that I first adopted the above view, and brought it forward in my Lectures, that the celebrated Leonard Euler had published a somewhat similar theory; and, though I suggested it without knowing that it had been previously advanced, I should have hesitated in reproducing it had I not found that it was sanctioned by so eminent a mathematician as Euler, who cannot be supposed to have overlooked any irresistible argument against it—the more so in a matter so much controverted and discussed as the undulatory theory of light was in his time.

Although this theory has been considered defective by a

philosopher of high repute, I cannot see the force of the arguments by which it has been assailed; and therefore, for the present, though with diffidence, I still adhere to it. The fact itself of the correlation of the different modes of force is to my mind a very cogent argument in favour of their being affections of the same matter; and though electricity, magnetism, and heat might be viewed as produced by undulations of the same ether as that by means of which light is supposed to be produced, yet this hypothesis offers greater difficulties with regard to the other affections than with regard to light: many of these difficulties I have already alluded to when treating of electricity; thus conduction and non-conduction are not explained by it; the transmission of electricity through long wires in preference to the air which surrounds them, and which must be at least equally pervaded by the ether, is irreconcilable with such an hypothesis. The phenomena exhibited by these forces afford, as I think, equally strong evidence with those of light, of ordinary matter acting from particle to particle, and having no action at a distance. I have already instanced the experiments of Faraday on electrical induction, showing it to be an action of contiguous particles, which are strongly in favour of this view, and many experiments which I have made on the voltaic arc, some of which I have mentioned in this Essay, are, to my mind, confirmatory of it.

If it be admitted that one of the so-called imponderables is a mode of motion, then the fact of its being able to produce the others, and be produced by them, renders it highly difficult to conceive some as molecular motions and others as fluids or undulations of an ether. To the main objection of Dr. Young, that all bodies would have the properties of solar phosphorus if light consisted in the undulations of ordinary matter, it may be answered that so many bodies have this property, and with so great a variety in its duration, that *non constat* all may not have it, though for a time so short that the eye cannot detect its duration. M. E. Becquerel has made many experiments which support this view; the fact of the phosphorescence by insolation of a large number of bodies, is in itself evidence of the matter of which they are composed being thrown into a state of undulation, or at all events molecularly affected by the impact of light, and is therefore an argument in support of the view to which objection is taken. Dr. Young admits that the phenomena of solar phosphorus appear to resemble greatly the sympathetic sounds of musical instruments, which are agitated by other sounds conveyed to them through the air, and I am not aware that he gives any explanation of these effects on the ethereal hypothesis.

Some curious experiments of M. Niepce de St. Victor seem also to present an analogy in luminous phenomena to sympathetic sounds. An engraving which has been kept for some days in the dark is half covered by an opaque screen, and then exposed to the sun; it is then removed from the light, the screen taken away, and the engraving placed opposite, and at a short distance from, photographic paper: an inverted image of that portion of the engraving which has been exposed to the sun is produced on the photographic paper, while the part which had been covered by the screen is not reproduced. If the engraving, after exposure, is allowed to remain in contact with white paper for some hours, and the white paper is then placed upon photographic paper, a faint image of the exposed portion of the engraving is reproduced. Similar results are produced by mottled marble exposed to the sun; an invisible tracing on paper by a fluorescent body, sulphate of quinine, is, after insolation, reproduced on the photographic paper. Insolated paper retains the power of producing an impression for a very long period, if it is kept in an opaque tube hermetically closed.

It is right to observe that these effects are supposed by many to be due to chemical emanations proceeding from the substances exposed to the sun, and which are believed to have undergone some chemical change by this exposure. It is desirable to await further experiment before forming a decided opinion.

The analogies in the progression of sound and light are very numerous: each proceed in straight lines, until interrupted; each is reflected in the same manner, the angles of incidence and reflexion being equal; each is alternately nullified and doubled in intensity by interference; each is capable of refraction when passing from media of different density: this last effect of sound, long ago theoretically determined, has been experimentally proved by Mr. Sondhauss, who constructed a lens of films of collodion, which, when filled with carbonic acid, enabled him to hear the ticking of a watch placed in one focus of the lens, the ear of the experimenter being in the opposite focus. The ticking was not heard when the watch was moved aside from the focal point, though it remained at an equal distance from the ear. An experiment of M. Dove seems, indeed, to show an effect of polarisation of sound.

The phenomena presented by heat, viewed according to the dynamic theory, cannot be explained by the motion of an imponderable ether, but involve the molecular actions of ordinary ponderable matter. The doctrine of propagation by undulations of ordinary matter is very generally admitted by those who support the dynamical theory of heat; but the analogies of the phenomena presented by heat and light are so close, that I cannot see how a theory applied to the one agent should not be applicable to the other. When heat is transmitted, reflected, refracted, or polarised, can we view that as an affection of ordinary matter, and when the same effects take place with light, view the phenomena as produced by an imponderable ether, and by that alone?

An objection that immediately occurs to the mind in reference to the ethereal hypothesis of light is, that the most porous bodies are opaque ; cork, charcoal, pumice stone, dried and moist wood, &c., all very porous and very light, are all opaque. This objection is not so superficial as it might seem at first sight. The theory which assumes that light is an undulation of an ethereal medium pervading gross matter, assumes the distances between the molecules or atoms of matter to be very great. Matter has been likened by Democritus, and by many modern philosophers, to the starry firmament, in which, though the individual monads are at immense distances from each other, yet they have in the aggregate a character of unity, and are firmly held by attraction in their respective positions and at definite distances. Now, if matter be built up of separate molecules, then, as far as our knowledge extends, the lightest bodies would be those in which the molecules are at the greatest distances, and those in which any undulation of a pervading medium would be the least interfered with by the separated particles—such bodies should consequently be the most transparent.

If, again, the analogy of the starry firmament held good, in this case an undulation or wave proportioned to the individual monads would be broken up by the number of them, and the very appearance of continuity which results, as in the milky way, from each point of vision being occupied by one of the monads, would show that at some portion of its progress the wave is interrupted by one of them, so that the whole may be viewed in some respect as a sheet of ordinary matter interposed in the ethereal expanse.

Even then, if it be admitted that a highly elastic medium pervades the interspaces, the separate masses as a whole must exercise an important influence on the progress of the wave.

Sound or vibrations of air meeting with a screen, or, as it were, sponge of diffused particles, would be broken up and dispersed by them; but if they be sufficiently continuous to take up the vibration and propagate it themselves, the sound continues comparatively unimpaired.

* With regard, however, to liquid and gaseous bodies, there are very great difficulties in viewing them as consisting of separate and distant molecules. If, for instance, we assume with Young that the particles in water are at least as distant from each other comparatively as 100 men would be if dispersed at equal distances over the surface of England, the distance of these particles, when the water is expanded into steam, would be increased more than forty times, so that the 100 men would be reduced to two, and by further increasing the temperature this distance may be indefinitely increased; adding to the effects of temperature rarefaction by the air-pump, we may again increase the distance, so that, if we assume any original distance, we ought, by expansion, to increase it to a point at which the distance between molecule and molecule should become measurable. But no extent of rarefaction, whether by heat or the air-pump, or both, makes the slightest change in the apparent continuity of matter; and gases, I find, retain their peculiar character, as far as a judgment of it can be formed from its effect on the electric spark, throughout any extent of rarefaction which can experimentally be applied to them: thus the electric spark in protoxide of nitrogen, however attenuated, presents a crimson tint, that in carbonic oxide a greenish tint.

Without, however, entering on the metaphysical enquiry as to the constitution of matter (or whether the atomic philosophers or the followers of Boscovich are right), a question which probably human appliances will never answer: and even admitting that an ethereal medium, not absolutely imponderable as asserted by many, but of extreme tenuity, pervades matter, still ordinary or non-ethereal matter itself must exercise a most important action upon the transmission of light; and Dr. Young, who opposed the theory of Euler, that light was transmitted by undulations of gross matter itself, just as sound is, was afterwards obliged to call to his assistance the vibrations of the ponderable matter of the refracting media, to explain why rays of all colours were not equally refracted, and other difficulties. One of his arguments in support of the existence of a permeating ether was, "that a medium resembling in many properties that which has been denominated Ether does exist, is undeniably proved by the phenomena of electricity." This seems to me, if I may venture to say so of anything proceeding from so eminent a man, scarcely logical: it is supporting one hypothesis by another, and considering that to be proved which its most strenuous advocates admit to be surrounded by very many difficulties.

If it be said that there is not sufficient elasticity in ordinary matter for the transmission of undulations with such velocity as light is known to travel, this may be so if the vibrations be supposed exactly analogous to those of sound; but that molecular motion *can* travel with equal and even greater velocity than light, is shown by the rapidity with which electricity traverses a metal wire where each particle of metal is undoubtedly affected. It has, moreover, been shown by the experiments of Mr. Latimer Clarke upon a length of wire of 760 miles, that whatever be the intensity of electrical currents, they are propagated with the same velocity provided the effects of lateral induction be the same—a striking analogy with one of the effects observed in the propagation of light and sound. The effects observed by MM. Fizeau and Foucault, of the slower progression of light in proportion as the transmitting medium is more dense, seem to me in favour of the view here advocated; as a greater degree of heat would be produced by light in proportion to the density of the medium, force would be thus carried off, and the molecular system disturbed so that the progress of the motion should be more slow; but so many considerations enter into this question, and the phenomena are so extremely complex, that it would be rash to hazard any positive opinion.

Dr. Young ultimately came to the conclusion that it was simplest to consider the ethereal medium, together with the material atoms of the substance, as constituting together a compound medium denser than pure ether, but not more elastic. Ether might thus be viewed as performing the functions which oil does with tracing paper, giving continuity to the particles of gross matter, and in the interplanetary spaces forming itself the medium which transmits the undulations.

Since the period when Huyghens, Euler, and Young, the fathers of the undulatory theory, applied their great minds to this subject, a mass of experimental data has accumulated, all tending to establish the propositions, that whenever matter transmitting or reflecting light undergoes a structural change, the light itself is affected, and that there is a connection or parallelism between the change in the matter and the change in the affection of light, and conversely that light will modify or change the structure of matter and impress its molecules with new characteristics.

Transparency, opacity, refraction, reflection, and colour were phenomena known to the ancients, but sufficient attention does not appear to have been paid by them to the molecular states of the bodies producing these effects; thus the transparency or opacity of a body appears to depend entirely upon its molecular arrangement. If striæ occur in a lens or glass through which objects are viewed, the objects are distorted: increase the number of these striæ, the distortion is so increased that the objects become invisible, and the glass ceases to be transparent, though remaining translucent; but alter completely the molecular structure, as by slow solidification, and it becomes opaque. Take, again, an example of a liquid and a gas: a solution of soap is transparent, air is transparent, but agitate them together so as to form a froth or lather, and this, though consisting of two transparent bodies, is opaque; and the reflection of light from the surface of these bodies, when so intermixed, is strikingly different from its reflection before mixture, in the one case giving to the eye a mere general effect of whiteness, in the other the images of objects in their proper shapes and colours.

To take a more refined instance: nitrogen is perfectly colourless, oxygen is perfectly colourless, but chemically united in certain proportions they form nitrous acid, a gas which has a deep orange brown colour. I know not how the colour of this gas, or of such gases as chlorine or vapour of iodine, can be accounted for by the ethereal hypothesis, without calling in aid molecular affections of the matter of these gases.

Colour in many instances depends upon the thickness of the plate or film of transparent matter upon which light is incident; as in all those cases which are termed the colours of thin plates, of which the soap bubble affords a beautiful instance.

When we arrive at the more recent discoveries of double refraction and polarisation, the effects of light are found to trace out as it were the structure of the matter affected, and the crystalline form of a body can be determined by the effects which a minute portion of it exercises on a ray of light.

Let a piece of good glass be placed in what is called a polariscope, or instrument in which light that has undergone polarisation is transmitted through the substance to be examined, and the emergent light is afterwards submitted to another substance capable of polarising light, or, as it is termed, an analyser; no change in effect will be observed. Remove the glass, heat it and suddenly or quickly cool it as to render it unannealed, in which state its molecules are in a state of tension or strain, and the glass highly brittle, on replacing it in the polariscope, a beautiful series of colours is perceptible. Instead of subjecting the glass to heat and sudden cooling, let it be bent or strained by mechanical pressure, and the colours will be equally visible, modified, according to the direction of the flexure, and indicating by their course the curves where the molecular state has been changed by pressure. So if tough glue be elongated and allowed to cool in a stretched state, it doubly refracts light, and the colours are shown as in the instance of glass.

Submit a series of crystals to the same examination, and different figures will be formed by different crystals, bearing a constant and definite relation to the structure of the particular crystal examined, and to the direction in which, with reference to crystalline form, the ray crosses the crystal.

In the crystallised salts of paratartaric acid, M. Pasteur noticed two sets of crystals which were hemihedral in opposite directions, i. e. the crystals of one set were to those of the other as to their own image reflected in a mirror; on making a separate solution of each of these classes of crystals, he found that the solution of the one class rotated the plane of polarisation to the right, while that of the other class rotated to the left, and that a mixture in proper proportions of the two solutions produced no deviation in the plane of polarisation. Yet all these three solutions are what is termed isomeric, that is, have as far as can be discovered the same chemical constitution.

In the above, and in innumerable other cases, it is seen that an alteration in the structure of a transparent substance alters the character and effects of the transmitted light. The phenomena of photography prove that light alters the structure of matter submitted to it; with regard even to vision itself, the persistence of images on the retina of the eye would seem to show that its structure was changed by the impact of light, the luminous impressions being as it were branded on the retina, and the memory of the vision being the scar of such brand. The science of photography has reference mainly to solid substances, yet there are many instances of liquid and gaseous bodies being changed by the action of light: thus hydrocyanic acid, a liquid, undergoes a chemical change and deposits a solid carbonaceous compound by the action of light. Chlorine and hydrogen gases, when mixed and preserved in darkness, do not unite, but when exposed to light rapidly combine, forming hydrochloric acid.

The above facts—and many others might have been given—go far to connect light with motion of ordinary matter, and to show that many of the evidences which our senses receive of the existence of light result from changes in matter itself. When the matter is in the solid state, these changes are more or less permanent; when in the liquid or gaseous state, they are temporary in the greater number of instances, unless there be some chemical change effected, which is, as it were, seized upon during its occurrence, and a resulting compound formed, which is more stable than the original compound or mixture.

I might weary my reader with examples, showing that, in every case which we can trace out, the effects of light are changed by any and every change of structure, and that light has a definite connection with the structure of the bodies affected by it. I cannot but think that it is a strong assumption to regard ether, a purely hypothetical creation, as changing its elasticity for each change of structure, and to regard it as penetrating the pores of bodies of whose porosity we have in many cases no proof; the which pores must, moreover, have a definite and peculiar communication, also assumed for the purpose of the theory.

Ether is a most convenient medium for hypothesis: thus, if to account for a given phenomenon the hypothesis requires that the ether be more elastic, it is said to be more elastic; if more dense, it is said to be more dense; if it be required by hypothesis to be less elastic, it is pronounced to be less elastic; and so on.

The advocates of the ethereal hypothesis certainly have this advantage, that the ether, being hypothetical, can have its characters modified or changed without any possibility of disproof either of its existence or modifications.

It may be that the refined mathematical labours on light, as on electricity, have given an undue and adventitious strength to the hypotheses on which they are based.

An objection to which the view I have been advocating is open, and a formidable one, is, the necessity involved in it of an universal plenum; for if light, heat, electricity, &c., be affections of ordinary matter, then matter must be supposed to be everywhere where these phenomena are apparent, and consequently there can be no vacuum.

These forces are transmitted through what are called vacua, or through the interplanetary spaces, where matter, if it exist, must be in a highly attenuated state.

It may be safely stated that hitherto all attempts at procuring a perfect vacuum have failed. The ordinary air-pump gives us only highly rarefied air; and, by the principle of construction, even of the best, the operation depends upon the indefinite expansion of the volume of air in the receiver; even in the vacuum which is formed in this, so great is the tendency of matter to fill up space, that I have observed distilled water contained in a vessel within the exhausted receiver of a good air-pump has a taste of tallow, derived from the grease, or an essential oil contained in it, which is used to form an air-tight junction between the edges of the receiver and the pump-plate.

The Torricellian vacuum, or that of the ordinary barometer, is filled with the vapour of mercury; but it might be worth the trouble to ascertain what would be the effect of a good Torricellian vacuum, when the mercury in the tube is frozen, which might, without much difficulty, be now effected by the use of solid carbonic acid and ether; the only probable difficulty would be the different rates of contraction of mercury and glass, at such a degree of cold, and more particularly the contraction of mercury at the period of its solidification. Davy, however, endeavoured to form a vacuum, in a somewhat similar manner, over fused tin, with but partial success; he also made many other attempts to obtain a perfect vacuum; his main object being to ascertain what would be the effect of electricity across empty space:

he admits that he could not succeed in procuring a vacuum, but found electricity much less readily conducted or transmitted by the best vacuum he could procure than by the ordinary Boylean vacuum.

Morgan found no conduction by a good Torricellian vacuum; and, although Davy does not seem to place much reliance on Morgan's experiments, there was one point in which they were less liable to error than those of Davy. Morgan, whose experiments seem to have been carefully conducted, operated with hermetically-sealed glass tubes and by induced electricity, while Davy sealed a platinum wire into the extremity of the tube in which he sought to produce a vacuum. I have found in very numerous experiments which I made to exclude air from water, that platinum wires, most carefully sealed into glass, allow liquids to pass between them and the glass; and this gives every reason to believe that gases may equally pass through; I have observed such effect in the gas battery when it has been in action for a long period. Davy supposed that the particles of bodies may be detached, and so produce electrical effects in a vacumm; and such effects would more readily take place in his experiments, where a wire projected into the exhausted space, than in Morgan's, where the induced electricity was diffused over the surface of the glass.

M. Masson found that the barometric vacuum does not conduct a current of electricity, or even a discharge, unless the tension is considerable and sufficient to detach particles from the electrodes; and by adopting a plan of Dr. Andrews, viz. absorbing carbonic acid by potash, M. Gassiot has recently succeeded in forming vacua across which the powerful discharge from the Rhumkorf coil will not pass.

The odour which many metals, such as iron, tin, and zinc emit, and the so-called thermographic radiations, we can hardly explain upon any other theory than the evaporation of an infinitesimally small portion of the metal itself.

So universal is the tendency of matter to diffuse itself into space, that it gave rise to the old saying that nature abhors a vacuum; an aphorism which, though cavilled at and ridiculed by the self-sufficiency of some modern philosophers, contains in a terse, though somewhat metaphorical, form of expression a comprehensive truth, and evinces a large extent of observation in those who, with few of the advantages which we possess, first generalised by this sentence the facts of which they had become cognisant.

It has been argued that, if matter were capable of infinite divisibility, the earth's atmosphere would have no limit, and that consequently portions of it would exist at points of space where the attraction of the sun and planets would be greater than that of the earth, and whence it would fly off to those bodies and form atmospheres around them. This was supposed to be negatived by the argument of the well-known paper of Dr. Wollaston; in which, from the absence of notable refraction near the margin of the sun and of the planet Jupiter, he considered himself entitled to conclude that the expansion of the earth's atmosphere had a definite limit, and was balanced at a certain point by gravitation: this deduction has been shown to be inconclusive by Dr. Whewell, and has also been impugned upon others grounds by Dr. Wilson. There is a point not adverted to in these papers, and which Wollaston does not seem to have considered, viz. that there is no evidence that the apparent discs of the sun and of Jupiter show us their real discs or bodies. Sir. W. Herschel regards the margin of the visible discs as that of clouds or a peculiar state of atmosphere, and the rapidly changing character of the apparent surfaces render some such conclusion necessary. If this be so, refraction of an occulted star could not be detected—at all events, in the denser portion of the atmosphere.

Sir W. Herschel's observations go to prove that the sun and Jupiter have dense atmospheres, while Wollaston's were believed to prove that they have no appreciable atmospheres.

If it be admitted, or considered proved, that the sun and planets have atmospheres—and little doubt now exists on this point—then the grounds upon which Wollaston founded his arguments are untenable; and there appears no reason why the atmosphere of the different planets should not be, with reference to each other, in a state of equilibrium. Ether, or the highly-attenuated matter existing in the interplanetary spaces, being an expansion of some or all of these atmospheres, or of the more volatile portions of them, would thus furnish matter for the transmission of the modes of motion which we call light, heat, &c.; and possibly minute portions of these atmospheres may, by gradual changes, pass from planet to planet, forming a link of material communication between the distant monads of the universe.

The view given above would approximate the theory of the transmission of light by the undulations of ordinary matter to the other two theories, which equally suppose the non-existence of a vacuum; for, according to the emissive or corpuscular theory, the vacuum is filled by the matter itself, of light, heat, &c.; according to the ethereal, it is filled by the all-penetrating ether. Of the existence of matter in the interplanetary spaces we have some evidence in the diminishing periods of comets; and where, from its highly attenuated state, the character of the medium by which the forces are conveyed cannot be tested, the term ether is a most appropriate generic name for such medium.

Newton has some curious passages on the subject matter of light. In the 'Queries to the Optics' he says:—

'Are not gross bodies and light convertible into one another, and may not bodies receive much of their activity from the particles of light which enter their composition? * * * The changing of bodies into light and light into bodies is very conformable to the course of nature, which seems delighted with transmutations. Water, which is a very fluid, tasteless salt, she changes by heat into vapour, which is a sort of air, and by cold into ice, which is a hard, pellucid, brittle, fusible stone, and this stone returns into water by heat, and vapour returns into water by cold. * * And, among such various and strange transmutations, why may not nature change bodies into light, and light into bodies?'

Newton has here seemingly in his mind the emissive theory of light; but the passages might be applied to either theory; the analogy he saw in the change of state of matter, as in ice, water, and vapour, with the hypothetic change into light, is very striking, and would seem to show that he regarded the change or transmutation of which he speaks as one analogous to the known changes of state, or consistence, in ordinary matter.

The difference between the view which I am advocating and that of the ethereal theory as generally enunciated is, that the matter which in the interplanetary spaces serves as the means of transmitting by its undulations light and heat, I should regard as possessing the qualities of ordinary, or as it has sometimes been called gross, matter, and particularly weight; though, from its extreme rarefaction, it would manifest these properties in an indefinitely small degree; whilst, on the surface of the earth, that matter attains a density cognisable by our means of experiment, and the dense matter is itself, in great part, the conveyer of the undulations in which these agents consist. Doubtless, in very many of the forms which matter assumes it is porous, and pervaded by more volatile essences, which may differ as much in kind as matter does. In these cases a composite medium, such as that indicated by Dr. Young, would result; but even on such a supposition, the denser matter would probably exercise the more important influence on the undulations. Returning to the somewhat strained hypothesis, that the particles of dense matter in a so-called solid are as distant as the stars in heaven, still a certain depth or thickness of such solid would present at every point of space a particle or rock in the successive progress of a wave, which particles, to carry on the movement, must vibrate in unison with it.

At the utmost, our assumption, on the one hand, is that wherever light, heat, &c., exist, ordinary matter exists, though it may be so attenuated that we cannot recognise it by the tests of other forces, such as gravitation, and that to the expansibility of matter no limit can be assigned. On the other hand, a specific matter without weight must be assumed, of the existence of which there is no evidence, but in the phenomena for the explanation of which its existence is supposed. To account for the phenomena the ether is assumed, and to prove the existence of the ether the phenomena are cited. For these reasons, and others above given, I think that the assumption of the universality of ordinary matter is the least gratuitous.

Ουδεν τι του παντος κενον πελει ουδε περισσον.

A question has often occurred to me and possibly to others: Is the continuance of a luminous impulse in the interplanetary spaces perpetual, or does it after a certain distance dissipate itself and become lost as light—I do not mean by mere divergence directly as the squares of the distances it travels, but does the physical impulse itself lose force as it proceeds? Upon the view I have advocated, and indeed upon any undulatory hypothesis, there must be some resistance to its progress; and unless the matter or ether in the interplanetary spaces be infinitely elastic, and there be no lateral action of a ray of light, there must be some loss. That it is exceedingly minute is proved by the distance light travels. Stars whose parallax is ascertained are at such a distance from the earth that their light, travelling at the rate of 192,500 miles in a second, takes more than ten years to reach the earth; so that we see them as they existed ten years ago. The distance of most visible stars is probably far greater than this, and yet their brilliance is great, and increases when their rays are collected by the telescope in proportion *ceteris paribus* to the area of the object-glass or speculum. There is, however, an argument of a somewhat speculative character, by which light would seem to be lost or transformed into some other force in the interplanetary spaces.

Every increase of space-penetrating power in the telescope gives us a new field of visible stars. If this expansion of the stellar universe go on indefinitely and no light be lost, then, assuming the fixed stars to be of an average equal brightness with our sun, and no light lost other than by divergence, the night ought to be equally luminous with the day; for though the light from each point diminishes in intensity as the square of the distance, the number of luminous points would fill up the whole space around us; and if every point of space is occupied by an equally brilliant point of light, the distance of the points becomes immaterial. The loss of light intercepted by stellar bodies would make no difference in the total quantity of light, for each of these would yield from its own self-luminosity at least as much light as it intercepted. Light may, however, be intercepted by opaque bodies, such as planets; but, making every allowance for these, it is difficult to understand why we get so little light at night from the stellar universe, without assuming that some light is lost in its progress through space—not lost absolutely, for that would be an annihilation of force—but converted into some other mode of motion.

It may be objected that this hypothesis assumes the stellar universe to be illimitable: if pushed to its extreme so as to make the light of night equal that of day, provided no stellar light be lost, it does make this assumption; but even this is a far more rational assumption to make than that the stellar universe is limited. Our experience gives no indication of a limit; each improvement in telescopic power gives us new realms of stars or of nebulæ, which, if not stellar clusters, are at all events self-luminous matter; and if we assume a limit, what is it? We cannot conceive a physical boundary, for then immediately comes the question, what bounds the boundary? and to suppose the stellar universe to be bounded by infinite space or by infinite chaos, that is to say, to suppose a spot—for it would then become so—of matter in definite forms, with definite forces, and probably teeming with definite organic beings, plunged in a universe of nothing, is to my mind at least far more unphilosophical than to suppose a boundless universe of matter existing in forms and actions analogous to those which, as far as our examination goes, pervade space. But without speculating on topics in which the mind loses itself, it may not unreasonably be expected that a greater amount of light would reach us from the surrounding self-luminous spheres were not some portion lost as light, by its action on the medium which conveys the impulses. What force this becomes, or what it effects, it would be idle to speculate upon.

VI.—MAGNETISM.

MAGNETISM, as was proved by the important discovery of Faraday, will produce *electricity*, but with this peculiarity—that in itself it is static; and, therefore, to produce a dynamic force, motion must be superadded to it: it is, in fact, directive, not motive, altering the direction of other forces, but not, in strictness, initiating them. It is difficult to convey a definite notion of the force of magnetism, and of the mode in which it affects other forces. The following illustration may give a rude idea of magnetic polarity. Suppose a number of wind-vanes, say of the shape of arrows, with the spindles on which they revolve arranged in a row, but the vanes pointing in various directions: a wind blowing from the same point with an uniform velocity will instantly arrange these vanes in a definite direction, the arrow-heads or narrow parts pointing one way, the swallow-tails or broad parts another. If they be delicately suspended on their spindles, a very gentle breeze will so arrange them, and a very gentle breeze will again deflect them; or, if the wind cease, and they have been originally subject to other forces, such as gravity from unequal suspension, they will return to irregular positions, themselves creating a slight breeze by their return. Such a state of things will represent the state of the molecules of soft iron; electricity acting on them—not indeed in straight lines, but in a definite direction—produces a polar arrangement, which they will lose as soon as the dynamic inducing force is removed.

Let us now suppose the vanes, instead of turning easily, to be more stiffly fixed to the axles, so as to be turned with difficulty: it will require a stronger wind to move them and arrange them definitely; but when so arranged, they will retain their position; and should a gentle breeze spring up in another direction, it will not alter their position, but will itself be definitely deflected. Should the conditions of force and stability be intermediate, both the breeze and the vanes will be slightly deflected; or, if there be no breeze, and the spindles be all moved in any direction, preserving their linear relation, they will themselves create a breeze. Thus it is with the molecules of hard iron or steel in permanent magnets; they are polarised with greater difficulty, but, when so polarised, they cannot be affected by a feeble current of electricity. Again, if the magnets be moved, they themselves originate a current of electricity; and, lastly, the magnetic polarity and the electric current may be both mutually affected, if the degrees of motion and stability be intermediate.

The above instance will, of course, be taken only as an approximation, and not as binding me to any closer analogy than is generally expected of a mechanical illustration. It is difficult to convey by words a definite idea of the dual or antithetic character of force involved in the term polarity. The illustration I have employed may, I hope, somewhat aid in elucidating the manner in which magnetism acts on the other dynamic forces; i. e., definitely directing them, but not initiating them, except while in motion.

Magnets being moved in the direction of lines, joining their poles, produce electrical currents in such neighbouring bodies as are conductors of electricity, in directions transverse to the line of motion; and if the direction of motion or the position of the magnetic poles be reversed, the current of electricity flows in a reverse direction. So if the magnet be stationary, conducting bodies moved across any of the lines of magnetic force, i. e. lines in the direction of which the mutual action of the poles of the magnet would place minute portions of iron, have currents of electricity developed in them, the direction of which is dependent upon that of the motion of the substance with reference to the magnetic poles. Thus, as bodies affected by an electrical current are definitely moved by a magnet in proximity to them, so conversely bodies moved near a magnet have an electrical current developed in them. Magnetism can, then, through the medium of electricity, produce *heat*, *light*, and *chemical affinity*. *Motion* it can directly produce under the above conditions; i. e. a magnet being itself moved will move other ferreous bodies: these will acquire a static condition of equilibrium, and be again moved when the magnet is also moved. By motion or arrested motion only, could the phenomena of magnetism ever have become known to us. A magnet, however powerful, might rest for ever unnoticed and unknown, unless it were moved near to iron, or iron moved near to it, so as to come within the sphere of its attraction.

But even with other than either magnetic or electrified substances, all bodies will be moved when placed near the poles of very powerful magnets—some taking a position axially, or in the line from pole to pole of the magnet; others equatorially, or in a direction transverse to that line—the former being attracted, the latter apparently repelled, by the poles of the magnet. These effects, according to the views of Faraday, show a generic difference between the two classes of bodies, magnetics and diamagnetics; according to others, a difference of degree or a resultant of magnetic action; the less magnetic substance being forced into a transverse position by the magnetisation of the more magnetic medium which surrounds it.

According to the view given above, magnetism may be produced by the other forces, just as the vanes in the instance given are definitely deflected, but cannot produce them except when in motion: motion, therefore, is to be regarded in this case as the initiative force. Magnetism will, however, directly affect the other forces—light, heat, and chemical affinity, and change their direction or mode of action, or, at all events, will so affect matter subjected to these forces, that their direction is changed. Since these lectures were delivered, Faraday has discovered a remarkable effect of the magnetic force in occasioning the deflection of a ray of polarised light.

If a ray of polarised light pass through water, or through any transparent liquid or solid which does not alter or turn aside the plane of polarisation, and the column, say of water, through which it passes be subjected to the action of a powerful magnet, the line of magnetic force, or that which would unite the poles of the magnet, being in the same direction as the ray of polarised light, the water acquires, with reference to the light, similar, though not quite identical, properties to oil of turpentine—the plane of polarisation is rotated, and the direction of this rotation is changed by changing the direction of the magnetic force: thus, if we suppose a polarised ray to pass first in its course the north pole of the magnet, then between that and the south pole it will be deflected, or curved to the right; while if it meets the south pole first in its course, it will, in its journey between that and the north pole, be turned to the left. If the substance through which the ray is transmitted be of itself capable of deflecting the plane of polarisation, as, for instance, oil of turpentine, then the magnetic influence will increase or diminish this rotation, according to its direction. A similar effect to this is observed with polarised heat when the medium through which it is transmitted is subjected to magnetic influence.

Whether this effect of magnetism is rightly termed an effect upon light and heat, or is a molecular change of the matter transmitting the light and heat, is a question the resolution of which must be left to the future; at present, the answer to it would depend upon the theory we adopt. If the view of light and heat which I have stated be adopted, then we may fairly say that magnetism, in these experiments, directly affects the other forces; for light and heat being, according to that view, motions of ordinary matter, magnetism, in affecting these movements, affects the forces which occasion them. If, however, the other theories be adhered to, it would be more consistent with the facts to view these results as exhibiting an action upon the matter itself, and the heat and light as secondarily affected.

When substances are *undergoing* chemical changes, and a magnet is brought near them, the direction or lines of action of the chemical force will be changed. There are many old experiments which probably depended on this effect, but which were erroneously considered to prove that permanent magnetism could produce or increase chemical action: these have recently been extended and explained by Mr. Hunt and Mr. Wartmann, and are now better understood.

The above cases are applicable to the subject of the present Essay, inasmuch as they show a relation to exist between magnetic and the other forces, which relation is, in all probability, reciprocal; but in these cases there is not a production of light, heat, or chemical affinity, by magnetism, but a change in their direction or mode of action.

There is, however, that which may be viewed as a dynamic condition of magnetism; i. e. its condition at the commencement and the termination, or during the increment or decrement of its development. While iron or steel is being rendered magnetic, and as it progresses from its non-magnetic to its maximum magnetic state, or recedes from its maximum to zero, it exhibits a dynamic force; the molecules are, it may be inferred, in motion. Similar effects can then be produced to those which are produced by a magnet whilst in motion.

An experiment which I published in 1845 tends, I think, to illustrate this, and in some degree to show the character of the motion impressed upon the molecules of a magnetic metal at the period of magnetisation. A tube filled with the liquid in which magnetic oxide of iron had been prepared, and terminated at each end by plates of glass, is surrounded by a coil of coated wire. To a spectator looking through this tube a flash of light is perceptible whenever the coil is electrised, and less light is transmitted when the electrical current ceases, showing a symmetrical arrangement of the minute particles of magnetic oxide while under the magnetic influence.

In this experiment it should be borne in mind, that the particles of oxide of iron are not shaped by the hand of man, as would be the case with iron filings, or similar minute portions of magnetic matter, but being chemically precipitated, are of the form given to them by nature.

While magnetism is in the state of change above described, it will produce the other forces; but it may be said, while magnetism is thus progressive, some other force is acting on it, and therefore it does not initiate: this is true, but the same may be said of all the other forces; they have no commencement that we can trace. We must ever refer them back to some antecedent force equal in amount to that produced, and therefore the word initiation cannot in strictness apply, but must only be taken as signifying the force selected as the first: this is another reason why the idea of abstract causation is inapplicable to physical production. To this point I shall again advert.

Electricity may thus be produced directly by magnetism, either when the magnet as a mass is in motion, or when its magnetism is commencing, increasing, decreasing, or ceasing; and heat may similarly be directly produced by magnetism. I have, since the first edition of this Essay was published, communicated to the Royal Society a paper by which I think

I have satisfactorily proved, that whenever any metal susceptible of magnetism is magnetised or demagnetised, its temperature is raised. This was shown, first, by subjecting a bar of iron, nickel, or cobalt to the influence of a powerful electromagnet, which was rapidly magnetised and demagnetised in reverse directions, the electro-magnet itself being kept cool by cisterns of water, so that the magnetic metal subjected to the influence of magnetism was raised to a higher temperature than the electro-magnet itself, and could not, therefore, have acquired its increased temperature by conduction or radiation of heat from the electro-magnet; and secondly, by rotating a permanent steel magnet with its pole opposite to a bar of iron, a thermo-electric pile being placed opposite the latter.

Dr. Maggi covered a plate of homogeneous soft iron with a thin coating of wax mixed with oil, a tube traversed the centre through which the vapour of boiling water was passed. The plate was made to rest on the poles of an electro-magnet, with card interposed. When the iron is not magnetised, the melted wax assumes a circular form, the tube occupying the centre, but when the electro-magnet is put in action, the curve marking the boundary of the melted substance changes its form and becomes elongated in a direction transverse to the line joining the poles, showing that the conducting power of the iron for heat is changed by magnetisation.

Thus we get heat produced by magnetism and the conduction of heat altered by it in a direction having a definite relation to the direction of the magnetism. Is it necessary to call in aid ether or the substance 'caloric' to explain these results? is it not more rational to regard the calorific effects as changes in the molecular arrangements of the matter subjected to magnetism?

There is every probability that magnetism, in the dynamic state, either when the magnet is in motion, or when the magnetic intensity is varying, will also directly produce chemical affinity and light, though, up to the present time, such has not been proved to be the case; the reciprocal effect, also, of the direct production of magnetism by light and heat has not yet been experimentally established.

I have used, in contradistinction, the terms dynamic and static to represent the different states of magnetism. The applications I have made of these terms may be open to some exception, but I know of no other words which will so nearly express my meaning.

The static condition of magnetism resembles the static condition of other forces: such as the state of tension existing in the beam and a cord of a balance, or in a charged Leyden phial. The old definition of force was, that which caused change in motion; and yet even this definition presents a difficulty: in a case of static equilibrium, such, for instance, as that which obtains in the two arms of a balance, we get the idea of force without any palpable apparent motion: whether there be really an absence of motion may be a doubtful question, as such absence would involve in this case perfect elasticity, and, in all other cases, a stability which, in a long course of time, nature generally negatives, showing, as I believe, an inseparable connection of motion with matter, and an impossibility of a perfectly immobile or durable state. So with magnetism: I believe no magnet can exist in an absolutely stable state, though the duration of its stability will be proportionate to its original resistance to assuming a polarised condition. This, however, must be taken merely as a matter of opinion: we have, in support of it, the general facts that magnets do deteriorate in the course of years; and we have the further general fact of the instability, or fluxional state, of all nature, when we have an opportunity of fairly investigating it at different and remote periods: in many cases, however, the action is so slow that the changes escape human observation, and, until this can be brought to bear over a proportionate period of time, the proposition cannot be said to be experimentally or inductively proved, but must be left to the mental conviction of those who examine it by the light of already acknowledged facts.

All cases of static force present the same difficulty: thus, two springs pressing against each other would be said to be exercising force; and yet there is no resulting action, no heat, no light, &c.

So if gas be compressed by a piston, at the time of compression heat is given off; but when this is abstracted, although the pressure continues, no further heat is eliminated. Thus, by an equilibrium produced by opposing forces, motion is locked up, or in abeyance, as it were, and may be again developed when the forces are relieved from the tension. But in the first instance, in producing the state of tension, force has to be employed; and as we have said in treating of mechanical force, so with the other forces the original change which disturbs equilibrium produces other changes which go on without end. Thus, by the act of charging a Leyden phial, the cylinder, the rubber, and the adjoining portions of the electrical machine have each and all their states changed, and thence produce changes in surrounding bodies *ad infinitum;* when the jar is discharged, converse changes are again produced.

As with heat, light, and electricity, the daily accumulating observations tend to show that each change in the phenomena to which these names are given is accompanied by a change either temporary or permanent in the matter affected by them; so many recent experiments on magnetism have connected magnetic phenomena with a molecular change in the subject matter. Thus M. Wertheim has shown that the elasticity of iron and steel is altered by magnetisation; the co-efficient of elasticity in iron being temporarily, in steel permanently diminished.

He has also examined the effects of torsion upon magnetised iron, and concludes, from his experiments, that in a bar of iron arrived at a state of magnetic equilibrium, temporary torsion diminishes the magnetism, and that the untwisting or return to its primitive state restores the original degree of magnetisation.

M. Guillemin observed that a bar slightly curved by its own weight is straightened by being magnetised. Mr. Page and Mr. Marrion discovered that a sound is emitted when iron or steel is rapidly magnetised or demagnetised; and Mr. Joule found that a bar of iron is slightly elongated by magnetisation.

Again, with regard to diamagnetic bodies, M. Matteucci found that the mechanical compression of glass altered the rotatory power upon a ray of polarised light which it transmitted. He further considered that a change took place in the temper of portions of glass which he submitted to the influence of powerful magnets.

The same arguments which have been submitted to the reader as to the other affections of matter being modes of molecular motion, are therefore equally applicable to magnetism.

VII.—CHEMICAL AFFINITY.

CHEMICAL AFFINITY, or the force by which dissimilar bodies tend to unite and form compounds differing generally in character from their constituents, is that mode of force of which the human mind has hitherto formed the least definite idea. The word itself—*affinity*—is ill chosen, its meaning, in this instance, bearing no analogy to its ordinary sense; and the mode of its action is conveyed by certain conventional expressions, no dynamic theory of it worthy of attention having been adopted. Its action so modifies and alters the character of matter, that the changes it induces have acquired, not perhaps very logically, a generic contradistinction from other material changes, and we thus use, as contradistinguished, the terms physical and chemical.

The main distinction between chemical affinity and physical attraction or aggregation, is the difference of character of the chemical compound from its components. This is, however, but a vague line of demarcation; in many cases, which would be classed by all as chemical actions, the change of character is but slight; in others, as in the effects of neutralisation, the difference of character would be a result which would equally follow from physical attraction of dissimilar substances, the previous characters of the constituents depending upon this very attraction or affinity: thus an acid corrodes because it tends to unite with another body; when united, its corrosive power, i. e. its tendency to unite, being satiated, it cannot, so to speak, be further attracted, and it necessarily loses its corrosive power. But there are other cases where no such result could *à priori* be anticipated, as where the attraction or combining tendency of the compound is higher than that of its constituents: thus, who could, by physical reasoning, anticipate a substance like nitric acid from the combination of nitrogen and oxygen?

The nearest approach, perhaps, that we can form to a comprehension of chemical action, is by regarding it (vaguely perhaps) as a molecular attraction or motion. It will directly produce *motion* of definite masses, by the resultant of the molecular changes it induces: thus, the projectile effects of gunpowder may be cited as familiar instances of motion produced by chemical action. It may be a question whether, in this case, the force which occasions the motion of the mass is a conversion of the force of chemical affinity, or whether it is not, rather, a liberation of other forces existing in a state of static equilibrium, and having been brought into such state by previous chemical actions; but, at all events, through the medium of electricity chemical affinity may be directly and quantitatively converted into the other modes of force. By chemical affinity, then, we can directly produce *electricity;* this latter force was, indeed, said by Davy to be chemical affinity acting on masses: it appears, rather, to be chemical affinity acting in a definite direction through a chain of particles; but by no definition can the exact relation of chemical affinity and electricity be expressed; for the latter, however closely related to the former, yet exists where the former does not, as in a metallic wire, which when electrified, or conducting electricity, is, nevertheless, not chemically altered, or, at least, not known to be chemically altered.

Volta, the antitype of Prometheus, first enabled us definitely to relate the forces of chemistry and electricity. When two dissimilar metals in contact are immersed in a liquid belonging to a certain class, and capable of acting chemically on one of them, what is termed a voltaic circuit is formed, and, by the chemical action, that peculiar mode of force called an electric current is generated, which circulates from metal to metal, across the liquid, and through the points of contact.

Let us take, as an instance of the conversion of chemical force into electrical, the following, which I made known some years ago. If gold be immersed in hydrochloric acid, no chemical action takes place. If gold be immersed in nitric acid, no chemical action takes place; but mix the two acids, and the immersed gold is chemically attacked and dissolved: this an is ordinary chemical action, the result of a double chemical affinity. In hydrochloric acid, which is composed of chlorine and hydrogen, the affinity of chlorine for gold being less than its affinity for hydrogen, no change takes place; but when the nitric acid is added, this latter containing a great quantity of oxygen in a state of feeble combination, the affinity of oxygen for hydrogen opposes that of hydrogen for chlorine, and then the affinity of the latter for gold is enabled to act, the gold combines with the chlorine, and chloride of gold remains in solution in the liquid. Now, in order to exhibit this chemical force in the form of electrical force, instead of mixing the liquids, place them in separate vessels or compartments, but so that they may be in contact, which may be effected by having a porous material, such as unglazed porcelain, amianthus, &c., between them. Immerse in each of these liquids a strip or wire of gold: as long as these pieces of gold remain separated, no chemical or electrical effect takes place; but the instant they are brought into metallic contact, either immediately or by connecting each with the same metallic wire, chemical action takes place—the gold in the hydrochloric acid is dissolved, electrical action also takes place, the nitric acid is deoxidised by the transferred hydrogen, and a current of electricity may be detected in the metals or connecting metal by the application of a galvanometer or any instrument appropriate for detecting such effect.

There are few, if any, chemical actions which cannot be experimentally made to produce electricity: the oxidation of metals, the burning of combustibles, the combination of oxygen and hydrogen, &c., may all be made sources of electricity. The common mode in which the electricity of the voltaic battery is generated is by the chemical action of water upon zinc; this action is increased by adding certain acids to the water, which enable it to act more powerfully upon the zinc, or in some cases act themselves upon it; and one of the most powerful chemical actions known—that of nitric acid upon oxidable metals—is that which produces the most powerful voltaic battery, a combination which I made known in the year 1839: indeed, we may safely say, that when the chemical force is utilised, or not wasted, but all converted into electrical force, the more powerful the chemical action, the more powerful is the electrical action which results.

If, instead of employing manufactured products or educts, such as zinc and acids, we could realise as electricity the whole of the chemical force which is active in the combustion of cheap and abundant raw materials, such as coal, wood, fat, &c., with air or water, we should obtain one of the greatest practical desiderata, and have at our command a mechanical power in every respect superior in its applicability to the steam engine.

I have shown that the flame of the common blowpipe gives rise to a very marked electrical current, capable not only of affecting the galvanometer, but of producing chemical decomposition: two plates or coils of platinum are placed, the one in the portion of the flame near the orifice of the jet, or at the points where combustion commences, the other in the full yellow flame where combustion is at its maximum; this latter should be kept cool, to enable a thermo-electric current, which is produced by the different temperature of the platinum plates, to co-operate with the flame current; wires attached to the plates of platinum form the terminals or poles. By a row of jets a flame battery may be formed, yielding increased effects; but in these experiments, though theoretically interesting, so small a fraction of the power, actually at work in the combustion, has been thrown into an electrical form, that there is no immediate promise of a practical result.

The quantity of the electrical current, as measured by the quantity of matter it acts upon in its different phenomenal effects, is proportionate to the quantity of chemical action which generated it; and its intensity, or power of overcoming resistance, is also proportionate to the intensity of chemical affinity when a single voltaic pair is employed, or to the number of reduplications when the well-known instrument called the voltaic battery is used.

The mode in which the voltaic current is increased in intensity by these reduplications, is in itself a striking instance of the mutual relations and dynamic analogies of different forces. Let a plate of zinc or other metal possessing a strong affinity for oxygen, and another of platinum or other metal possessing little or no affinity for oxygen, be partially immersed in a vessel, A, containing dilute nitric acid, but not in contact with each other; let platinum wires touching each of these plates have their extremities immersed in another vessel, B, containing also dilute nitric acid: as the acid in vessel A is decomposed, by the chemical affinity of the zinc for the oxygen of the acid, the acid in vessel B is also decomposed, oxygen appearing at the extremity of the wire which is connected with the platinum: the chemical power is conveyed or transferred through the wires, and, abstracting certain local effects, for every unit of oxygen which combines with the zinc in the one vessel, a unit of oxygen is evolved from the platinum wire in the other. The platinum wire is thus thrown into a condition analogous to zinc, or has a power given to it of determining the oxygen of the liquid to its surface, though it cannot, as is the case with zinc, combine with it under similar circumstances. If we now substitute for the platinum wire which was connected with the platinum plate, a zinc wire, we have in addition to the determining tendency by which the platinum was affected, the chemical affinity of the oxygen in vessel B for the zinc wire thus we have, added to the force which was originally produced by the zinc of the combination in vessel A, a second force, produced by the zinc in vessel B, co-operating with the first; two pairs of zinc and platinum thus connected produce, therefore, a more intense effect than one pair; and if we go on adding to these alternations of zinc, platinum, and liquid, we obtain an indefinite exaltation of chemical power, just as in mechanics we obtain accelerated motion by adding fresh impulses to motion already generated.

The same rule of proportion which holds good in chemical combinations also obtains in electrical effects, when these are produced by chemical actions. Dalton and others proved that the constituents of a vast number of compound substances always bore a definite quantitative relation to each other: thus, water, which consists of one part by weight of hydrogen united to eight parts of oxygen, cannot be formed by the same elements in any other than these proportions; you can neither add to nor subtract from the normal ratio of the elements, without entirely altering the nature of the compound. Further, if any element be selected as unity, the combining ratios of other elements will bear an invariable quantitative relation to that and to each other: thus if hydrogen be chosen as 1, oxygen will be 8, chlorine will be 36; that is, oxygen will unite with hydrogen in the proportion of 8 parts by weight to 1, while chlorine will unite with hydrogen in the proportion of 36 to 1, or with oxygen in the proportion of 36 to 8. Numbers expressing their combining weights, which are thus relative, not absolute, may by a conventional assent as to the point of unity, be fixed for all chemical reagents; and, when so fixed, it will be found that bodies, at least in inorganic compounds, generally unite in those proportions, or in simple multiples of them: these proportions are termed *Equivalents*.

Now a voltaic battery, which consists usually of alternations of two metals, and a liquid capable of acting chemically upon one of them, has, as we have seen, the power of producing chemical action in a liquid connected with it by metals upon which this liquid is incapable of acting: in such case the constituents of the liquid will be eliminated at the surfaces of the immersed metals, and at a distance one from the other. For example, if the two platinum terminals of a voltaic battery be immersed in water, oxygen will be evolved at one and hydrogen at the other terminal, exactly in the proportions in which they form water; while, to the most minute examination, no action is perceptible in the stratum of liquid. It was known before Faraday's time that, while this chemical action was going on in the subjected liquid, a chemical action was going on in the cells of the voltaic battery; but it was scarcely if at all known that the amount of chemical action in the one bore a constant relation to the amount of action in the other. Faraday proved that it bore a direct equivalent relation: that is, supposing the battery to be formed of zinc, platinum, and water, the amount of oxygen which united with the zinc in each cell of the battery was exactly equal to the amount evolved at the one platinum terminal, while the hydrogen evolved from each platinum plate of the battery was equal to the hydrogen evolved from the other platinum terminal.

Supposing the battery to be charged with hydrochloric acid, instead of water, while the terminals are separated by water, then for every 36 parts by weight of chlorine which united with each plate of zinc, eight parts of oxygen would be evolved from one of the platinum terminals: that is, the weights would be precisely in the same relation which Dalton proved to exist in their chemical combining weights. This may be extended to all liquids capable of being decomposed by the voltaic force, thence called *Electrolytes:* and as no voltaic effect is produced by liquids incapable of being thus decomposed, it follows that voltaic action is chemical action taking place at a distance, or transferred through a chain of media, and that the chemical equivalent numbers are the exponents of the amount of voltaic action for corresponding chemical substances.

As heat, light, magnetism, or motion, can be produced by the requisite application of the electric current, and as this is definitely produced by chemical action, we get these forces very definitely, though not immediately, produced by chemical action. Let us, however, here enquire, as we have already done with respect to the other forces, how far other forces may directly emanate from chemical affinity.

Heat is an immediate product of chemical affinity. I know of no exception to the general proposition that all bodies in chemically combining produce heat; i. e. if solution be not considered as chemical action, and even in that case, when cold results, it is from a change of consistence, as from the solid to the liquid state, and not from chemical action.

We shall find that the same view of the expenditure of force which we have considered in treating of latent heat holds good as to the expenditure of chemical force when regarded with reference to the amount of heat or repulsive force which it engenders, the chemical force being here exhausted by chemical expansion—that is, by heat. Thus, in the chemical action of the ordinary combustion of coal and oxygen, the expenditure of fuel will be in proportion to the expansibility of the substances heated; water passing freely into the steam will consume more fuel than if it be confined and kept at a temperature above its boiling point.

Why chemical action produces heat, or what is the action of the molecules of matter when chemically uniting, is a question upon which many theories have been proposed and which may possibly be never more than approximately resolved.

Some authors explain it by the condensation which takes place; but this will not account for the many instances where, from the liberation of gases, a great increase of volume ensues upon chemical combustion, as in the familiar instance of the explosion of gunpowder: others explain it as resulting from the union of atmospheres of positive and negative electricity which are assumed to surround the atoms of bodies; but this involves hypothesis upon hypothesis. Dr. Wood has lately thrown out a view of the heat of chemical action which is more in accordance with a dynamic theory of heat, and as such demands some notice. Starting with his proposition, which I have previously mentioned, 'that the nearer the particles of bodies are to each other the less they require to move to produce a given motion in the particles of another body,' his argument, if I rightly understand it, assumes something of this form.

In the mechanical approximation of the particles of a homogeneous body heat results; the particles *a a* of the body A would, by their approximation, produce expansion in the neighbouring body B, the more so in proportion as they themselves were previously nearer to each other. In chemically combining, *a a* the particles of A are brought into very close proximity with *b b* the particles of B; heat should therefore result, and the greater because the proximity may fairly be assumed to be greater in the case of chemical combination than in that of mechanical compression. In cases, then, where there is no absolute diminution of bulk ensuing on chemical combination, if the greater proximity of the combining particles be such that the correlative expansion ought to be greater (if there were no chemical combination) than that occupied by the total volume of the new compound, an extra expanding power is evolved, and heat or expansion ought to be produced in surrounding bodies. In other words, if *a a* could be brought by physical attraction as near each other as they are by chemical attraction brought near to *b b*, they would, from their increased proximity, produce an expansive power *ultra* the volume occupied by the actual chemical compound A and B. The question, however, immediately occurs, why should the volume of the compound be limited and not occupy the full space equivalent to the expanding power induced by the contraction or approximation of the particles. As the distance of the particles is the resultant of the contending contracting and expanding powers, this result ought to express itself in terms of the actual volume produced by the combination, which it certainly does not.

Though I see some difficulties in Dr. Wood's theory, and perhaps have not rightly conceived it, his views have to my mind great interest, his mode of regarding natural phenomena being analogous to that which I have in this Essay, and for many years, advocated, viz. to divest physical science as much as possible of hypothetic fluids, ethers, latent entities, occult qualities, &c. My own notion of the heat produced by chemical combination, though I scarcely dare venture an opinion upon a subject so controverted, is, that it is analogous to the heat of friction, that the particles of matter in close approximation and rapid motion *inter se* evolve heat as a continuation of the motion interrupted by the friction or intestinal motion of the particles: heat would thus be produced, whether the resulting compound were of greater or less bulk than the sum of the components, though of course when the compound is of greater bulk less heat would be apparent in neighbouring bodies, the expansion taking place in one of the substances themselves—I say in one of them, for it is stated in books of authority that there is no instance of two or more solids or liquids, or a solid and a liquid, combining and producing a compound which is entirely gaseous at ordinary temperatures and pressures. The substance gun-cotton, however, discovered by Dr. Schoenbein, very nearly realises this proposition.

Dr. Andrews has arrived at the conclusion, after careful experiment, that in chemical combinations where acids and alkalies or analogous substances are employed, the amount of heat produced is determined by the basic ingredient, and his experiments have received general assent; although it should be stated that M. Hess arrived at contrary results, the acid constituent according to his experiments furnishing the measure of the heat developed.

Light is directly produced by chemical action, as in the flash of gunpowder, the burning of phosphorus in oxygen gas, and all rapid combustions: indeed, wherever intense heat is developed, light accompanies it. In many cases of slow combustion, such as the phenomena of phosphorescence, the light is apparently much more intense than the heat; the former being obvious, the latter so difficult of detection that for a long time it was a question whether any heat was eliminated; and I am not aware that at the present day, any thermic effects from certain modes of phosphorescence, such as those of phosphorescent wood, putrescent fish, &c., have been detected.

Chemical action produces *magnetism* whenever it is thrown into a definite direction, as in the phenomenon of electrolysis. I may adduce the gas voltaic battery, as presenting a simple instance of the direct production of magnetism by chemical synthesis. Oxygen and hydrogen in that combination chemically unite; but instead of combining by intimate molecular admixture, as in the ordinary cases, they act upon water, i. e. combined oxygen and hydrogen, placed between them so as to produce a line of chemical action; and a magnet adjacent to this line of action is deflected, and places itself at right angles to it. What a chain of molecules does here, there can be no doubt all the molecules entering into combination would produce in ordinary chemical actions; but in such cases, the direction of the lines of combination being irregular and confused, there is no general resultant by which the magnet can be affected.

What the exact nature of the transference of chemical power across an electrolyte is, we at present know not, nor can we form any more definite idea of it than that given by the theory of Grotthus. We have no knowledge as to the exact nature of any mode of chemical action, and, for the present must leave it as an obscure action of force, of which future researches may simplify our apprehension.

We have seen that an equivalent or proportionate electrical effect is produced by a given amount of chemical action; if we, in turn, produce heat and magnetism and motion by the electricity resulting from chemical action, we shall be able to measure these forces far more accurately than when they are directly produced, and thus to deduce their equivalent relation to the initial chemical action. Thus M. Favre, after ascertaining the quantity of heat produced by the oxidation of a quantity of zinc, and finding, as have others, that the heat is the same when evolved from a voltaic battery by the same consumption of zinc forming its positive element, makes the following experiment.

A voltaic battery and electro-magnet are immersed in calorimeters, and the heat produced when the connection with the magnet is effected is noted.

The electro-magnet is then made to raise a weight, and thus perform mechanical work, and the heat produced is again noted. It is found in the latter case that less heat is evolved than in the former, a certain quantity of heat has therefore been replaced by the mechanical work; and by estimating the amount of heat subtracted, and the amount of work produced, he deduces the relative equivalent of work to heat. These experiments give a production of mechanical work by chemical action, not, it is true, a direct production, but, as the heat and work are in inverse ratios, and each has its source in chemical action, they prove that they are definite for a definite amount of chemical action, and as each is produced respectively by electricity and magnetism, these forces must also bear a definite relation to the initial chemical force.

The doctrine of definite combining proportions, which so beautifully serves to relate chemistry to voltaic electricity, led to the atomic theory, which, though adopted in its universality by a large majority of chemists, presents great difficulties when extended to all chemical combinations.

The equivalent ratios in which a great number of substances chemically combine, hold good in so many instances, that the atomic doctrine is believed by many to be universally applicable, and called a law; and yet, when followed in the combinations of substances whose natural chemical attractions are very feeble, the relation fades away, and is sought to be recovered by applying a separate and arbitrary multiplier to the different constituents.

Thus, when it was found that a vast number of substances combined in definite volumes and weights, and in definite volumes and weights only, it was argued that their ultimate molecules or atoms had a definite size, as otherwise there was no apparent reason why this equivalent ratio should hold good: why, for instance, water should only be formed of two volumes or one unit by weight of hydrogen, and of one volume or eight units by weight of oxygen; why, unless there were some ultimate limits to the divisibility of its molecules, should not water, or a fluid substance approximating to water in character, be formed by a half, a third, or a tenth part of hydrogen, with eight parts of oxygen?

It was perfectly consistent with the atomic view that a substance might be formed with one part combined with eight parts, or with sixteen, or with twenty-four, for in such a substance there would be no subdivision of the (supposed indivisible) molecule; and this held good with many compounds: thus fourteen parts by weight, say grains of nitrogen, will combine respectively with eight, sixteen, twenty-four, thirty-two, and forty parts by weight, or grains, of oxygen.

So, again, twenty-seven grains of iron will combine with eight grains of oxygen or with twenty-four grains, i. e. three proportionals of oxygen. No compound is known in which twenty-seven grains of iron will combine with two proportionals or sixteen grains of oxygen; but this does not much affect the theory, as such a compound may be yet discovered, or there may be reasons at present unknown why it cannot be formed.

But now comes a difficulty: twenty-seven parts by weight of iron *will* combine with twelve parts by weight of oxygen, and twenty-seven parts of iron will also combine with ten and two-third parts of oxygen. Thus if we retain the unit of iron we must subdivide the unit of oxygen, or if we retain the unit of oxygen we must subdivide the unit of iron, or we must subdivide both by a different divisor. What then becomes of the notion of an atom or molecule physically indivisible?

If iron were the only substance to which this difficulty applied, it might be viewed as an unexplained exception, or as a mixture of two oxides; or recourse might be had to a more minute subdivision to form the units or equivalents of other substances; but numerous other substances fall under a similar category; and in organic combinations, to preserve the atomic nomenclature we must apply a separate multiplier or divisor to far the greater number of the elementary constituents, i. e. we must divide that which is, *ex hypothesi*, indivisible.

Thus, to take a more complex substance than any formed by the combination of iron and oxygen, let us select the substance albumen, composed of carbon, hydrogen, nitrogen, oxygen, phosphorus, and sulphur. In this case we must either divide the atoms of phosphorus and sulphur so as to reduce them to small fractions, or multiply the atoms of the other substances by extravagant numbers; thus to preserve the unit of one of the constituents of this substance, chemists say it is composed of 400 atoms of carbon, 310 of hydrogen, 120 of oxygen, 50 of nitrogen, 2 of sulphur, and 1 of phosphorus. This is a somewhat extreme case, but similar difficulties will be found in different degrees to prevail among organic compounds; in very many no constituent can be taken as a unit to which simple multiples of any of the others will give their relative proportions. By the mode of notation adopted, if any conceivable substance be selected, it could, whatever be the proportions of its constituents, be termed atomic. A solution of an ounce of sugar in a pound of water, in a pound and a half, in a pound and a quarter, in a pound and a tenth, might be expressed in an atomic form, if we select arbitrarily a multiplier or divisor.

It is true that in the case of solution, different proportions can be united up to the point of saturation without any difference in the character of the compound, though the same may be predicated to some extent of an acid and an alkali; but even where the steps are sudden, and compounds only exist with definite proportions, they cannot, in a multitude of cases, be reconciled with the true idea of an atomic combination, i. e. one to one, one to two, &c.

Although, therefore, nature presents us with facts which show that there is some restrictive law of combination which in numerous cases limits the ratios in which substances will combine, nay, further, shows many instances of a proportion between the combining weights of one compound and those of another; although she shows also a remarkable simplicity in the combining volumes of numerous gases, she also gives numerous cases to which the doctrine of atomic combinations cannot fairly be applied.

That there must be something in the constitution of matter, or in the forces which act on it, to account for the *per saltum* manner in which chemical combinations take place, is inevitable; but the idea of atoms does not seem satisfactorily to account for it.

By selecting a separate multiplier or divisor, chemists may denote every combination in terms derived from the atomic theory; but they have passed from the original law, which contemplated only definite multiples, and the very hypothetic expressions of atoms, which the apparently simple relations of combining weights first led them to adopt, they are obliged to vary and to contradict in terms, by dividing that which their hypothesis and the expression of it assumed to be indivisible.

While, therefore, I fully recognise a great natural truth in the definite ratios presented by a vast number of chemical combinations, and in the *per saltum* steps in which nearly all take place, I cannot accept as an argument in favour of an atomic theory, those combinations which are made to support it by the application of an arbitrary notation.

A similar straining of theory seems gradually obtaining in regard to the doctrine of compound radicals. The discovery of cyanogen by Gay-Lussac was probably the first inducement to the doctrine of compound radicals; a doctrine which is now generally, perhaps too generally, received in organic chemistry. As, in the case of cyanogen, a body obviously compound discharged in almost all its reactions the functions of an element, so in many other cases it was found that compound bodies in which a great number of elements existed, might be regarded as binary combinations, by considering certain groups of these elements as a compound radical; that is, as a simple body when treated of in relation to the other complex substances of which it forms part, and only as non-elementary when referred to its internal constitution.

Undoubtedly, by approximating in theory the reactions of inorganic and of organic chemistry, by keeping the mind within the limits of a beaten path, instead of allowing it to wander through a maze of isolated facts, the doctrine of compound radicals has been of service; but, on the other hand, the indefinite variety of changes which may be rung upon the composition of an organic substance, by different associations of its primary elements, makes the binary constituents vary as the minds of the authors who treat of them, and makes their grouping depend entirely upon the strength of the analogies presented to each individual mind. From this cause, and from the extreme license which has been taken in theoretic groupings deduced from this doctrine, a serious question arises whether it may not ultimately, unless carefully restricted, produce confusion rather than simplicity, and be to the student an embarrassment rather than an assistance.

VIII.—OTHER MODES OF FORCE.

CATALYSIS, or the chemical action induced by the mere presence of a foreign body, embraces a class of facts which must considerably modify many of our notions of chemical action: thus oxygen and hydrogen, when mixed in a gaseous state, will remain unaltered for an indefinite period; but the introduction to them of a slip of clean platinum will cause more or less rapid combination, without being in itself in any respect altered. On the other hand, oxygenated water, which is a compound of one equivalent of hydrogen plus two of oxygen, will, when under a certain temperature, remain perfectly stable; but touch it with platinum in a state of minute division, and it is instantly decomposed, one equivalent of oxygen being set free. Here, again, the platinum is unaltered, and thus we have synthesis and analysis effected apparently by the mere contact of a foreign body. It is not improbable that the increased electrolytic power of water by the addition of some acids, such as the sulphuric and phosphoric, where the acids themselves are not decomposed, depends upon a catalytic effect of these acids; but we know too little of the nature and rationale of catalysis to express any confident opinion on its modes of action, and possibly we may comprehend very different molecular actions under one and the same name. In no case does catalysis yield us new power or force: it only determines or facilitates the action of chemical force, and, therefore, is no creation of force by contact.

The force so developed by catalysis may be converted into a voltaic form thus: in a single pair of the gas battery above alluded to, one portion of a strip of platinum is immersed in a tube of oxygen, the other in one of hydrogen, both the gases and the extremities of the platinum being connected by water or other electrolyte; a voltaic combination is thus formed, and electricity, heat, light, magnetism, and motion, produced at the will of the experimenter.

In this combination we have a striking instance of correlative expansions and contractions, analogous, though in a much more refined form, to the expansions and contractions by heat and cold detailed in the early part of this essay, and illustrated by the alternations of two bladders partially filled with air: thus, as by the effect of chemical combination in each pair of tubes of the gas battery the gases oxygen and hydrogen lose their gaseous character and shrink into water, so at the platinum terminals of the battery, when immersed in water, water is decomposed, and expands into oxygen and hydrogen gases. The correlate of the force which changes gas into liquid at one point of space, changes liquid into gas at another, and the exact volume which disappears in the one place reappears in the other; so that it would appear to an inexperienced eye as though the gases passed through solid wires.

Gravitation, inertia, and aggregation, were but cursorily alluded to in my original lectures; their relation to the other modes of force seemed to be less definitely traceable; but the phenomenal effects of gravitation and inertia, being motion and resistance to motion, in considering motion I have in some degree included their relations to the other forces.

To my mind gravitation would only produce other force when the motion caused by it ceases. Thus, if we suppose a meteor to be a mass rotating in an orbit round the earth, and with no resisting medium, then, as long as that rotation continues, the motion of the meteoric mass itself would be the exponent of the force impelling it; if there be a resisting medium, part of this motion would be arrested and taken up by the medium, either as motion, heat, electricity, or some other mode of force; if the meteor approach the earth sufficiently to fall upon it, the perceptible motion of the meteor is stopped, but is taken up by the earth which vibrates through its mass; part also reappears as heat in both earth and meteor, and part in the change in the earth's position consequent on its increase of gravity, and so on. Gravitation is but the subjective idea, and its relation to other modes of force seems to me to be identical with that of pressure or motion. Thus, when arrested motion produces heat, it matters not whether the motion has been produced by a falling body, i. e. by gravitation, or a body projected by an explosive compound, &c.; the heat will be the same, provided the mass and velocity at the time of arrest be the same. In no other sense can I conceive a relation between gravitation and the other forces, and, with all diffidence, I cannot agree with those who seek a more mysterious link.

Mosotti has mathematically treated of the identity of gravitation with *cohesive attraction*, and Plücker has recently succeeded in showing that crystalline bodies are definitely affected by magnetism, and take a position in relation to the lines of magnetic force dependent upon their optical axis or axis of symmetry.

What is termed the optic axis is a fixed direction through crystals, in which they do not doubly refract light, and which direction, in those crystals which have one axis of figure, or a line around which the figure is symmetrical, is parallel to the axis of symmetry. When submitted to magnetic influence such crystals take up a position, so that their optic axis points diamagnetically or transversely to the lines of magnetic force; and when, as is the case in some crystals, there is more than one optic axis, the resultant of these axes points diamagnetically. The mineral cyanite is influenced by magnetism in so marked a manner that when suspended it will arrange itself definitely with reference to the direction of terrestrial magnetism, and may, according to Plücker, be used as a compass-needle.

There is scarcely any doubt that the force which is concerned in *aggregation* is the same which gives to matter its crystalline form; indeed, a vast number of inorganic bodies, if not all, which appear amorphous are, when closely examined, found to be crystalline in their structure: we thus get a reciprocity of action between the force which unites the molecules of matter and the magnetic force, and through the medium of the latter the correlation of the attraction of aggregation with the other modes of force may be established.

I believe that the same principles and mode of reasoning as have been adopted in this essay might be applied to the organic as well as the inorganic world; and that muscular force, animal and vegetable heat, &c., might, and at some time will, be shown to have similar definite correlations; but I have purposely avoided this subject, as pertaining to a department of science to which I have not devoted my attention. I ought, however, while alluding to this subject, shortly to mention some experiments of Professor Matteucci, communicated to the Royal Society in the year 1850, by which it appears that whatever mode of force it be which is propagated along the nervous filaments, this mode of force is definitely affected by currents of electricity. His experiments show that when a current of positive electricity traverses a portion of the muscle of a living animal in the same direction as that in which the nerves ramify—i. e. a direction from the brain to the extremities—a muscular contraction is produced in the limb experimented on, showing that the nerve of motion is affected; while, if the current, as it is termed, be made to traverse the muscle in the reverse direction, or towards the nervous centres, the animal utters cries, and exhibits all the indications of suffering pain, scarcely any muscular movement being produced; showing that in this case the nerves of sensation are affected by the electric current, and therefore that some definite pólar condition exists, or is induced, in the nerves, to which electricity is correlated, and that probably this polar condition constitutes nervous agency. There are other analogies given in the papers of M. Matteucci, and derived from the action of the electrical organs of fishes, which tend to corroborate and develope the same view.

By an application of the doctrine of the Correlation of Forces, Dr. Carpenter has shown how a difficulty arising from the ordinary notions of the developement of an organised being from its germ-cell may be lessened. It has been thought by many physiologists that the *nisus formativus*, or organising force of an animal or vegetable structure, lies dormant in the primordial germ-cell. 'So that the organising force required to build up an oak or a palm, an elephant or a whale, is concentrated in a minute particle only discernible by microscopic aid.'

Certain other views of nearly equal difficulty have been propounded. Dr. Carpenter suggests the probability of extraneous forces, as heat, light, and chemical affinity, continuously operating upon the material germ; so that all that is required in this is a structure capable of receiving, directing, and converting these forces into those which tend to the assimilation of extraneous matter and the definite developement of the particular structure. In proof of this position he shows how dependent the process of germ developement is upon the presence and agency of external forces, particularly heat and light, and how it is regulated by the measure of these forces supplied to it.

It certainly is far less difficult so to conceive the supply of force yielded to organised beings in their gradual process of growth, than to suppose a store of dormant or latent force pent up in a microscopic monad.

As by the artificial structure of a voltaic battery, chemical actions may be made to cooperate in a definite direction, so, by the organism of a vegetable or animal, the mode of motion which constitutes heat, light, &c., may, without extravagance, be conceived to be appropriated and changed into the forces which induce the absorption, and assimilation of nutriment, and into nervous agency and muscular power. Indications of similar thoughts may be detected in the writings of Liebig.

Some difficulty in studying the correlations of vital with inorganic physical forces arises from the effects of sensation and consciousness, presenting a similar confusion to that alluded to, when, in treating of heat, I ventured to suggest, that observers are too apt to confound the sensations with the phenomena. Thus, to apply some of the considerations on force, given in the introductory portion of this essay, to cases where vitality or consciousness intervenes. When a weight is raised by the hand, there should, according to the doctrine of non-creation of force, have been somewhere an expenditure equivalent to the amount of gravitation overcome in raising the weight. That there is expenditure we can prove, though in the present state of science we cannot measure it. Thus, prolong the effort, raise weights for an hour or two, the vital powers sink, food, i. e. fresh chemical force, is required to supply the exhaustion. If this supply is withheld and the exertion is continued, we see the consumption of force in the supervening weakness and emaciation of the body.

The consciousness of effort, which has formed a topic of argument by some writers when treating of force, and is by them believed to be that which has originated the idea of force, may by the physical student be regarded as feeling is in the phenomena of heat and cold, viz. a sensation of the struggle of opposing molecular motions in overcoming the resistance of the masses to be moved. When we say we feel hot, we feel cold, we feel that we are exerting ourselves, our expressions are intelligible to beings who are capable of experiencing similar sensations; but the physical changes accompanying these sensations are not thereby explained. Without pretending to know what probably we shall never know, the actual *modus agendi* of the brain, nerves, muscles, &c., we may study vital as we do inorganic phenomena, both by observation and experiment. Thus, Sir Benjamin Brodie has examined the effect of respiration on animal heat by inducing artificial respiration after the spinal cord has been severed; in which case he finds the animal heat declines, notwithstanding the continuance of the chemical action of respiration, carbonic acid being formed as usual; but he also finds that under such circumstances the struggles or muscular actions of the animal are very great, and sufficient probably to account for the force eliminated by the chemical action in digestion and respiration; and Liebig, by measuring the amount of chemical action in digestion and respiration, and comparing it with the labour performed, has to some extent established their equivalent relations.

Mr. Helmholtz has found that the chemical changes which take place in muscles are greater when these are made to undergo contractions than when they are in repose; and that, as would be expected, the consumption of the matter of the muscles, or, in other terms, the waste or excrementitious matter thrown off, is greater in the former than in the latter case.

M. Matteucci has ascertained that the muscles of recently killed frogs absorb oxygen and exhale carbonic acid, and that when they are thrown into a state of contraction, and still more when they perform mechanical work, the absorption is increased; and he even calculates the equivalents of work so performed.

M. Beclard finds that the quantity of heat produced by voluntary muscular contraction in man is greater when that contraction is what he terms static, that is, when it produces no external work, but is effort alone, than when that effort and contraction are employed dynamically, so as to raise a weight or produce mechanical work.

Thus, though we may see no present promise of being able to resolve sensations into their ultimate elements, or to trace, physically, the link which unites volition with exertion or effort, in terms of our own consciousness of it, we may hope to approximate the solution of these deeply interesting questions.

In the same individual the chemical and physical state of the secretions in the warm may be compared with those in the cold parts of the body. The changes in digestion and respiration, when the body is in a state of rest, may be compared with those which obtain when it is in a state of activity. The relations with external matter, maintaining, by the constant play of natural forces, the vital nucleus, or the organisation by means of which matter and force receive, for a definite period, a definite incorporation and direction, may be ascertained, while the more minute structural changes are revealed to us by the ever-improving powers of the microscope; and thus step by step we may learn that which it is given to us to learn, boundless in its range and infinite in its progress, and therefore never giving a response to the ultimate —Why?

As the first glimpse of a new star is caught by the eye of the astronomer while directing his vision to a different point of space, and disappears when steadfastly gazed at, only to have its position and figure ultimately ascertained by the employment of more penetrative powers, so the first scintillations of new natural phenomena frequently present themselves to the eye of the observer, dimly seen when viewed askance, and disappearing if directly looked for. When new powers of thought and experiment have developed and corrected the first notions, and given a character to the new image, probably very different from the first impression, fresh objects are again glanced at in the margin of the new field of vision, which in their turn have to be verified, and again lead to new extensions; thus the effort to establish one observation leads to the imperfect perception of new and wider fields of research; and, instead of approaching finality, the more we discover, the more infinite appears the range of the undiscovered!

IX.—CONCLUDING REMARKS.

I HAVE now gone through the affections of matter for which distinct names have been given in our received nomenclature: that other forces may be detected, differing as much from them as they differ from each other, is highly probable, and that when discovered, and their modes of action fully traced out, they will be found to be related *inter se*, and to these forces as these are to each other, I believe to be as far certain as certainty can be predicted of any future event.

It may in many cases be a difficult question to determine what constitutes a distinct affection of matter or mode of force. It is highly probable that different lines of demarcation would have been drawn between the forces already known, had they been discovered in a different manner, or first observed at different points of the chain which connects them. Thus, radiant heat and light are mainly distinguished by the manner in which they affect our senses: were they viewed according to the way in which they affect inorganic matter, very different notions would possibly be entertained of their character and relation. Electricity, again, was named from the substance in which, and magnetism from the district where, it first happened to be observed, and a chain of intermediate phenomena have so connected electricity with galvanism that they are now regarded as the same force, differing only in the degree of its intensity and quantity, though for a long time they were regarded as distinct.

The phenomenon of attraction and repulsion by amber, which originated the term *electricity*, is as unlike that of the decomposition of water by the voltaic pile, as any two natural phenomena can well be. It is only because the historical sequence of scientific discoveries has associated them by a number of intermediate links, that they are classed under the same category. What is called voltaic electricity might equally, perhaps more appropriately, be called voltaic chemistry. I mention these facts to show that the distinction in the name may frequently be much greater than the distinction of the subject which it represents, and vice versâ, not as at all objecting to the received nomenclature on these points; nor do I say it would be advisable to depart from it: were we to do so, inevitable confusion would result, and objections equally forcible might be found to apply to our new terminology.

Words, when established to a certain point, become a part of the social mind; its powers and very existence depend upon the adoption of conventional symbols; and were these suddenly departed from, or varied, according to individual apprehensions, the acquisition and transmission of knowledge would cease. Undoubtedly, neology is more permissible in physical science than in any other branch of knowledge, because it is more progressive; new facts or new relations require new names, but even here it should be used with great caution.

Si forte necesse est
Indiciis monstrare recentibus abdita rerum,
Fingere cinctutis non exaudita Cethegis,
Continget; dabiturque licentia, sumpta pudenter.

Even should the mind ever be led to dismiss the idea of various forces, and regard them as the exertion of one force, or resolve them definitely into motion; still we could never avoid the use of different conventional terms for the different modes of action of this one pervading force.

Reviewing the series of relations between the various forces which we have been considering, it would appear that in many cases where one of these is excited or exists, all the others are also set in action: thus, when a substance, such as sulphuret of antimony, is electrified, at the instant of electrisation it becomes *magnetic* in directions at right angles to the lines of electric force; at the same time it becomes *heated* to an extent greater or less according to the intensity of the electric force. If this intensity be exalted to a certain point the sulphuret becomes luminous, or *light* is produced: it expands, consequently *motion* is produced; and it is decomposed, therefore *chemical action* is produced. If we take another substance, say a metal, all these forces except the last are developed; and although we can scarcely apply the term mechanical action to a substance hitherto undecomposed, and which, under the circumstances we are considering, enters into no new combination, yet it undergoes that species of polarisation which, as far as we can judge, is the first step towards chemical action, and which, if the substance were decomposable, would resolve it into its elements. Perhaps, indeed, some hitherto undiscovered chemical action is produced in substances which we regard as undecomposable: there are experiments to show that metals which have been electrised are permanently changed in their molecular constitution. Oxygen, we have seen, is changed by the electric spark into ozone, and phosphorus into allotropic phosphorus, both which changes were for a long time unknown to those familiar with electrical science.

Thus, with some substances, when one mode of force is produced all the others are simultaneously developed. With other substances, probably with all matter, some of the other forces are developed, whenever one is excited, and all may be so were the matter in a suitable condition for their developement, or our means of detecting them sufficiently delicate.

This simultaneous production of several different forces seems at first sight to be irreconcileable with their mutual and necessary dependence, and it certainly presents a formidable experimental difficulty in the way of establishing their equivalent relations; but when examined closely, it is not in fact inconsistent with the views we have been considering, but is indeed a strong argument in favour of the theory which regards them as modes of motion.

Let us select one or two cases in which this form of objection may be prominently put forward. A voltaic battery decomposing water in a voltameter, while the same current is employed at the same time to make an electro-magnet, gives nevertheless in the voltameter an equivalent of gas, or decomposes an equivalent of an electrolyte for each equivalent of chemical decomposition in the battery cells, and will give the same ratios if the electro-magnet be removed. Here, at first sight, it would appear that the magnetism was an extra force produced, and that thus more than the equivalent power was obtained from the battery. In answer to this objection it may be said, that in the circumstances under which this experiment is ordinarily performed, several cells of the battery are used, and so there is a far greater amount of force generated in the cells than is indicated by the effect in the voltameter. If, moreover, the magnet be not interposed, still the magnetic force is equally existent throughout the whole current; for instance, the wires joining the plates will attract iron filings, deflect magnetic needles, &c., and produce diamagnetic effects on surrounding matter. By the iron core a small portion of the force is, indeed, absorbed *while* it is being made a magnet, but this ceases to be absorbed when the magnet is made; this has been proved by the observation of Mr. Latimer Clarke, who has found that along the wires of the electric telegraph the magnetic needles placed at different stations remained fixed after the connection with the battery was made, and while the electric current acted by induction on surrounding conducting matter, separated from the wires by their gutta percha coating, so that a sort of Leyden phial was formed; but as soon as this induction had produced its effect between each station, or, so to speak, the phial was charged, the needles successively were deflected: it is like the case of a pulley and weight, which latter exhausts force while it is being raised; but when raised, the force is free, and may be used for other purposes.

If a battery of one cell, just capable of decomposing water and no more, be employed, this will cease to decompose while making a magnet. There must, in every case, be preponderating chemical affinity in the battery cells, either by the nature of its elements or by the reduplication of series, to effect decomposition in the voltameter; and if the point is just reached at which this is effected, and the power is then reduced by any resistance, decomposition ceases: were it otherwise, were the decomposition in the voltameter the exponent of the entire force of the generating cells, and these could independently produce magnetic force, this latter force would be got from nothing, and perpetual motion be obtained.

To take another and different example: A piece of zinc dissolved in dilute sulphuric acid gives somewhat less heat than when the zinc has a wire of platinum attached to it, and is dissolved by the same quantity of acid. The argument is deduced that, as there is more electricity in the second than in the first case, there should be less heat; but as, according to our received theories, the heat is a product of the electric current, and in consequence of the impurity of zinc electricity is generated in the first case molecularly, in what is called local action, though not thrown into a general direction, there should be more of both heat and electricity in the second than in the first case, as the heat and electricity due to the voltaic combination of zinc and platinum are added to that excited on the surface of the zinc, and the zinc should be, as in fact it is, more rapidly dissolved; so that the extra heat and electricity is produced by extra chemical force. Many additional cases of a similar description might be suggested. But although it is difficult, and perhaps impossible, to restrict the action of any one force to the production of one other force, and of one only—yet if the whole of one force, say chemical action, be supposed to be employed in producing its full equivalent of another force, say heat, then as this heat is capable in its turn of reproducing chemical action, and in the limit, a quantity equal or at least only infinitely short of the initial force: if this could at the same time produce independently another force, say magnetism, we could, by adding the magnetism to the total heat, get more than the original chemical action, and thus create force or obtain perpetual motion.

The term Correlation, which I selected as the title of my Lectures in 1843, strictly interpreted, means a necessary mutual or reciprocal dependence of two ideas, inseparable even in mental conception: thus, the idea of height cannot exist without involving the idea of its correlate, depth; the idea of parent cannot exist without involving the idea of offspring. It has been scarcely, if at all, used by writers on physics, but there are a vast variety of physical relations to which, if it does not in its strictest original sense apply, cannot certainly be so well expressed by any other term. There are, for example, many facts, one of which cannot take place without involving the other; one arm of a lever cannot be depressed without the other being elevated—the finger cannot press the table without the table pressing the finger. A body cannot be heated without another being cooled, or some other force being exhausted in an equivalent ratio to the production of heat; a body cannot be positively electrified without some other body being negatively electrified, &c.

The probability is, that, if not all, the greater number of physical phenomena are correlative, and that, without a duality of conception, the mind cannot form an idea of them: thus motion cannot be perceived or probably imagined without parallax or relative change of position. The world was believed fixed, until by comparison with the celestial bodies, it was found to change its place with regard to them: had there been no perceptible matter external to the world, we should never have discovered its motion. In sailing along a river, the stationary vessels and objects on the banks seem to move past the observer: if at last he arrives at the conviction that he is moving, and not these objects, it is by correcting his senses by reflection derived from a more extensive previous use of them: even then he can only form a notion of the motion of the vessel he is in, by its change of position with regard to the objects it passes—that is, provided his body partakes of the motion of the vessel, which it only does when its course is perfectly smooth, otherwise the relative change of position of the different parts of the body and the vessel inform him of its alternating, though not of its progressive movement. So in all physical phenomena, the effects produced by motion are all in proportion to the relative motion: thus, whether the rubber of an electrical machine be stationary, and the cylinder mobile, or the rubber mobile and the cylinder stationary, or both mobile in different directions, or in the same direction with different degrees of velocity, the electrical effects are, *cæteris paribus*, precisely the same, provided the relative motion is the same, and so, without exception, of all other phenomena. The question of whether there can be absolute motion, or, indeed, any absolute isolated force, is purely the metaphysical question of idealism or realism—a question for our purpose of little import; sufficient for the purely physical inquirer, the maxim '*de non apparentibus et non existentibus eadem est ratio.*'

The sense I have attached to the word correlation, in

treating of physical phenomena, will, I think, be evident from the previous parts of this essay, to be that of a necessary reciprocal production: in other words, that any force capable of producing another may, in its turn, be produced by it—nay, more, can be itself resisted by the force it produces, in proportion to the energy of such production, as action is ever accompanied and resisted by reaction: thus, the action of an electro-magnetic machine is reacted upon by the magneto-electricity developed by its action.

To many, however, of the cases we have been considering, the term correlation may be applied in a more strict accordance with its original sense: thus, with regard to the forces of electricity and magnetism in a dynamic state, we cannot electrise a substance without magnetising it—we cannot magnetise it without electrising it:—each molecule, the instant it is affected by one of these forces, is affected by the other; but, in transverse directions, the forces are inseparable and mutually dependent—correlative, but not identical.

The evolution of one force or mode of force into another has induced many to regard all the different natural agencies as reducible to unity, and as resulting from one force which is the efficient cause of all the others: thus, one author writes to prove that electricity is the cause of every change in matter; another, that chemical action is the cause of everything; another, that heat is the universal cause, and so on. If, as I have stated it, the true expression of the fact is, that each mode of force is capable of producing the others, and that none of them can be produced but by some other as an anterior force, then any view which regards either of them as abstractedly the efficient cause of all the rest, is erroneous; the view has, I believe, arisen from a confusion between the abstract or generalised meaning of the term cause, and its concrete or special sense; the word itself being indiscriminately used in both these senses.

Another confusion of terms has arisen, and has, indeed,

much embarrassed me in enunciating the propositions put forth in these pages, on account of the imperfection of scientific language; an imperfection in great measure unavoidable, it is true, but not the less embarrassing. Thus, the words light, heat, electricity, and magnetism, are constantly used in two senses—viz. that of the force producing, or the subjective idea of force or power, and of the effect produced, or the objective phenomenon. The word motion, indeed, is only applied to the effect, and not to the force, and the term chemical affinity is generally applied to the force, and not to the effect; but the other four terms are, for want of a distinct terminology, applied indiscriminately to both.

I may have occasionally used the same word at one time in a subjective, at another in an objective sense; all I can say is, that this cannot be avoided without a neology, which I have not the presumption to introduce, or the authority to enforce. Again, the use of the term forces in the plural might be objected to by those who do not attach to the term force the notion of a specific agency, but of one universal power associated with matter, of which its various phenomena are but diversely modified effects.

Whether the imponderable agents, viewed as force, and not as matter, ought to be regarded as distinct forces or as distinct modes of force, is probably not very material, for, as far as I am aware, the same result would follow either view; I have therefore used the terms indiscriminately, as either happened to be the more expressive for the occasion.

Throughout this essay I have placed motion in the same category as the other affections of matter. The course of reasoning adopted in it, however, appears to me to lead inevitably to the conclusion that these affections of matter are themselves modes of motion; that, as in the case of friction, the gross or palpable motion, which is arrested by the contact of another body, is subdivided into molecular motions or vibrations, which vibrations are heat or electricity, as the case may be; so the other affections are only matter moved or molecularly agitated in certain definite directions. We have already considered the hypothesis that the passage of electricity and magnetism causes vibrations in an ether permeating the bodies through which the current is transmitted, or the application of the same ethereal hypothesis to these imponderables which had previously been applied to light; many, in speaking of some of the effects, admit that electricity and magnetism cause or produce by their passage vibrations in the particles of matter, but regard the vibrations produced as an occasional, though not always a necessary, effect of the passage of electricity, or of the increment or decrement of magnetism. The view which I have taken is, that such vibrations, molecular polarisations, or motions of some sort from particle to particle, are themselves electricity or magnetism; or, to express it in the converse, that dynamic electricity and magnetism are themselves motion, and that permanent magnetism, and Franklinic electricity, are static conditions of force bearing a similar relation to motion which tension or gravitation do.

This theory might well be discussed in greater detail than has been used in this work; but to do this and to anticipate objections would lead into specialities foreign to my present object, in the course of this essay my principal aim having been rather to show the relation of forces as evinced by acknowledged facts, than to enter upon any detailed explanation of their specific modes of action.

Probably man will never know the ultimate structure of matter or the minutiæ of molecular actions; indeed it is scarcely conceivable that the mind can ever attain to this knowledge; the monad irresolvable by a given microscope may be resolved by an increase in power. Much harm has already been done by attempting hypothetically to dissect matter and to discuss the shapes, sizes, and numbers of atoms, and their atmospheres of heat, ether, or electricity.

Whether the regarding electricity, light, magnetism, &c., as simply motions of ordinary matter, be or be not admissible, certain it is, that all past theories have resolved, and all existing theories do resolve, the actions of these forces into motion. Whether it be that, on account of our familiarity with motion, we refer other affections to it, as to a language which is most easily construed and most capable of explaining them; whether it be that it is in reality the only mode in which our minds, as contradistinguished from our senses, are able to conceive material agencies; certain it is, that since the period at which the mystic notions of spiritual or preternatural powers were applied to account for physical phenomena, all hypotheses framed to explain them have resolved them into motion. Take, for example, the theories of light to which I have before alluded: one of these supposes light to be a highly rare matter, emitted from—i. e. put in *motion* by—luminous bodies; a second supposes that the matter is not emitted from luminous bodies, but that it is put into a state of vibration or undulation, i. e. *motion*, by them; and thirdly, light may be regarded as an undulation or *motion* of ordinary matter, and propagated by undulation of air, glass, &c., as I have before stated. In all these hypotheses, matter and motion are the only conceptions. Nor, if we accept terms derived from our own sensations, the which sensations themselves may be but modes of motion in the nervous filaments, can we find words to describe phenomena other than those expressive of matter and motion. We in vain struggle to escape from these ideas; if we ever do so, our mental powers must undergo a change of which at present we see no prospect.

If we apply to any other force the mode of reasoning which we have applied to heat, we shall arrive at the same conclusion, and see that a given source of power can, supposing it to be fully utilised in each case, yield no more by employing it as an exciter of one force than of another. Let us take electricity as an example. Suppose a pound of mercury at 400° be employed to produce a thermo-electric current, and the latter be in its turn employed to produce mechanical force; if this latter force be greater than that which the direct effect of heat would produce, then it could by compression raise the temperature of the mercury itself, or of a similar quantity equally heated, to a higher point than its original temperature, the 400° to 401°, for example, which is obviously impossible; nor, if we admit force to be indestructible, can it produce less than 400°, or cool the second body except by some portion of it being converted into another form or mode of force.

But as the mechanical effect here is produced through the medium of electricity, and the mechanical effect is definite, so the quantity of electricity producing it must be definite also, for unequal quantities of electricity could only produce an equal mechanical effect by a loss or gain of their own force into or out of nothing. The same reasoning will apply to the other forces, and will lead, it appears to me, necessarily and inevitably to the conclusion, that each force is definitely and equivalently convertible into any other, and that where experiment does not give the full equivalent, it is because the initial force has been dissipated, not lost, by conversion into other unrecognised forces. The equivalent is the limit never practically reached.

The great problem which remains to be solved, in regard to the correlation of physical forces, is this establishment of their equivalents of power, or their measurable relation to a given standard. The progress made in some of the branches of this inquiry has been already noticed. Viewed in their static relations, or in the conditions requisite for producing equilibrium or quantitative equality of force, a remarkable relation between chemical affinity and heat is that discovered in many simple bodies by Dulong and Petit, and extended to compounds by Neumann and Avogadro. Their researches have shown that the specific heats of certain substances, when multiplied by their chemical equivalents, give a constant quantity as product—or, in other words, that the combining weights of such substances are those weights which require equal accessions or abstractions of heat, equally to raise or lower their temperature. To put the proposition more in accordance with the view we have taken of the nature of heat: each body has a power of communicating or receiving molecular repulsive power, exactly equal, weight for weight, to its chemical or combining power. For instance, the equivalent of lead is 104, of zinc 33, or, in round numbers, as 3 to 1: these numbers are therefore inversely the exponents of their chemical power, three times as much lead as zinc being required to saturate the same quantity of an acid or substance combining with it; but their power of communicating or abstracting heat or repulsive power is precisely the same, for three times as much lead as zinc is required to produce the same amount of expansion or contraction in a given quantity of a third substance, such as water.

Again, a great number of bodies chemically combine in equal volumes, i. e. in the ratios of their specific gravities; but the specific gravities represent the attractive powers of the substance, or are the numerical exponents of the forces tending to produce motion in masses of matter towards each other; while the chemical equivalents are the exponents of the affinities or tendencies of the molecules of dissimilar substances to combine, and saturate each other; consequently, here we have to some extent an equivalent relation between these two modes of force—gravitation and chemical attraction.

Were the above relations extended into an universal law, we should have the same numerical expression for the three forces of heat, gravity, and affinity; and as electricity and magnetism are quantitatively related to them, we should have a similar expression for these forces: but at present the bodies in which this parity of force has been discovered, though in themselves numerous, are small compared with the exceptions, and, therefore, this point can only be indicated as promising a generalisation, should subsequent researches alter our knowledge as to the elements and combining equivalents of matter.

With regard to what may be called dynamic equivalents, i. e. the definite relation to time of the action of these varied forces upon equivalents of matter, the difficulty of establishing them is still greater. If the proposition which I stated at the commencement of this paper be correct, that motion may be subdivided or changed in character, so as to become heat, electricity, &c., it ought to follow that when we collect the dissipated and changed forces, and reconvert them, the initial motion, minus an infinitesimal quantity affecting the same amount of matter with the same velocity, should be reproduced, and so of the changes in matter produced by the other forces; but the difficulties of proving the truth of this by experiment will, in many cases, be all but insuperable; we cannot imprison motion as we can matter, though we may to some extent restrain its direction.

The term perpetual motion, which I have not unfrequently employed in these pages, is itself equivocal. If the doctrines here advanced be founded, all motion is, in one sense, perpetual. In masses whose motion is stopped by mutual concussion, heat or motion of the particles is generated; and thus the motion continues, so that if we could venture to extend such thoughts to the universe, we should assume the same amount of motion affecting the same amount of matter for ever. Where force opposes force, as in cases of static equilibrium, the balance of pre-existing equilibrium is affected, and fresh motion is started equivalent to that which is withdrawn into a state of abeyance.

But the term perpetual motion is applied, in ordinary parlance (and in such sense I have used it), to a perpetual recurrent motion, e.g. a weight which by its fall would turn a wheel, which wheel would, in its turn, raise the initial weight, and so on forever, or until the material of which the machine is made be worn out. It is strange that to common apprehension the impossibility of this is not self-evident: if the initial weight is to be raised by the force it has itself generated, it must necessarily generate a force greater than that of its own weight or centripetal attraction; in other words, it must be capable of raising a weight heavier than itself: so that, setting aside the resistance of friction, &c., a weight, to produce perpetual recurrent motion, must be heavier than an equal weight of matter, in short, heavier than itself.

Suppose two equal weights at each end of an equi-armed lever, there is no motion; cut off a fraction of one of them, and it rises while the other falls. How, now, is the lesser weight to bring back the greater without any extraneous application of force? If, as is obvious, it cannot do so in this simple form of experiment, it is *à fortiori* more impossible if machinery be added, for increased resistances have then to be overcome. Can we again mend this by employing any other force? Suppose we employ electricity, the initial weight in descending turns a cylinder against a cushion, and so generates electricity; to make this force recurrent, the electricity so generated must, in its turn, raise the initial weight, or one heavier than it, i. e. the initial weight must, through the medium of electricity, raise a weight heavier than itself. The same problem, applied to any other forces, will involve the same absurdity: and yet simple as the matter seems, the world is hardly yet disabused of an idea little removed from superstition.

But the importance of the deductions to be derived from the negation of perpetual motion seems scarcely to have impressed philosophers, and we only find here and there a scattered hint of the consequences necessarily resulting from that which to the thinking mind is a conviction. Some of these I have ventured to put forward in the present essay, but many remain, and will crowd upon the mind of those who pursue the subject. Does not, for instance, the impossibility of perpetual motion, when thought out, involve the demonstration of the impossibility, to which I have previously alluded, of any event identically recurring?

The pendulum in vacuo, at each beat leaves a portion of the force which started it in the form of heat at its point of suspension: this force, though ever existent, can never be restored in its integrity to the ball of the pendulum, for in the process of restoration it must affect other matter, and alter the condition of the universe. To restore the initial force to its integrity, everything as it existed at the moment of the first beat of the pendulum must be restored in its integrity: but how can this be—for while the force was escaping from the pendulum by radiating heat from the point of suspension, surrounding matter has not stood still; the very attraction which caused the beat of the pendulum has changed in degree, for the pendulum is nearer to or further from the sun, or from some planet or fixed star.

It might be an interesting and not profitless speculation to follow out these and other consequences; it would, I believe, lead us to the conviction that the universe is ever changing, and that notwithstanding secular recurrences which would primâ facie seem to replace matter in its original position, nothing in fact ever returns or can return to a state of existence identical with a previous state. But the field is too illimitable for me to venture further.

The inevitable dissipation or throwing off a portion of the initial force presents a great experimental difficulty in the way of establishing the equivalents of the various natural forces. In the steam-engine, for instance, the heat of the furnace not only expands the water and thereby produces the motion of the piston, but it also expands the iron of the boiler, of the cylinder and all surrounding bodies. The force expended in expanding this iron to a very small extent is equal to that which expands the vapour to a very large extent: this expansion of the iron is capable, in its turn, of producing a great mechanical force, which is practically lost. Could all the force be applied to the vapour, an enormous addition of power would be gained for the same expenditure: and perhaps even with our present means more might be done in utilising the expansion of the iron.

Another great difficulty in experimentally ascertaining the dynamic equivalents of different forces arises from the effects of disruption, or the overcoming an existing force. Thus, when a part of the initial force employed is engaged in twisting or tearing asunder matter previously held together by cohesive attraction, or in overcoming gravitation or inertia, the same amount of heat or electricity would not be evolved as if such obstacle were non-existent, and the initial force were wholly employed in producing, not in opposing. There is a difficulty apparently extreme in devising experiments in which some portion of the force is not so employed.

The initial force, however, that has been employed for such disruption is not lost, as at the moment of disruption the bodies producing it fly off, and carry with them their force. Thus, let two weights be attached to a cord placed across a bar; when their force is sufficient to break the cord or the bar, the weights fall down and strike the earth, making it vibrate, and so conveying away or continuing the force expressed by the cohesion of the bar or cord. If, instead of breaking a cord, the weights be employed to bend a bar, their gravitating force, instead of making the earth vibrate, produces heat in the bar, and so with whatever other force be employed to produce effects of disruption, torsion, &c., so that, though difficult in practice, the numerical problem of the equivalent of the force is not theoretically irresolvable

The voltaic battery affords us the best means of ascertaining the dynamic equivalents of different forces, and it is probable that by its aid the best theoretical and practical results will be ultimately attained.

In investigating the relation of the different forces, I have in turn taken each one as the initial force or starting-point, and endeavoured to show how the force thus arbitrarily selected could mediately or immediately produce and be merged into the others: but it will be obvious to those who have attentively considered the subject, and brought their minds into a general accordance with the views I have submitted to them, that no force can, strictly speaking, be initial, as there must be some anterior force which produced it: we cannot create force or motion any more than we can create matter.

Thus, to take an example previously noticed, and recede backwards; the spark of light is produced by electricity, electricity by motion, and motion is produced by something else, say a steam-engine—that is, by heat. This heat is produced by chemical affinity, i.e. the affinity of the carbon of the coal for the oxygen of the air: this carbon and this oxygen have been previously eliminated by actions difficult to trace, but of the pre-existence of which we cannot doubt, and in which actions we should find the conjoint and alternating effects of heat, light, chemical affinity, &c. Thus, tracing any force backwards to its antecedents, we are merged in an infinity of changing forms of force; at some point we lose it, not because it has been in fact created at any definite point, but because it resolves itself into so many contributing forces, that the evidence of it is lost to our senses or powers of detection; just as in following it forward into the effect it produces, it becomes, as I have before stated, so subdivided and dissipated as to be equally lost to our means of detection.

Can we, indeed, suggest a proposition, definitely conceivable by the mind, of force without antecedent force? I cannot, without calling for the interposition of created power, any more than I can conceive the sudden appearance of a mass of matter come from nowhere, and formed from nothing. The impossibility, humanly speaking, of creating or annihilating matter, has long been admitted, though, perhaps, its distinct reception in philosophy may be set down to the overthrow of the doctrine of Phlogiston, and the reformation of chemistry at the time of Lavoisier. The reasons for the admission of a similar doctrine as to force appear to be equally strong. With regard to matter, there are many cases in which we never practically prove its cessation of existence, yet we do not the less believe in it: who, for instance, can trace, so as to re-weigh, the particles of iron worn off the tire of a carriage wheel? who can re-combine the particles of wax dissipated and chemically changed in the burning of a candle? By placing matter undergoing physical or chemical changes under special limiting circumstances, we may, indeed, acquire evidence of its continued existence, weight for weight—and so we may in some instances of force, as in definite electrolysis: indeed the evidence we acquire of the continued existence of matter is by the continued exertion of the force it exercises, as, when we weigh it, our evidence is the force of attraction; so, again, our evidence of force is the matter it acts upon. Thus, matter and force are correlates, in the strictest sense of the word; the conception of the existence of the one involves the conception of the existence of the other: the quantity of matter again, and the degree of force, involve conceptions of space and time. But to follow out these abstract relations would lead me too far into the alluring paths of metaphysical speculation.

That the theoretical portions of this essay are open to objection I am fully conscious. I cannot, however, but think that the fair way to test a theory is to compare it with other theories, and to see whether upon the whole the balance of probability is in its favour. Were a theory open to no objection it would cease to be a theory, and become a law; and were we not to theorise, or to take generalised views of natural phenomena until those generalizations were sure and unobjectionable—in other words, were laws—science would be lost in a complex mass of unconnected observations, which would probably never disentangle themselves. Excess on either side is to be avoided; although we may often err on the side of hasty generalisation, we may equally err on the side of mere elaborate collection of observations, which, though sometimes leading to a valuable result, yet, when cumulated without a connecting link, frequently occasion a costly waste of time, and leave the subject to which they refer in greater obscurity than that in which it was involved at their commencement.

Collections of facts differ in importance, as do theories: the former, in many instances, derive their value from their capability of generalisation; while, conversely, theories are valuable as methods of co-ordinating given series of facts, and more valuable in proportion as they require fewer exceptions and fewer postulates. Facts may sometimes be as well explained by one view as by another, but without a theory they are unintelligible and incommunicable. Let us use our utmost effort to communicate a fact without using the language of theory, and we fail; theory is involved in all our expressions; the knowledge of bygone times is imported into succeeding times by terms involving theoretic conceptions. As the knowledge of any particular science developes itself our views of it become more simple; hypotheses, or the introduction of supposititious views, are more and more dispensed with; words become applicable more directly to the phenomena, and, losing the hypothetic meaning which they necessarily possessed at their reception, acquire a secondary sense, which brings more immediately to our minds the facts of which they are indices. The scaffolding has served its purpose. The hypothesis fades away, and a theory, or generalised view of phenomena, more independent of supposition, but still full of gaps and difficulties, takes its place. This in its turn, should the science continue to progress, either gives place to a more simple and wider generalisation, or becomes, by the removal of objections, established as a law. Even in this more advanced stage, words importing theory must be used, but phenomena are now intelligible and connected, though expressed by varied forms of speech.

To think on nature is to theorise; and difficult it is not to be led on by the continuities of natural phenomena to theories which appear forced and unintelligible to those who have not pursued the same path of thought: which, moreover, if allowed to gain an undue influence, seduce us from that truth which is the sole object of our pursuit.

Where to draw the line—where to say thus far we may go, and no farther, in any particular class of analogies or relations which Nature presents to us; how far to follow the progressive indications of thought, and where to resist its allurements—is a question of degree which must depend upon the judgment of each individual or of each class of thinkers; yet it is consolatory that thought is seldom expended in vain.

I have throughout endeavoured to discard the hypotheses of subtle or occult entities; if in this endeavour some of my views have been adopted upon insufficient data, I still hope that this essay will not prove valueless.

The conviction that the so-called imponderables are modes of motion, will, at all events, lead the observer of natural phenomena to look for changes in these affections, wherever the intimate structure of matter is changed; and, conversely, to seek for changes in matter, either temporary or permanent, whenever it is affected by these forces. I believe he will seldom do this in vain. It was not until I had long reflected on the subject, that I ventured to publish my views: their publication may induce others to think on their subject-matter. They are not put forward with the same objects, nor do they aim at the same elaboration of detail, as memoirs on newly-discovered physical facts: they purport to be a method of mentally regarding known facts, some few of which I have myself made known on other occasions, but the great mass of which have been accumulated by the labours of others, and are admitted as established truths. Every one has a right to view these facts through any medium he thinks fit to employ, but some theory must exist in the minds of those who reflect upon the many new phenomena which have recently, and more particularly during the present century, been discovered. It is by a generalised or connected view of past acquisitions in natural knowledge that deductions can best be drawn as to the probable character of the results to be anticipated. It is a great assistance in such investigations to be intimately convinced that no physical phenomena can stand alone: each is inevitably connected with anterior changes, and as inevitably productive of consequential changes, each with the other, and all with time and space; and, either in tracing back these antecedents or following up their consequents, many new phenomena will be discovered, and many existing phenomena, hitherto believed distinct, will be connected and explained: explanation is, indeed, only relation to something more familiar, not more known—i.e. known as to causative or creative agencies. In all phenomena the more closely they are investigated the more are we convinced that, humanly speaking, neither matter nor force can be created or annihilated, and that an essential cause is unattainable.—Causation is the will, Creation the act, of God.

NOTES AND REFERENCES.

PAGE

13. The reader who is curious as to the views of the ancients, regarding the objects of science, will find clues to them in the second book of Aristotle's Physics, and in the first three books of the Metaphysics. See also the Timæus of Plato, and Ritter's History of Ancient Philosophy, where a sketch of the Philosophy of Leucippus and Democritus will be found.

14. Bacon's Novum Organum, book ii. aph. 5 and 6.

16 Hume's Enquiry concerning Human Understanding, S. 7, London, 1768.

Brown's Enquiry into the Relations of Cause and Effect, London, 1835.

The illustration I have used of floodgate has been objected to, as being one to which the term cause would scarcely be applied, but after some consideration I have retained it: if cause be viewed only as sequence, it must be limited to sequence under given conditions or circumstances, and here, given the conditions, the sequence is invariable. I see no difference *quoad* the argument, between this illustration and that of Brown of a lighted match and gunpowder (4th edit. p. 27), to which my reasoning would equally well apply.

Herschel's Discourse on the Study of Natural Philosophy, pp. 88 and 149.

17. Quarterly Review, vol. lxviii. p. 212.

Whewell, On the Question 'Are Cause and Effect Successive or Simultaneous? (Cambridge Philosophical Transactions, vol. vii. p. 319.)

18. Herschel's Discourse, p. 93.

Ampere, Théorie des Phénomènes Electro-dynamiques, Memoirs in

PAGE

the Ann. de Chimie et de Physique, and works from 1820 to 1826 Paris.

23. LAMARCK, 'Sur la Matière du Son' (Journal de Physique, vol. xlix. p. 397).

25. D'ALEMBERT, Traité de Dynamique, pp. 3 and 4, Paris, 1796.

28. BABBAGE, On the Permanent Impression of our Words and Actions on the Globe we inhabit, 9th Bridgewater Treatise, ch. ix.

30. MAYER, Annalen der Pharmacie Leibig und Wohler, May 1852.

33. JOULE on the Mechanical Equivalent of Heat (Phil. Trans. 1850, p. 61.)

33. ERMAN, Influence of Friction upon Thermo-electricity (Reports of the British Association, 1845.)

35. BECQUEREL, Dégagement de l'Electricité par Frottement, Traité de l'Electricité, tom. ii. p. 113 et seq.

36. SULLIVAN, Currents produced by the vibration of metals (Archiv. de l'Electricité, t. 10, p. 480). LEROUX, Vibrations arrested produce heat (Cosmos, March 30, 1860).

37. WHEATSTONE on the Prismatic Decomposition of Electrical Light (Notices of Communications to the British Association, p. 11, 1835).

39. BACON, De Formâ Calidi, Nov. Org. book 2, aph. 20.

RUMFORD, An Enquiry concerning the Source of Heat which is excited by Friction (Phil. Trans. p. 80, 1798).

DAVY, On the Conversion of Ice into Water by Friction (West of England Contributions, p. 16).

Of Heat or Calorific Repulsion (Elements of Chemical Philosophy, p. 69).

41. BADEN POWELL on the Repulsive Power of Heat (Phil. Trans. 1834, p. 485).

FRESNEL, Annales de Chimie, tom. xxix. pp. 57 and 107.

42. MOSER on Invisible Light (Taylor's Scientific Memoirs, vol. iii. pp. 461 and 465).

43. BLACK on Latent Heat (Elements of Chemistry, p. 144 et passim, 1803).

45. The experiments of HENRY and DONNY have shown that the cohesion of liquids, as far as their antagonism to rupture goes, is much greater than has been generally believed. These experiments, however, make no difference in the view I have put forth, as, whatever be the character of the attraction, there is a molecular attraction to be overcome in changing bodies from the solid to the liquid state, which must require and exhaust force.

PAGE

DONNY, Sur la Cohésion des Liquides (Mémoires de l'Académie Royale de Bruxelles, 1843).

HENRY, Proceedings of the American Philosophical Society, April 1844 (Silliman's Journal, vol. xlviiii. p. 215).

48. THILORIER, Solidification de l'Acide carbonique (Ann. de Ch. et de Phys. tom. lx. p. 432).

50. I. WEDGWOOD, Thermometer for measuring the Higher Degrees of Heat (Phil. Trans. 1782, p. 305; and 1785, p. 390.

TYNDALL, on the physical properties of Ice (Phil. Trans. 1858, p. 211).

DESPRETZ, Recherches sur le Maximum de Densité de l'Eau pure et des Dissolutions aqueuses (Ann. de. Ch. et de Ph. tom. lxx. p. 45, and tom. lxxiii. p. 295).

51. BIOT (Comptes rendus de l'Académie des Sciences, Paris 1850, p. 281). The experiments on circular polarisation by water were, I believe, by Dr. Leeson.

52. I. THOMPSON, Trans. R. S. Edin. vol. xvi. p. 575.

W. THOMPSON, Phil. Mag. August 1850, p. 123.

BUNSEN, Pogg. Ann. vol. lxxxi. p. 562; Ann. de Ch. et de Phys. vol. xxxv. p. 383. Effects of Pressure on the Freezing Point.

53. JOULE, Phil. Trans. 1852, p. 99.

Although, taking the phenomena as they are known to exist, the mechanical laws may be deduced, yet in any physical conception of the nature of heat the expansion by cold has always been a great stumbling-block to me, and I believe to many others.

DULONG and PETIT, and REGNAULT. See their Memoirs abstracted and referred to in Gmelin's Handbook of Chemistry, translated by Watts for the Cavendish Society, vol. i. p. 242 et seq.

54. WOOD, Phil. Mag. 1851, 1852.

56. SENARMONT, Conduction of Heat by Crystals (Gmelin's Handbook vol. i. p. 222).

56. KNOBLAUCH, Ann. de Ch. et de Ph. vol. xxxvi. p. 124.

TYNDALL, Transmission of Heat through Organic Structures (Phil. Trans. vol. cxliii. p. 217).

58. GROVE, Electricity produced by approximating Metals: Report of a Lecture at the London Institution (Literary Gazette, 1843, p. 39).

GASSIOT, Phil. Mag. October 1844.

ROGET, On the Improbability of the Contact exciting Force: Treatise on Galvanism (Library of Useful Knowledge, S. 113).

FARADAY, Phil. Trans. 1840, p. 126.

PAGE

60. MELLONI, Sur la Polarisation de la Chaleur: Recherches sur plusieurs Phénomènes calorifiques (Annales de Chimie et de Ph. tom. xlv. pp. 5—68; tom. xli. pp. 375–410; tom. xlviii. pp. 198, 218).

FORBES, On the Refraction and Polarisation of Heat (Transactions of the Royal Society of Edinburgh, vol. xiii. pp. 131, 168).

61. KIRCHOFF Trans. Belin Acad. 1861.

BALFOUR STEWART on the theory of Exchanges (Report British Association, 1861).

63. T. WEDGWOOD, On the Production of Light and Heat by different Bodies (Phil. Trans. vol. lxxxii. p. 272).

65. GROVE, On the Decomposition of Water into its Constituent Gases by Heat (Phil. Trans. 1847, p. 1).

ROBINSON, On the Effect of Heat in lessening the Affinities of the Elements of Water (Transactions of the Royal Irish Academy, vol. xxi. p. 2).

67. GROVE, Water decomposed by Chlorine and Heat (Phil. Trans. 1847, p. 20).

70. CARNOT, Réflexions sur la Puissance motrice du Feu, Paris, 1824.

76. SEGUIN, Influence des Chemins de Fer, p. 378 et seq.

77. ROGERS, Consumption of Coal for Man power (Cosmos, vol. ii. p. 56).

80. Mr. WATERSTON has suggested that solar heat may arise from the mechanical action of meteoric stones falling into the sun, and Mr. THOMPSON has written an elaborate paper on the subject (Trans. Brit. Assoc. 1853). If a number of gravitating bodies exist in the neighbourhood of the sun, and form, as is conjectured, the zodiacal light, it is difficult to conceive how comets as they approach this region steer clear of such bodies, and are not even deflected from their orbits.

For Mr. THOMPSON'S various and valuable papers, see Phil. Mag. 1851 to 1854 inclusive.

81. POISSON, Comptes rendus, Paris, January 30, 1837.

83. DUFAYE, SYMMER, WATSON, and FRANKLIN, Theories of Electric Fluid and Electric Fluids (Priestley's History of Electricity, pp. 429—441).

83. GROTTHUS, Sur la Décomposition de l'Eau et des Corps qu'elle tient en dissolution à aide de l'Electricité galvanique (Ann. de Chimie, tom. lviii. p. 54).

FARADAY, On the Question whether Electrolytes conduct without Decomposition (Proceedings of the Weekly Meetings of the Royal Institution, 1855).

GROVE (Comptes rendus, Paris, 1839).

PAGE

84. Faraday, On Induction as an Action of contiguous Particles (Phil. Trans. 1838, p. 30).

85. Matteucci, Plates of Mica polarised by Electricity (De la Rive's Electricity, p. 140).

Grove, Electrolysis across Glass (Phil. Mag. Aug. 1860).

85. Karsten on Electrical Figures (Archiv. de l'Elec. vols. ii. iii. and iv).

87. Grove, Etching Electrical Figures and transferring them to Collodion (Phil. Mag. January 1857).

88. Fusinieri, Du Transport des Matières pondérable qui s'opère dans les Décharges électriques (Archives de l'Electricité ; Supplément à la Bibliothèque universelle de Genève, tom. iii. p. 597).

88. Grove, On the Voltaic Arc (Report of Lecture at the Royal Institution, Lit. Gaz. and Athenæum, Feb. 7, 1845 ; Phil. Trans. 1847, p. 16).

90 to 94. Grove, On the Electro-chemical Polarity of Gases (Phil. Trans. 1852, p. 87).

94. Fremy and E. Becquerel, Oxygen changed to Ozone by the Electric Spark (Ann. de Ch. et de Phys. 1852). This subject and the nature of Ozone was first investigated by Dr. Schönbein. See also a paper by Mr. Brodie On the Conditions of certain Elements at the Moment of Chemical Change (Phil. Trans. 1850).

95, 96. Molecular Changes in Electrised Metals (Nairne, Phil. Trans. 1780, p. 334, and 1793, p. 223 ; Grove, Electrical Mag. vol. i. p. 120 ; Peltier, Archives de l'Electricité, vol. v. p. 182 ; Fusinieri, id. p. 516).

96. Wertheim, Change in Elasticity of Metals by Electrisation (Ann. de Ch. et de Phys. vol. xii. p. 623 ; Arch. Elec. vol. iv. p. 490).

Dufour, Alteration in Tenacity of Metals by Electrisation (Bibl. univ. de Genève, Fev. 1855, p. 156).

97. Matteucci, Conduction of Electricity by Crystals (Comptes rendus de l'Acad., Paris, March, 5, 1855, p. 541).

98. E. Becquerel, Transmission of Electricity by heated Gases (Ann. de. Ch. et de Phys. vol. xxxix. p. 355).

Grove, Proceedings of the Royal Inst. (1854, p. 361).

Becquerel, Divergence of Gold-Leaves in Vacuo (Traité d'Electricité, vol. v.; part ii. p. 53).

Newton, Thirty-first Query to the Optics.

99. Grove, Particles of Metals and Metallic Oxids detached in Liquids by Electricity (Elec. Mag. vol. i. p. 119).

100. Matteucci, Relations of Electricity and Nervous Force (Phil. Trans.

PAGE

1845, p. 285, 1846, p. 497; Phénomènes physiques des Corps vivants, p. 305; Lezioni di Fisica, p. 360).

GALVANI VOLTA MARIANINI et NOBILI on Physiological Effects of Electricity (Ann. de Ch. et de Phys. vols. 23, 25, 29, 38, 40, 43, 44, 56).

102. BECQUEREL, Chemical Changes by Friction (Traité de l'Elec. vol. v. part 1, p. 16).

106. DE LA RIVE, Heat of the Voltaic Pile (Bibl. univ., vol. xiii. p. 389).

DAVY, On the Properties of Electrified Bodies in their relations to Conducting Powers and Temperature (Phil. Trans. 1821, p. 428).

106. GROVE, On the Effects of surrounding Media on Voltaic Ignition (Phil. Trans. 1849, p. 49).

107. OERSTED, Expérience sur l'Effet du Conflict électrique sur l'Aiguille aimantée (Ann. de Ch. et de Phys., tom. xiv. p. 417).

108. COLERIDGE, Table Talk, vol. i. p. 65.

109. LENZ and JACOBI, Pogg. Ann. vol. xvlii. p. 403; Bulletin de l'Acad. St. Petersburg, 1839; Harris, Magnetism, part 2, p. 63.

DAVY, Decomposition of the fixed Alkalies (Phil. Trans. 1808, p. 1).

BECQUEREL Des Composés électro-chimiques (Traité de l'Electricité, vol. iii. c. 13).

CROSSE, Transactions of the British Association, vol. v. p. 47; Proceedings of the Electrical Society, p. 320.

110. MALUS, Polarisation of Light by Reflection (Mémoires d'Arcueil, tom. ii. p. 143).

ARAGO, Circular Polarisation by Solids (Mémoires de l'Institut, 1811).

111. BIOT, Circular Polarisation by Liquids (Mémoires de l'Institut, 1817).

111. NIEPCE and DAGUERRE, Historique et Description des Procédés du Daguerréotype, Paris, 1839.

TALBOT, Photogenic Drawing and Calotype (Phil. Mag. March. 1839, and August 1841).

113. HERSCHEL, Chemical Action of the Solar Spectrum on various Substances (Phil. Trans. 1840, p. i. and 1842, p. 181).

HUNT, Researches on Light, London, 1844.

116. GROVE, Other Forces produced by Light (Lit. Gaz. January 1844).

117. GROVE, Influence of Light on the Polarised Electrode (Phil. Mag. December 1858).

SOMERVILLE (Mrs.), On the Magnetising Power of the more Refrangible Solar Rays (Phil. Trans. 1862, p. 132).

MORICHINI's experiments are given in Mrs. Somerville's paper.

118. HERSCHEL, On the Absorption of Light in Coloured Media viewed

PAGE

in connection with the Undulatory Theory (Phil. Mag. December 1863).

SEEBECK, Heat of Coloured Rays (Brewster's Optics, p. 90).

118. KNOBLAUCH (Ann. de Ch. vol. xxxvi. p. 124, and Pogg. Ann. there referred to).

119. HERSCHEL, Epipolised Light (Phil. Trans. vol. cxxxv. pp. 143, 147).

STOKES, Change in Refrangibility of Light (Phil. Trans. vols. cxlii. cxliii.)

123. For the first enunciations of the Corpuscular and Undulatory Theories, see NEWTON'S Optics, HOOKE'S Micographia, and HUYGHENS' Tractatus de Lumine. See also BREWSTER'S Optics, p. 138.

124. YOUNG, Lectures edited by Kelland, p. 358, et seq.; Phil. Trans. 1800, p. 126; HERSCHEL, Encyc. Metro. art. Light, pp. 450 and 738; NEWTON'S Optics, p. 322; WHEWELL'S Hist. Induc. Sc. vol. ii. p. 449; FOUCAULT, Comptes rendus, Paris, 1850, p. 65; HARRISON, Phil. Mag. November 1856; Camb. Phil. Trans.

126. SONDHAUSS, Refraction of Sound (Ann. de Ch. et de Phys. vol. xxxv. p. 505); DOVÉ, Polarisation of Sound (Cosmos, May 13, 1859).

132. PASTEUR, Rotation of Plane of Polarised Light by Solutions of Hemihedral Crystals (Ann. de Ch. et de Phys. vol. xxiv. p. 442).

134 to 135. WOLLASTON, Phil. Trans. 1822, p. 89; WHEWELL, Phil. of the Induct. Sc. vol. i. p. 419; WILSON, Trans. of the Roy. Soc. of Edin. vol. xvi. p. 79; Sir W. HERSCHEL, Phil. Trans. 1793, p. 201, and 1801, p. 300; MORGAN, Phil. Trans. vol. lxxv. p. 272; DAVY, Phil. Trans. 1822, p. 64; Elements of Chemical Philosophy, p. 97; GASSIOT, Phil. Trans. 1859, p. 157.

137. Diminishing Periods of Comets (Herschel's Outlines of Astronomy, p. 357).

140. Since writing the passage in the text, I find that STRUVE has been led, from his astronomical researches, to the conclusion that some light is lost in the interplanetary spaces. He gives as an approximation one per cent. as lost by the passage of light from a star of the first magnitude, assuming a mean or average distance (Etudes d'Astronomie Stellaire, 1847).

NEWTON, Thirtieth Query to the Optics.

142. FARADAY, Evolution of Electricity from Magnetism (Phil. Trans. 1832, p. 125).

144. FARADAY, Magnetic Condition of all Matter (Phil. Trans. 1846, p. 21; Phil. Mag. 1846, p. 249).

BECQUEREL, Ann. de Ch. et de Ph. tom. xxxvi. p. 337; Comptes rendus, Paris, 1846, p. 147; and 1850, p. 201.

PAGE

145. Faraday, On the Magnetism of Light (Phil. Trans. 1846, p. 1).

145. Wartmann, Rotation of the Plane of Polarisation of Heat by Magnetism (Journal de l'Institute, No. 644).
Provostaye and Dessaines, Ann. de Ch. et de Phys. October 1849.

146. Hunt, Influence of Magnetism on Molecular Arrangement (Phil. Mag 1846, vol. xxviii. p. 1; Memoirs of the Geological Society, vol. i p. 433).
Wartmann, Phil. Mag. 1847, vol. xxx. p. 263.

147. Grove, Experiment on Molecular Motion of a Magnetic Substance (Electrical Mag. 1845, vol. i. p. 601).

147. On the direct Production of Heat by Magnetism (Proceedings of the Royal Society, 1849, p. 826).
After this paper was communicated and ordered to be printed in the Philosophical Transactions, I found that I had been anticipated by Mr. Van Breda, who communicated, in 1845, a paper to the Institut on the subject: his paper appears in the Comptes rendus under an erroneous title, which accounts for its having been overlooked: he does not give thermometric measures of the heat he obtained, nor did he produce heating effects by a permanent steel magnet, or with other metals than iron. (Comptes rendus, October 27, 1845). See also an earlier experiment by Mr. Joule (Phil. Mag. 1843), to which he called my attention after my paper was read.

148, 151. The Experiments on the effects of Magnetism on the Matter magnetised, are collected by Mr. De la Rive in his recently-published Treatise on Electricity, vol. i.

153. Davy, Electricity defined as Chemical affinity acting on Masses (Phil. Trans. 1826, p. 009).
Volta, Electricity excited by the mere Contact of conducting Substances (Phil. Trans. 1800, p. 403).

154. Grove, Gold-Leaf Experiment (Comptes rendus, Paris, 1839, p. 567).

155. Grove, Voltaic Action of Sulphur, Phosphorus, and Hydrocarbons (Phil. Trans. 1845, p. 351).
Grove, New Voltaic Combination (Phil. Mag. vol. xiv. p. 388; vol. xv. p. 287).

155. Grove, Electricity of Blowpipe Flame (Proceedings of the Royal Institution, February 1854), Phil. Mag.

157. Dalton, New System of Chemistry, London, 1810.

158. I have here and elsewhere used whole numbers, as sufficiently approximate for the argument, but without intending to express any opinion as to the law of Prout.

158. Faraday, Definite Electrolysis (Phil. Trans. 1834, p. 77).

PAGE

160. WOOD, Heat disengaged in Chemical Combinations (Phil. Mag. 1852)

162. ANDREWS, Phil. Trans. 1844, p. 21.
HESS, Poggendoff's Annalen, Bd. lii. p. 197.

163. FAVRE, Ann. de Ch. et de Phys. vols. 39, 40; Comptes rendus, Paris, vol. 45, p. 56, and vol. 46, p. 337.

169. CATALYSIS by Platinum (DOBEREIMER, Ann. de Ch. et de Phys. tom. xxiv. p. 93; DULONG and THENARD, Ann. de Ch. et de Phys. tom. xxiii. p. 440).

170. GROVE, Gas Voltaic Battery (Phil. Mag. February 1839, and December 1842; Phil. Trans. 1843, p. 91).

171. MOSOTTI, Forces which regulate the Internal Constitution of Bodies (Taylor's Scientific Memoirs, vol. i. p. 448).

172. PLUCKER, Repulsion of the Optic Axes of Crystals by the Poles of a Magnet (Taylor's Scientific Memoirs, vol. v. p. 353).
Magnetic Action of Cyanite (Lit. Gaz. 1849, p. 431).

172. MATTEUCCI, Correlation of Electric Current and Nervous Force (Phil. Trans. 1850, p. 287).

173. CARPENTER, On the Mutual Relations of the Vital and Physical Forces (Phil. Trans. 1850, p. 751).

174. On Effort. See BROWN, Cause and Effect; HERSCHEL'S Discourse; and QUARTERLY REVIEW, June 1841.

175. HELMHOLTZ, Muller's Archives, 1845; MATTEUCCI, Comptes rendus, Paris, 1856; BECLARD, Archives de Medicine, 1861.

189. DULONG and PETIT, Relation between Specific Heat and Chemical Equivalents (Ann. de Ch. et de Phys. tom. x. p. 395).

189. NEUMANN, Poggendorff's Annalen, Bd. xxiii. p. 1.
AVOGADRO, Ann. de Ch. et de Phys. tom. lv. p. 80.

ON THE

INTERACTION OF NATURAL FORCES.

By Prof. H. L. F. HELMHOLTZ.

Translated by JOHN TYNDALL, F.R.S.

HERMAN LUDWIG FERDINAND HELMHOLTZ was born at Pottsdam, August 31, 1821. He was first military physician, and afterwards assistant of the Astronomical Museum in Berlin (1848), and subsequently Professor Extraordinary of Physiology at the University of Königsberg (1849 to 1852). He became Professor of Physiology at the University of Bonn in 1855, and in 1858 accepted the physiological chair in the University of Heidelberg. The lecture which follows was delivered at Königsberg in 1854. He is an eminent investigator, and an able promoter of the recent philosophy of forces; but of his life we have fewer particulars than of his accomplished translator.

The ancestors of JOHN TYNDALL emigrated from England to the eastern or Saxon border of Ireland about the middle of the last century. He was born at the village of Leighlin Bridge in 1820, where he received his early education and acquired a taste for mathematics. In 1839 he left school and joined the Ordnance Survey as a civil assistant, where he became in turn draughtsman, computer, surveyor, and trigometrical observer. He was five years connected with the survey, and for three years occupied as railroad engineer. In 1847 he became teacher in Queenswood College in Hampshire, a school for agriculturists and engineers, where he was distinguished for his mild but efficient discipline. Professor Frankland, the chemist, was here joined with him in the work of instruction, and in 1848 the two friends left the institution and went to the University of Marburg in Hesse Cassel, to study with the eminent chemist, Bunsen. In 1851 Professor Tyndall went to Berlin and worked at the subject of diamagnetism in the laboratory of Professor Magnus. He returned to London the same year, and was elected Fellow of the Royal Society in 1852.

Through the influence of Dr. Bence Jones, General Sabine, and Professor Faraday, he was appointed Professor of Natural Philosophy in the Royal Institution in 1853, an appointment which he now holds. In company with his friend, Professor Huxley, he visited the Alps in 1856; and returning each succeeding year, he accumulated the observations and adventures which are so graphically described in his "Glaciers of the Alps," published in 1860. Professor Tyndall has worked with eminent success at various scientific questions, but he is chiefly distinguished for his original and elaborate researches on the relations of radiant heat to gaseous and vaporous matter. These researches are given in his able work on "Heat as a mode of Motion," issued in 1863. As an experimenter, Professor Tyndall is marked for his caution, accuracy, and tireless perseverance under difficulties; as a writer, for his clear, vivid, and vigorous style.

INTERACTION OF NATURAL FORCES.

A NEW conquest of very general interest has been recently made by natural philosophy. In the following pages, I will endeavour to give a notion of the nature of this conquest. It has reference to a new and universal natural law, which rules the action of natural forces in their mutual relations towards each other, and is as influential on our theoretic views of natural processes as it is important in their technical applications.

Among the practical arts which owe their progress to the development of the natural sciences, from the conclusion of the middle ages downwards, practical mechanics, aided by the mathematical science which bears the same name, was one of the most prominent. The character of the art was, at the time referred to, naturally very different from its present one. Surprised and stimulated by its own success, it thought no problem beyond its power, and immediately attacked some of the most difficult and complicated. Thus it was attempted to build automaton figures which should perform the functions of men and animals. The wonder of the last century was Vaucanson's duck, which fed and digested its food; the flute-player of the same artist, which moved all its fingers correctly; the writing boy of the older, and the piano-forte player of the younger Droz: which latter, when performing, followed its hands with his eyes, and at the conclusion of the piece bowed courteously to the audience. That men like those mentioned, whose talent might bear comparison with the most inventive heads of the present age, should spend so much time in the construction of these figures, which we at present regard as the merest trifles, would be incomprehensible, if they had not hoped in solemn earnest to solve a great problem. The writing boy of the elder Droz was publicly exhibited in Germany some years ago. Its wheel-work is so complicated, that no ordinary head would be sufficient to decipher its manner of action. When, however, we are informed that this boy and its constructor, being suspected of the black art, lay for a time in the Spanish Inquisition, and with difficulty obtained their freedom, we may infer that in those days even such a toy appeared great enough to excite doubts as to its natural origin. And though these artists may not have hoped to breathe into the creature of their ingenuity a soul gifted with moral completeness, still there were many who would be willing to dispense with the moral qualities of their servants, if, at the same time, their immoral qualities could also be got rid of; and accept, instead of the mutability of flesh and bones, services which should combine the regularity of a machine with the durability of brass and steel. The object, therefore, which the inventive genius of the past century placed before it with the fullest earnestness, and not as a piece of amusement merely, was boldly chosen, and was followed up with an expenditure of sagacity which has contributed not a little to enrich the mechanical experience which a later time knew how to take advantage of. We no longer seek to build machines which shall fulfil the thousand services required of *one* man, but desire, on the contrary, that a machine shall perform *one* service, but shall occupy in doing it the place of a thousand men.

From these efforts to imitate living creatures, another idea, also by a misunderstanding, seems to have developed itself, which, as it were, formed the new philosopher's stone of the seventeenth and eighteenth centuries. It was now the endeavour to construct a perpetual motion. Under this term was understood a machine, which, without being wound up, without consuming in the working of it, falling water, wind, or any other natural force, should still continue in motion, the motive power being perpetually supplied by the machine itself. Beasts and human beings seemed to correspond to the idea of such an apparatus, for they moved themselves energetically and incessantly as long as they lived, were never wound up, and nobody set them in motion. A connection between the taking-in of nourishment and the development of force did not make itself apparent. The nourishment seemed only necessary to grease, as it were, the wheelwork of the animal machine, to replace what was used up, and to renew the old. The development of force out of itself seemed to be the essential peculiarity, the real quintessence of organic life. If, therefore, men were to be constructed, a perpetual motion must first be found.

Another hope also seemed to take up incidentally the second place, which, in our wiser age, would certainly have claimed the first rank in the thoughts of men. The perpetual motion was to produce work inexhaustibly without corresponding consumption, that is to say, out of nothing. Work, however, is money. Here, therefore, the practical problem which the cunning heads of all centuries have followed in the most diverse ways, namely, to fabricate money out of nothing, invited solution. The similarity with the philosopher's stone sought by the ancient chemists was complete. That also was thought to contain the quintessence of organic life, and to be capable of producing gold.

The spur which drove men to inquiry was sharp, and the talent of some of the seekers must not be estimated as small. The nature of the problem was quite calculated to entice poring brains, to lead them round a circle for years, deceiving ever with new expectations, which vanished upon nearer approach, and finally reducing these dupes of hope to open insanity. The phantom could not be grasped. It would be impossible to give a history of these efforts, as the clearer heads, among whom the elder Droz must be ranked, convinced themselves of the futility of their experiments, and were naturally not inclined to speak much about them. Bewildered intellects, however, proclaimed often enough that they had discovered the grand secret; and as the incorrectness of their proceedings was always speedily manifest, the matter fell into bad repute, and the opinion strengthened itself more and more that the problem was not capable of solution; one difficulty after another was brought under the dominion of mathematical mechanics, and finally a point was reached where it could be proved, that, at least by the use of pure mechanical forces, no perpetual motion could be generated.

We have here arrived at the idea of the driving force or power of a machine, and shall have much to do with it in future. I must, therefore, give an explanation of it. The idea of work is evidently transferred to machines by comparing their arrangements with those of men and animals to replace which they were applied. We still reckon the work of steam engines according to horse-power. The value of manual labor is determined partly by the force which is expended in it (a strong laborer is valued more highly than a weak one), partly however, by the skill which is brought into action. A machine, on the contrary, which executes work skilfully, can always be multiplied to any extent; hence its skill has not the high value of human skill in domains where the latter cannot be supplied by machines. Thus the idea of the quantity of work in the case of machines has been limited to the consideration of the expenditure of force; this was the more important, as indeed most machines are constructed for the express purpose of exceeding, by the magnitude of their effects, the powers of men and animals. Hence, in a mechanical sense, the idea of work is become identical with that of the expenditure of force, and in this way I will apply it.

How, then, can we measure this expenditure, and compare it in the case of different machines?

I must here conduct you a portion of the way—as short a portion as possible—over the uninviting field of mathematico-mechanical ideas, in order to bring you to a point of view from which a more rewarding prospect will open. And though the example which I shall here choose, namely, that of a water-mill with iron hammer, appears to be tolerably romantic, still, alas, I must leave the dark forest valley, the spark-emitting anvil, and the black Cyclops wholly out of sight, and beg a moment's attention to the less poetic side of the question, namely, the machinery. This is driven by a water-wheel which in its turn is set in motion by the falling water. The axle of the water-wheel has at certain places small projections, thumbs, which, during the rotation, lift the heavy hammer and permit it to fall again. The falling hammer belabors the mass of metal, which is introduced beneath it. The work therefore done by the machine consists, in this case, in the lifting of the hammer, to do which the gravity of the latter must be overcome. The expenditure of force will, in the first place, other circumstances being equal, be proportioned to the weight of the hammer; it will, for example, be double when the weight of the hammer is doubled. But the action of the hammer depends not upon its weight alone, but also upon the height from which it falls. If it falls through two feet, it will produce a greater effect than if it falls through only one foot. It is, however, clear that if the machine, with a certain expenditure of force, lifts the hammer a foot in height, the same amount of force must be expended to raise it a second foot in height. The work is therefore not only doubled when the weight of the hammer is increased twofold, but also when the space through which it falls is doubled. From this it is easy to see that the work must be measured by the product of the weight into the space through which it ascends. And in this way, indeed, do we measure in mechanics.

The unit of work is a foot-pound, that is, a pound weight raised to the height of one foot.

While the work in this case consists in the raising of the heavy hammer-head, the driving force which sets the latter in motion, is generated by falling water. It is not necessary that the water should fall vertically, it can also flow in a moderately inclined bed; but it must always, where it has water-mills to set in motion, move from a higher to a lower position. Experiment and theory coincide in teaching, that when a hammer of a hundred weight is to be raised one foot, to accomplish this at least a hundred weight of water must fall through the space of one foot; or what is equivalent to this, two hundred weight must fall full half a foot, or four hundred weight a quarter of a foot, etc. In short, if we multiply the weight of the falling water by the height through which it falls, and regard, as before, the product as the measure of the work, then the work performed by the machine in raising the hammer, can, in the most favourable case, be only equal to the number of foot-pounds of water which have fallen in the same time. In practice, indeed, this ratio is by no means attained; a great portion of the work of the falling water escapes unused, inasmuch as part of the force is willingly sacrificed for the sake of obtaining greater speed.

I will further remark, that this relation remains unchanged whether the hammer is driven immediately by the axle of the wheel, or whether—by the intervention of wheel-work, endless screws, pulleys, ropes—the motion is transferred to the hammer. We may, indeed, by such arrangements, succeed in raising a hammer of ten hundred weight, when by the first simple arrangement, the elevation of a hammer of one hundred weight might alone be possible; but either this heavier hammer is raised to only one tenth of the height, or tenfold the time is required to raise it to the same height; so that, however we may alter, by the interposition of machinery, the intensity of the acting force, still in a certain time, during which the mill-stream furnishes us with a definite quantity of water, a certain definite quantity of work, and no more, can be performed.

Our machinery, therefore, has, in the first place, done nothing more than make use of the gravity of the falling water in order to overpower the gravity of the hammer, and to raise the latter. When it has lifted the hammer to the necessary height, it again liberates it, and the hammer falls upon the metal mass which is pushed beneath it. But why does the falling hammer here exercise a greater force than when it is permitted simply to press with its own weight on the mass of metal? Why is its power greater as the height from which it falls is increased? We find, in fact, that the work performed by the hammer is determined by its velocity. In other cases, also, the velocity of moving masses is a means of producing great effects. I only remind you of the destructive effects of musket-bullets, which, in a state of rest, are the most harmless things in the world. I remind you of the wind-mill, which derives its force from the moving air. It may appear surprising that motion, which we are accustomed to regard as a non-essential and transitory endowment of bodies, can produce such great effects. But the fact is, that motion appears to us, under ordinary circumstances, transitory, because the movement of all terrestrial bodies is resisted perpetually by other forces, friction, resistance of the air, etc., so that motion is incessantly weakened and finally neutralized. A body, however, which is opposed by no resisting force, when once set in motion, moves onward eternally with undiminished velocity. Thus we know that the planetary bodies have moved without change, through space, for thousands of years. Only by resisting forces can motion be diminished or destroyed. A moving body, such as the hammer or the musket-ball, when it strikes against another, presses the latter together, or penetrates it, until the sum of the resisting forces which the body struck presents to its pressure, or to the separation of its particles, is sufficiently great to destroy the motion of the hammer or of the bullet. The motion of a mass regarded as taking the place of working force is called the living force (*vis viva*) of the mass. The word "living" has of course here no reference whatever to living beings, but is intended to represent solely the force of the motion as distinguished from the state of unchanged rest—from the gravity of a motionless body, for example, which produces an incessant pressure against the surface which supports it, but does not produce any motion.

In the case before us, therefore, we had first power in the form of a falling mass of water, then in the form of a lifted hammer, and, thirdly, in the form of the living force of the fallen hammer. We should transform the third form into the second, if we, for example, permitted the hammer to fall upon a highly elastic steel beam strong enough to resist the shock. The hammer would rebound, and in the most favourable case would reach a height equal to that from which it fell, but would never rise higher. In this way its mass would ascend: and at the moment when its highest point has been attained, it would represent the same number of raised foot-pounds as before it fell, never a greater number; that is to say, living force can generate the same amount of work as that expended in its production. It is therefore equivalent to this quantity of work.

Our clocks are driven by means of sinking weights, and our watches by means of the tension of springs. A weight which lies on the ground, an elastic spring which is without tension, can produce no effects; to obtain such we must first raise the weight or impart tension to the spring, which is accomplished when we wind up our clocks and watches. The man who winds the clock or watch communicates to the weight or to the spring a certain amount of power, and exactly so much as is thus communicated is gradually given out again during the following twenty-four hours, the original force being thus slowly consumed to overcome the friction of the wheels and the resistance which the pendulum encounters from the air. The wheel-work of the clock therefore exhibits no working force which was not previously communicated to it, but simply distributes the force given to it uniformly over a longer time.

Into the chamber of an air-gun we squeeze, by means of a condensing air-pump, a great quantity of air. When we afterwards open the cock of a gun and admit the compressed air into the barrel, the ball is driven out of the latter with a force similar to that exerted by ignited powder. Now we may determine the work consumed in the pumping-in of the air, and the living force which, upon firing, is communicated to the ball, but we shall never find the latter greater than the former. The compressed air has generated no working force, but simply gives to the bullet that which has been previously communicated to it. And while we have pumped for perhaps a quarter of an hour to charge the gun, the force is expended in a few seconds when the bullet is discharged; but because the action is compressed into so short a time, a much greater velocity is imparted to the ball than would be possible to communicate to it by the unaided effort of the arm in throwing it.

From these examples you observe, and the mathematical theory has corroborated this for all purely mechanical, that is to say, for moving forces, that all our machinery and apparatus generate no force, but simply yield up the power communicated to them by natural forces,—falling water, moving wind, or by the muscles of men and animals. After this law had been established by the great mathematicians of the last century, a perpetual motion, which should make only use of pure mechanical forces, such as gravity, elasticity, pressure of liquids and gases, could only be sought after by bewildered and ill-instructed people. But there are still other natural forces which are not reckoned among the purely moving forces,—heat, electricity, magnetism, light, chemical forces, all of which nevertheless stand in manifold relation to mechanical processes. There is hardly a natural process to be found which is not accompanied by mechanical actions, or from which mechanical work may not be derived. Here the question of a perpetual motion remained open; the decision of this question marks the progress of modern physics.

In the case of the air-gun, the work to be accomplished in the propulsion of the ball was given by the arm of the man who pumped in the air. In ordinary firearms, the condensed mass of air which propels the bullet is obtained in a totally different manner, namely, by the combustion of the powder. Gunpowder is transformed by combustion for the most part into gaseous products, which endeavor to occupy a much larger space than that previously taken up by the volume of the powder. Thus, you see, that, by the use of gunpowder, the work which the human arm must accomplish in the case of the air-gun is spared.

In the mightiest of our machines, the steam engine, it is a strongly compressed aëriform body, water vapour, which, by its effort to expand, sets the machine in motion. Here also, we do not condense the steam by means of an external mechanical force, but by communicating heat to a mass of water in a closed boiler, we change this water into steam, which, in consequence of the limits of the space, is developed under strong pressure. In this case, therefore, it is the heat communicated which generates the mechanical force. The heat thus necessary for the machine we might obtain in many ways; the ordinary method is to procure it from the combustion of coal.

Combustion is a chemical process. A particular constituent of our atmosphere, oxygen, possesses a strong force of attraction, or, as it is named in chemistry, a strong affinity for the constituents of the combustible body, which affinity, however, in most cases, can only exert itself at high temperatures. As soon as a portion of the combustible body, for example the coal, is sufficiently heated, the carbon unites itself with great violence to the oxygen of the atmosphere and forms a peculiar gas, carbonic acid, the same which we see foaming from beer and champagne. By this combination, light and heat are generated; heat is generally developed by any combination of two bodies of strong affinity for each other; and when the heat is intense enough, light appears. Hence, in the steam engine, it is chemical processes and chemical forces which produce the astonishing work of these machines. In like manner the combustion of gunpowder is a chemical process, which, in the barrel of the gun, communicates living force to the bullet.

While now the steam engine develops for us mechanical work out of heat, we can conversely generate heat by mechanical forces. A skilful blacksmith can render an iron wedge red hot by hammering. The axles of our carriages must be protected by careful greasing, from ignition through friction. Even lately this property has been applied on a large scale. In some factories, where a surplus of water power is at hand, this surplus is applied to cause a strong iron plate to rotate swiftly upon another, so that they become strongly heated by the friction. The heat so obtained warms the room, and thus a stove without fuel is provided. Now, could not the heat generated by the plates be applied to a small steam engine, which, in its turn, should be able to keep the rubbing plates in motion? The perpetual motion would thus be at length found. This question might be asked, and could not be decided by the older mathematico-mechanical investigations. I will remark, beforehand, that the general law which I will lay before you answers the question in the negative.

By a similar plan, however, a speculative American set

some time ago the industrial world of Europe in excitement. The magneto-electric machines often made use of in the case of rheumatic disorders are well known to the public. By imparting a swift rotation to the magnet of such a machine, we obtain powerful currents of electricity. If those be conducted through water, the latter will be reduced into its two components, oxygen and hydrogen. By the combustion of hydrogen, water is again generated. If this combustion takes place, not in atmospheric air, of which oxygen only constitutes a fifth part, but in pure oxygen, and if a bit of chalk be placed in the flame, the chalk will be raised to a white heat, and give us the sun-like Drummond's light. At the same time, the flame develops a considerable quantity of heat. Our American proposed to utilize in this way the gases obtained from electrolytic decomposition, and asserted that by the combustion a sufficient amount of heat was generated to keep a small steam engine in action, which again drove his magneto-electric machine, decomposed the water, and thus continually prepared its own fuel. This would certainly have been the most splendid of all discoveries; a perpetual motion which, besides the force which kept it going, generated light like the sun, and warmed all around it. The matter was by no means badly cogitated. Each practical step in the affair was known to be possible; but those who at that time were acquainted with the physical investigations which bear upon this subject could have affirmed, on the first hearing the report, that the matter was to be numbered among the numerous stories of the fable-rich America; and indeed, a fable it remained.

It is not necessary to multiply examples further. You will infer from those given, in what immediate connection heat, electricity, magnetism, light, and chemical affinity, stand with mechanical forces.

Starting from each of these different manifestations of natural forces, we can set every other in motion, for the most part not in one way merely, but in many ways. It is here as with the weaver's web,—

> Where a step stirs a thousand threads,
> The shuttles shoot from side to side,
> The fibres flow unseen,
> And one shock strikes a thousand combinations.

Now it is clear that if by any means we could succeed, as the above American professed to have done, by mechanical forces, to excite chemical, electrical, or other natural processes, which, by any circuit whatever, and without altering permanently the active masses in the machine, could produce mechanical force in greater quantity than that at first applied, a portion of the work thus gained might be made use of to keep the machine in motion, while the rest of the work might be applied to any other purpose whatever. The problem was, to find in the complicated net of reciprocal actions, a track through chemical, electrical, magnetical, and thermic processes, back to mechanical actions, which might be followed with a final gain of mechanical work; thus would the perpetual motion be found.

But, warned by the futility of former experiments, the public had become wiser. On the whole, people did not seek much after combinations which promised to furnish a perpetual motion, but the question was inverted. It was no more asked, How can I make use of the known and unknown relations of natural forces so as to construct a perpetual motion? but it was asked, If a perpetual motion be impossible, what are the relations which must subsist between natural forces? Everything was gained by this inversion of the question. The relations of natural forces rendered necessary by the above assumption, might be easily and completely stated. It was found that all known relations of force harmonize with the consequences of that assumption, and a series of unknown relations were discovered at the same time, the correctness of which remained to be proved. If a single one of them could be proved false, then a perpetual motion would be possible.

The first who endeavoured to travel this way was a Frenchman, named Carnot, in the year 1824. In spite of a too limited conception of his subject, and an incorrect view as to the nature of heat, which led him to some erroneous conclusions, his experiment was not quite unsuccessful. He discovered a law which now bears his name, and to which I will return further on.

His labors remained for a long time without notice, and it was not till eighteen years afterwards, that is, in 1842, that different investigators in different countries, and independent of Carnot, laid hold of the same thought.

The first who saw truly the general law here referred to, and expressed it correctly, was a German physician, J. R. Mayer, of Heilbronn, in the year 1842. A little later, in 1843, a Dane, named Colding, presented a memoir to the Academy of Copenhagen, in which the same law found utterance, and some experiments were described for its further corroboration. In England, Joule began about the same time to make experiments having reference to the same subject. We often find, in the case of questions to the solution of which the development of science points, that several heads, quite independent of each other, generate exactly the same series of reflections.

I myself, without being acquainted with either Mayer or Colding, and having first made the acquaintance of Joule's experiments at the end of my investigation, followed the same path. I endeavoured to ascertain all the relations between the different natural processes, which followed from our regarding them from the above point of view. My inquiry was made public in 1847, in a small pamphlet bearing the title, "On the Conservation of Force."

Since that time the interest of the scientific public for this subject has gradually augmented. A great number of the essential consequences of the above manner of viewing the subject, the proof of which was wanting when the first theoretic notions were published, have since been confirmed by experiment, particularly by those of Joule; and during the last year the most eminent physicist of France, Regnault, has adopted the new mode regarding the question, and by fresh investigations on the specific heat of gases has contributed much to its support. For some important consequences the experimental proof is still wanting, but the number of confirmations is so predominant, that I have not deemed it too early to bring the subject before even a non-scientific audience.

How the question has been decided you may already infer from what has been stated. In the series of natural processes there is no circuit to be found, by which mechanical force can be gained without a corresponding consumption. The perpetual motion remains impossible. Our reflections, however, gain thereby a higher interest.

We have thus far regarded the development of force by natural processes, only in its relation to its usefulness to man, as mechanical force. You now see that we have arrived at a general law, which holds good wholly independent of the application which man makes of natural forces; we must therefore make the expression of our new law correspond to this more general significance. It is in the first place clear, that the work which, by any natural process whatever, is performed under favourable conditions by a machine, and which may be measured in the way already indicated, may be used as a measure of force common to all. Further, the important question arises, "If the quantity of force cannot be augmented except by corresponding consumption, can it be diminished or lost? For the purpose of our machines it certainly can, if we neglect the opportunity to convert natural processes to use, but as investigation has proved, not for a nature as a whole."

In the collision and friction of bodies against each other, the mechanics of former years assumed simply that living force was lost. But I have already stated that each collision and each act of friction generates heat; and, moreover, Joule has established by experiment the important law, that for every foot-pound of force which is lost, a definite quantity of heat is always generated, and that when work is performed by the consumption of heat, for each foot-pound thus gained a definite quantity of heat disappears. The quantity of heat necessary to raise the temperature of a pound of water a degree of the centigrade thermometer, corresponds to a mechanical force by which a pound weight would be raised to the height of 1350 feet; we name this quantity the mechanical equivalent of heat. I may mention here that these facts conduct of necessity to the conclusion, that the heat is not, as was formerly imagined, a fine imponderable substance, but that, like light, it is a peculiar shivering motion of the ultimate particles of bodies. In collision and friction, according to this manner of viewing the subject, the motion of the mass of a body which is apparently lost is converted into a motion of the ultimate particles of the body; and conversely, when mechanical force is generated by heat, the motion of the ultimate particles is converted into a motion of the mass.

Chemical combinations generate heat, and the quantity of this heat is totally independent of the time and steps through which the combination has been effected, provided that other actions are not at the same time brought into play. If, however, mechanical work is at the same time accomplished, as in the case of the steam engine, we obtain as much less heat as is equivalent to this work. The quantity of work produced by chemical force is in general very great. A pound of the purest coal gives, when burnt, sufficient heat to raise the temperature of 8086 pounds of water one degree of the centigrade thermometer; from this we can calculate that the magnitude of the chemical force of attraction between the particles of a pound of coal and the quantity of oxygen that corresponds to it, is capable of lifting a weight of one hundred pounds to a height of twenty miles. Unfortunately, in our steam engines, we have hitherto been able to gain only the smallest portion of this work; the greater part is lost in the shape of heat. The best expansive engines give back as mechanical work only eighteen per cent. of the heat generated by the fuel.

From a similar investigation of all the other known physical and chemical processes, we arrive at the conclusion that Nature as a whole possesses a store of force which cannot in any way be either increased or diminished. And that, therefore, the quantity of force in nature is just as eternal and unalterable as the quantity of matter. Expressed in this form, I have named the general law "The Principle of the Conservation of Force."

We cannot create mechanical force, but we may help ourselves from the general store-house of Nature. The brook and the wind, which drive our mills, the forest and the coal-bed, which supply our steam engines and warm our rooms, are to us the bearers of a small portion of the great natural supply which we draw upon for our purposes, and the actions of which we can apply as we think fit. The possessor of a mill claims the gravity of the descending rivulet, or the living force of the moving wind, as his possession. These portions of the store of Nature are what give his property its chief value.

Further, from the fact that no portion of force can be absolutely lost, it does not follow that a portion may not be inapplicable to human purposes. In this respect the inferences drawn by William Thomson from the law of Carnot are of importance. This law, which was discovered by Carnot during his endeavours to ascertain the relations between heat and mechanical force, which, however, by no means belongs to the necessary consequences of the conservation of force, and which Clausius was the first to modify in such a manner that it no longer contradicted the above general law, expresses a certain relation between the compressibility, the capacity for heat, and the expansion by heat of all bodies. It is not yet considered as actually proved, but some remarkable deductions having been drawn from it, and afterwards proved to be facts by experiment, it has attained thereby a great degree of probability. Besides the mathematical form in which the law was first expressed by Carnot, we can give it the following more general expression:—"Only when heat passes from a warmer to a colder body, and even then only partially, can it be converted into mechanical work."

The heat of a body which we cannot cool further, cannot be changed into another form of force; into the electric or chemical force, for example. Thus, in our steam engines, we convert a portion of the heat of the glowing coal into work, by permitting it to pass to the less warm water of the boiler. If, however, all the bodies in nature had the same temperature, it would be impossible to convert any portion of their heat into mechanical work. According to this, we can divide the total force store of the universe into two parts, one of which is heat, and must continue to be such; the other, to which a portion of the heat of the warmer bodies, and the total supply of chemical, mechanical, electrical, and magnetical forces belong, is capable of the most varied changes of form, and constitutes the whole wealth of change which takes place in nature.

But the heat of the warmer bodies strives perpetually to pass to bodies less warm by radition and conduction, and thus to establish an equilibrium of temperature. At each motion of a terrestrial body, a portion of mechanical force passes by friction or collision into heat, of which only a part can be converted back again into mechanical force. This is also generally the case in every electrical and chemical process. From this, it follows that the first portion of the store of force, the unchangeable heat, is augmented by every natural process, while the second portion, mechanical, electrical, and chemical force, must be diminished; so that if the universe be delivered over to the undisturbed action of its physical processes, all force will finally pass into the form of heat, and all heat come into a state of equilibrium. Then all possibility of a further change would be at an end, and the complete cessation of all natural processes must set in. The life of men, animals, and plants, could not of course continue if the sun had lost its high temperature, and with it his light,—if all the components of the earth's surface had closed those combinations which their affinities demand. In short, the universe from that time forward would be condemned to a state of eternal rest.

These consequences of the law of Carnot are, of course, only valid, provided that the law, when sufficiently tested, proves to be universally correct. In the mean time there is little prospect of the law being proved incorrect. At all events we must admire the sagacity of Thomson, who, in the letters of a long known little mathematical formula, which only speaks of the heat, volume, and pressure of bodies, was able to discern consequences which threatened the universe, though certainly after an infinite period of time, with eternal death.

I have already given you notice that our path lay through a thorny and unrefreshing field of mathematico-mechanical developments. We have now left this portion of our road behind us. The general principle which I have sought to lay before you has conducted us to a point from which our view is a wide one, and, aided by this principle, we can now at pleasure regard this or the other side of the surrounding world, according as our interest in the matter leads us. A glance into the narrow laboratory of the physicist, with its small appliances and complicated abstractions, will not be so attractive as a glance at the wide heaven above us, the clouds, the rivers, the woods, and the living beings around us. While regarding the laws which have been deduced from the physical processes of terrestrial bodies, as applicable also to the heavenly bodies, let me remind you that the same force which, acting at the earth's surface, we call gravity (*Schwere*), acts as gravitation in the celestial spaces, and also manifests its power in the motion of the immeasurably distant double stars which are governed by exactly the same laws as those subsisting between the earth and moon; that, therefore, the light and heat of terrestrial bodies do not in any way differ essentially from those of the sun, or of the most distant fixed star; that the meteoric stones which sometimes fall from external space upon the earth are composed of exactly the same simple chemical substances as those with which we are acquainted. We need, therefore, feel no scruple in granting that general laws to which all terrestrial natural processes are subject, are also valid for other bodies than the earth. We will, therefore, make use of our law to glance over the household of the universe with respect to the store of force, capable of action, which it possesses.

A number of singular peculiarities in the structure of our planetary system indicate that it was once a connected mass with a uniform motion of rotation. Without such an assumption, it is impossible to explain why all the planets move in the same direction round the sun, why they all rotate in the same direction round their axes, why the planes of their orbits, and those of their satellites and rings all nearly coincide, why all their orbits differ but little from circles; and much besides. From these remaining indications of a former state, astronomers have shaped an hypothesis regarding the formation of our planetary system, which, although from the nature of the case it must ever remain an hypothesis, still in its special traits is so well supported by analogy, that it certainly deserves our attention. It was Kant, who, feeling great interest in the physical description of the earth and the planetary system, undertook the labour of studying the works of Newton, and as an evidence of the depth to which he had penetrated into the fundamental ideas of Newton, seized the notion that the same attractive force of all ponderable matter which now supports the motion of the planets, must also aforetime have been able to form from matter loosely scattered in space the planetary system. Afterwards, and independent of Kant, Laplace, the great author of the *Mécanique Céleste*, laid hold of the same thought, and introduced it among astronomers.

The commencement of our planetary system, including the sun, must, according to this, be regarded as an immense nebulous mass which filled the portion of space which is now occupied by our system, far beyond the limits of Neptune, our most distant planet. Even now we perhaps see similar masses in the distant regions of the firmament, as patches of nebulæ, and nebulous stars; within our system also, comets, the zodiacal light, the corona of the sun during a total eclipse, exhibit remnants of a nebulous substance, which is so thin that the light of the stars passes through it unenfeebled and unrefracted. If we calculate the density of the mass of our planetary system, according to the above assumption, for the time when it was a nebulous sphere, which reached to the path of the outmost planet, we should find that it would require several cubic miles of such matter to weigh a single grain.

The general attractive force of all matter must, however, impel these masses to approach each other, and to condense, so that the nebulous sphere became incessantly smaller, by which, according to mechanical laws, a motion of rotation originally slow, and the existence of which must be assumed, would gradually become quicker and quicker. By the centrifugal force which must act most energetically in the neighbourhood of the equator of the nebulous sphere, masses could from time to time be torn away, which afterwards would continue their courses separate from the main mass, forming themselves into single planets, or, similar to the great original sphere, into planets with satellites and rings, until finally the principal mass condensed itself into the sun. With regard to the origin of heat and light, this view gives us no information.

When the nebulous chaos first separated itself from other fixed star masses, it must not only have contained all kinds of matter which was to constitute the future planetary system, but also, in accordance with our new law, the whole store of force which at one time must unfold therein its wealth of actions. Indeed in this respect an immense dower was bestowed in the shape of the general attraction of all the particles for each other. This force, which on the earth exerts itself as gravity, acts in the heavenly spaces as gravitation. As terrestrial gravity when it draws a weight downwards performs work and generates *vis viva*, so also the heavenly bodies do the same when they draw two portions of matter from distant regions of space towards each other.

The chemical forces must have been also present, ready to act; but as these forces can only come into operation by the most intimate contact of the different masses, condensation must have taken place before the play of chemical forces began.

Whether a still further supply of force in the shape of heat was present at the commencement we do not know. At all events, by aid of the law of the equivalence of heat and work, we find in the mechanical forces, existing at the time to which we refer, such a rich source of heat and light, that there is no necessity whatever to take refuge in the idea of a store of these forces originally existing. When through condensation of the masses their particles came into collision, and clung to each other, the *vis viva* of their motion would be thereby annihilated, and must reappear as heat. Already in old theories, it has been calculated, that cosmical masses must generate heat by their collision, but it was far from any body's thought, to make even a guess at the amount of heat to be generated in this way. At present we can give definite numerical values with certainty.

Let us make this addition to our assumption; that, at the commencement, the density of the nebulous matter was a vanishing quantity, as compared with the present density of the sun and planets; we can then calculate how much work has been performed by the condensation; we can further calculate how much of this work still exists in the form of mechanical force, as attraction of the planets towards the sun, and as *vis viva* of their motion, and find, by this, how much of the force has been converted into heat.

The result of this calculation is, that only about the 454th part of the original mechanical force remains as such, and that the remainder, converted into heat, would be sufficient to raise a mass of water equal to the sun and planets taken together, not less than twenty-eight millions of degrees of the centigrade scale. For the sake of comparison, I will mention that the highest temperature which we can produce by the oxyhydrogen blowpipe, which is sufficient to fuse and vaporize even platina, and which but few bodies can endure, is estimated at about two thousand centigrade degrees. Of the action of a temperature of twenty-eight millions of such degrees we can form no notion. If the mass of our entire system were pure coal, by the combustion of the whole of it only the 3500th part of the above quantity would be generated. This is also clear, that such a development of heat must have presented the greatest obstacle to the speedy union of the masses, that the larger part of the heat must have been diffused by radiation into space, before the masses could form bodies possessing the present density of the sun and planets, and that these bodies must once have been in a state of fiery fluidity. This notion is corroborated by the geological phenomena of our planet; and with regard to the other planetary bodies, the flattened form of the sphere, which is the form of equilibrium of a fluid mass, is indicative of a former state of fluidity. If I thus permit an immense quantity of heat to disappear without compensation from our system, the principle of the conservation of force is not thereby invaded. Certainly for our planet it is lost, but not for the universe. It has proceeded outwards, and daily proceeds outwards into infinite space; and we know not whether the medium which transmits the undulations of light and heat possesses an end where the rays must return, or whether they eternally pursue their way through infinitude.

The store of force at present possessed by our system, is also equivalent to immense quantities of heat. If our earth were by a sudden shock brought to rest on her orbit—which is not to be feared in the existing arrangements of our system—by such a shock a quantity of heat would be generated equal to that produced by the combustion of fourteen such earths of solid coal. Making the most unfavourable assumption as to its capacity for heat, that is, placing it equal to that of water, the mass of the earth would thereby be heated 11,200 degrees; it would therefore be quite fused and for the most part reduced to vapour. If, then, the earth, after having been thus brought to rest, should fall into the sun, which of course would be the case, the quantity of heat developed by the shock would be four hundred times greater.

Even now, from time to time, such a process is repeated on a small scale. There can hardly be a doubt that meteors, fire-balls, and meteoric stones, are masses which belong to the universe, and before coming into the domain of our earth, moved like the planets round the sun. Only when they enter our atmosphere do they become visible and fall sometimes to the earth. In order to explain the emission of light by these bodies, and the fact that for some time after their descent they are very hot, the friction was long ago thought of which they experience in passing through the air. We can now calculate that a velocity of 3000 feet a second, supposing the whole of the friction to be expended in heating the solid mass, would raise a piece of meteoric iron 1000° C. in temperature, or, in other words, to a vivid red heat. Now the average velocity of the meteors seems to be thirty or forty times the above amount. To compensate this, however, the greater portion of the heat is, doubtless, carried away by the condensed mass of air which the meteor drives before it. It is known that bright meteors generally leave a luminous trail behind them, which probably consists of several portions of the red-hot surfaces. Meteoric masses which fall to the earth often burst with a violent explosion, which may be regarded as a result of the quick heating. The newly-fallen pieces have been for the most part found hot, but not red-hot, which is easily explainable by the circumstance, that during the short time occupied by the meteor in passing through the atmosphere, only a thin, superficial layer is heated to redness, while but a small quantity of heat has been able to penetrate to the interior of the mass. For this reason the red heat can speedily disappear.

Thus has the falling of the meteoric stone, the minute remnant of processes which seems to have played an important part in the formation of the heavenly bodies, conducted us to the present time, where we pass from the darkness of hypothetical views to the brightness of knowledge. In what we have said, however, all that is hypothetical is the assumption of Kant and Laplace, that the masses of our system were once distributed as nebulæ in space.

On account of the rarity of the case, we will still further remark, in what close coincidence the results of science here stand with the earlier legends of the human family, and the forebodings of poetic fancy. The cosmogony of ancient nations generally commences with chaos and darkness.

Neither is the Mosaic tradition very divergent, particularly when we remember that that which Moses names heaven is different from the blue dome above us, and is synonymous with space, and that the unformed earth, and the waters of the great deep, which were afterwards divided into waters above the firmament, and waters below the firmament, resembled the chaotic components of the world.

Our earth bears still the unmistakable traces of its old fiery fluid condition. The granite formations of her mountains exhibit a structure, which can only be produced by the crystallization of fused masses. Investigation still shows that the temperature in mines, and borings, increases as we descend; and if this increase is uniform, at the depth of fifty miles, a heat exists sufficient to fuse all our minerals. Even now our volcanoes project, from time to time, mighty masses of fused rocks from their interior, as a testimony of the heat which exists there. But the cooled crust of the earth has already become so thick, that, as may be shown by calculations of its conductive power, the heat coming to the surface from within, in comparison with that reaching the earth from the sun, is exceedingly small, and increases the temperature of the surface only about one thirtieth of a degree centigrade; so that the remnant of the old store of force which is enclosed as heat within the bowels of the earth, has a sensible influence upon the processes at the earth's surface, only through the instrumentality of volcanic phenomena. *These processes owe their power almost wholly to the action of other heavenly bodies, particularly to the light and heat of the sun, and partly also, in the case of the tides, to the attraction of the sun and moon.*

Most varied and numerous are the changes which we owe to the light and heat of the sun. The sun heats our atmosphere irregularly, the warm rarefied air ascends, while fresh cool air flows from the sides to supply its place: in this way winds are generated. This action is most powerful at the equator, the warm air of which incessantly flows in the upper regions of the atmosphere towards the poles: while just as persistently, at the earth's surface, the trade wind carries new and cool air to the equator. Without the heat of the sun all winds must, of necessity, cease. Similar currents are produced by the same cause in the waters of the sea. Their power may be inferred from the influence which in some cases they exert upon climate. By them the warm water of the Antilles is carried to the British Isles, and confers upon them a mild, uniform warmth and rich moisture; while, through similar causes, the floating ice of the North Pole is carried to the coast of Newfoundland, and produces cold. Further, by the heat of the sun, a portion of the water is converted into vapour which rises in the atmosphere, is condensed to clouds, or falls in rain and snow upon the earth, collects in the form of springs, brooks, and rivers, and finally reaches the sea again, after having gnawed the rocks, carried away the light earth, and thus performed its part in the geologic changes of the earth; perhaps, besides all this it has driven our water-mill upon its way. If the heat of the sun were withdrawn, there would remain only a single motion of water, namely, the tides, which are produced by the attraction of the sun and moon.

How is it, now, with the motions and the work of organic beings. To the builders of the automata of the last century, men and animals appeared as clockwork which was never wound up, and created the force which they exerted out of nothing. They did not know how to establish a connection between the nutriment consumed and the work generated. Since, however, we have learned to discern in the steam-engine this origin of mechanical force, we must inquire whether something similar does not hold good with regard to men. Indeed, the continuation of life is dependent on the consumption of nutritive materials: these are combustible substances, which, after digestion and being passed into the blood, actually undergo a slow combustion, and finally enter into almost the same combinations with the oxygen of the atmosphere that are produced in an open fire. As the quantity of heat generated by combustion is independent of the duration of the combustion and the steps in which it occurs, we can calculate from the mass of the consumed material how much heat, or its equivalent work is thereby generated in an animal body. Unfortunately, the difficulty of the experiments is still very great; but within those limits of accuracy which have been as yet attainable, the experiments show that the heat generated in the animal body corresponds to the amount which would be generated by the chemical processes. The animal body therefore does not differ from the steam-engine, as regards the manner in which it obtains heat and force, but does differ from it in the manner in which the force gained is to be made use of. The body is, besides, more limited than the machine in the choice of its fuel; the latter could be heated with sugar, with starch-flour, and butter, just as well as with coal or wood; the animal body must dissolve its materials artificially, and distribute them through its system; it must, further, perpetually renew the used-up materials of its organs, and as it cannot itself create the matter necessary for this, the matter must come from without. Liebig was the first to point out these various uses of the consumed nutriment. As material for the perpetual renewal of the body, it seems that certain definite albuminous substances which appear in plants, and form the chief mass of the animal body, can alone be used. They form only a portion of the mass of nutriment taken daily; the remainder, sugar, starch, fat, are really only materials for warming, and are perhaps not to be superseded by coal, simply because the latter does not permit itself to be dissolved.

If, then, the processes in the animal body are not in this respect to be distinguished from inorganic processes, the question arises, whence comes the nutriment which constitutes the source of the body's force? The answer is, from the vegetable kingdom; for only the material of plants, or the flesh of plant-eating animals, can be made use of for food. The animals which live on plants occupy a mean position between carnivorous animals, in which we reckon man, and vegetables, which the former could not make use of immediately as nutriment. In hay and grass the same nutritive substances are present as in meal and flour, but in less quantity. As, however, the digestive organs of man are not in a condition to extract the small quantity of the useful from the great excess of the insoluble, we submit, in the first place, these substances to the powerful digestion of the ox, permit the nourishment to store itself in the animal's body, in order in the end to gain it for ourselves in a more agreeable and useful form. In answer to our question, therefore, we are referred to the vegetable world. Now when what plants take in and what they give out are made the subjects of investigation, we find that the principal part of the former consists in the products of combustion which are generated by the animal. They take the consumed carbon given off in respiration, as carbonic acid, from the air, the consumed hydrogen as water, the nitrogen in its simplest and closest combination as ammonia; and from these materials, with the assistance of small ingredients which they take from the soil, they generate anew the compound combustible substances, albumen, sugar, oil, on which the animal subsists. Here, therefore, is a circuit which appears to be a perpetual store of force. Plants prepare fuel and nutriment, animals consume these, burn them slowly in their lungs, and from the products of combustion the plants again derive their nutriment. The latter is an eternal source of chemical, the former of mechanical forces. Would not the combination of both organic kingdoms produce the perpetual motion? We must not conclude hastily: further inquiry shows, that plants are capable of producing combustible substances only when they are under the influence of the sun. A portion of the sun's rays exhibits a remarkable relation to chemical forces,—it can produce and destroy chemical combinations; and these rays, which for the most part are blue or violet, are called therefore chemical rays. We make use of their action in the production of photographs. Here compounds of silver are decomposed at the place where the sun's rays strike them. The same rays overpower in the green leaves of plants the strong chemical affinity of the carbon of the carbonic acid for oxygen, give back the latter free to the atmosphere, and accumulate the other, in combination with other bodies, as woody fibre, starch, oil, or resin. These chemically active rays of the sun disappear completely as soon as they encounter the green portions of the plants, and hence it is that in daguerrotype images the green leaves of plants appear uniformly black. Inasmuch as the light coming from them does not contain the chemical rays, it is unable to act upon the silver compounds.

Hence a certain portion of force disappears from the sunlight, while combustible substances are generated and accumulated in plants; and we can assume it as very probable, that the former is the cause of the latter. I must indeed remark, that we are in possession of no experiments from which we might determine whether the *vis viva* of the sun's rays which have disappeared, corresponds to the chemical forces accumulated during the same time; and as long as these experiments are wanting, we cannot regard the stated relation as a certainty. If this view should prove correct, we derive from it the flattering result, that all force, by means of which our bodies live and move, finds its source in the purest sunlight; and hence we are all, in point of nobility, not behind the race of the great monarch of China, who heretofore alone called himself Son of the Sun. But it must also be conceded that our lower fellow-beings, the frog and leech, share the same ethereal origin, as also the whole vegetable world, and even the fuel which comes to us from the ages past, as well as the youngest offspring of the forest with which we heat our stoves and set our machines in motion.

You see, then, that the immense wealth of ever-changing meteorological, climatic, geological, and organic processes of our earth are almost wholly preserved in action by the light and heat-giving rays of the sun; and you see in this a remarkable example, how Proteus-like the effects of a single cause, under altered external conditions, may exhibit itself in nature. Besides these, the earth experiences an action of another kind from its central luminary, as well as from its satellite the moon, which exhibits itself in the remarkable phenomenon of the ebb and flow of the tide.

Each of these bodies excites, by its attraction upon the waters of the sea, two gigantic waves, which flow in the same direction round the world, as the attracting bodies themselves apparently do. The two waves of the moon, on account of her greater nearness, are about three and a half times as large as those excited by the sun. One of these waves has its crest on the quarter of the earth's surface which is turned towards the moon, the other is at the opposite side. Both these quarters possess the flow of the tide, while the regions which lie between have the ebb. Although in the open sea the height of the tide amounts to only about three feet, and only in certain narrow channels, where the moving water is squeezed together, rises to thirty feet, the might of the phenomena is nevertheless manifest from the calculation of Bessel, according to which a quarter of the earth covered by the sea possesses, during the flow of the tide, about 25,000 cubic miles of water more than during the ebb, and that therefore such a mass of water must, in six and a quarter hours, flow from one quarter of the earth to the other.

The phenomena of the ebb and flow, as already recognized by Mayer, combined with the law of the conservation of force, stand in remarkable connection with the question of the stability of our planetary system. The mechanical theory of the planetary motions discovered by Newton teaches, that if a solid body in absolute *vacuo*, attracted by the sun, move around him in the same manner as the planets, this motion will endure unchanged through all eternity.

Now we have actually not only one, but several such

planets, which move around the sun, and by their mutual attraction create little changes and disturbances in each other's paths. Nevertheless Laplace, in his great work, the *Mécanique Céleste*, has proved that in our planetary system all these disturbances increase and diminish periodically, and can never exceed certain limits, so that by this cause the eternal existence of the planetary system is unendangered.

But I have already named two assumptions which must be made: first that the celestial spaces must be absolutely empty; and secondly, that the sun and planets must be solid bodies. The first is at least the case as far as astronomical observations reach, for they have never been able to detect any retardation of the planets, such as would occur if they moved in a resisting medium. But on a body of less mass, the comet of Encke, changes are observed of such a nature: this comet describes ellipses round the sun which are becoming gradually smaller. If this kind of motion, which certainly corresponds to that through a resisting medium, be actually due to the existence of such a medium, a time will come when the comet will strike the sun; and a similar end threatens all the planets, although after a time, the length of which baffles our imagination to conceive of it. But even should the existence of a resisting medium appear doubtful to us, there is no doubt that the planets are not wholly composed of solid materials which are inseparably bound together. Signs of the existence of an atmosphere are observed on the Sun, on Venus, Mars, Jupiter, and Saturn. Signs of water and ice upon Mars; and our earth has undoubtedly a fluid portion on its surface, and perhaps a still greater portion of fluid within it. The motions of the tides, however, produce friction, all friction destroys *vis viva*, and the loss in this case can only affect the *vis viva* of the planetary system. We come thereby to the unavoidable conclusion, that every tide, although with infinite slowness, still with certainty, diminishes the store of mechanical force of the system; and as a consequence of this, the rotation of the planets in question round their axes must become more slow; they must therefore approach the sun, or their satellites must approach them. What length of time must pass before the length of our day is diminished one second by the action of the tide cannot be calculated, until the height and time of the tide in all portions of the ocean are known. This alteration, however, takes place with extreme slowness, as is known by the consequences which Laplace has deduced from the observations of Hipparchus, according to which, during a period of 2000 years, the duration of the day has not been shortened by the one three hundredth part of a second. The final consequence would be, but after millions of years, if in the mean time the ocean did not become frozen, that one side of the earth would be constantly turned towards the sun, and enjoy a perpetual day, whereas the opposite side would be involved in eternal night. Such a position we observe in our moon with regard to the earth, and also in the case of the satellites as regards their planets; it is, perhaps, due to the action of the mighty ebb and flow to which these bodies, in the time of their fiery fluid condition, were subjected.

I would not have brought forward these conclusions, which again plunge us in the most distant future, if they were not unavoidable. Physico-mechanical laws are, as it were, the telescopes of our spiritual eye, which can penetrate into the deepest night of time, past and to come.

Another essential question as regards the future of our planetary system has reference to its future temperature and illumination. As the internal heat of the earth has but little influence on the temperature of the surface, the heat of the sun is the only thing which essentially affects the question. The quantity of heat falling from the sun during a given time upon a given portion of the earth's surface may be measured, and from this it can be calculated how much heat in a given time is sent out from the entire sun. Such measurements have been made by the French physicist Pouillet, and it has been found that the sun gives out a quantity of heat per hour equal to that which a layer of the densest coal ten feet thick would give out by its combustion; and hence in a year a quantity equal to the combustion of a layer of seventeen miles. If this heat were drawn uniformly from the entire mass of the sun, its temperature would only be diminished thereby one and one third of a degree centigrade per year, assuming its capacity for heat to be equal to that of water. These results can give us an idea of the magnitude of the emission, in relation to the surface and mass of the sun; but they cannot inform us whether the sun radiates heat as a glowing body, which since its formation has its heat accumulated within it, or whether a new generation of heat by chemical processes takes place at the sun's surface. At all events the law of the conservation of force teaches us that no process analogous to those known at the surface of the earth, can supply for eternity an inexhaustible amount of light and heat to the sun. But the same law also teaches that the store of force at present existing, as heat, or as what may become heat, is sufficient for an immeasurable time. With regard to the store of chemical force in the sun, we can form no conjecture, and the store of heat there existing can only be determined by very uncertain estimations. If, however, we adopt the very probable view, that the remarkably small density of so large a body is caused by its high temperature, and may become greater in time, it may be calculated that if the diameter of the sun were diminished only the ten-thousandth part of its present length, by this act a sufficient quantity of heat would be generated to cover the total emission for 2100 years. Such a small change besides it would be difficult to detect even by the finest astronomical observations.

Indeed, from the commencement of the period during which we possess historic accounts, that is, for a period of about 4000 years, the temperature of the earth has not sensibly diminished. From these old ages we have certainly no thermometric observations, but we have information regarding the distribution of certain cultivated plants, the vine, the olive tree, which are very sensitive to changes of the mean annual temperature, and we find that these plants at the present moment have the same limits of distribution that they had in the times of Abraham and Homer; from which we may infer backwards the constancy of the climate.

In opposition to this it has been urged, that here in Prussia the German knights in former times cultivated the vine, cellared their own wine and drank it, which is no longer possible. From this the conclusion has been drawn, that the heat of our climate has diminished since the time referred to. Against this, however, Dove has cited the reports of ancient chroniclers, according to which, in some peculiarly hot years, the Prussian grape possessed somewhat less than its usual quantity of acid. The fact also speaks not so much for the climate of the country as for the throats of the German drinkers.

But even though the force store of our planetary system is so immensely great, that by the incessant emission which has occurred during the period of human history it has not been sensibly diminished, even though the length of the time which must flow by, before a sensible change in the state of our planetary system occurs, is totally incapable of measurement, still the inexorable laws of mechanics indicate that this store of force, which can only suffer loss and not gain, must be finally exhausted. Shall we terrify ourselves by this thought? Men are in the habit of measuring the greatness and the wisdom of the universe by the duration and the profit which it promises to their own race; but the past history of the earth already shows what an insignificant moment the duration of the existence of our race upon it constitutes. A Nineveh vessel, a Roman sword awakes in us the conception of grey antiquity. What the museums of Europe show us o the remains of Egypt and Assyria we gaze upon with silent astonishment, and despair of being able to carry our thoughts back to a period so remote. Still must the human race have existed for ages, and multiplied itself before the pyramids of Nineveh could have been erected. We estimate the duration of human history at 6000 years; but immeasurable as this time may appear to us, what is it in comparison with the time during which the earth carried successive series of rank plants and mighty animals, and no men; during which in our neighbourhood the amber-tree bloomed, and dropped its costly gum on the earth and in the sea; when in Siberia, Europe and North America groves of tropical palms flourished; where gigantic lizards, and after them elephants, whose mighty remains we still find buried in the earth, found a home? Different geologists, proceeding from different premises, have sought to estimate the duration of the above creative period, and vary from a million to nine million years. And the time during which the earth generated organic beings is again small when we compare it with the ages during which the world was a ball of fused rocks. For the duration of its cooling from 2000° to 200° centigrade, the experiments of Bishop upon basalt show that about 350 millions of years would be necessary. And with regard to the time during which the first nebulous mass condensed into our planetary system, our most daring conjectures must cease. The history of man, therefore, is but a short ripple in the ocean of time. For a much longer series of years than that during which man has already occupied this world, the existence of the present state of inorganic nature favourable to the duration of man seems to be secured, so that for ourselves and for long generations after us, we have nothing to fear. But the same forces of air and water, and of the volcanic interior, which produced former geological revolutions, and buried one series of living forms after another, act still upon the earth's crust. They more probably will bring about the last day of the human race than those distant cosmical alterations of which we have spoken, and perhaps force us to make way for new and more complete living forms, as the lizards and the mammoth have given place to us and our fellow-creatures which now exist.

Thus the thread which was spun in darkness by those who sought a perpetual motion has conducted us to a universal law of nature, which radiates light into the distant nights of the beginning and of the end of the history of the universe. To our own race it permits a long but not an endless existence; it threatens it with a day of judgment, the dawn of which is still happily obscured. As each of us singly must endure the thought of his death, the race must endure the same. But above the forms of life gone by, the human race has higher moral problems before it, the bearer of which it is, and in the completion of which it fulfils its destiny.

I.

REMARKS ON

THE FORCES OF INORGANIC NATURE.

BY DR. J. R. MAYER.

TRANSLATED BY J. C. FOSTER, B.A.

II.

ON CELESTIAL DYNAMICS.

BY DR. J. R. MAYER.

TRANSLATED BY DR. H. DEBUS, F.R.S.

III.

REMARKS ON

THE MECHANICAL EQUIVALENT OF HEAT.

BY DR. J. R. MAYER.

TRANSLATED BY J. C. FOSTER, B.A.

Julius Robert Mayer was born at Heilbronn, November 25, 1814. He received a medical education, and became first, county wound-physician and afterwards city physician of Heilbronn. But few particulars of his life have been obtained. In 1840 he made a voyage on a Dutch freighter to Java, and it was the accident of bleeding a feverish patient in this country, and observing that the venous blood in the tropics was of a much brighter red than in colder latitudes, that led him to those investigations of natural forces, the chief results of which are given in the following essays. Two years after his attention was drawn to the subject—in 1842, he published his first paper on the "Forces of Inorganic Nature." It was put together briefly, and published in Liebig's journal to secure the public recognition of his claims. His second publication, "On Organic Motion and Nutrition" (1845), an able essay of one hundred and twelve pages, is not yet translated. His third paper, on "Celestial Dynamics," was published in 1848; and his fourth, on the "Mechanical Equivalent of Heat," appeared in 1851.

These vast and rapid labors were too much for his strength. His overtasked mind gave way, and he was taken to an insane asylum. He, however, fortunately recovered, and is now reported as occupied with the cultivation of the vine in Heilbronn.

I.

THE FORCES OF INORGANIC NATURE.

THE following pages are designed as an attempt to answer the questions, What are we to understand by "Forces"? and how are different forces related to each other? Whereas the term *matter* implies the possession, by the object to which it is applied, of very definite properties, such as weight and extension; the term *force* conveys for the most part the idea of something unknown, unsearchable, and hypothetical. An attempt to render the notion of force equally exact with that of matter, and so to denote by it only objects of actual investigation, is one which, with the consequences that flow from it, ought not to be unwelcome to those who desire that their views of nature may be clear and unencumbered by hypotheses.

Forces are causes: accordingly, we may in relation to them make full application of the principle—*causa æquat effectum.* If the cause c has the effect e, then $c=e$; if, in its turn, e is the cause of a second effect f, we have $e=f$, and so on: $c=e=f\ldots=c$. In a chain of causes and effects, a term or a part of a term can never, as plainly appears from the nature of an equation, become equal to nothing. This first property of all causes we call their *indestructibility*.

If the given cause c has produced an effect e equal to itself, it has in that very act ceased to be: c has become e; if, after the production of e, c still remained in whole or in part, there must be still further effects corresponding to this remaining cause: the total effect of c would thus be $>e$, which would be contrary to the supposition $c=e$. Accordingly, since c becomes e, and e becomes f, &c., we must regard these various magnitudes as different forms under which one and the same object makes its appearance. This capability of assuming various forms is the second essential property of all causes. Taking both properties together, we may say, causes are (quantitatively) *indestructible* and (qualitatively) *convertible* objects.

Two classes of causes occur in nature, which, so far as experience goes, never pass one into another. The first class consists of such causes as possess the properties of weight and impenetrability; these are kinds of Matter: the other class is made up of causes which are wanting in the properties just mentioned, namely Forces, called also Imponderables, from the negative property that has been indicated. Forces are therefore *indestructible, convertible, imponderable objects.*

We will in the first instance take matter, to afford us an example of causes and effects. Explosive gas, $H+O$, and water, HO, are related to each other as cause and effect, therefore $H+O=HO$. But if $H+O$ becomes HO, heat, *cal.*, makes its appearance as well as water; this heat must likewise have a cause, x, and we have therefore $H+O+x=HO+cal.$ It might, however, be asked whether $H+O$ is really $=HO$, and $x=cal.$, and not perhaps $H+O=cal.$, and $x=HO$, whence the above equation could equally be deduced; and so in many other cases. The phlogistic chemists recognized the equation between *cal.* and x, or Phlogiston as they called it, and in so doing made a great step in advance; but they involved themselves again in a system of mistakes by putting $-x$ in place of O; thus, for instance, they obtained $H=HO+x$.

Chemistry, whose problem it is to set forth in equations the causal connection existing between the different kinds of matter, teaches us that matter, as a cause, has matter for its effect; but we are equally justified in saying that to force as cause, corresponds force as effect. Since $c=e$, and $e=c$, it is unnatural to call one term of an equation a force, and the other an effect of force or phenomenon, and to attach different notions to the expressions Force and Phenomenon. In brief, then, if the cause is matter, the effect is matter; if the cause is a force, the effect is also a force.

A cause which brings about the raising of a weight is a force; its effect (*the raised weight*) is, accordingly, equally *a force;* or, expressing this relation in a more general form, *separation in space of ponderable objects is a force;* since this force causes the fall of bodies, we call it *falling force.* Falling force and fall, or, more generally still, falling force and motion, are forces which are related to each other as cause and effect—forces which are convertible one into the other—two different forms of one and the same object. For example, a weight resting on the ground is not a force: it is neither the cause of motion, nor of the lifting of another weight; it becomes so, however, in proportion as it is raised above the ground: the cause—the distance between a weight and the earth—and the effect—the quantity of motion produced—bear to each other, as we learn from mechanics, a constant relation.

Gravity being regarded as the cause of the falling of bodies, a gravitating force is spoken of, and so the notions of *property* and of *force* are confounded with each other: precisely that which is the essential attribute of every force—the *union* of indestructibility with convertibility—is wanting in every property: between a property and a force, between gravity and motion, it is therefore impossible to establish the equation required for a rightly-conceived causal relation. If gravity be called a force, a cause is supposed which produces effects without itself diminishing, and incorrect conceptions of the causal connections of things are thereby fostered. In order that a body may fall, it is no less necessary that it should be lifted up, than that it should be heavy or possess gravity; the fall of bodies ought not therefore to be ascribed to their gravity alone.

It is the problem of Mechanics to develop the equations which subsist between falling force and motion, motion and falling force, and between different motions: here we will call to mind only one point. The magnitude of the falling force v is directly proportional (the earth's radius being assumed$=\infty$) to the magnitude of the mass m, and the height d to which it is raised; that is, $v=md$. If the height $d=1$, to which the mass m is raised, is transformed into the final velocity $c=1$ of this mass, we have also $v=mc$; but from the known relations existing between d and c, it results that, for other values of d or of c, the measure of the force v is mc^2; accordingly $v=md=mc^2$: the law of the conservation of *vis viva* is thus found to be based on the general law of the indestructibility of causes.

In numberless cases we see motion cease without having caused another motion or the lifting of a weight; but a force once in existence cannot be annihilated, it can only change its form; and the question therefore arises, What other forms is force, which we have become acquainted with as falling force and motion, capable of assuming? Experience alone can lead us to a conclusion on this point. In order to experiment with advantage, we must select implements which, besides causing a real cessation of motion, are as little as possible altered by the objects to be examined. If, for example, we rub together two metal plates, we see motion disappear, and heat, on the other hand, make its appearance, and we have now only to ask whether *motion* is the cause of heat. In order to come to a decision on this point, we must discuss the question whether, in the numberless cases in which the expenditure of motion is accompanied by the appearance of heat, the motion has not some other effect than the production of heat, and the heat some other cause than the motion.

An attempt to ascertain the effects of ceasing motion has never yet been seriously made; without, therefore, wishing to exclude *à priori* the hypothesis which it may be possible to set up, we observe only that, as a rule, this effect cannot be supposed to be an alteration in the state of aggregation of the moved (that is, rubbing, &c.) bodies. If we assume that a certain quantity of motion v is expended in the conversion of a rubbing substance m into n, we must then have $m+v=n$, and $n=m+v$; and when n is reconverted into m, v must appear again in some form or other. By the friction of two metallic plates continued for a very long time, we can gradually cause the cessation of an immense quantity of movement; but would it ever occur to us to look for even the smallest trace of the force which has disappeared in the metallic dust that we could collect, and to try to regain it thence? We repeat, the motion cannot have been annihilated; and contrary, or positive and negative, motions cannot be regarded as $=0$, any more than contrary motions can come out of nothing, or a weight can raise itself.

Without the recognition of a causal connection between motion and heat, it is just as difficult to explain the production of heat as it is to give any account of the motion that disappears. The heat cannot be derived from the diminution of the volume of the rubbing substances. It is well known that two pieces of ice may be melted by rubbing them together *in vacuo*; but let any one try to convert ice into water by pressure,* however enormous. Water undergoes, as was

* Since the original publication of this paper, Prof. W. Thomson has shown that pressure has a sensible effect in liquefying ice (*Conf.* Phil. Mag. S. 3, vol. xxxvii. p. 123); but the experiments of Bunsen and of Hopkins have shown that the melting-points of bodies which expand on becoming liquid are raised by pressure, which is all that Mayer's argument requires.—G. C. F.

found by the author, a rise of temperature when violently shaken. The water so heated (from 12° to 13° C.) has a greater bulk after being shaken than it had before; whence now comes this quantity of heat, which by repeated shaking may be called into existence in the same apparatus as often as we please? The vibratory hypothesis of heat is an approach toward the doctrine of heat being the effect of motion, but it does not favour the admission of this causal relation in its full generality; it rather lays the chief stress on uneasy oscillations (*unbehagliche Schwingungen*).

If it be now considered as established that in many cases (*exceptio confirmat regulam*) no other effect of motion can be traced except heat, and that no other cause than motion can be found for the heat that is produced, we prefer the assumption that heat proceeds from motion, to the assumption of a cause without effect and of an effect without a cause—just as the chemist, instead of allowing oxygen and hydrogen to disappear without further investigation, and water to be produced in some inexplicable manner, establishes a connection between oxygen and hydrogen on the one hand and water on the other.

The natural connection existing between falling force, motion, and heat may be conceived of as follows: We know that heat makes its appearance when the separate particles of a body approach nearer to each other; condensation produces heat. And what applies to the smallest particles of matter, and the smallest intervals between them, must also apply to large masses and to measurable distances. The falling of a weight is a diminution of the bulk of the earth, and must therefore without doubt be related to the quantity of heat thereby developed; this quantity of heat must be proportional to the greatness of the weight and its distance from the ground. From this point of view we are very easily led to the equations between falling force, motion, and heat, that have already been discussed.

But just as little as the connection between falling force and motion authorizes the conclusion that the essence of falling force is motion, can such a conclusion be adopted in the case of heat. We are, on the contrary, rather inclined to infer that, before it can become heat, motion—whether simple, or vibratory as in the case of light and radiant heat, &c. —must cease to exist as motion.

If falling force and motion are equivalent to heat, heat must also naturally be equivalent to motion and falling force. Just as heat appears as an *effect* of the diminution of bulk and of the cessation of motion, so also does heat disappear as a *cause* when its effects are produced in the shape of motion, expansion, or raising of weight.

In water-mills, the continual diminution in bulk which the earth undergoes, owing to the fall of the water, gives rise to motion, which afterwards disappears again, calling forth unceasingly a great quantity of heat; and inversely, the steam-engine serves to decompose heat again into motion or the raising of weights. A locomotive engine with its train may be compared to a distilling apparatus; the heat applied under the boiler passes off as motion, and this is deposited again as heat at the axles of the wheels.

We will close our disquisition, the propositions of which have resulted as necessary consequences from the principle "causa æquat effectum," and which are in accordance with all the phenomena of Nature, with a practical deduction. The solution of the equations subsisting between falling force and motion requires that the space fallen through in a given time, *e. g.* the first second, should be experimentally determined; in like manner, the solution of the equations subsisting between falling force and motion on the one hand and heat on the other, requires an answer to the question, How great is the quantity of heat which corresponds to a given quantity of motion or falling force? For instance, we must ascertain how high a given weight requires to be raised above the ground in order that its falling force may be equivalent to the raising of the temperature of an equal weight of water from 0° to 1° C. The attempt to show that such an equation is the expression of a physical truth may be regarded as the substance of the foregoing remarks.

By applying the principles that have been set forth to the relations subsisting between the temperature and the volume of gases, we find that the sinking of a mercury column by which a gas is compressed is equivalent to the quantity of heat set free by the compression; and hence it follows, the ratio between the capacity for heat of air under constant pressure and its capacity under constant volume being taken as $=1{\cdot}421$, that the warming of a given weight of water from 0° to 1° C. corresponds to the fall of an equal weight from the height of about 365 metres.* If we compare with this result the working of our best steam-engines, we see how small a part only of the heat applied under the boiler is really transformed into motion or the raising of weights; and this may serve as justification for the attempts at the profitable production of motion by some other method than the expenditure of the chemical difference between carbon and oxygen—more particularly by the transformation into motion of electricity obtained by chemical means.

* When the corrected specific heat of air is introduced into the calculation this number is increased, and agrees then with the experimental determinations of Mr. Joule.

II.

CELESTIAL DYNAMICS.

I.—INTRODUCTION.

EVERY incandescent and luminous body diminishes in temperature and luminosity in the same degree as it radiates light and heat, and at last, provided its loss be not repaired from some other source of these agencies, becomes cold and non-luminous.

For light, like sound, consists of vibrations which are communicated by the luminous or sounding body to a surrounding medium. It is perfectly clear that a body can only excite such vibrations in another substance when its own particles undergo a similar movement; for there is no cause for undulatory motion when a body is in a state of rest, or in a state of equilibrium with the medium by which it is surrounded. If a bell or a string is to be sounded, an external force must be applied; and this is the cause of the sound.

If the vibratory motion of a string could take place without any resistance, it would vibrate for all time; but in this case no sound could be produced, because sound is essentially the propagation of motion; and in the same degree as the string communicates its vibrations to the surrounding and resisting medium its own motion becomes weaker and weaker, until at last it sinks into a state of rest.

The sun has often and appropriately been compared to an incessantly sounding bell. But by what means is the power of this body kept up in undiminished force so as to enable him to send forth his rays into the universe in such a grand and magnificent manner? What are the causes which counteract or prevent his exhaustion, and thus save the planetary system from darkness and deadly cold?

Some endeavoured to approach "the grand secret," as Sir Wm. Herschel calls this question, by the assumption that the rays of the sun, being themselves perfectly cold, merely cause the "substance" of heat, supposed to be contained in bodies, to pass from a state of rest into a state of motion, and that in order to send forth such cold rays the sun need not be a hot body, so that, in spite of the infinite development of light, the cooling of the sun was a matter not to be thought of.

It is plain that nothing is gained by such an explanation; for, not to speak of the hypothetical "substance" of heat, assumed to be at one time at rest and at another time in motion, now cold and then hot, it is a well-founded fact that the sun does not radiate a cold phosphorescent light, but a light capable of warming bodies intensely; and to ascribe such rays to a cold body is at once at variance with reason and experience.

Of course such and similar hypotheses could not satisfy the demands of exact science, and I will therefore try to explain in a more satisfactory manner than has been done up to this time the connexion between the sun's radiation and its effects. In doing so, I have to claim the indulgence of scientific men, who are acquainted with the difficulties of my task.

II.—SOURCES OF HEAT.

Before we turn our attention to the special subject of this paper, it will be necessary to consider the means by which light and heat are produced. Heat may be obtained from very different sources. Combustion, fermentation, putrefaction, slaking of lime, the decomposition of chloride of nitrogen and of gun-cotton, &c. &c., are all of them sources of heat. The electric spark, the voltaic current, friction, percussion, and the vital processes are also accompanied by the evolution of this agent.

A general law of nature, which knows of no exception, is the following:—In order to obtain heat, something must be expended; this something, however different it may be in other respects, can always be referred to one of two categories: either it consists of some material expended in a chemical process, or of some sort of mechanical work.

When substances endowed with considerable chemical affinity for each other combine chemically, much heat is developed during the process. We shall estimate the quantity of heat thus set free by the number of kilogrammes of water which it would heat 1° C. The quantity of heat necessary to raise one kilogramme of water one degree is called a unit of heat.

It has been established by numerous experiments that the combustion of one kilogramme of dry charcoal in oxygen, so as to form carbonic acid, yields 7200 units of heat, which fact may be briefly expressed by saying that charcoal furnishes 7200° degrees of heat.

Superior coal yields 6000°, perfectly dry wood from 3300° to 3900°, sulphur 2700, and hydrogen 34,600° of heat.

According to experience, the number of units of heat only depends on the quantity of matter which is consumed, and not on the conditions under which the burning takes place. The same amount of heat is given out whether the combustion proceeds slowly or quickly, in atmospheric air or in pure oxygen gas. If in one case a metal be burnt in air and the amount of heat directly measured, and in another instance the same quantity of metal be oxidized in a galvanic battery, the heat being developed in some other place—say, the wire which conducts the current,—in both of these experiments the same quantity of heat will be observed.

The same law also holds good for the production of heat by mechanical means. The amount of heat obtained is only dependent on the quantity of power consumed, and is quite independent of the manner in which this power has been expended. If, therefore, the amount of heat which is produced by certain mechanical work is known, the quantity which will be obtained by any other amount of mechanical work can easily be found by calculation. It is of no consequence whether this work consists in the compression, percussion, or friction of bodies.

The amount of mechanical work done by a force may be expressed by a weight, and the height to which this weight would be raised by the same force. The mathematical expression for "work done," that is to say, a measure for this work, is obtained by multiplying the height expressed in feet or other units by the number of pounds or kilogrammes lifted to this height.

We shall take one kilogramme as the unit of weight, and one metre as the unit of height, and we thus obtain the weight of one kilogramme raised to the height of one metre as a unit measure of mechanical work performed. This measure we shall call a kilogrammetre, and adopt for it the symbol Km.

Mechanical work may likewise be measured by the velo city obtained by a given weight in passing from a state of rest into that of motion. The work done is then expressed by the product obtained by the multiplication of the weight by the square of its velocity. The first method, however, because it is the more convenient, is the one usually adopted; and the numbers obtained therefrom may easily be expressed in other units.

The product resulting from the multiplication of the number of units of weight and measures of height, or, as it is called, the product of mass and height, as well as the product of the mass and the square of its velocity, are called "*vis viva* of motion," "mechanical effect," dynamical effect," "work done," "*quantité de travail*," &c. &c.

The amount of mechanical work necessary for the heating of 1 kilogramme of water 1° C has been determined by experiment to be = 367 Km; therefore Km = 0·00273 units of heat.*

A mass which has fallen through a height of 367 metres possesses a velocity of 84·8 metres in one second; a mass, therefore, moving with this velocity originates 1° C. of heat when its motion is lost by percussion, friction, &c. If the velocity be two or three times as great, 4° or 9° of heat will be developed. Generally speaking, when the velocity is c metres, the corresponding development of heat will be expressed by the formula

$$0{\cdot}000139^{\circ} \times c^2.$$

* This essay was published in 1845. At that time de la Roche and Berard's determination of the specific heat of air was generally accepted. If the physical constants used by Mayer be corrected according to the results of more recent investigation, the mechanical equivalent of heat is found to be 771·4 foot-pounds. Mr. Joule finds it = 772 foot-pounds.—Tr.

III.—MEASURE OF THE SUN'S HEAT.

The actinometer is an instrument invented by Sir John Herschel for the purpose of measuring the heating efffect produced by the sun's rays. It is essentially a thermometer with a large cylindrical bulb filled with a blue liquid, which is acted upon by the sun's rays, and the expansion of which is measured by a graduated scale.

From observations made with this instrument, Sir John Herschel calculates the amount of heat received from the sun to be sufficient to melt annually at the surface of the globe a crust of ice 29·2 metres in thickness.

Pouillet has recently shown by some careful experiments with the lens pyrheliometer, an instrument invented by himself, that every square centimetre of the surface of our globe receives, on an average, in one minute an amount of solar heat which would raise the temperature of one gramme of water 0·4408°. Not much more than one-half of this quantity of heat, however, reaches the solid surface of our globe, since a considerable portion of it is absorbed by our atmosphere. The layer of ice which, according to Pouillet, could be melted by the solar heat which yearly reaches our globe would have a thickness of 30·89 metres.

A square metre of our earth's surface receives, therefore, according to Pouillet's results, which we shall adopt in the following pages, on an average in one minute 4·408 units of heat. The whole surface of the earth is = 9,260,500 geographical square miles* ; consequently the earth receives in one minute 2247 billions of units of heat from the sun.

In order to obtain smaller numbers, we shall call the quantity of heat necessary to raise a cubic mile of water 1°

* The geographical mile = 7420 metres, and one English mile = 1608 metres.

C. in temperature, a cubic mile of heat. Since one cubic mile of water weighs 408·54 billions of kilogrammes, a cubic mile of heat contains 408·54 billions of units of heat. The effect produced by the rays of the sun on the surface of the earth in one minute is therefore 5·5 cubic miles of heat.

Let us imagine the sun to be surrounded by a hollow sphere whose radius is equal to the mean distance of the earth from the sun, or 20,589,000 geographical miles; the surface of this sphere would be equal to 5326 billions of square miles. The surface obtained by the intersection of this hollow sphere and our globe, or the base of the cone of solar light which reaches our earth, stands to the whole surface of this hollow sphere as $\frac{9,260,500}{4}$: 5326 billions, or as 1 to 2300 millions. This is the ratio of the heat received by our globe to the whole amount of heat sent forth from the sun, which latter in one minute amounts to 12,650 millions of cubic miles of heat.

This amazing radiation ought, unless the loss is by some means made good, to cool considerably even a body of the magnitude of the sun.

If we assume the sun to be endowed with the same capacity for heat as a mass of water of the same volume, and its loss of heat by radiation to affect uniformly its whole mass, the temperature of the sun ought to decrease 1°·8 C. yearly, and for the historic time of 5000 years this loss would consequently amount to 9000° C.

A uniform cooling of the whole of the sun's huge mass cannot, however, take place; on the contrary, if the radiation were to occur at the expense of a given store of heat or radiant power, the sun would become covered in a short space of time with a cold crust, whereby radiation would be brought to an end. Considering the continued activity of the sun through countless centuries, we may assume with mathematical certainty the existence of some compensating influence to make good its enormous loss.

Is this restoring agency a chemical process?

If such were the case, the most favourable assumption would be to suppose the whole mass of the sun to be one lump of coal, the combustion of every kilogramme of which produces 6000 units of heat. Then the sun would only be able to sustain for forty-six centuries its present expenditure of light and heat, not to mention the oxygen necessary to keep up such an immense combustion, and other unfavourable circumstances.

The revolution of the sun on his axis has been suggested as the cause of his radiating energy. A closer examination proves this hypothesis also to be untenable.

Rapid rotation, without friction or resistance, cannot in itself alone be regarded as a cause of light and heat, especially as the sun is in no way to be distinguished from the other bodies of our system by velocity of axial rotation. The sun turns on his axis in about twenty-five days, and his diameter is nearly 112 times as great as that of the earth, from which it follows that a point on the solar equator travels but a little more than four times as quickly as a point on the earth's equator. The largest planet of the solar system, whose diameter is about $\frac{1}{10}$th that of the sun, turns on its axis in less than ten hours; a point on its equator revolves about six times quicker than one on the solar equator. The outer ring of Saturn exceeds the sun's equator more than ten times in velocity of rotation. Nevertheless no generation of light or heat is observed on our globe, on Jupiter, or on the ring of Saturn.

It might be thought that friction, though undeveloped in the case of the other celestial bodies, might be engendered by the sun's rotation, and that such friction might generate enormous quantities of heat. But for the production of friction two bodies, at least, are always necessary which are in immediate contact with one another, and which move with different velocities or in different directions. Friction, moreover, has a tendency to produce equal motion of the two rubbing bodies; and when this is attained, the generation of heat ceases. If now the sun be the one moving body, where is the other? and if the second body exist, what power prevents it from assuming the same rotary motion as the sun?

But could even these difficulties be disregarded, a weightier and more formidable obstacle opposes this hypothesis. The known volume and mass of the sun allow us to calculate the *vis viva* which he possesses in consequence of his rotation. Assuming his density to be uniform throughout his mass, and his period of rotation twenty-five days, it is equal to 182,300 quintillions of kilogrammetres (Km). But for one unit of heat generated, 367 Km are consumed; consequently the whole rotation-effect of the sun could only cover the expenditure of heat for the space of 183 years.

The space of our solar system is filled with a great number of ponderable objects, which have a tendency to move towards the centre of gravity of the sun; and in so doing, their rate of motion is more and more accelerated.

A mass, without motion, placed within the sphere of the sun's attraction, will obey this attraction, and, if there be no disturbing influences, will fall in a straight line into the sun. In reality, however, such a rectilinear path can scarcely occur, as may be shown by experiment.

Let a weight be suspended by a string so that it can only touch the floor in one point. Lift the weight up to a certain height, and at the same time stretch the string out to its full length; if the weight be now allowed to fall, it will be observed, almost in every case, not to reach at once the point on the floor towards which it tends to move, but to move round this point for some time in a curved line.

The reason of this phenomenon is that the slightest deviation of the weight from its shortest route towards the point on the floor, caused by some disturbing influence such as the resistance of the air against a not perfectly uniform surface, will maintain itself as long as motion lasts. It is nevertheless possible for the weight to move at once to the point; the probability of its doing so, however, becomes the less as the height from which it is allowed to drop increases, or the string, by means of which it is suspended, is lengthened.

Similar laws influence the movements of bodies in the space of the solar system. The height of the fall is here represented by the original distance from the sun at which the body begins to move; the length of the string by the sun's attraction, which increases when the distance decreases; and the small surface of contact on the floor by the area of the section of the sun's sphere. If now a cosmical mass within the physical limits of the sun's sphere of attraction begins its fall towards that heavenly body, it will be disturbed in its long path for many centuries, at first by the nearest fixed stars, and afterwards by the bodies of the solar system. Motion of such a mass in a straight line, or its perpendicular fall into the sun, would, therefore, under such conditions, be impossible. The observed movement of all planetary bodies in closed curves agrees with this.

We shall now return to the example of the weight suspended by a string and oscillating round a point towards which it is attracted. The diameters of the orbits described by this weight are observed to be nearly equal; continued observation, however, shows that these diameters gradually diminish in length, so that the weight will by degrees approach the point in which it can touch the floor. The weight, however, touches the floor not in a mathematical point, but in a small surface; as soon, therefore, as the diameter of the curve in which the weight moves is equal to the diameter of this surface, the weight will touch the floor. This final contact is no accidental or improbable event, but a necessary phenomenon caused by the resistance which the oscillating mass constantly suffers from the air and friction. If all resistance could be annihilated, the motion of the weight would of course continue in equal oscillations.

The same law holds good for celestial bodies.

The movements of celestial bodies in an absolute vacuum would be as uniform as those of a mathematical pendulum, whereas a resisting medium pervading all space would cause the planets to move in shorter and shorter orbits, and at last to fall into the sun.

Assuming such a resisting medium, these wandering celestial bodies must have on the periphery of the solar system their cradle, and in its centre their grave; and however long the duration, and however great the number of their revolutions may be, as many masses will on the average in a certain time arrive at the sun as formerly in a like period of time came within his sphere of attraction.

All these bodies plunge with a violent impetus into their common grave. Since no cause exists without an effect, each of these cosmical masses will, like a weight falling to the earth, produce by its percussion an amount of heat proportional to its *vis viva*.

From the idea of a sun whose attraction acts throughout space, of ponderable bodies scattered throughout the universe, and of a resisting æther, another idea necessarily follows—that, namely, of a continual and inexhaustible generation of heat on the central body of this cosmical system.

Whether such a conception be realized in our solar system—whether, in other words, the wonderful and permanent evolution of light and heat be caused by the uninterrupted fall of cosmical matter into the sun—will now be more closely examined.

The existence of matter in a primordial condition (*Urmaterie*), moving about in the universe, and assumed to follow the attraction of the nearest stellar system, will scarcely be denied by astronomers and physicists; for the richness of surrounding nature, as well as the aspect of the starry heavens, prevents the belief that the wide space which separates our solar system from the regions governed by the other fixed stars is a vacant solitude destitute of matter. We shall leave, however, all suppositions concerning subjects so distant from us both in time and space, and confine our attention exclusively to what may be learnt from the observation of the existing state of things.

Besides the fourteen known planets with their eighteen satellites, a great many other cosmical masses move within the space of the planetary system, of which the comets deserve to be mentioned first.

Kepler's celebrated statement that "there are more comets in the heavens than fish in the ocean," is founded on the fact that, of all the comets belonging to our solar system, comparatively few can be seen by the inhabitants of the earth, and therefore the not inconsiderable number of actually observed comets obliges us, according to the rules of the calculus of probabilities, to assume the existence of a great many more beyond the sphere of our vision.

Besides planets, satellites, and comets, another class of celestial bodies exists within our solar system. These are masses which, on account of their smallness, may be considered as cosmical atoms, and which Arago has appropriately called asteroids. They, like the planets and the comets, are governed by gravity, and move in elliptical orbits round the sun. When accident brings them into the immediate neighbourhood of the earth, they produce the phenomena of shooting-stars and fireballs.

It has been shown by repeated observation, that on a bright night twenty minutes seldom elapse without a shooting-star being visible to an observer in any situation. At certain times these meteors are observed in astonishingly great numbers; during the meteoric shower at Boston, which lasted nine hours, when they were said to fall "crowded together like snow-flakes," they were estimated as at least 240,000. On the whole, the number of asteroids which come near the earth in the space of a year must be computed to be many thousands of millions. This, without doubt, is only a small fraction of the number of asteroids that move round the sun, which number, according to the rules of the calculus of probabilities, approaches the infinite.

As has been already stated, on the existence of a resisting æther it depends whether the celestial bodies, the planets, the comets, and the asteroids move at constant mean distances round the sun, or whether they are constantly approaching that central body.

Scientific men do not doubt the existence of such an æther. Littrow, amongst others, expresses himself on this point as follows:—"The assumption that the planets and the comets move in an absolute vacuum can in no way be admitted. Even if the space between celestial bodies contained no other matter than that necessary for the existence of light (whether light be considered as emission of matter or the undulations of a universal æther), this alone is sufficient to alter the motion of the planets in the course of time and the arrangement of the whole system itself; the fall of all the planets and the comets into the sun and the destruction of the present state of the solar system must be the final results of this action."

A direct proof of the existence of such a resisting medium has been furnished by the academician Encke. He found that the comet named after him, which revolves round the sun in the short space of 1207 days, shows a regular acceleration of its motion, in consequence of which the time of each revolution is shortened by about six hours.

From the great density and magnitude of the planets, the shortening of the diameters of their orbits proceeds, as might be expected, very slowly, and is up to the present time inappreciable. The smaller the cosmical masses are, on the contrary, other circumstances remaining the same, the faster they move towards the sun; it may therefore happen that in a space of time wherein the mean distance of the earth from the sun would diminish one metre, a small asteroid would travel more than one thousand miles towards the central body.

As cosmical masses stream from all sides in immense numbers towards the sun, it follows that they must become more and more crowded together as they approach thereto. The conjecture at once suggests itself that the zodiacal light, the nebulous light of vast dimensions which surrounds the sun, owes its origin to such closely-packed asteroids. However it may be, this much is certain, that this phenomenon is caused by matter which moves according to the same laws as the planets round the sun, and it consequently follows that the whole mass which originates the zodiacal light is continually approaching the sun and falling into it.

This light does not surround the sun uniformly on all sides; that is to say, it has not the form of a sphere, but that of a thin convex lens, the greater diameter of which is in the plane of the solar equator, and accordingly it has to an observer on our globe a pyramidal form. Such lenticular distribution of the masses in the universe is repeated in a remarkable manner in the disposition of the planets and the fixed stars.

From the great number of cometary masses and asteroids and the zodiacal light on the one hand, and the existence of a resisting æther on the other, it necessarily follows that ponderable matter must continually be arriving on the solar surface. The effect produced by these masses evidently depends on their final velocity; and, in order to determine the latter, we shall discuss some of the elements of the theory of gravitation.

The final velocity of a weight attracted by and moving towards a celestial body will become greater as the height through which the weight falls increases. This velocity, however, if it be only produced by the fall, cannot exceed a certain magnitude; it has a maximum, the value of which depends on the volume and mass of the attracting celestial body.

Let r be the radius of a spherical and solid celestial body, and g the velocity at the end of the first second of a weight falling on the surface of this body; then the greatest velocity which this weight can obtain by its fall towards the celestial body, or the velocity with which it will arrive at its surface after a fall from an infinite height, is $\sqrt{2gr}$ in one second. This number, wherein g and r are expressed in metres, we shall call G.

For our globe the value of g is 9·8164 . . and that of r 6,369,800; and consequently on our earth

$$G = \sqrt{(2 \times 9{\cdot}8164 \times 6{,}369{,}800)} = 11{,}183.$$

The solar radius is 112·05 times that of the earth, and the velocity produced by gravity on the sun's surface is 28·36 times greater than the same velocity on the surface of our globe; the greatest velocity therefore which a body could obtain in consequence of the solar attraction, or

$$G = \sqrt{(28{\cdot}36 \times 112{\cdot}05)} \times 11{,}183 = 630{,}400;$$

that is, this maximum velocity is equal to 630,400 metres, or 85 geographical miles in one second.

By the help of this constant number, which may be called the *characteristic* of the solar system, the velocity of a body in central motion may easily be determined at any point of its orbit. Let a be the mean distance of the planetary body from the centre of gravity of the sun, or the greater semidiameter of its orbit (the radius of the sun being taken as unity); and let h be the distance of the same body at any point of its orbit from the centre of gravity of the sun; then the velocity, expressed in metres, of the planet at the distance h is

$$G \times \sqrt{\frac{2a - h}{2a \times h}}.$$

At the moment the planet comes in contact with the solar surface, h is equal to 1, and its velocity is therefore

$$G \times \sqrt{\frac{2a - 1}{2a}}.$$

It follows from this formula that the smaller $2a$ (or the major axis of the orbit of a planetary body) becomes, the less will be its velocity when it reaches the sun. This velocity, like the major axis, has a minimum; for so long as the planet moves outside the sun, its major axis cannot be shorter than the diameter of the sun, or, taking the solar radius as a unit, the quantity $2a$ can never be less than 2. The smallest velocity with which we can imagine a cosmical body to arrive on the surface of the sun is consequently

$$G\times\sqrt{\frac{1}{2}}=445,750,$$

or a velocity of 60 geographical miles in one second.

For this smallest value the orbit of the asteroid is circular; for a larger value it becomes elliptical, until finally, with increasing excentricity, when the value of $2a$ approaches infinity, the orbit becomes a parabola. In the last case the velocity is

$$G\times\sqrt{\frac{\infty-1}{\infty}}=G,$$

or, 85 geographical miles in one second.

If the value of the major axis become negative, or the orbit assume the form of a hyperbola, the velocity may increase without end. But this could only happen when cosmical masses enter the space of the solar system with a projected velocity, or when masses, having missed the sun's surface, move into the universe and never return; hence a velocity greater than G can only be regarded as a rare exception, and we shall therefore only consider velocities comprised within the limits of 60 and 80 miles.*

The final velocity with which a weight moving in a

* The relative velocity also with which an asteroid reaches the solar surface depends in some degree on the velocity of the sun's rotation. This, however, as well as the rotatory effect of the asteroid, is without moment, and may be neglected.

straight line towards the centre of the sun arrives at the solar surface is expressed by the formula

$$c = G \times \sqrt{\frac{h-1}{h}},$$

wherein c expresses the final velocity in metres, and h the original distance from the centre of the sun in terms of solar radius. If this formula be compared with the foregoing, it will be seen that a mass which, after moving in central motion, arrives at the sun's surface has the same velocity as it would possess had it fallen perpendicularly into the sun from a distance* equal to the major axis of its orbit; whence it is apparent that a planet, on arriving at the sun, moves at least as quickly as a weight which falls freely towards the sun from a distance as great as the solar radius, or 96,000 geographical miles.

What thermal effect corresponds to such velocities? Is the effect sufficiently great to play an important part in the immense development of heat on the sun?

This crucial question may be easily answered by help of the preceding considerations. According to the formula given at the end of Chapter II., the degree of heat generated by percussion is

$$= 0 \cdot 000139^{\circ} \times c^2,$$

where c denotes the velocity of the striking body expressed in metres. The velocity of an asteroid when it strikes the sun measures from 445,750 to 630,400 metres; the caloric effect of the percussion is consequently equal to from $27\frac{1}{2}$ to 55 millions of degrees of heat†.

An asteroid, therefore, by its fall into the sun developes

* This distance is to be counted from the centre of the sun.

† Throughout this memoir the degrees of heat are expressed in the Centigrade scale. Unless stated to the contrary, the measures of length are given in geographical miles. A geographical mile = 7420 metres, and an English mile = 1608 metres.—Tr.

from 4600 to 9200 times as much heat as would be generated by the combustion of an equal mass of coal.

IV.—ORIGIN OF THE SUN'S HEAT.

THE question why the planets move in curved orbits, one of the grandest of problems, was solved by Newton in consequence, it is believed, of his reflecting on the fall of an apple. This story is not improbable, for we are on the right track for the discovery of truth when once we clearly recognize that between great and small no qualitative but only a quantitative difference exists—when we resist the suggestions of an ever active imagination, and look for the same laws in the greatest as well as in the smallest processes of nature.

This universal range is the essence of a law of nature, and the touchstone of the correctness of human theories. We observe the fall of an apple, and investigate the law which governs this phenomenon; for the earth we substitute the sun, and for the apple a planet, and thus possess ourselves of the key to the mechanics of the heavens.

As the same laws prevail in the greater as well as in the smaller processes of nature, Newton's method may be used in solving the problem of the origin of the sun's heat. We know the connexion between the space through which a body falls, the velocity, the *vis viva*, and the generation of heat on the surface of this globe; if we again substitute for the earth the sun, with a mass 350,000 greater, and for a height of a few metres celestial distances, we obtain a generation of heat exceeding all terrestrial measures. And since we have sufficient reason to assume the actual existence of such mechanical processes in the heavens, we find therein the only tenable explanation of the origin of the heat of the sun.

The fact that the development of heat by mechanical means on the surface of our globe is, as a rule, not so great, and cannot be so great as the generation of the same agent by chemical means, as by combustion, follows from the laws already discussed; and this fact cannot be used as an argument against the assumption of a greater development of heat by a greater expenditure of mechanical work. It has been shown that the heat generated by a weight falling from a height of 367 metres is only $\frac{1}{6000}$th part of the heat produced by the combustion of the same weight of coal; just as small is the amount of heat developed by a weight moving with the not inconsiderable velocity of 85 metres in one second. But, according to the laws of mechanics, the effect is proportional to the square of the velocity; if therefore the weight move 100 times faster, or with a velocity of 8500 metres in one second, it will produce a greater effect than the combustion of an equal quantity of coal.

It is true that so great a velocity cannot be obtained by human means; everyday experience, however, shows the development of high degrees of temperature by mechanical processes.

In the common flint and steel, the particles of steel which are struck off are sufficiently heated to burn in air. A few blows directed by a skilful blacksmith with a sledge-hammer against a piece of cold metal may raise the temperature of the metal at the points of collision to redness.

The new crank of a steamer, whilst being polished by friction, becomes red-hot, several buckets of water being required to cool it down to its ordinary temperature.

When a railway train passes with even less than its ordinary velocity along a very sharp curve of the line, sparks are observed in consequence of the friction against the rails.

One of the grandest constructions for the production of motion by human art is the channel in which the wood was allowed to glide down from the steep and lofty sides of Mount

Pilatus into the plain below. This wooden channel which was built about thirty years ago by the engineer Rupp, was 9 English miles in length; the largest trees were shot down it from the top to the bottom of the mountain in about two minutes and a half. The momentum possessed by the trees on their escaping at their journey's end from the channel was sufficiently great to bury their thicker ends in the ground to the depth of from 6 to 8 metres. To prevent the wood getting too hot and taking fire, water was conducted in many places into the channel.

This stupendous mechanical process, when compared with cosmical processes on the sun, appears infinitely small. In the latter case it is the mass of the sun which attracts, and in lieu of the height of Mount Pilatus we have distances of a hundred thousand and more miles; the amount of heat generated by cosmical falls is therefore at least 9 million times greater than in our terrestrial example.

Rays of heat on passing through glass and other transparent bodies undergo partial absorption, which differs in degree, however, according to the temperature of the source from which the heat is derived. Heat radiated from sources less warm than boiling water is almost completely stopped by thin plates of glass. As the temperature of a source of heat increases, its rays pass more copiously through diathermic bodies. A plate of glass, for example, weakens the rays of a red-hot substance, even when the latter is placed very close to it, much more than it does those emanating at a much greater distance from a white-hot body. If the quality of the sun's rays be examined in this respect, their diathermic energy is found to be far superior to that of all artificial sources of heat. The temperature of the focus of a concave metallic reflector in which the sun's light has been collected is only diminished from one-seventh to one-eighth by the interposition of a screen of glass. If the same experiment be made with an artificial and luminous source of heat, it is found that, though the focus be very hot when the screen is away, the interposition of the latter cuts off nearly all the heat; moreover, the focus will not recover its former temperature when reflector and screen are placed sufficiently near to the source of heat to make the focus appear brighter than it did in the former position without the glass screen.

The empirical law, that the diathermic energy of heat increases with the temperature of the source from which the heat is radiated, teaches us that the sun's surface must be much hotter than the most powerful process of combustion could render it.

Other methods furnish the same conclusion. If we imagine the sun to be surrounded by a hollow sphere, it is clear that the inner surface of this sphere must receive all the heat radiated from the sun. At the distance of our globe from the sun, such a sphere would have a radius 215 times as great, and an area 46,000 times as large as the sun himself; those luminous and calorific rays, therefore, which meet this spherical surface at right angles retain only $\frac{1}{46,000}$th part of their original intensity. If it be further considered that our atmosphere absorbs a part of the solar rays, it is clear that the rays which reach the tropics of our earth at noonday can only possess from $\frac{1}{50,000}$th to $\frac{1}{60,000}$th of the power with which they started. These rays, when gathered from a surface of from 5 to 6 square metres, and concentrated in an area of one square centimetre, would produce about the temperature which exists on the sun, a temperature more than sufficient to vaporize platinum, rhodium, and similar metals.

The radiation calculated in Chapter III. likewise proves the enormous temperature of the solar surface. From the determination mentioned therein, it follows that each square centimetre of the sun's surface loses by radiation about 80 units of heat per minute—an immense quantity in comparison with terrestrial radiations.

A correct theory of the origin of the sun's heat must explain the cause of such enormous temperatures. This explanation can be deduced from the foregoing statements. According to Pouillet, the temperature at which bodies appear intensely white-hot is about 1500° C. The heat generated by the combustion of one kilogramme of hydrogen is, as determined by Dulong, 34,500, and according to the more recent experiments of Grassi, 34,666 units of heat. One part of hydrogen combines with eight parts of oxygen to form water; hence one kilogramme of these two gases mixed in this ratio would produce 3850°.

Let us now compare this heat with the amount of the same agent generated by the fall of an asteroid into the sun. Without taking into account the low specific heat of such masses when compared with that of water, we find the heat developed by the asteroid to be from 7000 to 15,000 times greater than that of the oxyhydrogen mixture. From data like these, the extraordinary diathermic energy of the sun's rays, the immense radiation from his surface, and the high temperature in the focus of the reflector are easily accounted for.

The facts above mentioned show that, unless we assume on the sun the existence of matter with unheard of chemical properties as a *deus ex machinâ*, no chemical process could maintain the present high radiation of the sun; it also follows from the above results, that the chemical nature of bodies which fall into the sun does not in the least affect our conclusions; the effect produced by the most inflammable substance would not differ by one-thousandth part from that resulting from the fall of matter possessing but feeble chemical affinities. As the brightest artificial light appears dark in comparison with the sun's light, so the mechanical processes of the heavens throw into the shade the most powerful chemical actions.

The quality of the sun's rays, as dependent on his temper

ature, is of the greatest importance to mankind. If the solar heat were originated by a chemical process, and amounted near its source to a temperature of a few thousand degrees, it would be possible for the light to reach us, whilst the greater part of the more important calorific rays would be absorbed by the higher strata of our atmosphere and then returned to the universe.

In consequence of the high temperature of the sun, however, our atmosphere is highly diathermic to his rays, so that the latter reach the surface of our earth and warm it. The comparatively low temperature of the terrestrial surface is the cause why the heat cannot easily radiate back through the atmosphere into the universe. The atmosphere acts, therefore, like an envelope, which is easily pierced by the solar rays, but which offers considerable resistance to the radiant heat escaping from our earth; its action resembles that of a valve which allows liquid to pass freely in one, but stops the flow in the opposite direction.

The action of the atmosphere is of the greatest importance as regards climate and meteorological processes. It must raise the mean temperature of the earth's surface. After the setting of the sun—in fact, in all places where his rays do not reach the surface, the temperature of the earth would soon be as low as that of the universe, if the atmosphere were removed, or if it did not exist. Even the powerful solar rays in the tropics would be unable to preserve water in its liquid state.

Between the great cold which would reign at all times and in all places, and the moderate warmth which in reality exists on our globe, intermediate temperatures may be imagined; and it is easily seen that the mean temperature would decrease if the atmosphere were to become more and more rare. Such a rarefaction of a valve-like acting atmosphere actually takes place as we ascend higher and higher above the level of the sea, and it is accordingly and necessarily accompanied by a corresponding diminution of temperature.

This well-known fact of the lower mean temperature of places of greater altitude has led to the strangest hypotheses. The sun's rays were not supposed to contain all the conditions for warming a body, but to set in motion the "substance" of heat contained in the earth. This "substance" of heat, cold when at rest, was attracted by the earth, and was therefore found in greater abundance near the centre of the globe. This view, it was thought, explained why the warming power of the sun was so much weaker at the top of a mountain than at the bottom, and why, in spite of his immense radiation, he retained his full powers.

This belief, which especially prevails amongst imperfectly informed people, and which will scarcely succumb to correct views, is directly contradicted by the excellent experiments made by Pouillet at different altitudes with the pyrheliometer. These experiments show that, everything else being equal, the generation of heat by the solar rays is more powerful in higher altitudes than near the surface of our globe, and that consequently a portion of these rays is absorbed on their passage through the atmosphere. Why, in spite of this partial absorption, the mean temperature of low altitudes is nevertheless higher than it is in more elevated positions, is explained by the fact that the atmosphere stops to a far greater degree the calorific rays emanating from the earth than it does those from the sun.

V.—CONSTANCY OF THE SUN'S MASS.

Newton, as is well known, considered light to be the emission of luminous particles from the sun. In the continued emission of light this great philosopher saw a cause tending to diminish the solar mass; and he assumed, in order to make good this loss, comets and other cosmical masses to be continually falling into the central body.

If we express this view of Newton's in the language of the undulatory theory, which is now universally accepted, we obtain the results developed in the preceding pages. It is true that our theory does not accept a peculiar "substance" of light or of heat; nevertheless, according to it, the radiation of light and heat consists also in purely material processes, in a sort of motion, in the vibrations of ponderable resisting substances. Quiescence is darkness and death; motion is light and life.

An undulating motion proceeding from a point or a plane and excited in an unlimited medium, cannot be imagined apart from another simultaneous motion, a translation of the particles themselves;* it therefore follows, not only from the emission, but also from the undulatory theory, that radiation continually diminishes the mass of the sun. Why, nevertheless, the mass of the sun does not really diminish has already been stated.

The radiation of the sun is a centrifugal action equivalent to a centripetal motion.

The caloric effect of the centrifugal action of the sun can be found by direct observation; it amounts, according to Chapter III., in one minute to 12,650 millions of cubic miles of heat, or 5·17 quadrillions of units of heat. In Chapter IV. it has been shown that one kilogramme of the mass of an asteroid originates from 27·5 to 55 millions of units of heat; the quantity of cosmical masses, therefore, which falls every minute into the sun amounts to from 94,000 to 188,000 billions of kilogrammes.

To obtain this remarkable result, we made use of a method

* This centrifugal motion is perhaps the cause of the repulsion of the tails on comets when in the neighbourhood of the sun, as observed by Bessel.

which is common in physical inquiries. Observation of the moon's motion reveals to us the external form of the earth. The physicist determines with the torsion-balance the weight of a planet, just as the merchant finds the weight of a parcel of goods, whilst the pendulum has become a magic power in the hands of the geologist, enabling him to discover cavities in the bowels of the earth. Our case is similar to these. By observation and calculation of the velocity of sound in our atmosphere, we obtain the ratio of the specific heat of air under constant pressure and under constant volume, and by the help of this number we determine the quantity of heat generated by mechanical work. The heat which arrives from the sun in a given time on a small surface of our globe serves as a basis for the calculation of the whole radiating effect of the sun; and the result of a series of observations and well-founded conclusions is the quantitative determination of those cosmical masses which the sun receives from the space through which he sends forth his rays.

Measured by terrestrial standards, the ascertained number of so many billions of kilogrammes per minute appears incredible. This quantity, however, may be brought nearer to our comprehension by comparison with other cosmical magnitudes. The nearest celestial body to us (the moon) has a mass of about 90,000 trillions of kilogrammes, and it would therefore cover the expenditure of the sun for from one to two years. The mass of the earth would afford nourishment to the sun for a period of from 60 to 120 years.

To facilitate the appreciation of the masses and the distances occurring in the planetary system, Herschel draws the following picture. Let the sun be represented by a globe 1 metre in diameter. The nearest planet (Mercury) will be about as large as a pepper-corn, 3½ millimetres in thickness, at a distance of 40 metres. 78 and 107 metres distant from the sun will move Venus and the Earth, each 9 millimetres in diameter, or a little larger than a pea. Not much more than a quarter of a metre from the Earth will be the Moon, the size of a mustard seed, $2\frac{1}{2}$ millimetres in diameter. Mars, at a distance of 160 metres, will have about half the diameter of the Earth; and the smaller planets (Vesta, Hebe, Astrea, Juno, Pallas, Ceres, &c.), at a distance of from 250 to 300 metres from the sun, will resemble particles of sand. Jupiter and Saturn, 560 and 1000 metres distant from the centre, will be represented by oranges, 10 and 9 centimetres in diameter. Uranus, of the size of a nut 4 centimetres across, will be 2000 metres; and Neptune, as large as an apple 6 centimetres in diameter, will be nearly twice as distant, or about half a geographical mile away from the sun. From Neptune to the nearest fixed star will be more than 2000 geographical miles.

To complete this picture, it is necessary to imagine finely-divided matter grouped in a diversified manner, moving slowly and gradually towards the large central globe, and on its arrival attaching itself thereto; this matter, when favourably illuminated by the sun, represents itself to us as the zodiacal light. This nebulous substance forms also an important part of a creation in which nothing is by chance, but wherein all is arranged with Divine foresight and wisdom.

The surface of the sun measures 115,000 millions of square miles, or $6\frac{1}{3}$ trillions of square metres; the mass of matter which in the shape of asteroids falls into the sun every minute is from 94,000 to 188,000 billions of kilogrammes; one square metre of solar surface, therefore, receives on an average from 15 to 30 grammes of matter per minute.

To compare this process with a terrestrial phenomenon, a gentle rain may be considered which sends down in one hour a layer of water 1 millimetre in thickness (during a thunderstorm the rainfall is often from ten to fifteen times this quantity); this amounts on a square metre to 17 grammes per minute.

The continual bombardment of the sun by these cosmical masses ought to increase its volume as well as its mass, if centripetal action only existed. The increase of volume, could scarcely be appreciated by man; for if the specific gravity of these cosmical masses be assumed to be the same as that of the sun, the enlargement of his apparent diameter to the extent of one second, the smallest appreciable magnitude, would require from 33,000 to 66,000 years.

Not quite so inappreciable would be the increase of the mass of the sun. If this mass, or the weight of the sun, were augmented, an acceleration of the motion of the planets in their orbits would be the consequence, whereby their times of revolution round the central body would be shortened. The mass of the sun is 2·1 quintillions of kilogrammes; and the mass of the cosmical matter annually arriving at the sun stands to the above as 1 to from 21 — 42 millions. Such an augmentation of the weight of the sun ought to shorten the sidereal year from $\frac{1}{42,000,000}$th to $\frac{1}{85,000,000}$th of its length, or from $\frac{3}{4}$ths to $\frac{3}{8}$ths of a second.

The observations of astronomers do not agree with this conclusion; we must therefore fall back on the theory mentioned at the beginning of this chapter, which assumes that the sun, like the ocean, is constantly losing and receiving equal quantities of matter. This harmonizes with the supposition that the *vis viva* of the universe is a constant quantity.

VI.—THE SPOTS ON THE SUN'S DISC.

THE solar disc presents, according to Sir John Herschel, the following appearance. "When the sun is observed through a powerful telescope provided with coloured glasses in order to lessen the heat and brightness which would be hurtful to the eyes, large dark spots are often seen surrounded by edges which are not quite so dark as the spots themselves, and which are called penumbræ. These spots, however, are neither permanent nor unchangeable. When observed from day to day, or even from hour to hour, their form is seen to change; they expand or contract, and finally disappear; on other parts of the solar surface new spots spring into existence where none could be discovered before. When they disappear, the darker part in the middle of the spot contracts to a point and vanishes sooner than the edge. Sometimes they break up into two or more parts that show all the signs of mobility characteristic of a liquid, and the extraordinary commotion which it seems only possible for gaseous matter to possess. The magnitude of their motion is very great. An arc of 1 second, as seen from our globe, corresponds to 465 English miles on the sun's disc; a circle of this diameter, which measures nearly 220,000 English square miles, is the smallest area that can be seen on the solar surface. Spots, however, more than 45,000 English miles in diameter, and, if we may trust some statements, of even greater dimensions, have been observed. For such a spot to disappear in the course of six weeks (and they rarely last longer), the edges, whilst approaching each other, must move through a space of more than 1000 miles per diem.

"That portion of the solar disc which is free from spots is by no means uniformly bright. Over it are scattered small dark spots or pores, which are found by careful observation to be in a state of continual change. The slow sinking of some chemical precipitates in a transparent liquid, when viewed from the upper surface and in a direction perpendicular thereto, resembles more accurately than any other phenomenon the changes which the pores undergo. The similarity is so striking, in fact, that one can scarcely resist the idea that the appearances above described are owing to a luminous medium moving about in a non-luminous atmosphere, either like the clouds in our air, or in wide-spread planes and flame-like columns, or in rays like the aurora borealis.

"Near large spots, or extensive groups of them, large spaces are observed to be covered with peculiarly marked lines much brighter than the other parts of the surface; these lines are curved, or deviate in branches, and are called faculæ. Spots are often seen between these lines, or to originate there. These are in all probability the crests of immense waves in the luminous regions of the solar atmosphere, and bear witness to violent action in their immediate neighbourhood."

The changes on the solar surface evidently point to the action of some external disturbing force; for every moving power resident in the sun itself ought to exhaust itself by its own action. These changes, therefore, are no unimportant confirmation of the theory explained in these pages.

At the same time it must be observed that our knowledge of physical heliography is, from the nature of the subject, very limited; even the meteorological processes and other phenomena of our own planet are still in many respects enigmatical. For this reason no special information could be given about the manner in which the solar surface is affected by cosmical masses. However, I may be allowed to mention some probable conjectures which offer themselves.

The extraordinarily high temperature which exists on the sun almost precludes the possibility of its surface being solid; it doubtless consists of an uninterrupted ocean of fiery fluid matter. This gaseous envelope becomes more rarefied in those parts most distant from the sun's centre.

As most substances are able to assume the gaseous state of aggregation at high temperatures, the height of the sun's atmosphere cannot be inconsiderable. There are, however, sound reasons for believing that the relative height of the solar atmosphere is not very great.

Since the gravity is 28 times greater on the sun's surface than it is on our earth, a column of air on the former must cause a pressure 28 times greater than it would on our globe. This great pressure compresses air as much as a temperature of 8000° would expand it.

In a still greater degree than this increased gravity do the qualities peculiar to gases affect the height of the solar atmosphere. In consequence of these properties, the density of our atmosphere rapidly diminishes as we ascend, and increases as we descend. Generally speaking, rarefaction increases in a geometrical progression when the heights are in an arithmetical progression. If we ascend or descend $2\frac{1}{2}$, 5, or 30 miles, we find our atmosphere 10, 100, or a billion times more rarefied or more dense.

This law, although modified by the unequal temperatures of the different layers of the photosphere, and the unknown chemical nature of the substances of which it is composed, must also hold good in some measure for the sun. As, however, the mean temperature of the solar atmosphere must considerably exceed that of our atmosphere, the density of the former will not vary so rapidly with the height as the latter does. If we assume this increase and decrease on the sun to be ten times slower than it is on our earth, it follows that at the heights of 25, 50, and 300 miles, a rarefaction of 10, 100, and a billion times respectively would be observed. The solar atmosphere, therefore, does not attain a height of 400 geographical miles, or it cannot be as much as $\frac{1}{240}$th of the sun's radius. For if we take the density of the lowest strata of the sun's atmosphere to be 1000 times greater that that of our own near the level of the sea, a density greater than that of water, and necessarily too high, then at a height of 400 miles this atmosphere would be 10 billion times less dense than the earth's atmosphere; that is to say, to human comprehension it has ceased to exist.

This discussion shows that the solar atmosphere, in comparison with the body of the sun, has only an insignificant height; at the same time it may be remarked that on the sun's surface, in spite of the great heat, such substances as water may possibly exist in the liquid state under a pressure thousands of times greater than that of our atmosphere.

Since gases, when free from any solid particles, emit, even at very high temperatures, a pale transparent light—the so-called *lumen philosophicum*—it is probable that the intense white light of the sun has its origin in the denser parts of his surface. If such be assumed to be the case, the sun's spots and faculæ seem to be the disturbances of the fiery liquid ocean, caused by most powerful meteoric processes, for which all necessary materials are present, and partly to be caused by the direct influence of streams of asteroids. The deeper and less heated parts of this fiery ocean become thus exposed, and perhaps appear to us as spots, whereas the elevations form the so-called faculæ.

According to the experiments made by Henry, an American physicist, the rays sent forth from the spots do not produce the same heating effect as those emitted by the brighter parts.

We have to mention one more remarkable circumstance. The spots appear to be confined to a zone which extends 30° on each side of the sun's equator. The thought naturally suggests itself that some connexion exists between those solar processes which produce the spots and faculæ, the velocity of rotation of the sun, and the swarms of asteroids, and to deduce therefrom the limitation of the spots to the zone mentioned. It still remains enigmatical by what means nature contrives to bring about the uniform radiation which pertains alike to the polar and equatorial regions of the sun.

VII—THE TIDAL WAVE.

In almost every case the forces and motions on the surface of the earth may be traced back to the rays of the sun. Some processes, however, form a remarkable exception.

One of these is the tides. Beautiful, and in some respects exhaustive researches on this phenomenon have been made by Newton, Laplace, and others. The tides are caused by the attraction exercised by the sun and the moon on the moveable parts of the earth's surface, and by the axial rotation of our globe.

The alternate rising and falling of the level of the sea may be compared to the ascent and descent of a pendulum oscillating under the influence of the earth's attraction.

The continual resistance, however weak it may be, which an instrument of this nature (a physical pendulum) suffers, constantly shortens the amplitude of the oscillations which it performs; and if the pendulum be required to continue in uniform motion, it must receive a constant supply of *vis viva* corresponding to the resistance it has to overcome.

Clocks regulated by a pendulum obtain such a supply, either from a raised weight or a bent spring. The power consumed in raising the weight or in bending the spring, which power is represented by the raised weight or the bent spring, overcomes for a time the resistance, and thus secures the uniform motion of the pendulum and clock. In doing so, the weight sinks down or the spring uncoils, and therefore force must be expended in winding the clock up again, or it would stop moving.

Essentially the same holds good for the tidal wave. The moving waters rub against each other, against the shore, and against the atmosphere, and thus, meeting constantly with resistance, would soon come to rest if a *vis viva* did not exist competent to overcome these obstacles. This *vis viva* is the rotation of the earth on its axis, and the diminution and final exhaustion thereof will be a consequence of such an action.

The tidal wave causes a diminution of the velocity of the rotation of the earth.

This important conclusion can be proved in different ways.

The attraction of the sun and the moon disturbs the equilibrium of the moveable parts of the earth's surface, so as to move the waters of the sea towards the point or meridian above and below which the moon culminates. If the waters could move without resistance, the elevated parts of the tidal wave would exactly coincide with the moon's meridian, and under such conditions no consumption of *vis viva* could take place. In reality, however, the moving waters experience resistance, in consequence of which the flow of the tidal wave is delayed, and high water occurs in the open sea on the average about 2½ hours after the transit of the moon through the meridian of the place.

The waters of the ocean move from west and east towards the meridian of the moon, and the more elevated wave is, for the reason above stated, always to the east of the moon's meridian; hence the sea must press and flow more powerfully from east to west than from west to east. The ebb and flow of the tidal wave therefore consists not only in an alternate rising and falling of the waters, but also in a slow progressive motion from east to west. The tidal wave produces a general western current in the ocean.

This current is opposite in direction to the earth's rotation, and therefore its friction against and collision with the bed and shores of the ocean must offer everywhere resistance to the axial rotation of the earth, and diminish the *vis viva* of its motion. The earth here plays the part of a fly-wheel. The moveable parts of its surface adhere, so to speak, to the relatively fixed moon, and are dragged in a direction opposite to that of the earth's rotation, in consequence of which, action takes place between the solid and liquid parts of this fly-wheel, resistance is overcome, and the given rotatory effect diminished.

Water-mills have been turned by the action of the tides; the effects produced by such an arrangement are distinguished in a remarkable manner from those of a mill turned by a mountain-stream. The one obtains the *vis viva* with which it works from the earth's rotation, the other from the sun's radiation.

Various causes combine to incessantly maintain, partly in an undulatory, partly in a progressive motion, the waters of the ocean. Besides the influence of the sun and the moon on the rotating earth, mention must be made of the influence of the movement of the lower strata of the atmosphere on the surface of the ocean, and of the different temperatures of the sea in various climates; the configuration of the shores and the bed of the ocean likewise exercise a manifold influence on the velocity, direction, and extent of the oceanic currents.

The motions in our atmosphere, as well as those of the ocean, presuppose the existence and consumption of *vis viva* to overcome the continual resistances, and to prevent a state of rest or equilibrium. Generally speaking, the power necessary for the production of aerial currents may be of threefold origin. Either the radiation of the sun, the heat derived from a store in the interior of the earth, or, lastly, the rotatory effect of the earth may be the source.

As far as quantity is concerned the sun is by far the most important of the above. According to Pouillet's measurements, a square metre of the earth's surface receives on the average 4·408 units of heat from the sun per minute. Since one unit of heat is equivalent to 367 Km, it follows that one square metre of the surface of our globe receives per minute an addition of *vis viva* equal to 1620 Km, or the whole of the earth's surface in the same time 825,000 billions of Km. A power of 75 Km per second is called a horse-power. According to this, the effect of the solar radiation in mechanical work on one square metre of the earth's surface would be equal to 0·36, and the total effect for the whole globe 180 billions of horse-powers. A not inconsiderable portion of this enormous quantity of *vis viva* is consumed in the production of atmospheric actions, in consequence of which numerous motions are set up in the earth's atmosphere.

In spite of their great variety, the atmospheric currents may be reduced to a single type. In consequence of the unequal heating of the earth in different degrees of latitude, the colder and heavier air of the polar regions passes in an under current towards the equator; whereas the heated air of the tropics ascends to the higher parts of the atmosphere, and flows from thence towards the poles. In this manner the air of each hemisphere performs a circuitous motion.

It is known that these currents are essentially modified by the motion of the earth on its axis. The polar currents, with their smaller rotatory velocity, receive a motion from east to west contrary to the earth's rotation, and the equatorial currents one from west to east in advance of the axial rotation of the earth. The former of these currents, the easterly winds, must diminish the rotatory effect of the globe, the latter, the westerly winds, must increase the same power. The final result of the action of these opposed influences is, as regards the rotation of the earth, according to well-known mechanical principles, $=0$; for these currents counteract each other, and therefore cannot exert the least influence on the axial rotation of the earth. This important conclusion was proved by Laplace.

The same law holds good for every imaginable action which is caused either by the radiant heat of the sun, or by the heat which reaches the surface from the earth's interior, whether the action be in the air, in the water, or on the land. The effect of every single motion produced by these means on the rotation of the globe, is exactly compensated by the effect of another motion in an opposite direction; so that the resultant of all these motions is, as far as the axial rotation of the globe is concerned, $= 0$.

In those actions known as the tides, such compensation, however, does not take place; for the pressure or pull by which they are produced is always stronger from east to west than from west to east. The currents caused by this pull may ebb and flow in different directions, but their motion predominates in that which is opposed to the earth's rotation.

The velocity of the currents caused by the tide of the atmosphere amounts, according to Laplace's calculation, to not more than 75 millimetres in a second, or nearly a geographical mile in twenty-four hours; it is clear that much more powerful effects produced by the sun's heat would hide this action from observation. The influence of these air-currents, however, on the rotatory effect of the earth is, according to the laws of mechanics, exactly the same as it would be were the atmosphere undisturbed by the sun's radiant heat.

The combined motions of air and water are to be regarded from the same point of view. If we imagine the influence of the sun and that of the interior of our globe not to exist, the motion of the air and ocean from east to west is still left as an obstacle to the axial rotation of the earth.

The motion of the waters of the ocean from east to west was long ago verified by observation, and it is certain that the tides are the most effectual of the causes to which this great westerly current is to be referred.

Besides the tidal wave, the lower air-currents moving in the same direction, the trade-winds of the tropics especially, may be assigned as causes of this general movement of the waters. The westerly direction of the latter, however, is not confined to the region of easterly winds; it is met with in the region of perpetual calms, where it possesses a velocity of several miles a day; it is observed far away from the tropics both north and south, in regions where westerly winds prevail, near the Cape of Good Hope, the Straits of Magellan, the arctic regions, &c.

A third cause for the production of a general motion of translation of the waters of the ocean is the unequal heating of the sea in different zones. According to the laws of hydrostatics, the colder water of the higher degrees of latitude is compelled to flow towards the equator, and the warmer water of the tropics towards the poles, in consequence of which, similar movements are produced in the ocean to those in the atmosphere. This is the cause of the cold under current from the poles to the equator, and of the warm surface-current from the equator to the poles. The waters of the latter, by virtue of the greater velocity of rotation at the equator, assume in their onward progress a direction from west to east. It is a striking proof of the preponderating influence of the tidal wave that, in spite of this, the motion of the ocean is on the whole in an opposite direction.

Theory and experience thus agree in the result that the influence of the moon on the rotating earth causes a motion of translation from east to west in both atmosphere and ocean. This motion must continually diminish the rotatory effect of the earth, for want of an opposite and compensating influence.

The continual pressure of the tidal wave against the axial rotation of the earth may also be deduced from statical laws.

The gravitation of the moon affects without exception all parts of the globe. Let the earth be divided by the plane of the meridian in which the moon happens to be into two hemispheres, one to the east, the other to the west of this meridian. It is clear that the moon, by its attraction of the eastern hemisphere, tends to retard the motion of the earth, and by its attraction of the western hemisphere, to accelerate the same rotation.

Under certain conditions both these tendencies compensate each other, and then the action of the moon on the earth's rotation becomes zero. This happens when both hemispheres are arranged in a certain manner symmetrically, or when no parts of the earth can change their relative position; in the latter case a sort of symmetry is produced by the rotation.

The form of the earth deviates from a perfectly symmetrical sphere on account of the three following causes:—(1) the flattening of the poles, (2) the mountains on the surface, and (3) the tidal wave. The first two causes do not change the velocity of the earth's axial rotation. In order to comprehend clearly the effect of the tidal wave, we shall imagine the earth to be a perfectly symmetrical sphere uniformly surrounded by water. The attraction of the sun and the moon disturbs the equilibrium of this mass, and two flat mountains of water are formed. The top of one of these is directed towards the moon, and the summit of the other is turned away from it. A straight line passing through the tops of these two mountains is called the major axis of this earth-spheroid.

In this state the earth may be imagined to be divided into three parts—a smaller sphere, and two spherical segments attached to the opposite sides of the latter, and representing the elevations of the tidal wave. The attraction of the moon on the small central sphere does not change the rotation, and we have therefore only to consider the influence of this attraction on the two tidal elevations. The upper elevation or mountain, the one nearest the moon, is attracted towards the west because its mass is principally situated to the east of the moon, and the opposite mountain, which is to the west of the moon, is attracted towards the east. The upper tidal elevation is not only more powerfully attracted because it is nearer to the moon, but also because the angle under which it is pulled aside is more favourable for lateral deflection than in the case of the opposite protuberance. The pressure from east to west of the upper elevation preponderates therefore over the pressure from west to east of the opposite mountain; according to calculation, these quantities stand to each other nearly as 14 to 13. From the relative position of these two tidal protuberances and the moon, or the unchangeable position of the major axis of the earth-spheroid towards the centre of gravity of the moon, a pressure results, which preponderates from east to west, and offers an obstacle to the earth's rotation.

If gravitation were to be compared with magnetic attraction, the earth might be considered to be a large magnet, one pole of which, being more powerfully attracted, would represent the upper, and the other pole the lower tidal elevation. As the upper tidal wave tends to move towards the moon, the earth would act like a galvanometer, whose needle has been deflected from the magnetic meridian, and which, while tending to return thereto, exerts a constant lateral pressure.

The foregoing discussion may suffice to demonstrate the influence of the moon on the earth's rotation. The retarding pressure of the tidal wave may quantitatively be determined in the same manner as that employed in computing the precession of the equinoxes and the nutation of the earth's axis. The varied distribution of land and water, the unequal and unknown depth of the ocean, and the as yet imperfectly ascertained mean difference between the time of the moon's culmination and that of high water in the open sea, enter, however, as elements into such a calculation, and render the desired result an uncertain quantity.

In the mean time this retarding pressure, if imagined to act at the equator, cannot be assumed to be less than 1000 millions of kilogrammes. In order to start with a definite conception, we may be allowed to use this round number as a basis for the following calculations.

The rotatory velocity of the earth at the equator is 464 metres, and the consumption of mechanical work, therefore, for the maintenance of the tides 464,000 millions of Km, or 6000 millions of horse-powers per second. The effect of the tides may consequently be estimated at $\frac{1}{80,000}$th of the effect received by the earth from the sun.

The rotatory effect which the earth at present possesses, may be calculated from its mass, volume, and velocity of rotation. The volume of the earth is 2,650,686,000 cubic miles, and its specific gravity, according to Reich, = 5·44. If, for the sake of simplicity, we assume the density of the earth to be uniform throughout its mass, we obtain from the above premises, and the known velocity of rotation, 25,840 quadrillions of kilogrammetres as the rotatory effect of the earth. If, during every second in 2500 years, 464,000 millions of Km of this effect were consumed by the ebb and flow of the tidal wave, it would suffer a diminution of 36,600 trillions of Km, or about $\frac{1}{700,000}$th of its quantity.

The velocities of rotation of a sphere stand to each other in the same ratio as the square roots of the rotatory effects, when the volume of the sphere remains constant. From this it follows that, in the assumed time of 2500 years, the length of a day has increased $\frac{1}{1,400,000}$th; or if a day be taken equal to 86,400 seconds, it has lengthened $\frac{1}{16}$th of a second, if the volume of the earth has not changed. Whether this supposition be correct or not, depends on the temperature of our planet, and will be discussed in the next chapter.

The tides also react on the motion of the moon. The stronger attraction of the elevation nearest to, and to the east of the moon, increases with the tangential velocity of our satellite; the mean distance of the earth and the moon, and the time of revolution of the latter, are consequently augmented. The effect of this action, however, is insignificant, and, according to calculation, does not amount to more than a fraction of a second in the course of centuries.

VIII.—THE EARTH'S INTERIOR HEAT.

Without doubt there was once a time when our globe had not assumed its present magnitude. According to this, by aid of this simple assumption, the origin of our planet may be reduced to the union of once separated masses.

To the mechanical combinations of masses of the second order, with masses of the second and third order, &c., the same laws as those enunciated for the sun apply. The collision of such masses must always generate an amount of heat proportional to the squares of their velocities, or to their mechanical effect.

Although we are not in a position to affirm anything certain respecting the primordial conditions under which the constituent parts of the earth existed, it is nevertheless of the greatest interest to estimate the quantities of heat generated by the collision and combination of these parts by a standard based on the simplest assumptions.

Accordingly we shall consider for the present the earth to have been formed by the union of two parts, which obtained their relative motions by their mutual attraction only. Let the whole mass of the present earth, expressed in kilogrammes, be T, and the masses of the two portions $T-x$ and x. The ratio of these two quantities may be imagined to assume various values. The two extreme cases are, when x is considered infinitely small in comparison with T, and when $x=T-x=\frac{1}{2}T$. These form the limits of all imaginable ratios of the parts $T-x$ and x, and will now be more closely examined.

Terrestrial heights are of course excluded from the following consideration. In the first place, let x, in comparison with $T-x$, be infinitely small. The final velocity with which x arrives on the surface of the large mass, after having passed through a great space in a straight line, or after previous central motion round it, is, according to the laws developed in relation to the sun in Chapter III., confined within the limits of 7908 and 11,183 metres. The heat generated by this process may amount to from $8685 \times x$ to $17{,}370 \times x$ units, according to the value of the major axis of the orbit of x. This heat, however, vanishes by its distribution through the greater mass, because x is, according to supposition, infinitely small in comparison with T.

The quantity of heat generated increases with x, and amounts in the second case, when $x = \frac{1}{2}T$, to from $6000 \times T$ to $8685 \times T$ units.

If we assume the earth to possess a very great capacity for heat, equal in fact to that of its volume of water, which when calculated for equal weights = 0·184, the above discussion leads to the conclusion that the difference of temperature of the constituent parts, and of the earth after their union, or, in other words, the heat generated by the collision of these parts, may range, according to their relative magnitude, from 0° to 32,000°, or even to 47,000° !

With the number of parts which thus mechanically combine, the quantity of heat developed increases. Far greater still would have been the generation of heat if the constituent parts had moved in separate orbits round the sun before their union, and had accidentally approached and met each other. For various reasons, however, this latter supposition is not very probable.

Several facts indicate that our earth was once a fiery liquid mass, which has since cooled gradually, down to a comparatively inconsiderable depth from the surface, to its present temperature. The first proof of this is the form of the earth. "The form of the earth is its history." According to the most careful measurements, the flattening at the poles is exactly such as a liquid mass rotating on its axis with the velocity of the earth would possess; from this we may conclude that the earth at the time it received its rotatory motion was in a liquid state; and, after much controversy, it may be considered as settled that this liquid condition was not that of an aqueous solution, but of a mass melted by a high temperature.

The temperature of the crust of the globe likewise furnishes proof of the existence of a store of heat in its interior. Many exact experiments and measurements show that the temperature of the earth increases with the depth to which we penetrate. In boring the artesian well at Grenelle, which is 546 metres deep, it was observed that the temperature augmented at the rate of 1° for every 30 metres. The same result was obtained by observations in the artesian well at Mondorf in Luxembourg: this well is 671 metres in depth, and its water 34° warm.

Thermal springs furnish a striking proof of the high temperature existing in the interior of the earth. Scientific men are agreed that the aqueous deposits from the atmosphere, rain, hail, dew, and snow, are the sole causes of the formation of springs. The water obeying the laws of gravity, percolates through the earth wherever it can, and reappears at the surface in places of a lower situation. When water sinks to considerable depths through vertical crevices in the rocks, it acquires the temperature of the surrounding strata, and returns as a thermal spring to the surface.

Such waters are frequently distinguished from the water of ordinary springs merely by their possessing a higher temperature. If, however, the water in its course meets with mineral or organic substances which it can dissolve and retain, it then reappears as a mineral spring. Examples of such are met with at Aachen, Carlsbad, &c.

In a far more decided manner than by the high temperature of the water of certain springs, the interior heat of our globe is made manifest by those fiery fluid masses which sometimes rise from considerable depths. The temperature of the earth's crust increases at the rate of 1° for every 30 metres we descend from the surface towards the centre. Although it is incredible that this augmentation can continue at the same rate till the centre be reached, we may nevertheless assume with certainty that it does continue to a considerable depth. Calculation based on this assumption shows that at a depth of a few miles a temperature must exist sufficiently powerful to fuse most substances. Such molten masses penetrate the cold crust of the globe in many places, and make their appearance as lava.

A distinguished scientific man has lately expressed himself on the origin of the interior heat of the earth as follows:—"No one of course can explain the final causes of things. This much, however, is clear to every thinking man, that there is just as much reason that a body, like the earth, for example, should be warm, warmer than ice or human blood, as there is that it should be cold or colder than the latter. A particular cause for this absolute heat is as little necessary as a cause for motion or rest. Change—that is to say, transition from one state of things to another—alone requires and admits of explanation."

It is evident that this reflection is not fitted to suppress the desire for an explanation of the phenomenon in question. As all matter has the tendency to assume the same temperature as that possessed by the substances by which it happens to be surrounded, and to remain in a quiescent state as soon as equilibrium has been established, we must conclude that, whenever we meet with a body warmer than its neighbours, such body must have received at a (relatively speaking) not far distant time, a certain degree of heat,—a process which certainly allows of, and requires explanation.

Newton's theory of gravitation, whilst it enables us to determine, from its present form, the earth's state of aggregation in ages past, at the same time points out to us a source of heat powerful enough to produce such a state of aggregation, powerful enough to melt worlds; it teaches us to consider the molten state of a planet as the result of the mechanical union of cosmical masses, and thus derive the radiation of the sun and the heat in the bowels of the earth from a common origin.

The rotatory effect of the earth also may be readily explained by the collision of its constituent parts; and we must accordingly subtract the *vis viva* of the axial rotation from the whole effect of the collision and mechanical combination, in order to obtain the quantity of heat generated. The rotatory effect, however, is only a small quantity in comparison with the interior heat of the earth. It amounts to about $4400 \times T$ kilogrammetres, T being the weight of the earth in kilogrammes, which is equivalent to $12 \times T$ units of heat, if we assume the density of the earth to be uniform throughout.

If we imagine the moon in the course of time, either in consequence of the action of a resisting medium or from some other cause, to unite herself with our earth, two principal effects are to be discerned. A result of the collision would be, that the whole mass of the moon and the cold crust of the earth would be raised some thousands of degrees in temperature, and consequently the surface of the earth would be converted into a fiery ocean. At the same time the velocity of the earth's axial rotation would be somewhat accelerated, and the position of its axis with regard to the heavens, and to its own surface, slightly altered. If the earth had been a cold body without axial rotation, the process of its combining with the moon would have imparted to it both heat and rotation.

It is probable that such processes of combination between different parts of our globe may have repeatedly happened before the earth attained its present magnitude, and that luxuriant vegetation may have at different times been buried under the fiery débris resulting from the conflict of these masses.

As long as the surface of our globe was in an incandescent state, it must have lost heat at a very rapid rate; gradually this process became slower; and although it has not yet entirely ceased, the rate of cooling must have diminished to a comparatively small magnitude.

Two phenomena are caused by the cooling of the earth, which, on account of their common origin, are intimately related. The decrease of temperature, and consequent contraction of the earth's crust, must have caused frequent disturbances and revolutions on its surface, accompanied by the ejection of molten masses and the formation of protuberances; on the other hand, according to the laws of mechanics, the velocity of rotation must have increased with the diminution of the volume of the sphere, or, in other words, the cooling of the earth must have shortened the length of the day.

As the intensity of such disturbances and the velocity of rotation are closely connected, it is clear that the youth of our planet must have been distinguished by continual violent transformations of its crust, and a perceptible acceleration of the velocity of its axial rotation; whilst in the present time the metamorphoses of its surface are much slower, and the acceleration of its axial revolution diminished to a very small amount.

If we imagine the times when the Alps, the chain of the Andes, and the Peak of Teneriffe were upheaved from the deep, and compare with such changes the earthquakes and volcanic eruptions of historic times, we perceive in these modern transformations but weak images of the analogous processes of bygone ages.

Whilst we are surrounded on every side by the monuments of violent volcanic convulsions, we possess no record of the velocity of the axial rotation of our planet in antediluvian times. It is of the greatest importance that we should have an exact knowledge of a change in this velocity, or in the length of the day during historic times. The investigation of this subject by the great Laplace forms a bright monument in the department of exact science.

These calculations are essentially conducted in the following manner:—In the first place, the time between two eclipses of the sun, widely apart from each other, is as accurately as possible expressed in days, and from this the ratio of the time of the earth's rotation to the mean time of the moon's revolution determined. If, now, the observations of ancient astronomers be compared with those of our present time, the least alteration in the absolute length of a day may be detected by a change in this ratio, or in a disturbance in the lunar revolution. The most perfect agreement of ancient records on the movements of the moon and the planets, on the eclipses of the sun, &c., revealed to Laplace the remarkable fact that in the course of 25 centuries, the time in which our earth revolves on its axis has not altered $\frac{1}{500}$th part of a sexagesimal second; and the length of a day therefore may be considered to have been constant during historic times.

This result, as important as it was convenient for astronomy, was nevertheless of a nature to create some difficulties for the physicist. With apparently good reason it was concluded that, if the velocity of rotation had remained constant, the volume of the earth could have undergone no change. The earth completes one revolution on its axis in 86,400 sidereal seconds; it consequently appears, if this time has not altered during 2500 years to the extent of $\frac{1}{500}$th of a second, or $\frac{1}{43,000,000}$th part of a day, that during this long space of time the radius of the earth also cannot have altered more than this fraction of its length. The earth's radius measures 6,369,800 metres, and therefore its length ought not to have diminished more than 15 centimetres in 25 centuries.

The diminution in volume, as a result of the cooling-process, is, however, closely connected with the changes on the earth's surface. When we consider that scarcely a day passes without the occurrence of an earthquake or shock in one place or another, and that of the 300 active volcanos some are always in action, it would appear that such a lively reaction of the interior of the earth against the crust is incompatible with the constancy of its volume.

This apparent discrepancy between Cordier's theory of the connexion between the cooling of the earth and the reaction of the interior on the exterior parts, and Laplace's calculation showing the constancy of the length of the day, a calculation which is undoubtedly correct, has induced most scientific men to abandon Cordier's theory, and thus to deprive themselves of any tenable explanation of volcanic activity.

The continued cooling of the earth cannot be denied, for it takes place according to the laws of nature; in this respect the earth cannot comport itself differently from any other mass, however small it may be. In spite of the heat which it receives from the sun, the earth will have a tendency to cool so long as the temperature of its interior is higher than the mean temperature of its surface. Between the tropics the mean temperature produced by the sun is about 28°, and the sun therefore is as little able to stop the cooling-tendency of the earth as the moderate warmth of the air can prevent the cooling of a red-hot ball suspended in a room.

Many phenomena, for instance the melting of the glaciers near the bed on which they rest, show the uninterrupted emission of heat from the interior towards the exterior of the earth; and the question is, Has the earth in 25 centuries actually lost no more heat than that which is requisite to shorten a radius of more than 6 millions of metres only 15 centimetres?

In answering this question, three points enter into our calculation;—(1) the absolute amount of heat lost by the earth in a certain time, say one day; (2) the earth's capacity for heat; and (3) the coefficient of expansion of the mass of the earth.

As none of these quantities can be determined by direct

measurements, we are obliged to content ourselves with probable estimates; these estimates will carry the more weight the less they are formed in favour of some preconceived opinion.

Considering what is known about the expansion and contraction of solids and liquids by heat and cold, we arrive at the conclusion that for a diminution of 1° in temperature, the linear contraction of the earth cannot well be less than $\frac{1}{100,000}$th part, a number which we all the more readily adopt because it has been used by Laplace, Arago, and others.

If we compare the capacity for heat of all solid and liquid bodies which have been examined, we find that, both as regards volume and weight, the capacity of water is the greatest. Even the gases come under this rule; hydrogen, however, forms an exception, it having the greatest capacity for heat of all bodies when compared with an equal weight of water. In order not to take the capacity for heat of the mass of the earth too small, we shall consider it to be equal to that of its volume of water, which, when calculated for equal weights, amounts to 0·184.*

If we accept Laplace's result, that the length of a day has remained constant during the last 2500 years, and conclude

* The capacity for heat, as well as the coefficient of expansion of matter, as a rule, increases at higher temperatures. As, however, these two quantities act in opposite ways in our calculations, we may be allowed to dispense with the influence which the high temperature of the interior of the earth must exercise on these numbers. Even if, in consequence of the high temperature of the interior, the earth's mass could have a capacity two or three times as great as that which it has from 0° to 100°, it is to be considered, on the other hand, that the coefficient of expansion, $\frac{1}{100,000}$, only holds good for solids, and is even small for them, whilst in the case of liquids we have to assume a much greater coefficient: for mercury between 0° and 100°, it is about six times as great. Especially great is the contraction and expansion of bodies when they change their state of aggregation; and this should be taken into account when considering the formation of the earth's crust.

that the earth's radius has not diminished $1\frac{1}{2}$ decimetre in consequence of cooling, we are obliged to assume, according to the premises stated, that the mean temperature of our planet cannot have decreased $\frac{1}{480}°$ in the same period of time.

The volume of the earth amounts to 2650 millions of cubic miles. A loss of heat sufficient to cool this mass $\frac{1}{430}°$ would be equal to the heat given off when the temperature of 6,150,000 cubic miles of water decreases 1°; hence the loss for one day would be equal to 6·74 cubic miles of heat.

Fourier has investigated the loss of heat sustained by the earth. Taking the observation that the temperature of the earth increases at the rate of 1° for every 30 metres as the basis of his calculations, this celebrated mathematician finds the heat which the globe loses by conduction through its crust in the space of 100 years to be capable of melting a layer of ice 3 metres in thickness and covering the whole surface of the globe; this corresponds in one day to 7·7 cubic miles of heat, and in 2500 years to a decrease of 17 centimetres in the length of the radius.

According to this, the cooling of the globe would be sufficiently great to require attention when the earth's velocity of rotation is considered.

At the same time it is clear that the method employed by Fourier can only bring to our knowledge one part of the heat which is annually lost by the earth; for simple conduction through *terra firma* is not the only way by which heat escapes from our globe.

In the first place, we may make mention of the aqueous deposits of our atmosphere, which, as far as they penetrate our earth, wash away, so to speak, a portion of the heat, and thus accelerate the cooling of the globe. The whole quantity of water which falls from the atmosphere upon the land in one day, however, cannot be assumed to be much more than half a cubic mile in volume, hence the cooling effect produced by this water may be neglected in our calculation. The heat carried off by all the thermal springs in the world is very small in comparison with the quantities which we have to consider here.

Much more important is the effect produced by active volcanos. As the heat which accompanies the molten matter to the surface is derived from the store in the interior of the earth, their action must influence considerably the diminution of the earth's heat. And we have not only to consider here actual eruptions which take place in succession or simultaneously at different parts of the earth's surface, but also volcanos in a quiescent state, which continually radiate large quantities of heat abstracted from the interior of the globe. If we compare the earth to an animal body, we may regard each volcano as a place where the epidermis has been torn off, leaving the interior exposed, and thus opening a door for the escape of heat.

Of the whole of the heat which passes away through these numerous outlets, too low an estimate must not be made. To have some basis for the estimation of this loss, we have to recollect that in 1783 Skaptar-Jokul, a volcano in Iceland, emitted sufficient lava in the space of six weeks to cover 60 square miles of country to an average depth of 200 metres, or, in other words, about 1½ cubic miles of lava. The amount of heat lost by this one eruption of one volcano must, when the high temperature of the lava is considered, be estimated to be more than 1000 cubic miles of heat; and the whole loss resulting from the action of all the volcanos amounts, therefore, in all probability, to thousands of cubic miles of heat per annum. This latter number, when added to Fourier's result, produces a sum which evidently does not agree with the assumption that the volume of our earth has remained unchanged.

In the investigation of the cooling of our globe, the influence of the water of the ocean has to be taken into account. Fourier's calculations are based on the observations of the increase of the temperature of the crust of our earth, from the surface towards the centre. But two-thirds of the surface of our globe are covered with water, and we cannot assume *à priori* that this large area loses heat at the same rate as the solid parts; on the contrary, various circumstances indicate that the cooling of our globe proceeds more quickly through the waters of the ocean resting on it than from the solid parts merely in contact with the atmosphere.

In the first place, we have to remark that the bottom of the ocean is, generally speaking, nearer to the store of heat in the interior of the earth than the dry land is, and hence that the temperature increases most probably in a greater ratio from the bottom of the sea towards the interior of the globe, than it does in our observations on the land. Secondly, we have to consider that the whole bottom of the sea is covered by a layer of ice-cold water, which moves constantly from the poles to the equator, and which, in its passage over sand-banks, causes, as Humboldt aptly remarks, the low temperatures which are generally observed in shallow places. That the water near the bottom of the sea, on account of its great specific heat and its low temperature, is better fitted than the atmosphere to withdraw the heat from the earth, is a point which requires no further discussion.

We have plenty of observations which prove that the earth suffers a great loss of heat through the waters of the ocean. Many investigations have demonstrated the existence of a large expanse of sea, much visited by whalers, situated between Iceland, Greenland, Norway, and Spitzbergen, and extending from lat. 76° to 80° N., and from long. 15° E. to 15° W. of Greenwich, where the temperature was observed to be higher in the deeper water than near the surface—an experience which neither accords with the general rule, nor agrees with the laws of hydrostatics. Franklin observed, in lat. 77° N. and long. 12° E., that the temperature of the sea near the surface was $-\frac{1}{2}°$, and at a depth of 700 fathoms

+6°. Fisher, in lat. 80° N. and long. 11° E., noticed that the surface-water had a temperature of 0°, whilst at a depth of 140 fathoms it stood at +8°.

As sea-water, unlike pure water, does not possess a point of greatest density at some distance above the freezing-point, and as the water in lat. 80° N. is found at some depth to be warmer than water at the same depth 10° southward, we can only explain this remarkable phenomenon of an increase of temperature with an increase of depth by the existence of a source of heat at the bottom of the sea. The heat, however, which is required to warm the water at the bottom of an expanse of ocean more than 1000 square miles in extent to a sensible degree, must amount, according to the lowest estimate, to some cubic miles of heat a day.

The same phenomenon has been observed in other parts of the world, such as the west coast of Australia, the Adriatic, the Lago Maggiore, &c. Especial mention should here be made of an observation by Horner, according to whom the lead, when hauled up from a depth varying from 80 to 100 fathoms in the mighty Gulf-stream off the coast of America, used to be hotter than boiling water.

The facts above mentioned, and some others which might be added, clearly show that the loss of heat suffered by our globe during the last 2500 years is far too great to have been without sensible effect on the velocity of the earth's rotation. The reason why, in spite of this accelerating cause, the length of a day has nevertheless remained constant since the most ancient times, must be attributed to an opposite retarding action. This consists in the attraction of the sun and moon on the liquid parts of the earth's surface, as explained in the last chapter.

According to the calculations of the last chapter, the retarding pressure of the tides against the earth's rotation would cause, during the lapse of 2500 years, a sidereal day to be lengthened to the extent of $\frac{1}{16}$th of a second; as the length of a day, however, has remained constant, the cooling effect of the earth during the same period of time must have shortened the day $\frac{1}{16}$th of a second. A diminution of the earth's radius to the amount of $4\frac{1}{2}$ metres in 2500 years, and a daily loss of 200 cubic miles of heat, correspond to this effect. Hence, in the course of the last 25 centuries, the temperature of the whole mass of the earth must have decreased $\frac{1}{14}°$.

The not inconsiderable contraction of the earth resulting from such a loss of heat, agrees with the continual transformations of the earth's surface by earthquakes and volcanic eruptions; and we agree with Cordier, the industrious observer of volcanic processes, in considering these phenomena a necessary consequence of the continual cooling of an earth which is still in a molten state in its interior.

When our earth was in its youth, its velocity of rotation must have increased to a very sensible degree, on account of the rapid cooling of its then very hot mass. This accelerating cause gradually diminished, and as the retarding pressure of the tidal wave remains nearly constant, the latter must finally preponderate, and the velocity of rotation therefore continually decrease. Between these two states we have a period of equilibrium, a period when the influence of the cooling and that of the tidal pressure counterbalance each other; the whole life of the earth therefore may be divided into three periods—youth with increasing, middle age with uniform, and old age with decreasing velocity of rotation.

The time during which the two opposed influences on the rotation of the earth are in equilibrium can, strictly speaking, only be very short, inasmuch as in one moment the cooling, and in the next moment the pressure of the tides must prevail. In a physical sense, however, when measured by human standards, the influence of the cooling, and still more so that of the tidal wave, may for ages be considered constant, and there must consequently exist a period of many thousand years' duration during which these counteracting influences will appear to be equal. Within this period a sidereal day attains its shortest length, and the velocity of the earth's rotation its maximum—circumstances which, according to mathematical analysis, would tend to lengthen the duration of this period of the earth's existence.

The historical times of mankind are, according to Laplace's calculation, to be placed in this period. Whether we are at the present moment still near its commencement, its middle, or are approaching its conclusion, is a question which cannot be solved by our present data, and must be left to future generations.

The continual cooling of the earth cannot be without an influence on the temperature of its surface, and consequently on the climate; scientific men, led by Buffon, in fact, have advanced the supposition that the loss of heat sustained by our globe must at some time render it an unfit habitation for organic life. Such an apprehension has evidently no foundation, for the warmth of the earth's surface is even now much more dependent on the rays of the sun than on the heat which reaches us from the interior. According to Pouillet's measurements, mentioned in Chapter III., the earth receives 8000 cubic miles of heat a day from the sun, whereas the heat which reaches the surface from the earth's interior may be estimated at 200 cubic miles per diem. The heat therefore obtained from the latter source every day is but small in comparison to the diurnal heat received from the sun.

If we imagine the solar radiation to be constant, and the heat we receive from the store in the interior of the earth to be cut off, we should have as a consequence various changes in the physical constitution of the surface of our globe. The temperature of hot springs would gradually sink down to the mean temperature of the earth's crust, volcanic eruptions would cease, earthquakes would no longer be felt, and the temperature of the water of the ocean would be sensibly altered in many places—circumstances which would doubtless affect the climate in many parts of the world. Especially it may be presumed that Western Europe, with its present favourable climate, would become colder, and thus *perhaps* the seat of the power and culture of our race transferred to the milder parts of North America.

Be this as it may, for thousands of years to come we can predict no diminution of the temperature of the surface of our globe as a consequence of the cooling of its interior mass; and, as far as historic records teach, the climates, the temperatures of thermal springs, and the intensity and frequency of volcanic eruptions are now the same as they were in the far past.

It was different in prehistoric times, when for centuries the earth's surface was heated by internal fire, when mammoths lived in the now uninhabitable polar regions, and when the tree-ferns and the tropical shell-fish whose fossil remains are now especially preserved in the coal-formation were at home in all parts of the world.

III.

THE MECHANICAL EQUIVALENT OF HEAT

THE vast and magnificent structure of the experimental sciences has been erected on only a few pillars. History teaches us that the searching spirit of man required thousands of years for the discovery of the fundamental principles of the sciences, on which the superstructure was then raised in a comparatively short time. But these very fundamental propositions are nevertheless so clear and simple, that the discovery of them reminds us, in more than one respect, of Columbus's egg.

But if, now that we are at last in possession of the truth, we speak of a method by the application of which the most essential fundamental laws might have been discovered without waste of time, it is not that we would criticize in any light spirit the efforts and achievements of our forerunners: it is merely with the object of laying before the reader in an advantageous form one of the additions to our knowledge which recent times have brought forth.

The most important—not to say the only—rule for the genuine investigation of nature is, to remain firm in the conviction that the problem before us is to learn to *know* phenomena, before seeking for explanations or inquiring after higher causes. As soon as a fact is once known in all its relations, it is therein explained, and the problem of science is at an end.

Notwithstanding that some may pronounce this a trite assertion, and no matter how many arguments others may bring to oppose it, it remains none the less certain that this primary rule has been too often disregarded even up to the most modern times; while all the speculative operations of even the most highly gifted minds which, instead of taking firm hold of facts as such, have striven to rise above them, have as yet borne but barren fruit.

We shall not here discuss the modern naturalistic philosophy (*Naturphilosophie*) further than to say that its character is already sufficiently apparent from the ephemeral existence of its offspring. But even the greatest and most meritorious of the naturalists of antiquity, in order to explain, for example, the properties of the lever, took refuge in the assertion that a circle is such a marvellous thing that no wonder if motions, taking place in a circle, offer also in their turn most unusual phenomena. If Aristotle, instead of straining his extraordinary powers in meditations upon the fixed point and advancing line, as he calls the circle, had investigated the numerical relations subsisting between the length of the arm of the lever and the pressure exerted, he would have laid the foundation of an important part of human knowledge.

Such mistakes, committed as they were, in accordance with the spirit of those times, even by a man whose many positive services constitute his everlasting memorial, may serve to point us in the opposite road which leads us surely to the goal. But if, even by the most correct method of investigation, nothing can be attained without toil and industry, the cause is to be sought in that divine order of the world according to which man is made to labour. But it is certain that already immeasurably more means and more toil have been sacrificed to error than were needed for the discovery of the truth.

The rule which must be followed, in order to lay the foundations of a knowledge of nature in the shortest conceivable time, may be comprised in a few words. The natural phenomena with which we come into most immediate contact, and which are of most frequent occurrence, must be subjected to a careful examination by means of the organs of sense, and this examination must be continued until it results in quantitative determinations which admit of being expressed by *numbers.*

These numbers are the required foundations of an exact investigation of nature.

Among all natural operations, the free fall of a weight is the most frequent, the simplest, and—witness Newton's apple—at the same time the most important. When this process is analysed in the way that has been mentioned, we immediately see that the weight strikes against the ground the harder the greater the height from which it has fallen; and the problem now consists in the determination of the quantitative relations subsisting between the height from which the weight falls, the time occupied by it in its descent, and its final velocity, and in expressing these relations by *definite numbers.*

In carrying out this experimental investigation, various difficulties have to be contended with; but these must and can be overcome; and then the truth is arrived at, that for every body a fall of sixteen feet, or a time of descent of one second, corresponds to a final velocity of thirty-two feet per second.

A second phenomenon of daily occurrence, which is in apparent contradiction to the laws of falling bodies, is the ascent of liquids in tubes by suction. Here, again, the rule applies, not to allow the maxim, *velle rerum cognoscere causas*, to lead us into error through useless and therefore harmful speculations concerning the qualities of the vacuum, and the like; on the contrary, we must again examine the phenomenon with attention and awakened senses; and then we find, as soon as we put a tube to the mouth to raise a liquid, that the operation is at first quite easy, but that afterwards it requires an amount of exertion which rapidly increases as the column of liquid becomes higher. Is there, perchance, an ascertainable limit to the action of suction? As soon as we once begin to experiment in this direction, it can no longer escape us that there is a barometric height, and that it attains to about thirty inches. This number is a second chief pillar in the edifice of human knowledge.

Question now follows question, and answer, answer. We have learned that the pressure exerted by a column of fluid is proportional to its height and to the specific gravity of the fluid; we have thus determined the specific gravity of the atmosphere, and by this investigation we are led to carry up our measuring-instrument, the barometer, from the plain to the mountains, and to express numerically the effect produced by elevation above the sea-level upon the height of the mercury-column. Such experiments suggest the question, Whether the laws of falling bodies, with which we have become acquainted at the surface of the earth, do not likewise undergo modification at greater distances from the ground. And if, as *à priori* we cannot but expect, this should be really the case, the further question arises, In what manner is the number already found modified by distance from the earth? We have thus come upon a problem the solution of which is attended with many difficulties; for what has now to be accomplished, is to make observations and carry out measurements in places where no human foot can tread. History, however, teaches that the same man who put the question was also able to furnish the answer. Truly he could do so only through a rich treasure of astronomical knowledge. But how is this knowledge to be attained by us?

Astronomy is, without question, even in its first principles, the most difficult of all sciences. We have here to deal with objects and spaces which forbid all thought of experiment, while at the same time the motions of the innumerable heavenly bodies are of so complicated a kind, that astronomical science, in its stately unfolding, is rightly considered the highest triumph whereof human intellect here below is able to boast.

In accordance with the natural rule that, both in particulars and in general, man has to begin with that which is easiest and then to advance step by step to what is more difficult, it might well be supposed that astronomy must have arrived at a flourishing state of development later than any other branch of human knowledge. But it is well known that in reality the direct opposite was the case, inasmuch as it was precisely in astronomy, and in no other branch, that the earliest peoples attained to really sound knowledge, It may, indeed, be asserted that the science of the heavenly bodies had in antiquity reached as high a degree of perfection as the complete want of all the auxiliary sciences rendered possible.

This early occurrence of a vigorous development of astronomy, which, indeed, was a necessary forerunner of the other sciences, since it alone furnished the necessary data for the measurement of time, is observable among the most various races of mankind: the reason of it, moreover, lies in the nature of things, and in the constitution of the human mind. It furnishes a remarkable proof that a right method is the most important condition for the successful prosecution of scientific inquiry.

The explanation of this phenomenon lies in the fact that the need which was felt at a very early period, of a common standard for the computation of time, made it necessary to institute observations such that their results required to be expressed by definite *numbers*. There was a felt necessity of determining the time in which the sun accomplishes his circuit through the heavens, as well as the time in which the moon goes through her phases, and other similar questions.

In order to meet this necessity, there was no temptation to take up the Book of Nature, after the manner of expositors and critics, merely to cover it with glosses:

"Mit eitler Rede wird hier nichts geschafft."

It was *numbers* that were sought, and *numbers* that were found. The overpowering force of circumstances constrained the spirit of inquiry into the right path, and therein led it at once from success to success.

Now that after long-continued, accurate, and fortunate observations the needful knowledge of the courses and distances of the nearest heavenly bodies, as well as of the figure and size of the earth, has been acquired, we are in a position to treat the question, What is the numêrical influence exerted by increased distance from the earth upon the known laws of falling bodies? and we thus arrive at the pregnant discovery that, at a height equal to the earth's semidiameter, the distance fallen through and the final velocity, for the first second, is four times less than on the surface of the earth.

In order to pursue our inquiry, let us now return to the objects which immediately surround us. From the earliest times, the phenomena of combustion must have claimed in an especial degree the attention of mankind. In order to *explain* them, the ancients, in accordance with the method of their naturalistic philosophy, put forward a peculiar upward-striving element of Fire, which in conjunction with, and in opposition to, Air, Water, and Earth, constituted all that existed. The necessary consequence of this theory, which they discussed with the most acute sagacity, was, that in regard to the phenomena in question and all that related to them, they remained in complete ignorance.

Here, again, it is quantitative determinations, it is numbers alone, which put the Ariadne's clue in our hand. If we want to know what goes on during the phenomena of combustion, we must *weigh* the substances before and after they are burned; and here the knowledge we have already acquired of the weight of gaseous bodies comes to our aid. We then find that, in every case of combustion, substances which previously existed in a separate state enter into an intimate union with each other, and that the total weight of the substances remains the same both before and after the combination. We thus come to know the different bodies in their separate and in their combined states, and learn how to transform them from one of these states into the other; we learn, for instance, that water is composed of two kinds of air which combine with each other in the proportion of 1:8. An entrance into chemical science is thus opened to us, and the numerical laws which regulate the combinations of matter (*die Stöchiometrie*) hang like ripe fruit before us.

As we proceed further in our investigations, we find that in all chemical operations—combinations as well as decompositions—changes of temperature occur, which, according to the varying circumstances of different cases, are of all degrees of intensity, from the most violent heat downwards. We have measured quantitatively the heat developed, or counted the number of heat-units, and have so come into possession of the law of the evolution of heat in chemical processes.

We have long known, however, that in innumerable cases heat makes its appearance where no chemical action is going on; for instance, whenever there is friction, when unelastic bodies strike one another, and when aëriform bodies are compressed.

What then takes place when heat is evolved in such ways as these?

We are taught by history that in this case also the most sagacious hypotheses concerning the state and nature of a peculiar "matter" of heat, concerning a "thermal æther," whether at rest or in a state of vibration, concerning "thermal atoms," supposed to exercise their functions in the interstices between the material atoms, or other hypotheses of like nature, have not availed to solve the problem. It is, notwithstanding, of no less wonderfully simple a nature than the laws of the lever, about which the founder of the peripatetic philosophy cudgelled his brains in vain.

After what has gone before, the reader cannot be in any doubt about what is the course now to be pursued. We must again make quantitative determinations: we must measure and count.

If we proceed in this direction and measure the quantity of heat developed by mechanical agency, as well as the amount of force used up in producing it, and compare these quantities with each other, we at once find that they stand to each other in the simplest conceivable relation—that is to say, in an invariable direct proportion, and that the proportion also holds when, inversely, mechanical force is again produced by the aid of heat.

Putting these facts into brief and plain language, we may say,

Heat and motion are transformable one into the other.

We cannot and ought not, however, to let this suffice us. We require to know *how much* mechanical force is needed for the production of a given amount of heat, and conversely. In other words, the law of the invariable quantitative relation between motion and heat must be expressed *numerically*.

When we appeal hereupon to experiment, we find that raising the temperature of a given weight of water one degree of the Centigrade scale corresponds to the elevation of an equal weight to the height of about 1,200 [French] feet.

This number is THE MECHANICAL EQUIVALENT OF HEAT.

The production of heat by friction and other mechanical operations is a fundamental fact of such constant occurrence, that the importance of its establishment on a scientific basis will be recognized by naturalists without any preliminary enumeration of its useful applications; and, for the same reason, a few historical remarks touching the circumstances attending the discovery of the foregoing fundamental law, will not be out of place here.

In the summer of 1840, on the occasion of bleeding Europeans newly arrived in Java, I made the observation that the blood drawn from the vein of the arm possessed, almost without exception, a surprisingly bright red colour.

This phenomenon riveted my earnest attention. Starting from Lavoisier's theory, according to which animal heat is the result of a process of combustion, I regarded the twofold change of colour which the blood undergoes in the capillaries as a sensible sign—as the visible indication—of an oxidation going on in the blood. In order that the human body may be kept at a uniform temperature, the *development* of heat within it must bear a quantitative relation to the heat *which it loses*—a relation, that is, to the temperature of the surrounding medium; and hence both the production of heat and the process of oxidation, as well as the *difference in colour of the two kinds of blood*, must be on the whole less in the torrid zones than in colder regions.

In accordance with this theory, and having regard to the known physiological facts which bear upon the question, the blood must be regarded as a fermenting liquid undergoing slow combustion, whose most important function—that is, sustaining the process of combustion—is fulfilled without the constituents of the blood (with the exception, that is, of the products of decomposition) leaving the cavities of the blood-vessels or coming into such relation with the organs that an interchange of matter can take place. This may be thus stated in other words: by far the greater part of the assimilated food is burned in the cavities of the blood-vessels themselves, for the purpose of producing a physical effect, and a comparatively small quantity only serves the less important end of ultimately entering the substance of the organs themselves, so as to occasion growth and the renewal of the worn-out solid parts.

If hence it follows that a general balance must be struck in the organism between receipts and expenditure, or between work done and wear and tear, it is unmistakably one of the most important problems with which the physiologist has to deal, to make himself as thoroughly acquainted as it is possible for him to be with the budget of the object of his examination. The wear and tear consists in the amount of matter consumed; the work done is the evolution of heat. This latter effect, however, is of two kinds, inasmuch as the animal body evolves heat on the one hand directly in its own interior, and distributes it by communication to the objects immediately surrounding it; while, on the other hand, it possesses, through its organs of motion, the power of producing heat mechanically by friction or in similar ways, even at distant points. We now require to know

Whether the heat directly evolved is ALONE *to be laid to the account of the process of combustion, or whether it is the* SUM *of the heat evolved both directly and indirectly that it is to be taken into calculation.*

This is a question that touches the very foundations of science; and unless it receives a trustworthy answer, the healthy development of the doctrine concerned is not possible. For it has been already shown, by various examples, what are the consequences of neglecting primary quantitative determinations. No wit of man is able to furnish a substitute for what nature offers.

The physiological theory of combustion starts from the fundamental proposition, that the quantity of heat which results from the combustion of a given substance is *invariable*—that is, that its amount is *uninfluenced* by the circumstances which accompany the combustion; whence we infer, "*in specie,*" that the chemical effect of combustible matter can undergo no alteration in amount even by the vital process, or that the living organism, with all its riddles and marvels, cannot create heat out of nothing.

But if we hold firm to this physiological axiom, the answer to the question started above is already given. For, unless we wish to attribute again to the organism the power of creating heat which has just been denied to it, it cannot be assumed that the heat which it produces can ever amount to more than the chemical action which takes place. On the combustion-theory there is, then, no alternative, short of sacrificing the theory itself, but to admit that the *total* amount of heat evolved by the organism, partly directly, and partly indirectly by mechanical action, corresponds quantitatively, or is equal to the amount of combustion.

Hence it follows, no less inevitably, *that the heat produced mechanically by the organism must bear an invariable quantitative relation to the work expended in producing it.*

For if, according to the varying construction of the mechanical arrangements which serve for the development of the heat, the same amount of work, and hence the same amount of organic combustion, could produce *varying* quantities of heat, the quantity of heat produced from one and the same expenditure of material would come out smaller at one time and larger at another, which is contrary to our assumption. Further, inasmuch as there is no difference in kind between the mechanical performances of the animal body and those of other inorganic sources of work, it follows that

AN INVARIABLE QUANTITATIVE RELATION BETWEEN HEAT AND WORK IS A POSTULATE OF THE PHYSIOLOGICAL THEORY OF COMBUSTION.

While following in general the direction indicated, it was accordingly needful for me in the end to fix my attention chiefly on the physical connection subsisting between motion and heat; and it was thus impossible for the existence of the mechanical equivalent of heat to remain hidden from me. But, although I have to thank an accident for this discovery, it is none the less my own, and I do not hesitate to assert my right of priority.

In order to ensure what had been thus discovered against casualties, I put together the most important points in a short paper which I sent in the spring of 1842 to Liebig, with a request that he would insert it in the *Annalen der Chemie und Pharmacie*, in the forty-second volume of which, page 233, it may be found under the title "Bemerkungen über die Kräfte der unbelebten Natur."

It was a fortunate circumstance for me that the reception given to my unpretending work by this man, gifted with so deep an insight, at once secured for it an entrance into one of the first scientific organs, and I seize this opportunity of publicly testifying to the great naturalist my gratitude and my esteem.

Liebig himself, however, had about the same time already pointed out, in more general but still unmistakable terms, the connection subsisting between heat and work. In particular, he asserts that the heat produced mechanically by a steam-engine is to be attributed solely to the effect of combustion, which can never receive any increase through the fact of its producing mechanical effects, and, through these, again developing heat.

From these, and from similar expressions of other scientific men, we may infer that science has recently entered upon a direction in which the existence of the mechanical equivalent of heat could not in any case have remained longer unperceived.

In the paper to which reference has been made, the natural law with which we are now concerned is referred back to a few fundamental conceptions of the human mind. The proposition that a magnitude, which does not spring from nothing, cannot be annihilated, is so simple and clear that no valid argument can be urged against its truth, any more than against an axiom of geometry; and until the contrary is proved by some fact established beyond a doubt, we may accept it as true.

Now we are taught by experience, that neither motion nor heat ever takes its rise except at the expense of some measurable object, and that in innumerable cases motion disappears without any thing except heat making its appearance. The axiom that we have established leads, then, now to the conclusion that the motion that disappears becomes heat, or, in other words, that both objects bear to each other an invariable quantitative relation. The proof of this conclusion by the method of experiment, the establishment of it in all its details, the tracing of a complete harmony subsisting between the laws of thought and the objective world, is the most interesting, but at the same time the most comprehensive problem that it is possible to find. What I, with feeble powers and without any external support or encouragement, have effected in this direction is truly little enough; but—*ultra posse nemo obligatus.*

In the paper referred to (the first of Mayer's in the present volume) I have thus expressed myself with regard to the genetic connection of heat and moving force:

"If it be now considered as established that in many cases (*exceptio confirmat regulam*) no other effect of motion can be traced except heat, and that no other cause than motion can be found for the heat that is produced, we prefer the assumption that heat proceeds from motion, to the assumption of a cause without effect and of an effect without a cause—just as the chemist, instead of allowing oxygen and hydrogen to disappear without further investigation, and water to be produced in some inexplicable manner, establishes a connection between oxygen and hydrogen on the one hand and water on the other."

From this point there is but *one* step to be made to the goal. At page 257 it is said: "The solution of the equations subsisting between falling-force [that is, the raising of weight] and motion requires that the space fallen through in a given time, *e. g.* the first second, should be experimentally determined; in like manner, the solution of the equations subsisting between falling-force and motion on the one hand and heat on the other, requires an answer to the question, How great is the quantity of heat which corresponds to a given quantity of motion or falling-force? For instance, we must ascertain how high a given weight requires to be raised above the ground in order that its falling-force may be equivalent to the raising of the temperature of an equal weight of water from 0° to 1° C. The attempt to show that such an equation is the expression of a physical truth may be regarded as the substance of the foregoing remarks.

"By applying the principles that have been set forth to the relations subsisting between the temperature and the volume of gases, we find that the sinking of a mercury column by which a gas is compressed is equivalent to the quantity of heat set fire by the compression; and hence it follows, the ratio between the capacity for heat of air under constant pressure and its capacity under constant volume being taken as =1·421, that the warming of a given weight of water from 0° to 1° C. corresponds to the fall of an equal weight from the height of about 365 metres."

It is plain that the expression "equivalent" is here used in quite a different sense from what it bears in chemistry. The difference will be shown most distinctly by an example. When the same weight of potash is neutralized, first, with sulphuric acid, then with nitric acid, the numbers which express the ratio which the absolute weights of these three substances bear to one another are called their equivalents; but there is no thought here either of the quantitative equality or of the transformation of the bodies in question.

This peculiar signification which the word "equivalent" has acquired in chemistry, is doubtless connected with the fact that the chemist has been able to determine the object of his investigation by a common quantitative standard, their absolute weights. Let us suppose, however, that we could determine one body, for instance water, only by weight, and another, water-forming or explosive gas, only by volume, and that we had agreed to choose one pound as the unit of weight, and one cubic foot as the unit of volume; we should then have to ascertain how many cubic feet of explosive gas could be obtained from one pound of water, and conversely. This number, without which neither the formation nor the decomposition of water could be made the subject of calculation, might then be suitably called "the explosive-gas equivalent of water."

In this latter sense a raised weight might, in accordance with the known laws of mechanics, be called the "equivalent" of the motion resulting from its fall. Now, in order to compare these two objects, the raised and the moving weight, which admit of no common measure, we require that constant number which is generally denoted by g. This number, however, and the mechanical equivalent of heat, whereby the relation subsisting between heat and motion is defined, belong both of them to one and the same category of ideas.

In the paper that I have mentioned it is further shown how we may arrive at such a conception of force as admits of being consistently followed to its consequences and is scientifically tenable; and the importance of this subject induces me to return to it again here.

The word "force" (*Kraft*) is used in the higher or scientific mechanics in two distinct senses.

I. On the one hand, it denotes every push or pull, every effort of an inert body to change its state of rest or of motion; and this effort, when it is considered alone and apart from the result produced, is called "pushing force," "pulling force," or shortly "force," and also, in order to distinguish between this and the following conception, "dead force" (*vis mortua*).

II. On the other hand, the product of the pressure into the space through which it acts, or, again, the product—or half-product—of the mass into the square of the velocity, is named "force." In order that motion may actually occur, it is in fact necessary that the mass, whatever it may be, should under the influence of a pressure, and, in the direction of that pressure, traverse a certain space, "the effective space" (*Wirkungsraum*): and in this case a magnitude which is proportional to the "pushing force" *and* to the effective space, likewise receives the name "force;" but to distinguish it from the mere pushing force, by which alone motion is never actually brought about, it is also called the "*vis viva* of motion," or "moving force."

With the *generic conception* of "force," the higher mechanics, as an essentially analytic science, is not concerned. In order to arrive at it, we must, according to the general rule, collect together the characters possessed in common by the several species. As is well known, the definition so obtained runs thus—"Force is every thing which brings about or tends to bring about, alters or tends to alter motion."

This definition, however, it is easy to see, is tautological; for the last fourteen words of it might be omitted, and the sense would be still the same.

This erroneous solution is occasioned by the nature of the problem, which requires an impossibility. Mere pressure (dead force) and the product of the pressure into the effective space (living force) are magnitudes too thoroughly unlike to be by possibility combined into a generic conception. Pressure or attraction is, in the theory of motion, what affinity is in chemistry—an abstract conception: living force, like matter, is concrete; and these two kinds of force, however closely connected in the region of the association of ideas, are in reality so widely separated that a frame which should take them both in must be able to include the whole world.

There are several conceivable ways of escaping from the

difficulty. For instance, just as we speak of absolute weight, specific weight, and combining weight, without its ever entering any one's head to want to construct a generic idea out of these distinct notions, so two or more meanings may be attached to the word force. This is what is actually done in the higher mechanics, and hence in this branch of science we meet with no mention of a generic conception of "force."

There has been no lack of recommendations to carry, in like manner, the notions of "dead" and "living force" as distinct and separate through the other departments of science; it has, however, been found impossible to put in practice such recommendations; for the use of ambiguous expressions, which can in no case contribute any thing to clearness, is altogether inadmissible if confusion can possibly arise. It is true that the mathematician is in no danger of confounding in his calculations a product with one of its factors; but in other departments of knowledge a systematic confusion of ideas exists on this point; and if any thing is to be done toward clearing it up, the source of the error must be stopped; for if we once recognize two meanings of the word "force," it would be the labour of Sisyphus to try to distinguish between them in each separate case. In order, then, to arrive at any result, we must make up our minds to do without any common denomination of the magnitudes mentioned above, as I. and II., and either to give up the use of the word "force" altogether, or to employ it for *one* only of these two categories.

The notion of force was consistently employed in the latter sense by Newton. In solving his problems, he decomposes the product of the attraction into the effective space into its two factors, and calls the former by the name "force."

As an objection to this mode of proceeding, it must, however, be remarked that in many cases it is not possible thus to decompose the product in question. Let us take, for instance, the following very simple case: a mass M, originally at rest, is caused to move with the (uniform final) velocity c; from the knowledge of the magnitudes M and c it is certainly possible to deduce the value of the product of the force (in Newton's sense) into its effective space, but we are not thereby enabled to conclude as to the magnitude of this force itself.

As a matter of fact, the necessity soon made itself felt of treating and *naming* this product as a whole. It also has been called "force," and the expressions "*vis viva* of motion," "moving force," "working force," "horse-power" (or force), "muscular force," &c., have been long naturalized in science.

However happy we may, in many respects, think the choice of this word, there is still the objection that a new meaning has been fixed upon an already existing technical expression, without the old one having been called in from circulation at the same time. This formal error has become a Pandora's box, whence has sprung a Babylonian confusion of tongues.

Under existing circumstances no choice is left us but to withdraw the term "force" either from Newton's dead force or from Leibnitz's living force; but in either case we come into conflict with prevailing usage. But if once we have made up our minds to introduce into our science a logically accurate use of terms, even at the cost of existing expressions which have become easy and pleasant to us by long usage, we cannot long hesitate in the choice we have to make between the conceptions I. and II.

Let us consider the elementary case of a mass, originally at rest, which receives motion: this happens, as has been already said, by the mass being subjected to a certain push or pull under the influence of which it traverses a certain space, the effective space. Now, however, both the velocity and also the intensity of the push (Newton's force) always vary at every point of the effective space; and in order to multiply these variable magnitudes into effective space, that is, to deduce the quantity of motion from the intensity of the pushing force, we must call in the aid of the *higher* mathematics.

But hence it follows that, except in statics, where the effective space is nought and the pressure constant, the Newtonian conception of force is available only in the higher branches of mechanics; and it is plainly not advisable so to choose our conception of "force" that it cannot be consistently employed in that branch (namely, the elementary parts of the theory of motion) which of all others is chiefly concerned with fundamental notions.

It is, however, a totally mistaken method to try to adapt the idea of a force, such as gravity, conceived in Newton's sense, to the elementary parts of science, by leaving out of consideration one of its most important properties, namely its dependence on distance, and to make a "force" out of Galileo's gravity thus inexactly and in some relations most incorrectly conceived. Some such ideal force (No. III.) seems to hover before the minds of most writers on natural science as the original type of a "force of nature."

Such quantitative determinations as hold good only approximately and under certain conditions ought never to be employed to establish *definitions*. In a calculation, it is true, we may correctly enough take an arc, which is sufficiently small in comparison with the radius, as equal in size to the sine or to the tangent; but if we attempted to use such a relation in settling first principles, we should lay a foundation for fallacies and errors.

The Newtonian idea of force, however, transplanted in the manner that is commonly done into the region of elementary science, is no whit better than the notion of a straight curve. Newton's force, or attraction, *in specie* gravity, g, is equal to the differential quotient of the velocity by the time; that is, $g=\frac{dc}{dt}$. This expression is quite exact, but in order to understand and apply it a knowledge of the higher mathematics is required. On the other hand, it is quite true that, so long as we have to do only with cases in which the space fallen through is so small in comparison with the earth's semi-diameter that it may be disregarded, the equation just given may be abbreviated into the very convenient form $g=\frac{c}{t}$ without any considerable error; but this expression can never be mathematically exact so long as the space fallen through has any calculable magnitude. But on the strength of an equation thus radically inaccurate, there are planted in the receptive mind of youth such false notions as—that gravity is a uniformly accelerating (?) force, a moving (?) force whose action is proportional to the time (?); that force is directly proportional (?) to the velocity produced; and many other like errors.

It would certainly be a great merit if authors of treatises on physics would help to remedy this state of things, and in framing their definitions would start only from thoroughly exact determinations of magnitudes; for elementary physics in its present form, instead of being a well-grounded science, is only a sort of half-knowledge, such that on passing to the higher and strictly scientific departments the student must try to forget its principles and theorems as quickly as he can.

If we have once convinced ourselves by unprejudiced examination that the retention, under that name, of the conception of force distinguished above by I. has nothing but its origin to recommend it, but much to condemn it, the rest follows almost spontaneously. It accords with the laws of thought, as well as with the common usage of language, to connect every production of motion with an *expenditure* of force. Hence "force" is—

Something which is expended in producing motion; and this something which is expended is to be looked upon as a cause equivalent to the effect, namely, to the motion produced.

This definition not only corresponds perfectly with facts, but it accords as far as possible with that which already exists; for, as I shall show, it contains by implication the conception of force as met with in the higher mechanics, and referred to above by II.

If a mass M, originally at rest, while traversing the effective space s, under the influence and in the direction of the pressure p, acquires the velocity c, we have $ps=Mc^2$. Since, however, every production of motion implies the existence of a pressure (or of a pull) and an effective space, and also the exhaustion of one at least of these factors, the effective space, it follows that motion can never come into existence except at the cost of this product, $ps=Mc^2$. And this it is which for shortness I call "force."

The connection between expenditure and performance (in other words, the exhaustion of force in producing its effect) presents itself in the simplest form in the phenomena of gravitation. The necessary condition of every falling motion is that the centre of gravity of the two masses concerned in it (that is, of the earth and of the falling weight) should approach each other. But in the case of the falling together of the two masses, the approach of their centres of gravity reaches its natural limit, and hence the production of a falling movement is thus bound up with an expenditure, namely, with the exhaustion of the given falling-space, and thereby also of the product of that space into the attraction. The falling down of a weight upon the earth is a process of mechanical combination; and just as in combustion the capacity of performance (that is, the condition of the development of heat) ceases when the act of combination comes to an end, so also the production of motion ceases when the weight has fallen to its lowest position. The weight, when lying on the solid ground, is, like the carbonic acid formed in combustion, nothing but a *caput mortuum*. The affinity, whether mechanical or chemical, is still there after the union just as much as before, and opposes a certain resistance to the reduction of the compound; but its power of performance (*Leistungsfähigkeit*) is at an end as soon as there is no further available falling-space.

Whenever the attraction becomes indefinitely small, or ceases altogether, space is no longer effective space; and thus it follows, from the diminution which gravity undergoes with distance, that falling-space is limited in the centrifugal direction also, and hence that the cause of motion or "force" is, under all circumstances, a finite magnitude which becomes exhausted in producing its effect.

This fundamental physical truth will be most easily perceived when applied to a special case and reduced to figures. When a pound weight is lifted one foot from the ground, the available force is, as every one knows, =one foot-pound. If the falling-height of this weight amounts to n feet, n not being a large number, the force may be taken as approximately $=n$ foot-pounds. But supposing n, or the original distance of the weight from the earth, to be very considerable, or indeed infinite, the force (that is, the number of foot-pounds) does not by any means thereby become infinite, but, according to Newton's law of gravitation, it becomes at most $=r$ foot-pounds, where r is the number of feet contained in the earth's semidiameter. Thus how great soever the distance through which a weight falls against the earth, or the time occupied by its fall may be, it can acquire no higher final velocity than 34,450 Paris feet per second. On the other hand, were the mass of the earth four times as great as it is, its bulk remaining the same, the force would likewise become four times as great, and the maximum velocity would be 68,900 feet.

It is one of the essentials of a *good* terminology that it should put fundamental facts of this kind in a clear light; exactly the opposite, however, is done by the nomenclature at present in use. A few expressions, employed by a very meritorious naturalist in combating my views, may serve to support this assertion.

"Although," he says, "it is quite true that in nature no motion can be annihilated, or that, as it is commonly expressed, the quantity of motion once in existence continues unceasingly and without any lessening, and although in this sense the character of indestructibility belongs to every proximate cause even, every primary cause, that is, every true physical force, possesses the additional characteristic of being inexhaustible. These characteristics will best admit of being unfolded by the closer consideration of gravity, the most active and widely diffused of the natural forces (primary causes), which, as it were the soul of the world, indestructibly and inexhaustibly upholds the life of those great masses on whose motions depends the order of the universe, while requiring no food from without to call forth its ever renewed activity."

If these words are intended to contain a material contradiction of the views I have put forward, they must be meant to imply that, by virtue of its being inexhaustible, the attractive power of the earth must be capable of imparting to a falling weight, under certain conceivable circumstances, an infinite velocity. But our author himself in several places lets us see that he has a (quite well-founded) mistrust of any so decided a conclusion: this is shown in the following, among other passages: "If we follow up the chain of causes and effects to its first beginnings, we come at length to the true forces of nature, to those primary causes whose activity does not require that they should be preceded by any others, which ask for no nourishment, but which can ever call forth new motions, as it were, out of an inexhaustible soil, and can uphold and quicken those that are already in being."

Again: "If the moon every moment falls, at least virtually, a certain distance toward the earth, what is the force which the next moment pulls it away again, as it were, in order to give rise to a new falling force? It is precisely its indestructibility and inexhaustibility, its power at all times and under all circumstances to bring about without ceasing, at least virtually, the same effects, that is the essence of every true force or primary cause."

This "as it were" and "at least virtually," which always slips in at the critical moment, affords room for the suspicion that our author is himself not quite confident of the power of his "true natural causes" to give rise to an inexhaustible amount of motion (of actual exertion of force); and the indefiniteness of these expressions is quite characteristic of the Protean part which the force of gravity plays in writings on natural science. The most arbitrary explanations are given of this word, and then, when facts no longer admit of any thing else, a retreat is sought in the Newtonian conception.

Gravity being called a force, and at the same time the term force being connected, in accordance with the common use of language, with the conception of an object capable of producing motion, leads to the false assumption that a mechanical effect (the production of motion) can be produced without a corresponding expenditure of a measurable object; and here is likewise plainly the reason why our author could neither keep clear in his facts nor consistent in his reasoning. If once the production of motion out of nothing is granted, the annihilation of motion must also be admitted as a consequence; and the magnitude of motion must, in accordance with this assumption, be simply proportional to the velocity, or $=Mc$, and the "quantity of motion once in existence" must be $=+Mc-Mc=0$. But notwithstanding his "inexhaustible forces," the writer referred to expressly declares that motion is indestructible; but, instead of stating his opinion as to what becomes of motion which disappears by friction, he says in another place again that it remains "undecided" whether the effect of a force (the amount of motion produced by it) is measured by the first or by the second power of the velocity (that is, whether it is or is not destructible): he even appears, from repeated expressions, to hold it possible that a given quantity of heat can produce motion *ad infinitum!* If such were the case, it would certainly be useless to consider the convertibility of these magnitudes: the ground would rather have been won for the contact theory.

The polemics of my respected critic, whom I have here introduced as the representative and spokesman of prevailing views, and to whom I feel that my sincere thanks are due for his attentive examination of my first publication, appear to me to be necessarily without result, inasmuch as the first problem in combating my assertions, which all revolve about the *one* point of an invariable quantitative relation between heat and motion, must be to find out that this relation is variable, and in what cases. Formal controversy without a material basis is only beating the air; and as to what relates specially to the questions about force, the first point to consider is, not what sort of thing a "force" is, but to what thing we shall *give the name* "force." Backwards and forwards talk about gravity is fruitless, since all who understand the matter are agreed as to its nature; for gravity is and remains a differential quotient of the velocity by the time, directly proportional to the attracting mass, and inversely proportional to the square of the distance: on this point a final decision was come to long ago But whether it is expedient to call this magnitude a force is quite another question.

Since, whenever an innovation of essential importance is proposed, the public is so ready to misapprehend, I will here state once more, as clearly as I can, my reasons for saying that "the force of gravity" is an improper expression.

It is an unassailable truth that the production of every falling motion is connected with a corresponding expenditure of a measurable magnitude. This magnitude, if it is to be made an object of scientific investigation (and why should it not?), must have a name given to it; and in accordance with the logical instinct of man, as manifested in the genius of language, no other name can be here chosen than the word "force." But since this expression is already used in a quite different sense, we might be tempted to create for the conception which is as yet—in the fundamental parts of science at least—unnamed an entirely new name. But before betaking ourselves to this extreme course, which for reasons that are not far to seek would be the one whereby we should be brought most into conflict with existing usage, it is reasonable to inquire whether the word "force," which in itself answers so well to the requirements of the case, is in its right place where it was first put by the schools.

According to the common custom of speech, we understand by "force" something moving—a cause of motion; and if, on the one hand, the expression "moving force" is for this reason, strictly speaking, a pleonasm, the notion of a not moving or "dead" force is, on the other hand, a *contradictio in adjecto*. If it be said, for instance, that a load which presses with its weight on the ground exerts thereby a force—a force which, though never so great, is unable of itself to bring about the smallest movement—the mode of conception and of expression is quite justified by scholastic usage, but it is so far-fetched that it becomes the source of unnumbered misapprehensions.

Between gravity and the force of gravity there is, so far as I know, no difference; and hence I consider the second expression unscientific, inasmuch as it is tautological.

Let it not be objected that the "force" of pressure, the "force" of gravity, cohesive "force," &c., are the higher causes of pressure, gravity, and the like. The exact sciences are concerned with phenomena and measurable quantities. The first cause of things is Deity—a Being ever inscrutable by the intellect of man; while "higher causes," "supersensuous forces," and the rest, with all their consequences, belong to the delusive middle region of naturalistic philosophy and mysticism.

By a law that is universally true, waste and want go hand in hand. If to the case before us, where this rule likewise meets with confirmation, we apply an equalizing process, and take away the word "force" from the connection in which it is superfluous and hurtful, and bring it to where we are in want of it, we get rid at one time of two important obstacles. The higher mathematics at once cease to be required in order to gain *admittance* into the theory of motion: nature presents herself in simple beauty before the astonished eye, and even the less gifted may now behold many things which hitherto were concealed from the most learned philosophers.

Force and matter are indestructible objects. This law, to which individual facts may most simply be referred, and which therefore I might figuratively call the heliocentric standpoint, constitutes a natural basis for physics, chemistry, physiology, and philosophy.

Among the facts which, though known, have been hitherto only empirically established and have remained isolated, but which can be easily referred to this natural law, is the one that electric and magnetic attraction cannot be isolated any more than gravity, or that the strength of this attraction undergoes no alteration, so long as the distance remains the same, by the intervening of indifferent substances (non-conductors).

Among facts which have remained unknown up to the most recent times, I will refer only to the influence which the ebb and flow of the tide exerts, in accordance with the known laws of mechanics, on the motion of the earth about its axis. A fact of such importance, standing, as it does, in close relation with the fundamental law just stated, having been able to escape the attention of naturalists, is of itself a proof that the prevailing system has no *exclusive* title.

For the rest, it will not have escaped those who are acquainted with the modern literature of science that a modification of scientific language in the sense of my views is actually beginning to take place. But in matters of this kind the chief part of the work must be left to time.

According to what has been said thus far, the *vis viva* of motion must be called a force. But since the expression *vis viva* denotes in mechanics, not only a magnitude which is proportional to the mass and to the square of its velocity, but also one which is proportional to the mass and to the height from which it has fallen, force thus conceived naturally divides itself into two very easily distinguished species, each of which requires a distinct technical name, for which the words *motion* (*Bewegung*) and *falling-force* (*Fallkraft*) seem to me the most appropriate.*

Hence, according to this definition, "motion" is always measured by the product of the moved mass into the *square* of the velocity, never by the product of the mass into the velocity.

By "falling-force" we understand a raised weight, or still more generally, a distance in space between two ponderable

[* The distinction here drawn between "motion" and "falling-force" is the same as that made by Helmholtz (*Die Erhaltung der Kraft*, 1847) between "*vis viva*" (*lebendige Kraft*) and "tension" (*Spankraft*). The English expressions "dynamical energy" and "statical energy" were used by Prof. W. Thomson (Phil. Mag. S. vol. iv. p. 304, 1852) in the same sense, but were afterwards abandoned by him in favour of the terms "actual energy" and "potential energy" introduced by Prof. Rankine. More recently ("Good Words" for October, 1862) Professors Thomson and Tait have employed the expression "kinetic energy" in place of "actual energy." The German word *Kraft* in the text has been uniformly translated *force*, to which term the ambiguity of the German original has thus been transferred. This ambiguity, however, may be avoided in English by allowing the word "force" to retain the meaning which it bears in common language, that is, to denote all resistances which it requires the exertion of a *power* to overcome (whence the expressions gravitating force, cohesive force, &c.), and by using the word "energy" to denote force as defined by Mayer.—G. C. F.]

bodies. In many cases falling-force is measured with sufficient accuracy by the product of the raised weight into its height; and the expressions "foot-pound," "kilogramme-metre," "horse-power," and many others, are conventional units for the measurement of this force, which have of late come into general use, especially in practical mechanics. But in order to find the exact quantitative expression for the magnitude in question, we must consider (at least) two masses existing at a determinate distance from each other, which acquire motion by mutually approaching; and we must investigate the relation which exists between the conditions of the motion, namely, the magnitude of the masses and their original and final distance, and the amount of motion produced.

It very remarkably happens that this relation is the simplest conceivable; for, according to Newton's law of gravitation, the quantity of motion produced is directly proportional to the masses and to the space through which they fall, but inversely proportional to the distances of the centres of gravity of the masses before and after the movement. That is, if A and B are the two masses, c and c' the velocities which they respectively acquire, and h and h' their original and final distances apart, we have

$$\mathrm{A}c^2+\mathrm{B}c'^2=\frac{\mathrm{A.B}(h-h')}{h.h'};$$

or in words, *the falling-force is equal to the product of the masses into the space fallen through divided by the two distances.*

By help of this theorem, which, as will be easily seen, is nothing but a more general and convenient expression of Newton's law of gravitation,* the laws of the fall of bodies

* Newton's formula relates to the particular case in which the two distances (the initial and the final distance) are equal, so that their product becomes a square. In this case, however, both the space fallen through and the velocity become nought; and hence, when this expression has to

from cosmical elevations, and also the general laws of central motions, can be developed without its being needful to employ equations of more than the second degree.

Having now become acquainted with two species of force—motion and falling-force—we can arrive at a conception of "a force" in general, according to the well-known rule, by collecting together the common characteristics of the two species. To this end, we must consider the properties of these objects somewhat more closely. Their most important property depends on their mutual relation. Whenever a given quantity of falling force disappears, motion is produced; and by the expenditure of this latter, the falling-force can be reproduced in its original amount.

This constant proportion which exists between falling-force and motion, and is known in the higher mechanics under the name of "the principle of the conservation of *vis viva*," may be shortly and fitly denoted by the term "transformation" (*Umwandlung*). For instance, we may say that a planet, in passing from its aphelion to its perihelion, transforms a part of its falling-force into motion, and, as it moves away from the sun again, changes a part of its motion into falling-force. In using the word "transform" in this sense, nothing else can or is intended to be expressed but a constant numerical ratio.

But it follows from the axiom mentioned at page 326, that the production of a definite quantity of motion from a given quantity of falling-force, and *vice versâ*, implies that neither falling-force nor motion can be annihilated either totally or in part. We thus obtain the following definition:

Forces are transformable, indestructible, and (in contradis-

be taken as the starting-point for the calculation of real velocities, mathematical artifices become necessary which are inadmissible in the elementary branches of science.

tinction from matter) *imponderable objects.* (Conf. paper already quoted, pp. 328, 329.)

It is easy to see that this definition embraces, among other things, the fact that the motion which disappears in mechanical processes of different kinds bears a constant relation to the heat thereby produced, or that motion is convertible, as an indestructible magnitude, into heat. Thus heat is, like motion, a force; and motion, like heat, an imponderable.

I have characterized the relation which various forces bear to one another by saying (Phil. Mag. S. 4, vol. xxiv. p. 252) that they are "different forms under which one and the same object makes its appearance." At the same time I have expressly guarded myself from making the certainly plausible, but unproved, and, as it seems to me, hazardous deduction that thermal phenomena are to be regarded as merely phenomena of motion. The following is what I said upon this point (*loc. cit.*) p. 376:

"But just as little as the connection between falling-force and motion authorizes the conclusion that the essence of falling-force is motion, can such a conclusion be adopted in the case of heat. We are, on the contrary, rather inclined to infer that before it can become heat, motion—whether simple, or vibratory as in the case of light and radiant heat, &c.—must cease to exist as motion."

The relation which, as we have seen, subsists between heat and motion has regard to quantity, not to quality; for (to borrow the words of Euclid) things which are equal to one another are not therefore similar. Let us beware of leaving the solid ground of the objective, if we would not entangle ourselves in difficulties of our own making.

In the mean time it at least results from the foregoing considerations that the phenomena of heat, electricity, and magnetism do not owe their existence to any particular fluids; and the immateriality of heat, asserted half a century ago by

Rumford, becomes, through the discovery of its mechanical equivalent, a certainty.

The form of force denoted by the name "heat" is plainly not single, but includes several distinct, though mutually equivalent, objects, three principal forms of which are distinguished in common language: namely, I. Radiant Heat; II. Free (sensible) Heat, Specific Heat; and III. Latent Heat.

There can be no doubt that radiant heat must be regarded as a phenomenon of motion, especially since the recent detection of phenomena of interference in the radiation of heat. But whether there really exists, as is commonly assumed, a peculiar æther, of which the vibratory motion is perceived by us as radiant heat, or whether the seat of this motion is the particles of material bodies, is a question that is not yet made out.

Still greater obscurity hangs about the essential nature of specific heat, or what goes on in the interior of a heated body. Not only does the unanswered question of the æther enter again here, but, before we can be in a position to form any clear ideas on this subject, we require to have an exact knowledge of the internal constitution of matter. We are, however, still far from having reached this point; for, in particular, we do not know whether such things as atoms exist—that is, whether matter consists of such constituents as undergo no further change of form in chemical processes.

But a span of that time which stretches both backwards and forwards into eternity is meted out to man here on earth, and the space which his foot can tread is narrowly bounded above and below: so also his scientific knowledge finds natural limits in the direction of the infinitely small as well as of the infinitely great. The question of atoms seems to me to lead beyond these limits, and hence I consider it unpractical. An atom in itself can no more become an object of our investigation than a differential, notwithstanding that the *ratio* which such immensely small auxiliary magnitudes bear to one another may be represented by concrete numbers. In every case, however, the conception of an atom must be regarded as merely relative, and must be considered in connection with some definite process; for, as is well known, the particles of an acid and base may play the part of atoms in the formation and decomposition of a salt, while in another process these atoms may themselves undergo further division.

But assuming that, in a chemical sense, atoms have a real existence—an assumption which, among other things, the laws of isomorphism certainly render probable—the further question arises whether, by the continued division of matter, we can at last arrive at molecules which are atoms in relation to the *phenomena of heat*, such that heat cannot penetrate to their interior, and such that, when the whole mass is heated, they for their parts undergo no increase of bulk. But since we are unable to grapple with such preliminary questions as these, we are forced to confess that, whether the existence of an æther and of atoms be admitted or not, we are, so far as regards the nature of specific heat, in a state of ignorance.

The expression "latent heat" has reference to its correctly recognized property of indestructibility. In all cases in which thermometrically sensible specific heat disappears, it must be assumed that it eludes our perception only by taking on some other state of existence, and that by an appropriate process of inverse transformation the free heat can be reproduced in its original amount. These are the facts on which the doctrine of latent heat rests; and hence, if we have regard to them only, all the connected phenomena may be claimed as so many confirmations of the principle of the transformation and conservation of force.

The conception of latent heat is accordingly nothing else than the conception of something equivalent to free heat, and thus the doctrine of free and specific heat embraces pretty nearly the whole domain of physics. A few examples, chosen from among the abundance of facts, may serve to show

how, according to my view, the phenomena wherein heat becomes latent are to be regarded.

If heat is communicated to a gas retained under constant pressure, the free heat of the gas is increased, and at the same time a calculable quantity of heat becomes *latent;* the gas is thereby caused to expand, and there is consequently produced an amount of *vis viva* proportional to the pressure and to the space through which expansion takes place. Therefore as soon as we know how much of the heat that has become latent is to be attributed to the expansion of the gas, we know also the amount of the remainder of the latent heat corresponding to the *vis viva* produced. Now Gay-Lussac has proved by experiment that the specific heat of a gas undergoes *no* sensible alteration in flowing from a containing vessel into a vacuum. Hence it follows that a gaseous body opposes no perceptible resistance to the separation of its particles, and that the rarefaction of a gas does not of itself (that is, when it occurs without any evolution of force) cause any heat to become latent. The total quantity of heat which becomes latent by the expansion of a gas is therefore to be taken as the equivalent of the *vis viva* produced.

It results from the principle of the indestructibility of heat—a principle which no one calls in question—that the quantity of heat which has thus become latent must again become free when heat is in any way produced at the expense of the acquired *vis viva* of motion. Motion is latent heat, and heat is latent motion.

The celebrated law of Dulong, that the amount of heat produced by the compression of a gas is dependent on the amount of force expended, and not upon the chemical nature, tension, or temperature of the gas, is a special application of the above general principle. But in the communication so often mentioned I have shown that this law of nature is capable of a very much wider application, and that the heat which becomes latent in the expansion of a gas reappears again in every case, if the *vis viva* thereby produced is employed to generate heat, whether by the compression of air, by friction, or by the impact of nonelastic bodies; and I have there calculated the mechanical equivalent of heat upon principles of which the accuracy cannot be disputed. I also measured at that time, by way of control, the heat produced in the manufacture of paper in Holland, and compared it with the working force expended, and so found a sufficient degree of concordance between the two quantities. I have recently, moreover, succeeded in constructing, for the purpose of the direct determination of the mechanical equivalent of heat, a very simple thermal dynamometer on a small scale, with which the truth of the principle in question can be demonstrated *ad oculos;* and I have reason to believe that the efficiency of water-wheels and steam-engines might be easily and advantageously measured by means of a similar calorimotorial apparatus. It must, however, be left to the future judgment of practical men to decide whether, and to what extent, this method deserves to be preferred to Prony's.

Heat further becomes latent in certain changes of the state of aggregation of bodies. Since it is a settled fact that both solid and liquid bodies oppose a certain resistance to the separation of their parts, and since in general an expenditure of *vis viva* is required for the overcoming of mechanical resistances, we are led to conclude *à priori* that whenever the cohesion of a body is diminished or done away with, force or heat must become latent; and this, as is well known, perfectly accords with experience.

Starting from this point of view, the French physicist Person has attempted to detect a direct quantitative relation between the latent heat of metals, on which he has made a great number of observations, and their cohesion; but at present determinations of this kind are beset with almost insurmountable difficulties.

The heat which becomes latent in the evaporation of water

has been considered from quite a similar point of view by Holtzmann in his important memoir "On the Heat and Elasticity of Gases and Vapours." Starting from the principle that elevation of temperature is equivalent to the raising of a weight, this philosopher has likewise calculated the mechanical equivalent of heat from the quantity of heat which becomes latent by the expansion of a gas; and he very rightly conceives of the latent heat of steam as made up of two parts, whereof one, the smaller, is expended in overcoming the opposing pressure of the atmosphere, and can hence be easily calculated by means of the mechanical equivalent of heat, while the remaining part, the amount of which can also be calculated, is what Holtzmann calls the heat required to destroy the cohesion of the water. In all steam-engines this latter portion is wasted, and Holtzmann calculates from these data the superior efficiency of high-pressure compared with low-pressure engines.*

If the view here taken of the latent heat of fusion and evaporation is correct, heat must also become latent when hard bodies are reduced to powder; and when such substances pass into the liquid condition from a state of fine division, they must absorb a smaller quantity of heat than when they are liquefied without previous comminution. A few experiments that I have instituted in this direction have not hitherto given any decisive result.

It is also worthy of notice that certain solid bodies which are capable of assuming allotropic states, as, for instance, the oxygen-compounds of iron, evolve a considerable quantity of heat on passing from a less to a more hard condition. Such facts, the number of which will doubtless continually increase with time, agree perfectly with the above principle, that diminution of cohesion involves an *expenditure* of heat, and, on the other hand, increase of cohesion a *production* of heat.

* The engines which give the greatest useful effect must be those in which the steam receives an addition of heat during its expansion.

Customary language, according to which gravity is called a moving force and heat a substance, occasions, on the one hand, the significance of an important natural object, falling-space, or the space through which a body falls, to be kept as much as possible out of sight, and, on the other hand, heat to be removed to the greatest possible distance from the *vis viva* of motion. The sciences are thus reduced to an artificial system, over whose fissured surface we can advance in safety only by the powerful aid of the higher analysis.

Without doubt the fact that so simple and obvious a matter as the connection between heat and motion could remain unperceived up to the most recent times must also be attributed to the same defect. Nevertheless, as has been already pointed out, the quantitative determination of chemical heating-effects and of galvanic actions, as well as researches into vital phenomena, instituted in the spirit of those of Liebig, must soon have led to the law, not difficult to discover, of the equivalence of heat and motion.

In reality this law and its numerical expression, the mechanical equivalent of heat, were published almost simultaneously in Germany and in England.

Starting from the fact that the amount of chemical as well as of galvanic effect is dependent only and solely on the amount of material expenditure, the celebrated English physicist Joule was led to the principle that the phenomena of motion and of heat rest essentially upon one and the same foundation, or, as he expressed himself, in the same way as I have done, heat and motion are transformable one into the other.

Not only did this philosopher indisputably make an independent discovery of the natural law in question, but to him belongs the credit of having made numerous and important contributions towards its further establishment and development. Joule has shown that when motion is produced by means of electro-magnetism, the heating effect of the galvanic current is diminished in a corresponding and fixed proportion. He has further ascertained that by reversing the poles of a magnetic bar a quantity of heat is produced proportional to the square of the magnetic tension—a fact which was also discovered by myself, though at a later date. In particular, Joule has likewise demonstrated, by means of numerous experiments, that the heat evolved by friction under various circumstances stands in an unvarying proportion to the amount of force expended. According to his most recent experiments of this kind, he has fixed the mechanical equivalent of heat at 423.*

Joule has likewise investigated experimentally, in relation to this question, the thermal behaviour of elastic fluids when expanded, and has thereby confirmed the earlier results of other physicists.

The new subject soon began to excite the attention of learned men; but inasmuch as both at home and abroad the subject has been exclusively treated as a foreign discovery, I find myself compelled to make the claims to which priority entitles me; for although the few investigations which I have given to the public, and which have almost disappeared in the flood of communications which every day sends forth without leaving a trace behind, prove, by the very form of their publication, that I am not one who hankers after effect, it is not therefore to be assumed that I am willing to be deprived of intellectual property which documentary evidence proves to be mine.

By help of the mechanical equivalent of heat many problems can be solved which, without it, could not be attacked at all: among them, the calculation of the thermal effect of the falling together of cosmical masses may be especially mentioned. It will not be out of place to indicate here briefly a few results of such calculations.

* That is, 1 thermal unit = 423 kilogrammetres.

The following is one problem of this kind. It is assumed that a cosmical body enters the atmosphere of our earth with a velocity of four geographical miles per second, and that, in consequence of the resistance which it here encounters, it loses so much of its *vis viva* of motion that its remaining velocity when it again quits the atmosphere amounts to three miles: the question now arises, How great is the thermal effect which accompanies this process?

A simple calculation, based upon the mechanical equivalent of heat, shows that the quantity of heat required is about eight times as great as the heat of combustion of a mass of coal of equal weight with the body in question, one kilogramme of coal being taken as yielding 6,000 thermal units. Hence it follows that the velocity of the motion of shooting-stars and fire-balls, which, as is well-known, attains, according to astronomical observations, to from four to eight miles, is a cause fully sufficient to produce the most violent evolution of heat, and an insight into the nature of these remarkable phenomena is thereby afforded to us.*

The following is a problem of a similar kind: if two cosmical masses, moving in space about their common centre of gravity, were by any cause whatever, for example by the resistance of the surrounding medium, caused to fall together, the question again arises, How great is the thermal effect corresponding to this process of mechanical combination?

Even though the elements of the orbits (that is, their excentricity) may be unknown, we can nevertheless calculate from the given weight and volume of the masses in question the maximum and the minimum of the required effect. Thus let it be supposed, for the sake of an example, that our earth had been divided into two equal globes which had united in

* The idea that the meteors here referred to owe their light to a mechanical process—whether friction, or the compression of the air—is not new; but without a knowledge of the mechanical equivalent of heat it could have no scientific foundation.

the manner described: calculation teaches us that the amount of heat which would have been evolved in such a case would considerably exceed that which an equal weight of matter could furnish by the most intense process of chemical action.

It is more than probable that the earth has come into existence in some such way, and that in consequence our sun, as seen from the distance of the fixed stars, exhibited at that epoch a transient burst of light. But what took place in our solar system perhaps millions of years ago, still goes on at the present time here and there among the fixed stars; and the transient appearance of stars, which in some cases, like the celebrated star of Tycho Brahe, have at first an extraordinary degree of brilliance, may be satisfactorily explained by assuming the falling together of previously invisible double stars.

Contrasting with such explosive bursts of light is the steady radiation, shown continuously through enormous periods, by the greater number of fixed stars, and among them by our sun. Do these appearances, which in so special a manner tempt to higher speculations, constitute a real exception to the exhaustion of a cause in producing its effect, which, in accordance with the foregoing considerations, we have regarded as an established law of Nature? or does the small sum of human knowledge authorize us in supposing that here also there is an equivalence between performance and expenditure, and in searching for the conditions of that equivalent?

To enter further upon this subject would lead us beyond the intended scope of this publication; and I therefore close in the hope that the reader will please to supplement by his own reflection much that in this tract has been left unsaid.

SOME THOUGHTS

ON THE

CONSERVATION OF FORCE.

BY DR. FARADAY.

MICHAEL FARADAY, son of a smith, was born in London in 1791. He was taught reading, writing, and arithmetic at a day-school, and in all other things educated himself. At thirteen he was apprenticed to a bookbinder, choosing this vocation in order to be among books. He was early fond of experiment, and averse to trade; and being taken to hear some lectures of Sir Humphrey Davy at the Royal Institution, he resolved to pursue science, and wrote to Davy asking his assistance in obtaining a place. Davy favored his application, and in 1813, at the age of twenty, he was appointed assistant in the laboratory of the Royal Institution. In 1820 he discovered the chloride of carbon, and in 1823 effected the condensation of chlorine and other gases. On this account Davy became jealous of him, and discouraged the idea of recommending him for election to the Royal Society, which, however, took place in 1824. In 1820, Oersted announced his celebrated discovery of electro-magnetism, and Faraday at once entered upon an investigation of the relations of magnetism and electricity. In 1831 he commenced his celebrated series of Experimental Researches in Electricity, which extended to three volumes, published in 1839, 1844, and 1855. In 1827 he published his admirable work on "Chemical Manipulations," and, in 1830, a valuable paper on "The Manufacture of Glass for Optical Purposes." In 1833 he became Professor of Chemistry in the Royal Institution, and he has received numerous honors from the learned societies of Europe. In 1835 he received a pension of £300 a year, and in 1858 the Queen allotted him a residence in Hampton Court. Dr. Faraday has talents of a high order, both as an original investigator and as a lecturer. Advanced in years, he has now retired to a considerable extent from active duty, but is still in the vigor of his powers, as is shown by his recent lectures to juvenile audiences in the Royal Institution.

THE CONSERVATION OF FORCE.

VARIOUS circumstances induce me at the present moment to put forth a consideration regarding the conservation of force. I do not suppose that I can utter any truth respecting it that has not already presented itself to the high and piercing intellects which move within the exalted regions of science; but the course of my own investigations and views makes me think that the consideration may be of service to those persevering labourers (amongst whom I endeavour to class myself) who, occupied in the comparison of physical ideas with fundamental principles, and continually sustaining and aiding themselves by experiment and observation, delight to labour for the advance of natural knowledge, and strive to follow it into undiscovered regions.

There is no question which lies closer to the root of all physical knowledge than that which inquires whether force can be destroyed or not. The progress of the strict science of modern times has tended more and more to produce the conviction that "force can neither be created nor destroyed;" and to render daily more manifest the value of the knowledge of that truth in experimental research. To admit, indeed, that force may be destructible or can altogether disappear, would be to admit that matter could be uncreated; for we know matter only by its forces; and though one of these is most commonly referred to, namely, gravity, to prove its presence, it is not because gravity has any pretension, or any exemption, amongst the forms of force as regards the principle of *conservation*, but simply that being, as far as we perceive, inconvertible in its nature and unchangeable in its manifestation, it offers an unchanging test of the matter which we recognize by it.

Agreeing with those who admit the conservation of force to be a principle in physics, as large and sure as that of the indestructibility of matter, or the invariability of gravity, I think that no particular idea of force has a right to unlimited or unqualified acceptance that does not include *assent* to it; and also, to *definite amount* and *definite disposition of the force*, either in one effect or another, for these are necessary consequences; therefore I urge, that the conservation of force ought to be admitted as a physical principle in all our hypotheses, whether partial or general, regarding the actions of matter. I have had doubts in my own mind whether the considerations I am about to advance are not rather metaphysical than physical. I am unable to define what is metaphysical in physical science; and am exceedingly adverse to the easy and unconsidered admission of one supposition upon another, suggested as they often are by very imperfect induction from a small number of facts, or by a very imperfect observation of the facts themselves; but, on the other hand, I think the philosopher may be bold in his application of principles which have been developed by close inquiry, have stood through much investigation, and continually increase in force. For instance, *time* is growing up daily into importance as an element in the exercise of force. The earth moves in its orbit in time; the crust of the earth moves in time; light moves in time; an electro-magnet requires time for its charge by an electric current; to inquire, therefore, whether power, acting either at sensible or insensible distances, always acts in *time*, is not to be metaphysical; if it acts in time and across space, it must act by physical lines of force; and our view of the nature of the force may be affected to the extremest degree by the conclusions which experiment and observation on time may supply; being, perhaps, finally determinable only by them. To inquire after the possible time in which gravitating, magnetic, or electric force is exerted, is no more metaphysical than to mark the times of the hands of a clock in their progress; or that of the temple of Serapis and its ascents and descents; or the periods of the occultations of Jupiter's satellites; or that in which the light from them comes to the earth. Again, in some of the known cases of action in time, something happens whilst the *time* is passing which did not happen before, and does not continue after; it is, therefore, not metaphysical to expect an effect in *every* case, or to endeavour to discover its existence and determine its nature. So in regard to the principle of the conservation of force; I do not think that to admit it, and its consequences, whatever they may be, is to be metaphysical; on the contrary, if that word have any application to physics, then I think that any hypothesis, whether of heat, or electricity, or gravitation, or any other form of force, which either willingly or unwillingly dispenses with the principle of conservation, is more liable to the charge than those which, by including it, become so far more strict and precise.

Supposing that the truth of the principle of the conservation of force is assented to, I come to *its uses*. No hypothesis should be admitted, nor any assertion of a fact credited, that denies the principle. No view should be inconsistent or incompatible with it. Many of our hypotheses in the present state of science may not comprehend it, and may be unable to suggest its consequences; but none should oppose or contradict it.

If the principle be admitted, we perceive at once that a theory or definition, though it may not contradict the principle, cannot be accepted as sufficient or complete unless the former be contained in it; that however well or perfectly the definition may include and represent the state of things commonly considered under it, that state or result is only partial, and must not be accepted as exhausting the power or being the full equivalent, and therefore cannot be considered as representing its *whole nature;* that, indeed, it may express only a very small part of the whole, only a residual phenomenon, and hence give us but little indication of the full natural truth. Allowing the principle its force, we ought, in every hypothesis, either to account for its consequences by saying what the changes are when force of a given kind apparently disappears, as when ice thaws, or else should leave space for the idea of the conversion. If any hypothesis, more or less trustworthy on other accounts, is insufficient in expressing it or incompatible with it, the place of deficiency or opposition should be marked as the most important for examination, for there lies the hope of a discovery of new laws or a new condition of force. The deficiency should never be accepted as satisfactory, but be remembered and used as a stimulant to further inquiry; for conversions of force may here be hoped for. Suppositions may be accepted for the time, provided they are not in contradiction with the principle. Even an increased or diminished capacity is better than nothing at all, because such a supposition, if made, must be consistent with the nature of the original hypothesis, and may, therefore, by the application of experiment, be converted into a further test of probable truth. The case of a force simply removed or suspended, without a transferred exertion in some other direction, appears to me to be absolutely impossible.

If the principle be accepted as true, we have a right to pursue it to its consequences, no matter what they may be. It is, indeed, a duty to do so. A theory may be perfection, as far as it goes, but a consideration going beyond it, is not for that reason to be shut out. We might as well accept our limited horizon as the limits of the world. No magnitude, either of the phenomena or of the results to be dealt with, should stop our exertions to ascertain, by the use of the principle, that something remains to be discovered, and to trace in what direction that discovery may lie.

I will endeavour to illustrate some of the points which have been urged, by reference, in the first instance, to a case of power, which has long had great attractions for me, because of its extreme simplicity, its promising nature, its universal presence, and in its invariability under like circumstances; on which, though I have experimented* and as yet failed, I think experiment would be well bestowed, I mean the force of gravitation. I believe I represent the received idea of the gravitating force aright in saying that it is *a simple attractive force exerted between any two or all the particles or masses of matter, at every sensible distance, but with a strength varying inversely as the square of the distance.* The usual idea of the force implies *direct* action at a distance; and such a view appears to present little difficulty except to Newton, and a few, including myself, who in that respect may be of like mind with him.

This idea of gravity appears to me to ignore entirely the principle of the conservation of force; and by the terms of its definition, if taken in an absolute sense, "*varying* inversely as the square of the distance," to be in direct opposition to it, and it becomes my duty now to point out where this contradiction occurs, and to use it in illustration of the principle of conservation. Assume two particles of matter, A and B, in free space, and a force in each or in both by which they gravitate towards each other, the force being unalterable for an unchanging distance, but varying inversely as the square of the distance when the latter varies. Then, at the distance of ten, the force may be estimated as one; whilst at the distance of one, that is, one-tenth of the former, the force will be one

* Philosophical Transactions, 1851, p. 1.

hundred; and if we suppose an elastic spring to be introduced between the two as a measure of the attractive force, the power compressing it will be a hundred times as much in the latter case as in the former. But from whence can this enormous increase of power come? If we say that it is the character of this force, and content ourselves with that as a sufficient answer, then it appears to me we admit a *creation* of power and that to an enormous amount; yet by a change of condition, so small and simple as to fail in leading the least instructed mind to think that it can be a sufficient cause, we should admit a result which would equal the highest act our minds can appreciate of the working of infinite power upon matter; we should let loose the highest law in physical science which our faculties permit us to perceive, namely, the *conservation of force.* Suppose the two particles, A and B, removed back to the greater distance of ten, then the force of attraction would be only a hundredth part of that they previously possessed; this, according to the statement that the force varies inversely as the square of the distance, would double the strangeness of the above results; it would be an *annihilation* of force—an effect equal in its infinity and its consequences with *creation*, and only within the power of Him who has created.

We have a right to view gravitation under every form that either its definition or its effects can suggest to the mind; it is our privilege to do so with every force in nature; and it is only by so doing that we have succeeded, to a large extent, in relating the various forms of power, so as to derive one from another, and thereby obtain confirmatory evidence of the great principle of the conservation of force. Then let us consider the two particles, A and B, as attracting each other by the force of gravitation, under another view. According to the definition, the force depends upon both particles, and if the particle A or B were by itself, it could not gravitate, that is, it could have no attraction, no *force* of gravity. Supposing A to exist in that isolated state and without gravitating force, and then B placed in relation to it, gravitation comes on, as is supposed, on the part of both. Now, without trying to imagine *how* B, which had no gravitating force, can raise up gravitating force in A; and how A, equally without force beforehand, can raise up force in B, still, to imagine it as a fact done, is to admit a creation of force in both particles; and so to bring ourselves within the impossible consequences which have been already referred to.

It may be said we cannot have an idea of one particle by itself, and so the reasoning fails. For my part I can comprehend a particle by itself just as easily as many particles; and though I cannot conceive the relation of a lone particle to gravitation, according to the limited view which is at present taken of that force, I can conceive its relation to something which causes gravitation, and with which, whether the particle is alone, or one of a universe of other particles, it is always related. But the reasoning upon a lone particle does not fail; for as the particles can be separated, we can easily conceive of the particle B being removed to an infinite distance from A, and then the power in A will be infinitely diminished. Such removal of B will be as if it were annihilated in regard to A, and the force in A will be annihilated at the same time; so that the case of a lone particle and that where different instances only are considered become one, being identical with each other in their consequences. And as removal of B to an infinite distance is as regards A annihilation of B, so removal to the smallest degree is, in principle, the same thing with displacement through infinite space; the smallest increase in distance involves annihilation of power; the annihilation of the second particle, so as to have A alone, involves no other consequence in relation to gravity; there is difference in degree, but no difference in the character of the result.

It seems hardly necessary to observe, that the same line

of thought grows up in the mind, if we consider the mutua. gravitating action of one particle and many. The particle A will attract the particle B at the distance of a mile with a certain degree of force; it will attract a particle C at the same distance of a mile with a power equal to that by which it attracts B; if myriads of like particles be placed at the given distance of a mile, A will attract each with equal force; and if other particles be accumulated round it, within and without the sphere of two miles diameter, it will attract them all with a force varying inversely with the square of the distance. How are we to conceive of this force growing up in A to a million-fold or more, and if the surrounding particles be then removed, of its diminution in an equal degree? Or, how are we to look upon the power raised up in all these outer particles by the action of A on them, or by their action one on another, without admitting, according to the limited definition of gravitation, the facile generation and annihilation of force?

The assumption which we make for the time with regard to the nature of a power (as gravity, heat, etc.), and the form of words in which we express it, that is, its definition, should be consistent with the fundamental principles of force generally. The conservation of force is a fundamental principle; hence the assumption with regard to a particular form of force ought to imply what becomes of the force when its action is *increased* or *diminished*, or its *direction changed;* or else the assumption should admit that it is deficient on that point, being only half competent to represent the force; and, in any case, should not be opposed to the principle of conservation. The usual definition of gravity as *an attractive force between the particles of matter* VARYING *inversely as the square of the distance*, whilst it stands as a full *definition* of the power, is inconsistent with the principle of the conservation of force. If we accept the principle, such a definition must be an imperfect account of the whole of the force, and is probably only a description of one exercise of that power, whatever the nature of the force itself may be. If the definition be accepted as tacitly including the conservation of force, then it ought to admit that consequences must occur during the suspended or diminished degree in its power as gravitation, equal in importance to the power suspended or hidden; being in fact equivalent to that diminution. It ought also to admit, that it is incompetent to suggest or deal with any of the consequences of that changed part or condition of the force, and cannot tell whether they depend on, or are related to, conditions *external* or *internal* to the gravitating particle; and, as it appears to me, can say neither yes nor no to any of the arguments or probabilities belonging to the subject.

If the definition *denies* the occurrence of such contingent results, it seems to me to be unphilosophical; if it simply *ignores* them, I think it is imperfect and insufficient; if it *admits* these things, or any part of them, then it prepares the natural philosopher to look for effects and conditions as yet unknown, and is open to any degree of development of the consequences and relations of power; by denying, it opposes a dogmatic barrier to improvement; by ignoring, it becomes in many respects an inert thing, often much in the way; by admitting, it rises to the dignity of a stimulus to investigation, a pilot to human science.

The principle of the conservation of force would lead us to assume, that when A and B attract each other less, because of increasing distance, then some other exertion of power, either within or without them, is proportionately growing up; and again, that when their distance is diminished, as from ten to one, the power of attraction, now increased a hundred-fold, has been produced out of some other form of power which has been equivalently reduced. This enlarged assumption of the nature of gravity is not more metaphysical than the half assumption; and is, I believe, more philosophical and more in accordance with all physical considerations.

The half assumption is, in my view of the matter, more dogmatic and irrational than the whole, because it leaves it to be understood that power can be created and destroyed almost at pleasure.

When the equivalents of the various forms of force, as far as they are known, are considered, their differences appear very great; thus, a grain of water is known to have electric relations equivalent to a very powerful flash of lightning. It may therefore be supposed that a very large apparent amount of the force causing the phenomena of gravitation, may be the equivalent of a very small change in some unknown condition of the bodies, whose attraction is varying by change of distance. For my own part, many considerations urge my mind toward the idea of a cause of gravity, which is not resident in the particles of matter merely, but constantly in them, and all space. I have already put forth considerations regarding gravity which partake of this idea,* and it seems to have been unhesitatingly accepted by Newton.†

There is one wonderful condition of matter, perhaps its only true indication, namely, *inertia;* but in relation to the ordinary definition of gravity, it only adds to the difficulty. For if we consider two particles of matter at a certain distance apart, attracting each other under the power of gravity, and free to approach, they will approach; and when at only half the distance, each will have had stored up in it, because of its *inertia*, a certain amount of mechanical force. This must

* Proceedings of the Royal Institution, 1855, vol. ii., p. 10, etc.

† "That gravity should be innate, inherent, and essential to matter, so that one body may act upon another at a distance, through a *vacuum*, without the mediation of any thing else, by and through which their action and force may be conveyed from one to another, is to me so great an absurdity that I believe no man who has in philosophical matters a competent faculty of thinking, can ever fall into it. Gravity must be caused by an agent, acting constantly according to certain laws; but whether this agent be material or immaterial I have left to the consideration of my reader."—*See Newton's Third Letter to Bentley.*

be due to the force exerted, and, if the conservation principle be true, must have consumed an equivalent proportion of the cause of attraction; and yet, according to the definition of gravity, the attractive force is not diminished thereby, but increased four-fold, the force growing up within itself the more rapidly, the more it is occupied in producing other force. On the other hand, if mechanical force from without be used to separate the particles to twice their distance, this force is not stored up in momentum or by inertia, but disappears; and three-fourths of the attractive force at the first distance disappears with it. How can this be?

We know not the physical condition or action from which *inertia* results; but inertia is always a pure case of the conservation of force. It has a strict relation to gravity, as appears by the proportionate amount of the force which gravity can communicate to the inert body; but it appears to have the same strict relation to other forces acting at a distance as those of magnetism or electricity, when they are so applied by the tangential balance as to act independent of the gravitating force. It has the like strict relation to force communicated by impact, pull, or in any other way. It enables a body to take up and conserve a given amount of force until that force is transferred to other bodies, or changed into an equivalent of some other form; that is all that we perceive in it; and we cannot find a more striking instance amongst natural, or possible phenomena, of the necessity of the conservation of force as a law of nature; or one more in contrast with the assumed variable condition of the gravitating force supposed to reside in the particles of matter

Even gravity itself furnishes the strictest proof of the conservation of force in this, that its power is unchangeable for the same distance; and is by that in striking contrast with the variation which we assume in regard to the *cause of gravity*, to account for the *results* at different distances.

It will not be imagined for a moment that I am opposed

to what may be called the *law of gravitating action*, that is, the law by which all the known effects of gravity are governed; what I am considering is the definition of the *force* of gravitation. That the result of one exercise of a power may be inversely as the square of the distance, I believe and admit; and I know that it is so in the case of gravity, and has been verified to an extent that could hardly have been within the conception even of Newton himself when he gave utterance to the law; but that the *totality* of a force can be employed according to that law I do not believe, either in relation to gravitation, or electricity, or magnetism, or any other supposed form of power.

I might have drawn reasons for urging a continual recollection of, and reference to, the principle of the conservation of force from other forms of power than that of gravitation; but I think that when founded on gravitating phenomena, they appear in their greatest simplicity; and precisely for this reason, that gravitation has not yet been connected by any degree of convertibility with the other forms of force. If I refer for a few minutes to these other forms, it is only to point in their variations, to the proofs of the value of the principle laid down, the consistency of the known phenomena with it, and the suggestions of research and discovery which arise from it. *Heat*, for instance, is a mighty form of power, and its effects have been greatly developed; therefore, assumptions regarding its nature become useful and necessary, and philosophers try to define it. The most probable assumption is, that it is a motion of the particles of matter; but a view, at one time very popular, is, that it consists of a particular fluid of heat. Whether it be viewed in one way or the other, the principle of conservation is admitted, I believe, with all its force. When transferred from one portion to another portion of like matter, the full amount of heat appears. When transferred to matter of another kind an apparent excess or deficiency often results; the word "capacity" is then introduced, which, while it acknowledges the principle of conservation, leaves space for research. When employed in changing the state of bodies, the appearance and disappearance of the heat is provided for consistently by the assumption of enlarged or diminished motion, or else space is left by the term "capacity" for the partial views which remain to be developed. When converted into mechanical force, in the steam or air engine, and so brought into direct contact with gravity, being then easily placed in relation to it, still the conservation of force is fully respected and wonderfully sustained. The constant amount of heat developed in the whole of a voltaic current described by M. P. Favre,* and the present state of the knowledge of thermo-electricity, are again fine, partial, or subordinate illustrations of the principles of conservation. Even when rendered radiant, and for the time giving no trace or signs of ordinary heat action, the assumptions regarding its nature have provided for the belief in the conservation of force, by admitting either that it throws the ether into an equivalent state, in sustaining which for the time the power is engaged; or else, that the motion of the particles of heat is employed altogether in their own transit from place to place.

It is true that heat often becomes evident or insensible in a manner unknown to us; and we have a right to ask what is happening when the heat disappears in one part, as of the thermo-voltaic current, and appears in another; or when it enlarges or changes the state of bodies; or what would happen, if the heat being presented, such changes were purposely opposed. We have a right to ask these questions, but not to ignore or deny the conservation of force; and one of the highest uses of the principle is to suggest such inquiries. Explications of similar points are continually produced, and will be most abundant from the hands of those who, not desiring

* Comtes Rendus 1854, vol. xxxix., p. 1212.

to ease their labour by forgetting the principle, are ready to admit it, either tacitly, or, better still, effectively, being then continually guided by it. Such philosophers believe that heat must do its equivalent of work; that if in doing work it seem to disappear, it is still producing its equivalent effect, though often in a manner partially or totally unknown; and that if it give rise to another form of force (as we imperfectly express it), that force is equivalent in power to the heat which has disappeared.

What is called *chemical attraction* affords equally instructive and suggestive considerations in relation to the principle of the conservation of force. The indestructibility of individual matter is one case, and a most important one, of the conservation of chemical force. A molecule has been endowed with powers which give rise in it to various qualities, and these never change, either in their nature or amount. A particle of oxygen is ever a particle of oxygen—nothing can in the least wear it. If it enters into combination and disappears as oxygen—if it pass through a thousand combinations, animal, vegetable, mineral—if it lie hid for a thousand years and then be evolved, it is oxygen with its first qualities, neither more nor less. It has all its original force, and only that; the amount of force which it disengaged when hiding itself has again to be employed in a reverse direction when it is set at liberty; and if, hereafter, we should decompose oxygen, and find it compounded of other particles, we should only increase the strength of the proof of the conservation of force, for we should have a right to say of these particles, long as they have been hidden, all that we could say of the oxygen itself.

Again, the body of facts included in the theory of definite proportions, witnesses to the truth of the conservation of force; and though we know little of the cause of the change of properties of the acting and produced bodies, or how the forces of the former are hid amongst those of the latter, we do not for an instant doubt the conservation, but are moved to look for the manner in which the forces are, for the time, disposed, or if they have taken up another form of force, to search what that form may be.

Even chemical action at a distance, which is in such antithetical contrast with the ordinary exertion of chemical affinity, since it can produce effects miles away from the particles on which they depend, and which are effectual only by forces acting at insensible distances, still proves the same thing, the conservation of force. Preparations can be made for a chemical action in the simple voltaic circuit, but until the circuit be complete that action does not occur; yet in completing we can so arrange the circuit, that a distant chemical action, the perfect equivalent of the dominant chemical action, shall be produced; and this result, whilst it establishes the electro-chemical equivalent of power, establishes the principle of the conservation of force also, and at the same time suggests many collateral inquiries which have yet to be made and answered, before all that concerns the conservation in this case can be understood.

This and other instances of chemical action at a distance carry our inquiring thoughts on from the facts to the physical mode of the exertion of force; for the qualities which seem located and fixed to certain particles of matter appear at a distance in connection with particles altogether different. They also lead our thoughts to the *conversion* of one form of power into another; as, for instance, in the *heat* which the elements of a voltaic pile may either show at the place where they act by their combustion or combination together, or in the distance, where the electric spark may be rendered manifest; or in the wire of fluids of the different parts of the circuit.

When we occupy ourselves with the dual forms of power, electricity, and magnetism, we find great latitude of assumption, and necessarily so, for the powers become more and more complicated in their conditions. But still there is no apparent desire to let loose the force of the principle of conservation, even in those cases where the appearance and disappearance of force may seem most evident and striking. Electricity appears when there is consumption of no other force than that required for friction; we do not know how, but we search to know, not being willing to admit that the electric force can arise out of nothing. The two electricities are developed in equal proportions; and having appeared, we may dispose variously of the influence of one upon successive portions of the other, causing many changes in relation, yet never able to make the sum of the force of one kind in the least degree exceed or come short of the sum of the other. In that necessity of equality, we see another direct proof of the conservation of force, in the midst of a thousand changes that require to be developed in their principles before we can consider this part of science as even moderately known to us.

One assumption with regard to electricity is, that there is an electric fluid rendered evident by excitement in plus and minus proportions. Another assumption is, that there are two fluids of electricity, each particle of each repelling all particles like itself, and attracting all particles of the other kind always, and with a force proportionate to the inverse square of the distance, being so far analogous to the definition of gravity. This hypothesis is antagonistic to the law of the conservation of force, and open to all the objections that have been, or may be, made against the ordinary definition of gravity. Another assumption is, that each particle of the two electricities has a given amount of power, and can only attract contrary particles with the sum of that amount, acting upon each of two with only half the power it could in like circumstances exert upon one. But various as are the assumptions, the conservation of force (though wanting in the second) is, I think, intended to be included in all. I might repeat the same observations nearly in regard to magnetism-whether to be assumed as a fluid, or two fluids or electric currents—whether the external action be supposed to be action at a distance, or dependent on an external condition and lines of force—still, all are intended to admit the conservation of power as a principle to which the phenomena are subject.

The principles of physical knowledge are now so far developed as to enable us not merely to define or describe the *known*, but to state reasonable expectations regarding the *unknown;* and I think the principle of the conservation of force may greatly aid experimental philosophers in that duty to science, which consists in the enunciation of problems to be solved. It will lead us, in any case where the force remaining unchanged in form is altered in direction only, to look for the new disposition of the force; as in the cases of magnetism, static electricity, and perhaps gravity, and to ascertain that as a whole it remains unchanged in amount—or, if the original force disappear, either altogether or in part, it will lead us to look for the new condition or form of force which should result, and to develop its equivalency to the force that has disappeared. Likewise, when force is developed, it will cause us to consider the previously-existing equivalent to the force so appearing; and many such cases there are in chemical action. When force disappears, as in the electric or magnetic induction after more or less discharge, or that of gravity with an increasing distance, it will suggest a research as to whether the equivalent change is one within the apparently acting bodies, or one *external* (in part) to them. It will also raise up inquiry as to the nature of the internal or external state, both before the change and after. If supposed to be external, it will suggest the necessity of a physical process, by which the power is communicated from body to body; and in the case of external action, will lead to the inquiry whether, in any case, there can be truly action at a distance, or whether the ether, or some other medium, is not necessarily present.

We are not permitted as yet to see the nature of the source of physical power, but we are allowed to see much of the consistency existing amongst the various forms in which it is presented to us. Thus, if, in static electricity, we consider an act of induction, we can perceive the consistency of all other like acts of induction with it. If we then take an electric current, and compare it with this inductive effect, we see their relation and consistency. In the same manner we have arrived at a knowledge of the consistency of magnetism with electricity, and also of chemical action and of heat with all the former; and if we see not the consistency between gravitation with any of these forms of force, I am strongly of the mind that it is because of our ignorance only. How imperfect would our idea of an electric current now be, if we were to leave out of sight its origin, its static and dynamic induction, its magnetic influence, its chemical and heating effects; or our idea of any one of these results, if we left any of the others unregarded? That there should be a power of gravitation existing by itself, having *no relation to the other natural powers, and no respect to the law of the conservation of force*, is as little likely as that there should be a principle of levity as well as of gravity. Gravity may be only the residual part of the other forces of nature, as Mositi has tried to show; but that it should fall out from the law of all other force, and should be outside the reach either of further experiment or philosophical conclusions, is not probable. So we must strive to learn more of this outstanding power, and endeavour to avoid any definition of it which is incompatible with the principles of force generally, for all the phenomena of nature lead us to believe that the great and governing law is one. I would much rather incline to believe that bodies affecting each other by gravitation act by lines of force of definite amount (somewhat in the manner of magnetic or electric induction, though with polarity), or by an ether pervading all parts of space, than admit that the conservation of force could be dispensed with.

It may be supposed, that one who has little or no mathematical knowledge should hardly assume a right to judge of the generality and force of a principle such as that which forms the subject of these remarks. My apology is this: I do not perceive that a mathematical mind, simply as such, has any advantage over an equally acute mind not mathematical, in perceiving the nature and power of a natural principle of action. It cannot of itself introduce the knowledge of any new principle. Dealing with any and every amount of static electricity, the mathematical mind has balanced and adjusted them with wonderful advantage, and has foretold results which the experimentalist can do no more than verify. But it could not discover dynamic-electricity, nor electro-magnetism, nor magneto-electricity, or even suggest them; though when once discovered by the experimentalist, it can take them up with extreme facility.

So in respect of the force of gravitation, it has calculated the results of the power in such a wonderful manner as to trace the known planets through their courses and perturbations, and in so doing has *discovered* a planet before unknown; but there may be results of the gravitating force of other kinds than attraction inversely as the square of the distance, of which it knows nothing, can discover nothing, and can neither assert nor deny their possibility or occurrence. Under these circumstances, a principle which may be accepted as equally strict with mathematical knowledge, comprehensible without it, applicable by all in their philosophical logic, whatever form that may take, and above all, suggestive, encouraging, and instructive to the mind of the experimentalist, should be the more earnestly employed and the more frequently resorted to when we are labouring either to discover new regions of science, or to map out and develop those which are known into one harmonious whole; and if in such strivings, we, whilst applying the principle of conservation, see but imperfectly, still we should endeavour to see, for even an obscure and distorted vision is better than none. Let us, if we can, discover a new thing in *any shape;* the true appearance and character will be easily developed afterwards.

Some are much surprised that I should, as they think, venture to oppose the conclusions of Newton; but here there is a mistake. I do not oppose Newton on any point; it is rather those who sustain the idea of action at a distance, that contradict him. Doubtful as I ought to be of myself, I am certainly very glad to feel that my convictions are in accordance with his conclusions. At the same time, those who occupy themselves with such matters ought not to depend altogether upon authority, but should find reason within themselves, after careful thought and consideration, to use and abide by their own judgment. Newton himself, whilst referring to those who were judging his views, speaks of such as are competent to form an opinion in such matters, and makes a strong distinction between them and those who were incompetent for the case.

But after all, the principle of the conservation of force may by some be denied. Well, then, if it be unfounded even in its application to the smallest part of the science of force, the proof must be within our reach, for all physical science is so. In that case, discoveries as large or larger than any yet made, may be anticipated. I do not resist the search for them, for no one can do harm, but only good, who works with an earnest and truthful spirit in such a direction. But let us not admit the destruction or creation of force without clear and constant proof. Just as the chemist owes all the perfection of his science to his dependence on the certainty of gravitation applied by the balance, so may the physical philosopher expect to find the greatest security and the utmost aid in the principle of the conservation of force. All that we have that is good and safe, as the steam-engine, the electric-telegraph, &c., witness to that principle—it would require a perpetual motion, a fire without heat, heat without a source, action without reaction, cause with effect, or effect without a cause, to displace it from its rank as a law of nature.

During the year that has passed since the publication of the foregoing views regarding gravitation, &c., I have come to the knowledge of various observations upon them, some adverse, others favourable: these have given me no reason to change my own mode of viewing the subject; but some of them make me think that I have not stated the matter with sufficient precision. The word "force" is understood by many to mean simply "the tendency of a body to pass from one place to another," which is equivalent, I suppose, to the phrase "mechanical force;" those who so restrain its meaning must have found my argument very obscure. What I mean by the word "force," is the *cause* of a physical action; the source or sources of all possible changes amongst the particles or materials of the universe.

It seems to me that the idea of the conservation of force is absolutely independent of any notion we may form of the nature of force or its varieties, and is as sure and may be as firmly held in the mind, as, if we, instead of being very ignorant, understood perfectly every point about the cause of force and the varied effects it can produce. There may be perfectly distinct and separate causes of what are called chemical actions, or electrical actions, or gravitating actions, constituting so many forces; but if the "conservation of force" is a good and true principle, each of these forces must be subject to it: none can vary in its absolute amount; each must be definite at all times, whether for a particle, or for all the particles in the universe; and the sum also of the three forces must be equally unchangeable. Or, there may be but one cause for these three sets of actions, and in place of three forces we may really have but one, convertible in its manifestations; then the proportions between one set of actions and another, as the chemical and the electrical, may become very variable, so as to be utterly inconsistent with the idea of the conservation of two separate forces (the electrical and the chemical), but perfectly consistent with the conservation of a force, being the common cause of the two or more sets of action.

It is perfectly true that we cannot always trace a force by its actions, though we admit its conservation. Oxygen and hydrogen may remain mixed for years without showing any signs of chemical activity; they may be made at any given instant to exhibit active results, and then assume a new state, in which again they appear as passive bodies. Now, though we cannot clearly explain what the chemical force is doing, that is to say, what are its effects during the three periods before, at, and after the active combination, and only by very vague assumption can approach to a feeble conception of its respective states, yet we do not suppose the creation of a new portion of force for the active moment of time, or the less believe that the forces belonging to the oxygen and hydrogen exist unchanged in their amount at all these periods, though varying in their results. A part may at the active moment be thrown off as mechanical force, a part as radiant force, a part disposed of we know not how; but believing, by the principle of conservation, that it is not increased or destroyed, our thoughts are directed to search out what at all and every period it is doing, and how it is to be recognized and measured. A problem, founded on the physical truth of nature, *is stated*, and, being stated, is *on the way* to its solution.

Those who admit the possibility of the common origin of all physical force, and also acknowledge the principle of conservation, apply that principle to the sum total of the force Though the amount of mechanical force (using habitual language for convenience sake) may remain unchanged and definite in its character for a long time, yet when, as in the collision of two equal inelastic bodies, it appears to be lost, they find it in the form of heat; and whether they admit that heat to be a continued mechanical action (as is most probable), or assume some other idea, as that of electricity, or action of a heat-fluid, still they hold to the principle of conservation by admitting that the sum of force, *i. e.* of the "cause of action," is the same, whatever character the effects assume. With them the convertibility of heat, electricity, magnetism, chemical action and motion, is a familiar thought; neither can I perceive any reason why they should be led to exclude, *à priori*, the cause of gravitation from association with the cause of these other phænomena respectively. All that they are limited by in their various investigations, whatever directions they may take, is the necessity of making no assumption directly contradictory of the conservation of force applied to the sum of all the forces concerned, and to endeavour to discover the different directions in which the various parts of the total force have been exerted.

Those who admit separate forces inter-unchangeable, have to show that each of these forces is separately subject to the principle of conservation. If gravitation be such a separate force, and yet its power in the action of two particles be supposed to be diminished fourfold by doubling the distance, surely some new action, having true gravitation character, and that alone, ought to appear, for how else can the totality of the force remain unchanged? To define the force as "a simple attractive force exerted between any two or all the particles of matter, with a strength varying inversely as the square of the distance," is not to answer the question; nor does it indicate or even assume what are the other complementary results which occur; or allow the supposition that such are necessary: it is simply, as it appears to me, to *deny* the conservation of force.

As to the gravitating force, I do not presume to say that I have the least idea of what occurs in two particles when their power of mutually approaching each other is changed by their being placed at different distances; but I have a strong conviction, through the influence on my mind of the doctrine of conservation, that there is a change; and that the phenomena resulting from the change will probably appear some day as the result of careful research. If it be said that "'twere to consider too curiously to consider so," then I must dissent: to refrain to consider would be to ignore the principle of the conservation of force, and to stop the inquiry which it suggests—whereas to admit the proper logical force of the principle in our hypotheses and considerations, and to permit its guidance in a cautious yet courageous course of investigation, may give us power to enlarge the generalities we already possess in respect of heat, motion, electricity, magnetism, &c., to associate gravity with them, and perhaps enable us to know whether the essential force of gravitation (and other attractions) is internal or external as respects the attracted bodies.

Returning once more to the definition of the gravitating power as "*a simple attractive force exerted between any two or all the particles or masses of matter at every sensible distance, but with a* STRENGTH VARYING *inversely as the square of the distance*," I ought perhaps to suppose there are many who accept this as a true and sufficient description of the force, and who therefore, in relation to it, deny the principle of conservation. If both are accepted and are thought to be consistent with each other, it cannot be difficult to add words which shall make "varying strength" and "conservation" agree together. It cannot be said that the definition merely applies to the *effects* of gravitation as far as we know them. So understood, it would form no barrier to progress; for, that particles at different distances are urged toward each other with a power varying inversely as the square of the distance, is a truth: but the definition has not that meaning; and what I object to is the pretence of knowledge which the definition sets up when it assumes to describe, not the partial effects of the force, but the nature of the force as a whole.

ON

THE CONNECTION AND EQUIVALENCE OF FORCES

By Prof. J. VON LIEBIG.

Justus von Liebig, born at Darmstadt in 1803, after spending ten months in an apothecary's shop, entered the University of Bonn in 1819, and afterwards graduated in medicine in Erlangen. In 1822 he went to Paris, where he studied chemistry two years. In 1824 he read a paper on the Fulminates before the French Institute, which attracted the attention of Humboldt, by whose influence he was appointed adjunct Professor of Chemistry in the University of Giessen. He became professor of this institution in 1826, and established here the first laboratory in Germany for teaching practical chemistry. In 1840 he published his "Chemistry in its applications to Agriculture and Physiology," in the form of a report to the British Association. In 1842 he reported to the same body his work on "Animal Chemistry." About the same time appeared his "Familiar Letters on Chemistry," which has since been rewritten and much extended. He is the author also of various other valuable works. He remained at Giessen till 1852, when he became professor and president of the laboratory in the University of Munich. In 1854 his friends in Europe contributed and presented to him £1,000, and in 1860 he became President of the Academy of Sciences in Munich. Professor Liebig is a bold and intrepid investigator, and an ardent writer, who has made a profound impression upon his age. While some of his views have not been accepted in the chemical world, and indeed have been abandoned by himself, others have taken their place as valuable additions to the body of scientific truth. The charge that some of his doctrines have proved erroneous does not disturb him; in the true scientific spirit he replies, "Show me the man who makes no mistakes, and I will show you a man who has done nothing."

THE CONNECTION AND EQUIVALENCE OF FORCES.

IT is well known that our machines create no power, but only return what they have received. The motion of a clock is produced by a weight or a spring; but it is the power of the human arm applied to stretch the spring or elevate the weight, which is expended in the movement of the wheels and pendulum in twenty-four hours, or in eight or fourteen days.

A water-wheel sets in motion, in a mill, one or more millstones; in a foundry, one or more hammers; in saltworks or mines it pumps or raises weights to certain heights; in factories, it communicates movements to looms, spinning machines, and rollers. In all these instances, the work performed by the water-wheel is due to the force exerted by the falling water on the buckets, which sets the wheel in motion; and this force must be greater than the resistance presented by the different machines in operation. The performance of the machine is measurable by this force.

The work of a steam-engine is executed by the movement of a piston upwards and downwards by the pressure of steam, just as a water-wheel is moved by the pressure of water. The cause of this pressure is heat, which is derived from the chemical process of combustion, and is absorbed by water. By this heat, steam is produced, and the necessary expansion obtained for the movement of the piston. It is heat, in this last form, which performs the mechanical work of the machine.

Every force acts by producing pressure either from or towards the centre of motion. In every machine in operation the amount of power is always measurable by the resistance overcome; and this again can be expressed by corresponding weights, which that power is capable of raising to a certain height. If one man raises by a pump, in one minute, 150 lbs. of water, and another 200 lbs.; or if one horse draws to a certain distance a load of 20 cwt., and another a load of 30 cwt., it is evident that these numbers express the relative working power of these two men or horses. In mechanics, the working power of every machine is expressed in horse power, that is, a force capable of elevating in each second 75 kilogrammes ($=2\frac{1}{8}$ lbs. avoirdupois) to a height of one meter (39·37 inches).

The whole power communicated to a machine is not actually available, but is in part lost by friction. For if two machines possess the same power, it is found that the greater quantity of work will be executed by the one which has to overcome the smaller amount of friction. In mechanics, friction is always regarded as acting in direct opposition to motion in every machine. It was believed that the working power of a machine could be absolutely annihilated by it.

As the proximate cause of the cessation of motion, friction was a palpable fact, and could as such be taken into account; but a fatal error was committed in giving a theoretical view of its mode of action. For if a power could be annihilated, or, in other words, have *nothing* as its effect, then there would be no contradiction involved in the belief, that out of *nothing* also power could be created. To this erroneous idea we may partly trace the belief, held for centuries by most able men, in the possibility of discovering a machine which should renew within itself its own power as it was expended, and thus ever continue in motion, without the necessity for any external motive force. The discovery of such a perpetual motion was, indeed, worthy of every effort. It would be as valuable as the bird which lays the golden eggs; for by its means labour would be performed, and money made in abundance without any expenditure.

A mass of facts, hitherto unintelligible, have had much light thrown upon them by a more correct view of natural forces, for which we are indebted to a physician, Dr. Mayer, of Heilbronn, and which, by the investigations of the most eminent natural philosophers and mathematicians, has attained a significance and importance scarcely to be foreseen.

According to Dr. Mayer, forces are causes, in which full application of the axiom must be found, that every cause must produce an effect which corresponds and is equal to the cause. *Causa æquat effectum.* Thus if a cause C produces an effect E, then C = E. Should the effect E become the cause of another effect e, then also E = e = C. In such a chain of causes and effects no link, or part of a link, can ever become nothing = nothing. Should a given cause C have pro duced its corresponding effect E, then C ceases to exist, for it has been converted into E. Consequently, as C passes into E, and the latter into e, it follows that all these causes, as far as relates to their *quantity*, possess the property of *indestructibility*, and to their *quality* that of *convertibility*. In numberless cases we see a motion cease, without its usual effects being produced, such as lifting a weight or load; but as the force which has caused the motion cannot be reduced to nothing, the question arises, what form has it assumed. Experience gives the answer, by showing that wherever motion is arrested by friction, a blow, or concussion, heat is the result. The motion is the cause of the heat.

The rapid friction of two plates of metal can raise their temperature to redness, and cause the ebullition of water if the friction takes place below its surface. In like manner, by rapid motion the iron tires of carriage wheels become frequently so hot that they cannot be touched. In grinding needle-points the steel is heated to redness, and the detached particles burn with sparks. The wooden breaks of railway carriages become frequently so hot by friction that their surface emits an empyreumatic odour. By the friction of an iron grater, particles of white sugar can be melted and heated so far as to acquire the taste of burnt sugar (Caramel). The heat evolved by the friction of two pieces of ice is sufficient to melt them.

In the English steel-foundries a bar of steel 10 or 12 inches long, by being heated at one end in a forge, is welded by hammering to another slender bar, 10 or 12 feet long, without the necessity of further direct application of heat—a point of great importance for the preservation of the good quality of the steel. Every spot on which the powerful blows of the hammer rapidly descend, becomes red hot, and to the spectators the red glow of heat appears to run up and down the bar. This glow is produced by the blows of the hammer, and corresponds to an amount of heat sufficient to raise many pounds of water to the boiling point; whilst the end of the bar heated in the fire would scarcely by itself raise to the same temperature as many ounces of water.

According to the preceding views a precise connection exists between the blows of the hammer (the cause) and the heat produced (the effect); and natural philosophers have devised the most ingenious experiments to show this relation. The working power is in this case converted into heat. If the view of Mayer be correct, then should we by this amount of heat thus obtained, be able to reproduce the same amount of work, viz., the same number of blows of the hammer. But a closer view of the point shows that we require to elevate the hammer, and that therefore its working power was not inherent, but only lent to it. The hammer was elevated by a water-wheel set in motion by a certain weight of water falling on its buckets. Thus to raise a hammer weighing ten pounds to the height of one foot requires at least the fall of ten pounds weight of water from a height of a foot. It was then, properly speaking, this weight of falling water which produced the heat through means of the hammer. By simply altering the arrangement of the machinery, the same force would have caused a mill-stone to revolve with great rapidity on its axis, or raised by friction two iron disks to a red heat.

From experiments instituted to elucidate this point, it has been established that 13,500 blows of a hammer, weighing 10 pounds, falling on a bar of iron from a height of one foot, produce an amount of heat sufficient to raise one pound of water from the freezing point to that of ebullition. This fact may be represented in another way by saying, that 1,350 cwts. of water, falling from a height of one foot, will raise the temperature of 1 lb. of water from freezing to the boiling point; or 1,350 lbs. of water falling from the same height will raise one pound of water one degree in temperature, or in other words, that this amount of heat corresponds to a working power, capable of elevating 13½ cwt. to the height of one foot.

Wherever motion is lost in a machine by friction or by concussion, there is always produced a corresponding amount of heat. When, on the other hand, a certain quantity of work is performed by heat, there disappears, with the mechanical effect obtained, a certain amount of heat, which is expressed by saying that the heat lost by one pound of water in falling one degree in temperature, is equal to the elevation of 13½ cwt. to the height of one foot. This quantity of heat becomes then the equivalent or value of the working power expressed by the above numbers.

This constant relation between heat and mechanical movement has been confirmed in the most varied manner. A rod of metal is extended by a weight, and on its removal resumes its original length, provided certain limits be not exceeded. The same effect is produced by heat; and it is evident that an equal force must be exerted by the rod in its extension as in its contraction. Now, experiment has shown that the relation expressed by the numbers above given, must exist between a given extension of a bar of iron, and the heat or weight which has caused that extension, viz., that a quantity of heat sufficient to raise a pound of water one degree in temperature, will, when communicated to a bar of iron, enable it to elevate a weight of 1,350 lbs. to the height of one foot.

An interesting application of this fact was long ago made in the Conservatoire des Arts et Métiers, in Paris. In this building, which was formerly a convent, the nave of the church was converted into a museum for industrial products, machines, and implements. In its arch, traversing its length, appeared a crack, which gradually increased to the width of several inches, and permitted the passage of rain and snow. The opening could easily have been closed by stone and lime, but the yielding of the side walls would not have been prevented by these means. The whole building was on the point of being pulled down, when a natural philosopher proposed the following plan, by which the object was accomplished. A number of strong iron rods were firmly fixed at one end to a side wall of the nave, and after passing through the opposite wall were provided on the outside with large nuts, which were screwed up tightly to the wall. By applying burning straw to the rods, they extended in length. The nuts by this extension being now removed several inches from the wall, were again screwed tight to it. The rods on cooling contracted with enormous force, and made the side walls approach each other. By repeating the operation the crack entirely disappeared. This building with its retaining rods is still in existence.

The working power of a machine, set in motion by electricity, can be expressed by numbers, in the same way as the mechanical effect of heat. An electrical current is generated by a rotating magnet or by solution of zinc in the galvanic battery. Such a current, in circulating through a thick or thin wire, exhibits the same deportment as a fluid flowing through a wide or narrow tube. As a given quantity of fluid requires more time or greater pressure to pass through a narrow tube than through a large, so a thin wire offers a greater resistance than a thick one to the passage of a current of electricity. The current is thus retarded and diminished, one portion only passing through the conductor, the other being converted into heat. According to the amount of heat thus produced by the conversion of the electricity, a conducting wire of platinum can be fused, one of gold fused and converted into vapour, and a considerable quantity of water brought into violent ebullition by passing the current through a thin platinum wire wound round a glass tube in a spiral form.

If the electrical current circulates through a wire wound spirally round a bar of iron, the latter is converted into a powerful magnet capable of attracting and carrying several hundred weights of iron. The electrical is converted into the magnetic force, by which a machine may be set in motion. The power of attraction communicated to the iron bar is in exact proportion to the amount of electricity circulating in the surrounding wire, and this current is again dependent on the property of the conductor. That portion of electricity which in the conductor is converted into heat, produces no power of attraction in the iron bar. It follows, from the foregoing, that the quantity of electricity which circulates, of that which produces heat, and the amount of magnetic power convertible into working power, stand in the same relation to each other, as the working power produced in a machine by the pressure of falling water to the heat generated by friction and concussion in the same machine. The same amount of electricity which, when converted into heat by the resistance of the conductor, raises by one degree the temperature of one pound of water, generates a magnetic force capable of elevating a weight of 13½ cwt. to the height of one foot.

If the metallic wire through which the electricity is circulating, be cut, and both ends immersed in water, a chemical decomposition of the water into hydrogen and oxygen takes place. The circulating electricity is converted into chemical affinity, and into a power of attraction which causes the separation of the elements of water. With the evolution of the hydrogen and oxygen all traces of the electrical current disappear. The power to produce heat and magnetic force, the usual effects of the electrical current, is apparently in this case annihilated, and in its place we obtain two gases, one of which, hydrogen, when burned in oxygen, reproduces water and evolves heat. Now it has been proved, by careful experiments, that an electrical current of a given strength, which, when converted into heat in a conductor, is capable of raising the temperature of a pound of water by one degree, will produce by the decomposition of water a quantity of hydrogen, by the combustion of which one pound of water can also be elevated one degree in temperature.

The heat and power of attraction which were apparently lost by the decomposition of the water, had only become latent, so to speak, in the elements of water. This heat is again set free on the reunion of these elements, and if converted into working power, would produce the same result (viz., raising a given weight a foot high) as would have been effected by a magnetic power generated by a quantity of electricity circulating round a bar of iron, equal to that which was originally employed in the decomposition of the water.

The electrical current is the consequence of a chemical action, and the amount of electricity which circulates can therefore be measured by the quantity of zinc which is dissolved. The chemical force (affinity) is converted by the solution of the zinc into a corresponding quantity of electricity; and this again in the conductor into its equivalent of heat, or into magnetic force, or, as in the case of the decomposition of water, into chemical force. In no case is there a diminution or increase of force. If, according to the materialist, matter is indestructible, the same holds good with regard to force. It is not extinguished; its apparent annihilation, its disappearance, is only a conversion into some other form.

We know now the origin of the heat and light which warm and illuminate our dwellings, of the heat and power generated in our bodies by the vital process. Plants are the one source of all materials used for the production of heat and light, and of that nourishment which must be daily taken to maintain the phenomena of vitality. The elements of plants are earthy in their nature, and are obtained from water, earth, and air. In plants, certain inorganic compounds—carbonic acid, water, and ammonia—are decomposed. The carbon of the carbonic acid, the hydrogen of the water, and the nitrogen of the ammonia, are retained as constituents of their organs, but the oxygen of the carbonic acid and of the water are returned as gas to the air. With out light, however, plants cannot grow.

The vital process in plants exhibits itself as directly opposite in its character to the chemical process in the formation of salts.

Carbonic acid, *water*, and *zinc*, when brought together produce a certain effect on each other. In virtue of chemical affinity there is formed a white powdery compound, containing carbonic acid, zinc, and oxygen from the water, and *hydrogen* is at the same time evolved.

In plants, the living bud or part of the plant takes the place of the zinc. By their growth are formed, from carbonic acid and water, compounds containing carbon and hydrogen, or carbon and the elements of water, and *oxygen* is at the same time evolved. Sunlight acts in living plants like electricity, which arrests the natural attraction of the elements of water, and separates them from each other.

Without the light of the sun plants cannot grow. The living germ, the green leaf, owe to the sun their power of transforming earthy elements into living, vigorous structures. The germ may, indeed, be evolved under ground without the action of light, but only when it breaks through the surface of the soil does it first acquire the power, by the sun's rays, of converting inorganic elements into its own structure. The illuminating and heating rays of the sun, in thus bestowing life, lose their own light and heat. Their power now becomes latent in the new products of the frame, which have been produced under their influence from carbonic acid, water, and ammonia. The light and heat with which our dwellings are illuminated and warmed are but those bestowed by the sun.

The food of men and animals consists of two classes of materials, which differ totally in their nature. One class is destined to the production of blood and the maintenance of the structure of the body; the other is similar in composition to ordinary materials for combustion. Sugar, starch, the gum of bread, may be regarded as transformed woody fibre, for we can prepare them from this substance. Fat, in its amount of carbon, resembles closely mineral coal. We heat our bodies as we do stoves, by combustibles which possess the same elements as wood and coal, but which differ essentially from them by being soluble in the fluids of the body.

The elements of nutrition from which the temperature of the body is derived, evidently produce no mechanical power; because power is but converted heat, and the heat which maintains and elevates the temperature of the body does not produce any other effect than that of warmth.

All those mechanical operations constantly taking place in the living body, in the movement of organs and limbs, are dependent on an accompanying change in the composition and properties of those highly complex sulphur and nitrogen constituents of the muscles, which, though furnished by the blood, are in the first instance derived directly from the food of man. The change of position in the elements of these complex bodies, attendant on their rearrangement into new and simpler compounds, necessarily gives rise to motion; and the molecular movement of the particles in a state of change is transferred to the muscular mass. Chemical action is thus evidently the source of mechanical power in bodies.

The elements of the food of men and animals which give rise to power and heat, are produced in living plants only by the action of sunlight. The rays of the sun become latent, so to speak, in them in the same way as the current of electricity becomes latent in the hydrogen by decomposition of water.

Man, by food, not only maintains the perfect structure of his body, but he daily lays in a store of power and heat, derived in the first instance from the sun. This power and heat, latent for a time, reappears and again becomes active when the living structures are resolved by the vital processes into their original elements.

The rays of the sun add daily to the store of indestructible forces of our terrestrial body, maintaining life and motion. Thus, from beyond the limits of our earth, the body, the more earthly vessel, derives all that may be called good in it, and of this not a single particle is ever lost.

ON

THE CORRELATION

OF THE

PHYSICAL AND VITAL FORCES

By Dr. WILLIAM B. CARPENTER.

WILLIAM BENJAMIN CARPENTER, the eminent English physiologist, was born in the early part of this century, and graduated as doctor of medicine in Edinburgh in 1839. He commenced practice in Bristol, but has been chiefly occupied as a lecturer and author. His most important works are the "Principles of General and Comparative Physiology" (1839), the "Principles of Human Physiology" (1846), which reached a fifth edition in 1855, and "The Microscope, its Revelations and Uses" (1856). He is the author of various minor, but valuable works, and of many elaborate papers in the cyclopedias and scientific periodicals. For many years he was editor of the "British and Foreign Medico-Chirurgical Review." He was elected a member of the Royal Society in 1844, and is now Professor of Medical Jurisprudence in University College, London; Lecturer on General Anatomy and Physiology at the London Hospital and School of Medicine, and Examiner in Physiology and Comparative Anatomy in the University of London. In 1850 he published an able paper in the Transactions of the Royal Society on the "Mutual Relations of the Vital and Physical Forces," and has published upon the same general subject, the essays which close this volume, in the new Quarterly Journal of Science for the present year. Dr. Carpenter is an able and original thinker, as well as a voluminous writer, and has made many valuable contributions to the progress of physiological science.

ON THE CORRELATION OF THE PHYSICAL AND VITAL FORCES.

I.—RELATIONS OF LIGHT AND HEAT TO THE VITAL FORCES OF PLANTS.

IN every period of the history of Physiology, attempts have been made to identify all the forces acting in the Living Body with those operating in the Inorganic universe. Because muscular force, when brought to bear on the bones, moves them according to the mechanical laws of lever action, and because the propulsive power of the heart drives the blood through the vessels according to the rules of hydraulics, it has been imagined that the movements of living bodies may be explained on physical principles; the most important consideration of all, namely, the source of that contractile power which the living muscle possesses, but which the dead muscle (though having the same chemical composition) is utterly incapable of exerting, being altogether left out of view. So, again, because the digestive process, whereby food is reduced to a fit state for absorption, as well as the formation of various products of the decomposition that is continually taking place in the living body, may be initiated in the laboratory of the chemist; it has been supposed that the appropriation of the nutriment to the production of the living organized tissues of which the several parts of the body are composed, is to be regarded as a chemical action—as if any combination of albumen and gelatine, fat and starch, salt and bone-earth, could make a living Man without the constructive agency inherent in the germ from which his bodily fabric is evolved.

Another class of reasoners have cut the knot which they could not untie, by attributing all the actions of living bodies for which Physics and Chemistry cannot account, to a hypothetical "Vital principle;" a shadowy agency that does every thing in its own way, but refuses to be made the subject of scientific examination; like the "od-force" or the "spiritual power" to which the lovers of the marvellous are so fond of attributing the mysterious movements of turning and tilting tables.

A more scientific spirit, however, prevails among the best Physiologists of the present day; who, whilst fully recognizing the fact that many of the phenomena of living bodies can be accounted for by the agencies whose operation they trace in the world around, separate into a distinct category—that of *vital* actions—such as appear to differ altogether *in kind* from the phenomena of Physics and Chemistry, and seek to determine, from the study of the conditions under which these present themselves, the *laws* of their occurrence.

In the prosecution of this inquiry, the Physiologist will find it greatly to his advantage to adopt the method of philosophizing which distinguishes the Physical science of the present from that of the past generation; that, namely, which, whilst fully accepting the logical definition of the *cause* of any phenomenon, as "the antecedent, or the concurrence of antecedents on which it is invariably and unconditionally consequent" (Mill), draws a distinction between the *dynamical* and the *material* conditions; the former supplying the *power* which does the work, whilst the latter affords the *instrumental means* through which that power operates.

Thus if we inspect a Cotton Factory in full action, we find it to contain a vast number of machines, many of them but repetitions of one another, but many, too, presenting the most marked diversities in construction, in operation, and in resultant products. We see, for example, that one is supplied with the raw material, which it cleans and dresses; that another receives the cotton thus prepared, and "cards" it so as to lay its fibres in such an arrangement as may admit of its being spun; that another series, taking up the product supplied by the carding machine, twists and draws it out into threads of various degrees of fineness; and that this thread, carried into a fourth set of machines, is woven into a fabric which may be either plain or variously figured according to the construction of the loom. In every one of these dissimilar operations the *force* which is immediately concerned in bringing about the results is one and the same; and the variety of its products is dependent solely upon the diversity of the material instruments through which it operates. Yet these arrangements, however skilfully devised, are utterly valueless without the force which brings them into play. All the elaborate mechanism, the triumph of human ingenuity in devising, and of skill in constructing, is as powerless as a corpse without the *vis viva* which alone can animate it. The giant stroke of the steam-engine, or the majestic revolution of the water-wheel gives the required impulse; and the vast apparatus which was the moment previously in a state of death-like inactivity, is aroused to all the energy of its wondrous life—every part of its complex organization taking upon itself its peculiar mode of activity, and evolving its own special product, in virtue of the share it receives of the one general force distributed through the entire aggregate of machinery.

But if we carry back our investigation a stage further, and inquire into the origin of the force supplied by the steam-engine or the water-wheel, we soon meet with a new and most significant fact. At our first stage, it is true, we find only the same mechanical force acting through a different kind of instrumentality; the strokes of the piston of the steam-engine being dependent upon the elastic force of the vapour of water, whilst the revolution of the water-wheel is maintained by the downward impetus of water *en masse*. But to what antecedent dynamical agency can we trace *these* forces? That agency in each case is Heat; a force altogether dissimilar in its ordinary manifestations to the force which produces sensible motion, yet capable of being in turn converted into it and generated by it. For it is from the Heat applied beneath the boiler of the steam-engine that the non-elastic liquid contained in it derives all that potency as elastic vapour, which enables it to overcome the vast mechanical resistance that is set in opposition to it. And, in like manner, it is the heat of the solar rays which pumps up terrestrial waters in the shape of vapour, and thus supplies to Man a perrenial source of new power in their descent by the force of gravity to the level from which they have been raised.*

The power of the steam-engine, indeed, is itself derived more remotely from those same rays; for the Heat applied to its boilers is but the expression of the chemical change involved in combustion; that combustion is sustained either by the wood which is the product of the vegetative activity of the present day, or by the coal which represents the vegetative life of a remote geological epoch; and that vegetative activity, whether present or past, represents an equivalent amount of Solar Light and Heat, used up in the decomposition of the carbonic acid of the atmosphere, by the instrumentality of the growing plant.† Thus in either case we come, directly or indirectly, to Solar Radiation as the main-

* See on this subject the recent admirable address of Sir William Armstrong at the Meeting of the British Association at Newcastle.

† This was discerned by the genius of George Stephenson, before the general doctrine of the Correlation of Forces had been given to the world by Mayer and Grove.

spring of our mechanical power; the *vis viva* of our whole microcosm. Modern physical inquiry ventures even one step further, and seeks the source of Light and Heat of the Sun itself. Are these, as formerly supposed, the result of combustion, or are they, as surmised by Mayer and Thomson, the expression of the motive power continually generated in the fall of aërolites towards the Sun, and as continually annihilated by their impact on its surface? Leaving the discussion of this question to Physical Philosophers, I proceed now to my own proper subject.

It is now about twenty years since Dr. Mayer first broadly announced, in all its generality, the great principle now known as that of "Conservation of Force;" as a necessary deduction from two axioms or essential truths—*ex nihilo nil fit*, and *nil fit ad nihilum*—the validity of which no true philosopher would ever have theoretically questioned, but of which he was (in my judgment) the first to appreciate the full practical bearing. Thanks to the labours of Faraday, Grove, Joule, Thomson, and Tyndall, to say nothing of those of Helmholtz and other distinguished Continental savans, the great doctrine expressed by the term "Conservation of Force" is now amongst the best-established generalizations of Physical Science; and every thoughtful Physiologist must desire to see the same course of inquiry thoroughly pursued in regard to the phenomena of living bodies. This ground was first broken by Dr. Mayer in his remarkable treatise, "Die Organische Bewegung in ihrem Zusammenhange mit dem Stoffwechsel" ("On Organic Movement in its relation to Material Changes," Heilbronn, 1845); in which he distinctly set forth the principle that the source of all changes in the living Organism, animal as well as vegetable, lies in the forces acting upon it *from without*; whilst the changes in its own composition brought about by these agencies, he considers to be the immediate source of the forces which are generated by it.

In treating of these forces, however, he dwells chiefly on

the production of Motion, Heat, Light, and Electricity by living bodies; touching more slightly upon the phenomena of Growth and Development, which constitute, in the eye of the physiologist, the distinct province of vitality. In a memoir of my own, "On the Mutual Relations of the Vital and Physical Forces," published in the Philosophical Transactions for 1850,* I aimed to show that the general doctrine of the "Correlation of the Physical Forces" propounded by Mr. Grove, was equally applicable to those Vital forces which must be assumed as the moving powers in the production of purely physiological phenomena; these forces being generated in living bodies by the transformation of the Light, Heat, and Chemical Action supplied by the world around, and being given back to it again, either during their life, or after its cessation, chiefly in Motion and Heat, but also to a less degree in Light and Electricity. This memoir attracted but little attention at the time, being regarded, I believe, as too speculative; but I have since had abundant evidence that the minds of thoughtful Physiologists, as well as Physicists, are moving in the same direction; and as the progress of science since the publication of my former memoir, would lead me to present some parts of my scheme of doctrine in a different form,† I venture to bring it again before the public in the form of a sketch (I claim for it no other title), of the aspect in which the application of the principle of the "Conservation of Force" to Physiology now presents itself to my mind.

* At this date the labours of Dr. Mayer were not known either to myself or (so far as I am aware) to any one else in this country, save the late Dr. Baly, who a few months after the publication of my Memoir, placed in my hands the pamphlet, "Die Organische Bewegung;" to which I took the earliest opportunity in my power of drawing public attention in "The British and Foreign Medico-Chirurgical Review" for July, 1851, p. 237.

† I have especially profited by a Memoir on the Correlation of Physical, Chemical, and Vital Force, and the Conservation of Force in Vital Phenomena, by Prof. Le Conte (of South Carolina College), in Silliman's American Journal for Nov., 1859, reprinted in the Philosophical Magazine for 1860.

If, in the first place, we inquire what it is that essentially distinguishes Vital from every kind of Physical activity, we find this distinction most characteristically expressed in the fact that a germ endowed with Life, developes itself into an organism of a type resembling that of its parent; that this organism is the subject of incessant changes, which all tend in the first place to the evolution of its typical form, and subsequently to its maintenance in that form, notwithstanding the antagonism of Chemical and Physical agencies, which are continually tending to produce its disintegration; but that, as its term of existence is prolonged, its conservative power declines so as to become less and less able to resist these disintegrating forces, to which it finally succumbs, leaving the organism to be resolved by their agency into the components from which its materials were originally drawn. The history of a living organism, then, is one of *incessant change;* and the conditions of this change are to be found partly in the organism itself, and partly in the external agencies to which it is subjected. That condition which is inherent in the organism, being derived hereditarily from its progenitors, may be conveniently termed its *germinal capacity;* its parallel in the inorganic world being that fundamental difference in properties which constitutes the distinction between one substance, whether elementary or compound, and another; in virtue of which each "behaves" in its own characteristic manner when subjected to new conditions.

Thus, although there may be nothing in the aspect or sensible properties of the germ of a Polype, to distinguish from that of a Man, we find that each develops itself, if the requisite conditions be supplied, into its typical form, *and no other;* if the developmental conditions required by either be not supplied we do not find a different type evolved, but no evolution at all takes place.*

* It is quite true that among certain of the lower tribes, both of Plants

Now the difference between a being of *high* and a being of *low* organization essentially consists in this: that in the latter the constituent parts of the fabric evolved by the process of growth from the original germ, are similar to each other in structure and endowments, whilst in the former they are progressively differentiated with the advance of development, so that the fabric comes at last to consist of a number of *organs*, or instruments, more or less dissimilar in structure, composition, and endowments. Thus in the lowest forms of Vegetable life, the primordial germ multiplies itself by duplicative subdivision into an apparently unlimited number of cells, each of them similar to every other, and capable of maintaining its existence independently of them. And in that lowest Rhizopod type of Animal life, the knowledge of which is among the most remarkable fruits of modern biological research, "the Physiologist has a case in which those vital operations which he is elsewhere accustomed to see carried on by an elaborate apparatus, are performed without any special instruments whatever; a little particle of apparently homogeneous jelly changing itself into a greater variety of forms than the fabled Proteus, laying hold of its food without members, swallowing it without a mouth, digesting it without a stomach, appropriating its nutritious material without absorbent vessels or a circulating system, moving from place to place without muscles, feeling (if it has any power to do so) without nerves, propagating itself without genital apparatus, and

and Animals, especially the *Fungi* and *Entozoa*—similar germs may develop themselves into very dissimilar forms, according to the conditions under which they are evolved; but such diversities are only the same kind as those which manifest themselves among *individuals* in the higher Plants and Animals, and only show that in the types in question there is a less close conformity to one pattern. Neither in these groups, nor in that group of *Foraminifera*, in which I have been led to regard the range of variation as peculiarly great, does any tendency ever show itself to the assumption of the characters of any group fundamentally dissimilar.

not only this, but in many instances forming shelly coverings of a symmetry and complexity not surpassed by those of any testaceous animals,"* whilst the mere separation of a fragment of this jelly is sufficient to originate a new and independent organism, so that any number of these beings may be produced by the successive detachment of such particles from a single Rhizopod, each of them retaining (so far as we have at present the means of knowing) the characteristic endowments of the stock from which it was an offset.

When, on the other hand, we watch the evolution of any of the higher types of Organization, whether vegetable or animal, we observe that although in the first instance the primordial cell multiplies itself by duplicative subdivision into an aggregation of cells, which are apparently but repetitions of itself and of each other, this homogeneous extension has in each case a definite limit, speedily giving place to a structural differentiation, which becomes more and more decided with the progress of development, until in that most heterogeneous of all types—the Human Organism—no two parts are precisely identical, except those which correspond to each other on the opposite sides of the body. With this structural differentiation is associated a corresponding differentiation of function; for whilst in the life of the most highly developed and complex organism we witness no act which is not foreshadowed, however vaguely, in that of the lowest and simplest, yet we observe in it that same "division of labour" which constitutes the essential characteristic of the highest grade of civilization. For, in what may be termed the elementary form of Human Society, in which every individual relies upon himself alone for the supply of all his wants, no greater result can be obtained by the aggregate action of the entire community than its mere maintenance; but as each in-

* See the Author's Introduction to the Study of the Foraminifera, published by the Ray Society, 1862: Preface, p. vii.

dividual selects a special mode of activity for himself, and aims at improvement in that specialty, he finds himself attaining a higher and still higher degree of aptitude for it; and this specialization tends to increase as opportunities arise for new modes of activity, until that complex fabric is evolved which constitutes the most developed form of the Social State wherein every individual finds the work—mental or bodily—for which he is best fitted, and in which he may reach the highest attainable perfection; while the mutual dependence of the whole (which is the necessary result of this specialization of parts) is such that every individual works for the benefit of all his fellows, as well as for his own. As it is only in such a state of society that the greatest triumphs of human ability become possible, so is it only in the most differentiated types of Organization that Vital Activity can present its highest manifestations. In the one case, as in the other, does the result depend upon a process of gradual *development*, in which, under the influence of agencies whose nature constitutes a proper object of scientific inquiry, that *most general* form in which the fabric—whether corporeal or social—originates, evolves itself into that *most special* in which its development culminates.

But notwithstanding the wonderful diversity of structure and of endowments which we meet with in the study of any complex Organism, we encounter a harmonious unity or coördination in its entire aggregate of actions, which is yet more wonderful. It is in this harmony or coördination, whose tendency is to the conservation of the organism, that the state of Health or Normal life essentially consists. And the more profound our investigations of its conditions, the more definite becomes the conclusion to which we are led by the study of them—that it is fundamentally based on the common origin of all these diversified parts in the same germ, the vital endowments of which, equally diffused throughout the entire fabric in those lowest forms of organization in which every part is but a repetition of every other, are differentiated in the highest amongst a variety of organs, acquiring in virtue of this differentiation a much greater intensity.

Thus, then, we may take that mode of Vital Activity which manifests itself in the evolution of the germ into the complete organism repeating the type of its parent, and the subsequent maintenance of that organism in its integrity, in the one case as in the other, at the expense of materials derived from external sources—as the most universal and most fundamental characteristic of Life; and we have now to consider the nature and source of the *Force* or *Power* by which that evolution is brought about. The prevalent opinion has until lately been, that this power is inherent in the germ; which has been supposed to derive from its parent not merely its material substance, but a *nisus formativus*, *bildungstrieb*, or *germ force*, in virtue of which it builds itself up into the likeness of its parent, and maintains itself in that likeness until the force is exhausted, at the same time imparting a fraction of it to each of its progeny. In this mode of viewing the subject, all the organizing force required to build up an Oak or a Palm, an Elephant or a Whale, must be concentrated in a minute particle, only discernible by microscopic aid, and the aggregate of all the germ-forces appertaining to the descendants, however numerous, of a common parentage, must have existed in their original progenitors. Thus in the case of the successive viviparous broods of *Aphides*, a germ-force capable of organizing a mass of living structure, which would amount (it has been calculated)* in the tenth brood to the bulk of five hundred millions of stout men, must have been shut up in the single individual, weighing perhaps the 1-1000th of a grain, from which the first brood was evolved. And in like manner, the germ-force which has organized the

* See Prof. Huxley on the "Agamic Reproduction of Aphis," in Linn. Trans., vol. xxii., p. 215.

bodies of all the individual men that have lived from Adam to the present day, must have been concentrated in the body of their common ancestor. A more complete *reductio ad absurdum* can scarcely be brought against any hypothesis; and we may consider it proved that in some way or other, fresh organizing force is constantly being supplied *from without* during the whole period of the exercise of its activity.

When we look carefully into the question, however, we find that what the *germ* really supplies is not the force, but the *directive agency;* thus rather resembling the control exercised by the superintendent builder, who is charged with working out the design of the architect, than the bodily force of the workmen who labour under his guidance in the construction of the fabric. The actual constructive force, as we learn from an extensive survey of the phenomena of life, is supplied by Heat, the influence of which upon the rate of growth and development, both animal and vegetable, is so marked as to have universally attracted the attention of Physiologists, who, however, have for the most part only recognized in it a *vital stimulus* that calls forth the latent power of the germ, instead of looking upon it as itself furnishing the power that does the work. It has been from the narrow limitation of the area over which physiological research has been commonly prosecuted, that the intimacy of this relationship between Heat and the Organizing force has not sooner become apparent. Whilst the vital phenomena of Warm-blooded animals, which possess within themselves the means of maintaining a constant temperature, were made the sole, or at any rate the chief objects of study, it was not likely that the inquirer would recognize the full influence of external heat in accelerating, or of cold in retarding their functional activity. It is only when the survey is extended to Cold-blooded animals and to Plants, that the immediate and direct relation between Heat and Vital Activity, as manifested in the rate of growth and development, or of other changes peculiar to the living body, is unmistakably manifested. To some of those phenomena, which afford the best illustrations of the mode in which Heat acts upon the living organism, attention will now be directed.

Commencing with the Vegetable kingdom, we find that the operation of Heat as the motive power or dynamical agency, to which the phenomena of growth and development are to be referred, is peculiarly well seen in the process of Germination. The seed consists of an embryo which has already advanced to a certain stage of development, and of a store of nutriment laid up as the material for its further evolution; and in the fact that this evolution is carried on at the expense of organic compounds already prepared by extrinsic agency, until (the store of these being exhausted) the young plant is sufficiently far advanced in its development to be able to elaborate them for itself, the condition of the germinating embryo resembles that of an Animal. Now, the seed may remain (under favourable circumstances) in a state of absolute inaction during an unlimited period. If secluded from the free access of air and moisture, and kept at a low temperature, it is removed from all influences that would on the one hand occasion its disintegration, or on the other, would call it into active life. But when again exposed to air and moisture, and subjected to a higher temperature, it either germinates or decays, according as the embryo it contains has or has not preserved its vital endowments—a question which only experiment can resolve. The process of germination is by no means a simple one. The nutriment stored up in the seed is in great part in the condition of insoluble starch; and this must be brought into a soluble form before it can be appropriated by the embryo. The metamorphosis is effected by the agency of a ferment termed *diastase*, which is laid up in the immediate neighbourhood of the embryo, and which, when brought to act on starch, converts it in the first instance into soluble dextrine, and then (if its action be continued) into sugar. The dextrine and sugar, combined with the albuminous and oily compounds also stored up in the seed, form the "protoplasm," which is the substance immediately supplied to the young plant as the material of its tissues; and the conversion of this protoplasm into various forms of organized tissue, which become more and more differentiated as development advances, is obviously referable to the vital activity of the germ. Now it can be very easily shown experimentally that the *rate of growth* in the germinating embryo is so closely related (within certain limits) to the amount of heat supplied, as to place its dependence on that agency beyond reasonable question: so that we seem fully entitled to say that Heat, acting through the germ, supplies the constructive force or power by which the Vegetable fabric is built up.* But there appears to be another source of that power in the seed itself. In the conversion of the insoluble starch of the seed into sugar, and probably also in a further metamorphosis of a part of that sugar, a large quantity of carbon is eliminated from the seed by combining with the oxygen of the air, so as to form carbonic acid; this combination is necessarily attended with a disengagement of heat, which becomes very sensible when (as in molting) a large number of germinating seeds are aggregated together; and it cannot but be regarded as probable that the heat thus evolved within the seed concurs with that derived from without, in supplying to the germ the force that promotes its evolution.

* The effect of Heat is doubtless manifested very differently by different seeds; such variations being partly *specific*, partly *individual*. But these are no greater than we see in the inorganic world: the increment of temperature and the augmentation of bulk exhibited by different substances when subjected to the same absolute measure of heat, being as diverse as the substances themselves. The whole process of "Malting," it may be remarked, is based on the regularity with which the seeds of a particular species may be at any time forced to a definite rate of germination by a definite increment of temperature.

The condition of the Plant which has attained a more advanced stage of its development, differs from that of the germinating embryo essentially in this particular, that the organic compounds which it requires as the materials of the extension of the fabric are formed by itself, instead of being supplied to it from without. The tissues of the coloured surfaces of the leaves and stems, when acted on by light, have the peculiar power of generating—at the expense of carbonic acid, water, and ammonia—various ternary and quaternary organic compounds, such as chlorophyll, starch, oil, and albumen; and of the compounds thus generated, some are appropriated by the constructive force of the plant (derived from the heat with which it is supplied) to the formation of new tissues; whilst others are stored up in the cavities of those tissues, where they ultimately serve either for the evolution of parts subsequently developed, or for the nutrition of animals which employ them as food. Of the source of those peculiar affinities by which the components of the starch, albumen, &c., are brought together, we have no right to speak confidently; but looking to the fact that these compounds are not produced in any case by the direct union of their elements, and that a decomposition of binary compounds seems to be a necessary antecedent of their formation, it is scarcely improbable that, as suggested by Prof. Le Conte (*op. cit.*), that source is to be found in the chemical forces set free in the preliminary act of decomposition, in which the elements would be liberated in that "nascent condition" which is well known to be one of peculiar energy.

The influence of Light, then, upon Vegetable organism appears to be essentially exerted in bringing about what may be considered a higher mode of chemical combination between oxygen, hydrogen, and carbon, with the addition of nitrogen in certain cases; and there is no evidence that it extends beyond this. That the appropriation of the materials thus prepared, and their conversion into organized tissue in the operations of growth and development, are dependent on the agency of Heat, is just as evident in the stage of maturity as in that of germination. And there is reason to believe, further, that an additional source of organizing force is to be found in the retrograde metamorphosis of organic compounds that goes on during the whole life of the plant; of which metamorphosis the expression is furnished by the production of carbonic acid. This is peculiarly remarkable in the case of the *Fungi*, which, being incapable of forming new compounds under the influence of light, are entirely supported by the organic matters they absord, and which in this respect correspond on the one hand with the germinating embryo, and on the other with Animals. Such a decomposition of a portion of the absorbed material is the only conceivable source of the large quantity of carbonic acid they are constantly giving out; and it would not seem unlikely that the force supplied by this retrograde metamorphosis of the superfluous components of their food, which fall down (so to speak) from the elevated plane of "proximate principles," to the lower level of comparatively simple binary compounds, supplies a force which raises another portion to the rank of living tissue, thus accounting in some degree for the very rapid growth for which this tribe of Plants is so remarkable. This exhalation of carbonic acid, however, is not peculiar to Fungi and germinating embryos, for it takes place during the whole life of flowering plants, both by day and by night, in sunshine and in shade, and from their green as well as from their dark surfaces; and it is not improbable that, as in the case of the Fungi, its source lies partly in the organic matters absorbed, recent investigations * having rendered it probable that Plants really take up and assimilate soluble *humus*, which, being a more highly carbonized substance than starch, dextrine, or cellulose, can only be con-

* See the Memoir of M. Risler, "On the Absorption of Humus," in the "Bibliothèque Universelle," N. S., 1858, tom. i., p. 305.

verted into compounds of the latter kind by parting with some of its carbon. But it may also take place at the expense of compounds previously generated by the plant itself, and stored up in its tissues; of which we seem to have an example in the unusual production of carbonic acid which takes place at the period of flowering, especially in such plants as have a fleshy disk, or receptacle containing a large quantity of starch; and thus, it may be surmised, an extra supply of force is provided for the maturation of those generative products whose preparation seems to be the highest expression of the vital power of the vegetable organism.

The entire aggregate of organic compounds contained in the vegetable tissues, then, may be considered as the expression, not merely of a certain amount of the *material* elements, oxygen, hydrogen, carbon, and nitrogen, derived (directly or indirectly) from the water, carbonic acid, and ammonia of the atmosphere, but also of a certain amount of *force* which has been exerted in raising these from the lower plane of simple binary compounds, to the higher level of complex, "proximate principles;" whilst the portion of these actually converted into organized tissue may be considered as the expression of a further measure of force, which, acting under the directive agency of the germ, has served to build up the fabric in its characteristic type. This *constructive* action goes on during the whole Life of the Plant, which essentially manifests itself either in the extension of the original fabric (to which in many instances there seems no determinate limit), or in the production of the germs of new and independent organisms. It is interesting to remark that the development of the more permanent parts involves the successional decay and renewal of parts whose existence is temporary. The "fall of the leaf" is the effect, not the cause, of the cessation of that peculiar functional activity of its tissues, which consists in the elaboration of the nutritive material required for the production of wood. And it would seem as if the duration of their existence stands in an inverse ratio to the energy of their action; the leaves of "evergreens," which are not cast off until the appearance of a new succession, effecting their functional changes at a much less rapid rate than do those of "deciduous" trees, whose term of life is far more brief.

Thus, the final cause or purpose of the whole Vital Activity of the Plant, so far as the *individual* is concerned, is to produce an indefinite extension of the dense, woody, almost inert, but permanent portions of the fabric, by the successional development, decay, and renewal of the soft, active, and transitory cellular parenchyma; and according to the principles already stated, the descent of a portion of the materials of the latter to the condition of binary compounds, which is manifested in the largely-increased exhalation of carbonic acid that takes place from the leaves in the later part of the season, comes to the aid of external Heat in supplying the force by which another portion of those materials is raised to the condition of organized tissue. The vital activity of the Plant, however, is further manifested in the provision made for the propagation of its race, by the production of the germs of new individuals; and here, again, we observe that whilst a higher temperature is usually required for the development of the flower, and the maturation of the seed, than that which suffices to sustain the ordinary processes of vegetation, a special provision appears to be made in some instances for the evolution of force in the sexual apparatus itself, by the retrograde metamorphosis of a portion of the organic compounds prepared by the previous nutritive operations. This seems the nearest approach presented in the Vegetable organism, to what we shall find to be an ordinary mode of activity in the Animal. That the performance of the generative act involves an extraordinary expenditure of vital force appears from this remarkable fact, that blossoms which wither and die as soon as the ovules have been fertilized, may be kept fresh for a long period if fertilization be prevented.

The decay which is continually going on during the life of a Plant restores to the inorganic world, in the form of carbonic acid, water, and ammonia, a part of the materials drawn from it in the act of vegetation; and a reservation being made of those vegetable products which are consumed as food by Animals, or which are preserved (like timber, flax, cotton, &c.) in a state of permanence, the various forms of decomposition which take place after death complete that restoration. But in returning, however slowly, to the condition of water, carbonic acid, ammonia, &c., the constituents of Plants give forth an amount of heat equivalent to that which they would generate by the process of ordinary combustion; and thus they restore to the inorganic world, not only the *materials*, but the *forces*, at the expense of which the vegetable fabric was constructed. It is for the most part only in the humblest Plants, and in a particular phase of their lives, that such a restoration takes place in the form of *motion*, this motion being, like growth and development, an expression of the vital activity of the "Zoospores" of Algœ, and being obviously intended for their dispersion.

Hence we seem justified in affirming that the Correlation between heat and the organizing force of Plants is not less intimate than that which exists between heat and motion. The special attribute of the vegetable germ is its power of utilizing, after its own particular fashion, the heat which it receives, and of applying it as a constructive power to the building-up of its fabric after its characteristic type.

II.—RELATIONS OF LIGHT AND HEAT TO THE VITAL FORCES OF ANIMALS.

THOSE of our readers who accompanied us through the first part of our inquiry are aware that it was our object to show, that as force is never *lost* in the inorganic world, so force is never *created* in the organic; but that those various operations of vegetable life which are sometimes vaguely attributed to the agency of an occult "vital principle," and are referred by more exact thinkers to certain Vital Forces inherent in the organism of the plant, are really sustained by solar light and heat. These, we have argued, supply to each germ the *whole power* by which it builds itself up, at the expense of the materials it draws from the Inorganic Universe, into the complete organism; while the mode in which that power is exerted (*generally* as vital force, *specially* as the determining cause of the form peculiar to each type) depends upon the "germinal capacity" or directive agency inherent in each particular germ. The *first* stage in this constructive operation consists in the production of certain organic compounds of a purely chemical nature—such as gum, starch, sugar, chlorophyll, oil, and albumen—at the expense of the oxygen, hydrogen, carbon, and nitrogen derived from the water, carboñic acid, and ammonia of the atmosphere; whilst the *second* consists in the further elevation of a portion of these organic compounds to the rank of organized tissue possessing attributes distinctively vital. Of the whole amount of organic compounds generated by the plant, it is but a comparatively small part (*a*) that undergoes this *progressive* metamorphosis into living tissue. Another small proportion (*b*) undergoes a *retrograde* metamorphosis, by which the original binary components are reproduced; and in this descent of organic compounds to the lower plane, the power consumed in their elevation is given forth in the form of heat and organizing force (as is specially seen in germination), which help to raise the portion *a* to a higher level. But by far the larger part (*c*) of the organic compounds generated by plants remains stored up in their fabric, without undergoing any further elevation; and it is at the expense of these, rather than of the actual tissues of plants, that the life of animals is sustained.

When, instead of yielding up any portion of its substance for the sustenance of animals, the entire vegetable organism undergoes retrograde metamorphosis, it not only gives back to the inorganic world the binary compounds from which it derived its own constituents, but in the descent of the several components of its fabric to that simple condition—whether by ordinary combustion (as in the burning of coal) or by slow decay—it gives out the equivalents of the light and heat by which they were elevated in the first instance.

In applying these views to the interpretation of the phe nomena of animal life, we find ourselves, at the commencement of our inquiry, on a higher platform (so to speak) than that from which we had to ascend in watching the constructive processes of the plant. For, whilst the plant had first to prepare the *pabulum* for its developmental operations, the animal has this already provided for it, not only at the earliest phase of its development, but during the whole period of its existence; and all its manifestations of vital activity are dependent upon a constant and adequate supply of the same *pabulum*. The first of these manifestations is, as in the plant, the building-up of the organism by the appropriation of material supplied from external sources under the directive agency of the germ. The ovum of the animal, like the seed of the plant, contains a store of appropriate nutriment previously elaborated by the parent; and this store suffices for the development of the embryo, up to the period at which it can obtain and digest alimentary materials for itself. That period occurs, in the different tribes of animals, at very dissimilar stages of the entire developmental process. In many of the lower classes, the embryo comes forth from the egg, and commences its independent existence, in a condition which, as compared with the adult form, would be as if a human embryo were to be thrown upon the world to obtain its own subsistence only a few weeks after conception; and its whole subsequent growth and development takes place at the expense of the nutriment which it ingests for itself.

We have examples of this in the class of insects, many of which come forth from the egg in the state of extremely simple and minute worms, having scarcely any power of movement, but an extraordinary voracity. The eggs having been deposited in situations fitted to afford an ample supply of appropriate nutriment (those of the flesh-fly, for example, being laid in carcases, and those of the cabbage-butterfly upon a cabbage-leaf), each larva on its emersion is as well provided with alimentary material as if it had been furnished with a large supplemental yolk of its own; and by availing itself of this, it speedily grows to many hundred or even many thousand times its original size, without making any considerable advance in development. But having thus laid up in its tissues a large additional store of material, it passes into a state which, so far as the external manifestations of life are concerned, is one of torpor, but which is really one of great developmental activity: for it is during the *pupa* state that those new parts are evolved, which are characteristic of the perfect insect, and of which scarcely a trace was discoverable in the larva; so that the assumption of this state may be likened in many respects to a reëntrance of the larva into the ovum. On its termination, the imago or perfect insect comes forth complete in all its parts, and soon manifests the locomotive and sensorial powers by which it is specially distinguished, and of which the extraordinary predominance seems to justify our regarding insects as the types of purely *animal* life.

There are some insects whose imago-life has but a very short duration, the performance of the generative act being apparently the only object of this state of their existence: and such for the most part take no food whatever after their final emersion, their vital activity being maintained, for the short period it endures, by the material assimilated during their larva state.* But those whose period of activity is prolonged, and upon whose energy there are extraordinary demands, are scarcely less voracious in their imago than in their larva-condition; the food they consume not being applied to the *increase* of their bodies, which grow very little after the assumption of the imago-state, but chiefly to their *maintenance;* no inconsiderable portion of it, however, being appropriated in the female to the production of ova, the entire mass of which deposited by a single individual is sometimes enormous. That the performance of the generative act involves not merely a consumption of material, but a special expenditure of force, appears from a fact to be presently stated, corresponding to that already noticed in regard to plants.

Now if we look for the source of the various forms of vital force—which may be distinguished as constructive, sensori-motor, and generative—that are manifested in the different stages of the life of an insect, we find them to lie, on the one hand, in the heat with which the organism is supplied from external sources, and, on the other, in the food provided for it. The agency of heat, as the moving power of the *constructive* operations, is even more distinctly shown in the development of the larva within the egg, and in the development of the imago within its pupa-case, than it is in

* It is not a little curious that in the tribe of *Rotifera*, or Wheel-animalcules, all the males yet discovered are entirely destitute of digestive apparatus, and are thus incapable of taking any food whatever; so that not only the whole of their development within the egg, but the whole of their active life after their emersion from it, is carried on at the expense of the store of yolk provided by the parent.

the germinating seed; the rate of each of these processes being strictly regulated by the temperature to which the organism is subjected. Thus ova which are ordinarily not hatched until the leaves suitable for the food of their larvæ have been put forth, may be made, by artificial heat, to produce a brood in the winter; whilst, on the other hand, if they be kept at a low temperature, their hatching may be retarded almost indefinitely without the destruction of their vitality. The same is true of the pupa-state; and it it remarkable that during the latter part of that state, in which the developmental process goes on with extraordinary rapidity, there is in certain insects a special provision for an elevation of the temperature of the embryo by a process resembling incubation. Whether, in addition to the heat imparted from without, there is any addition of force developed within (as in the germinating seed) by the return of a part of the organic constituents of the food to the condition of binary compounds, cannot at present be stated with confidence: the probability is, however, that such a retrograde metamorphosis does take place, adequate evidence of its occurrence during the incubation of the bird's egg being afforded by the liberation of carbonic acid, which is there found to be an essential condition of the developmental process. During the larva-state there is very little power of maintaining an independent temperature, so that the sustenance of vital activity is still mainly due to the heat supplied from without. But in the active state of the perfect insect there is a *production of heat* quite comparable to that of warm-blooded animals; and this is effected by the retrograde metamorphosis of certain organic constituents of the food, of which we find the expression in the exhalation of carbonic acid and water. Thus the food of animals becomes an internal source of heat, which may render them independent of external temperature.

Further, a like retrograde metamorphosis of certain constituents of the food is the source of that *sensori-motor power* which is the peculiar characteristic of the animal organism; for on the one hand the demand for food, on the other the amount of metamorphosis indicated by the quantity of carbonic acid exhaled, bear a very close relation to the quantity of that power which is put forth. This relation is peculiarly manifest in insects, since their conditions of activity and repose present a greater contrast in their respective rates of metamorphosis, than do those of any other animals. Of the exercise of *generative* force we have no similar measure; but that it is only a special modification of ordinary vital activity appears from this circumstance, that the life of those insects which ordinarily die very soon after sexual congress and the deposition of the ova, may be considerably prolonged if the sexes be kept apart so that congress cannot take place. Moreover, it has been shown by recent inquiries into the agamic reproduction of insects and other animals, that the process of generation differs far less from those reproductive acts which must be referred to the category of the ordinary nutritive processes, than had been previously supposed.

Thus, then, we find that in the animal organism the demand for food has reference not merely to its use as a *material* for the construction of the fabric; food serves also as a generator of *force;* and this force may be of various kinds—heat and motor-power being the principal but by no means the only modes under which it manifests itself. We shall now inquire what there is peculiar in the sources of the vital force which animates the organisms of the higher animals at different stages of life.

That the developmental force which occasions the evolution of the germ in the higher vertebrata is really supplied by the heat to which the ovum is subjected, may be regarded as a fact established beyond all question. In frogs and other amphibia, which have no special means of imparting a high temperature to their eggs, the rate of development (which in the early stages can be readily determined with great exactness) is entirely governed by the degree of warmth to which the ovum is subjected. But in serpents there is a peculiar provision for supplying heat; the female performing a kind of incubation upon her eggs, and generating in her own body a temperature much above that of the surrounding air.* In birds, the developmental process can only be maintained by the steady application of external warmth, and this to a degree much higher than that which is needed in the case of cold-blooded animals; and we may notice two results of this application as very significant of the dynamical relation between heat and developmental force—first, that the period required for the evolution of the germ into the mature embryo is nearly constant, each species having a definite period of incubation—and second, that the grade of development attained by the embryo before its emersion is relatively much higher than it is in cold-blooded vertebrata generally; the only instances in which any thing like the same stage is attained without a special incubation, being those in which (as in the turtle and crocodile) the eggs are hatched under the influence of a high external temperature. This higher development is attained at the expense of a much greater consumption of nutrient material; the store laid up in the "food yolk" and "albumen" of the bird's egg, being many times greater in proportion to the size of the animal which laid it, than that contained in the whole egg of a frog or a fish. There is evidence in that liberation of carbonic acid which has been ascertained to go on in the egg (as in the germinating seed) during the whole of the developmental process, that the return of a portion of the organic substances provided for the suste-

* In the Viper the eggs are usually retained within the oviduct until they are hatched. In the Python, which recently went through the process of incubation in the Zoological Gardens, the eggs were imbedded in the coils of the body; the temperature to which they were subjected (as ascertained by a thermometer placed in the midst of them) averaging 90° F., whilst that of the cage averaged 60° F.

nance of the embryo, to the condition of simple binary compounds, is an essential condition of the process; and since it can scarcely be supposed that the object of this metamorphosis can be to furnish *heat* (an ample supply of that force being afforded by the body of the parent), it seems not unlikely that its purpose is to supply a force that concurs with the heat received from without in maintaining the process of organization.

The development of the embryo within the body, in the mammalia, imparts to it a steady temperature equivalent to that of the parent itself; and in all save the *implacental* orders of this class, that development is carried still further than in birds, the new-born mammal being yet more complete in all its parts, and its size bearing a larger proportion to that of its parent, than even in birds. It is doubtless owing in great part to the constancy of the temperature to which the embryo is subjected, that its rate of development (as shown by the fixed term of utero-gestation) is so uniform. The supply of organizable material here afforded by the ovum itself is very small, and suffices only for the very earliest stage of the constructive process; but a special provision is very soon made for the nutrition of the embryo by materials directly supplied by the parent; and the imbibition of these takes the place, during the whole remainder of fœtal life, of the appropriation of the materials supplied in the bird's egg by the "food yolk" and "albumen." To what extent a retrograde metamorphosis of nutrient material takes place in the fœtal mammal, we have no precise means of determining; since the products of that metamorphosis are probably for the most part imparted (through the placental circulation) to the blood of the mother, and got rid of through her excretory apparatus. But sufficient evidence of such a metamorphosis is afforded by the presence of urea in the amniotic fluid and of biliary matter in the intestines, to make it probable that it takes place not less actively (to say the least) in the fœtal mammal than it does in the chick *in ovo*. Indeed, it is impossible to study the growth of any of the higher organisms—which not merely consists in the formation of new parts, but also involves a vast amount of interstitial change—without perceiving that in the remodelling which is incessantly going on, the parts first formed must be removed to make way for those which have to take their place. And such removal can scarcely be accomplished without a retrograde metamorphosis, which, as in the numerous cases already referred to, may be considered with great probability as setting free constructive force to be applied in the production of new tissue.

If, now, we pass on from the intra-uterine life of the mammalian organism to that period of its existence which intervenes between birth and maturity, we see that a temporary provision is made in the acts of lactation and nursing for affording both food and warmth to the young creature, which is at first incapable of adequately providing itself with aliment, or of resisting external cold without fostering aid. And we notice that the offspring of man remains longer dependent upon parental care than that of any other mammal, in accordance with the higher grade of development to be ultimately attained. But when the period of infancy has passed, the child, adequately supplied with food, and protected by the clothing which makes up for the deficiency of other tegumentary covering, ought to be able to maintain its own heat, save in an extremely depressed temperature; and this it does by the metamorphosis of organic substances, partly derived from its own fabric, and partly supplied directly by the food, into binary compounds. During the whole period of growth and development, we find the producing power at its highest point; the circulation of blood being more rapid, and the amount of carbonic acid generated and thrown off being much greater in proportion to the bulk of the body, than at any subsequent period of life. We find, too, in the large amount of other excretions, the evidence of a rapid metamorphosis of tissue; and it can hardly be questioned (if our general doctrines be well founded) that the constructive force that operates in the completion of the fabric will be derived in part from the heat so largely generated by chemical change, and in part from the descent which a portion of the fabric itself is continually making from the higher plane of organized tissue to the lower plane of dead matter. This high measure of vital activity can only be sustained by an ample supply of food; which thus supplies both *material* for the construction of the organism, and the *force* by whose agency that construction is accomplished.

How completely dependent the constructive process still is upon heat, is shown by the phenomena of reparation in cold-blooded animals; since not only can the rate at which they take place be experimentally shown to bear a direct relation to the temperature to which these animals are subjected, but it has been ascertained that any extraordinary act of reparation (such as the reproduction of a limb in the salamander) will only be performed under the influence of a temperature much higher than that required for the maintenance of the ordinary vital activity. After the maturity of the organism has been attained, there is no longer any call for a larger measure of constructive force than is required for the *maintenance* of its integrity; but there seems evidence that even then the required force has to be supplied by a retrograde metamorphosis of a portion of the constituents of the food, over and above that which serves to generate animal heat. For it has been experimentally found that, in the ordinary life of an adult mammal, the quantity of food necessary to keep the body in its normal condition is nearly twice that which would be required to supply the "waste" of the organism, as measured by the total amount of *excreta* when food is withheld; and hence it seems almost certain that the descent of a portion of the organic constituents of this food to the lower level of simple binary compounds is a necessary condition of the elevation of another portion to the state of living organized tissue.

The conditions of animal existence, moreover, involve a constant expenditure of *motor* force through the instrumentality of the nervo-muscular apparatus; and the exercise of the purely *psychical* powers, through the instrumentality of the brain, constitutes a further expenditure of force, even when no bodily exertion is made as its result. We have now to consider the conditions under which these forces are developed, and the sources from which they are derived.

The doctrine at present commonly received among physiologists upon these points may be stated as follows:—The functional activity of the nervous and muscular apparatuses involves, as its necessary condition, the disintegration of their tissues; the components of which, uniting with the oxygen of the blood, enter into new and simpler combinations, which are ultimately eliminated from the body by the excretory operations. In such a retrograde metamorphosis of tissue, we have two sources of the liberation of force:—first, its descent from the condition of living, to that of dead matter, involving a liberation of that force which was originally concerned in its organization;*—and second, the further descent of its complex organic components to the lower plane of simple binary compounds. If we trace back these forces to their proximate source, we find both of them in the *food* at the

* It was by Liebig ("Animal Chemistry," 1842) that the doctrine was first distinctly promulgated which had been already more vaguely affirmed by various Physiologists, that every production of motion by an Animal involves a proportional disintegration of muscular substance. But he seems to have regarded the motor force produced as the expression only of the vital force by which the tissue was previously animated; and to have looked upon its disintegration by oxygenation as simply a consequence of its death. The doctrine of the "Correlation of Forces" being at that time undeveloped, he was not prepared to recognize a source of motor power in the ulterior chemical changes which the substance of the muscle undergoes; but seems to have regarded them as only concerned in the production of heat.

expense of which the animal organism is constructed; for besides supplying the material of the tissues, a portion of that food (as already shown) becomes the source, in its retrograde metamorphosis, of the production of the heat which supplies the constructive power, whilst another portion may afford, by a like descent, a yet more direct supply of organizing force. And thus we find in the action of solar light and heat upon plants—whereby they are enabled not merely to extend themselves almost without limit, but also to accumulate in their substance a store of organic compounds for the consumption of animals—the ultimate source not only of the materials required by animals for their nutrition, but also of the forces of various kinds which these exert.

Recent investigations have rendered it doubtful, however, whether the doctrine that every exertion of the functional power of the nervo-muscular apparatus involves the disintegration of a certain equivalent amount of tissue, really expresses the whole truth. It has been maintained, on the basis of carefully-conducted experiments, in the first place, that the amount of work done by an animal may be greater than can be accounted for by the ultimate metamorphosis of the azotized constituents of its food, their mechanical equivalent being estimated by the heat producible by the combustion of the carbon and oxygen which they contain;* and secondly, that whilst there is not a constant relation (as affirmed by Liebig) between the amount of motor force produced and the amount of disintegration of muscular tissue represented by the appearance of urea in the urine, such a constant relation does exist between the development of motor force and the increase of carbonic acid in the expired air, as shows that between these two phenomena there is a most intimate rela-

* This view has been expressed to the author by two very high authorities, Prof. Helmholtz and Prof. William Thomson, independently of each other, as an almost necessary inference from the data furnished by the experiments of Dr. Joule.

tionship.* And the concurrence of these independent indications seems to justify the inference that *motor force* may be developed, like heat, by the metamorphosis of constituents of food which are not converted into living tissue;—an inference which so fully harmonizes with the doctrine of the direct convertibility of these two forces, now established as one of the surest results of physical investigation, as to have in itself no inherent improbability. Of the conditions which determine the generation of motor force, on the one hand, from the disintegration of muscular tissue, on the other from the metamorphosis of the components of the food, nothing definite can at present be stated; but we seem to have a typical example of the former in the parturient action of the uterus, whose muscular substance, built up for this one effort, forthwith undergoes a rapid retrograde metamorphosis; whilst it can scarcely be regarded as improbable that the constant activity of the heart and of the respiratory muscles, which gives them no opportunity of renovation by rest, is sustained not so much by the continual renewal of their substance (of which renewal there is no histological evidence whatever) as by a metamorphosis of matters external to themselves, supplying a force which is manifested through their instrumentality.

To sum up: The life of man, or of any of the higher animals, essentially consists in the manifestation of forces of various kinds, of which the organism is the instrument; and these forces are developed by the retrograde metamorphosis of the organic compounds generated by the instrumentality of the plant, whereby they ultimately return to the simple binary forms (water, carbonic acid, and ammonia), which serve as the essential food of vegetables. Of these organic compounds, one portion (*a*) is converted into the

* On these last points reference is especially made to the recent experiments of Dr. Edward Smith.

substance of the living body, by a constructive force which (in so far as it is not supplied by the direct agency of external heat) is developed by the retrograde metamorphosis of another portion (*b*) of the food. And whilst the ultimate descent of the first-named portion (*a*) to the simple condition from which it was originally drawn, becomes one source of the peculiarly animal powers—the *psychical* and the *motor*—exerted by the organism, another source of these may be found in a like metamorphosis of a further portion (*c*) of the food which has never been converted into living tissue.

Thus, during the whole life of the animal, the organism is restoring to the world around both the *materials* and the *forces* which it draws from it; and after its death this restoration is completed, as in plants, by the final decomposition of its substance. But there is this marked contrast between the two kingdoms of organic nature in their material and dynamical relations to the inorganic world—that whilst the vegetable is constantly engaged (so to speak) in raising its component materials from a lower plane to the higher, by means of the power which it draws from the solar rays, the animal, whilst raising one portion of these to a still higher level by the descent of another portion to a lower, ultimately lets down the whole of what the plant had raised; in so doing, however, giving back to the universe, in the form of heat and motion, the equivalent of the light and heat which the plant had taken from it.

INDEX.

THE END.

CPSIA information can be obtained
at www.ICGtesting.com
Printed in the USA
LVHW100027190422
716387LV00030B/96

9 783752 590036